THE CLASS OF PERFECTION

CYNTHIA EKREN

For my mom, Patricia Martin.

CONTENTS

Prologue: *Kyiv, Russia 1873* 9

Chapter 1: *St. Petersburg, 1874* 13

Chapter 2: *St. Petersburg, April 1877* 27

Chapter 3: *St. Petersburg, February 1883* 31

Chapter 4: *St. Petersburg, September 1884* 37

Chapter 5: *St. Petersburg, September 1888* 49

Chapter 6: *St. Petersburg, January 1889* 79

Chapter 7: *Lisiy Nos, February 1889* 87

Chapter 8: *St. Petersburg, September 1901* 95

Chapter 9: *St. Petersburg, January 1902* 103

Chapter 10: *St. Petersburg January 1903* 111

Chapter 11: *St. Petersburg, February 1903* 117

Chapter 12: *St. Petersburg, March 1903* 131

Chapter 13: *St. Petersburg, Late March 1903* 143

Chapter 14: *St. Petersburg, April 1903* 161

Chapter 15: *St. Petersburg, January 1904* 177

Chapter 16: *St. Petersburg, Fall, 1904* 191

Chapter 17: *St. Petersburg, January 22, 1905* 209

Chapter 18: *St. Petersburg, Late February 1905* 223

Chapter 19: *St. Petersburg, October 1905* 237

Chapter 20: *St. Petersburg November 1905* 259

Chapter 21: *Petrograd, December 1915* 267

Chapter 22: *Petrograd, February 1916* 279

Chapter 23: *Petrograd, February 1917* 321

Chapter 24: *Petrograd, February 27, 1917* 337

Chapter 25: *Delray Beach, Florida, USA, February 1, 1952* 347

Acknowledgements 359

About the Author 361

PROLOGUE

Kyiv, Russia 1873

One sunny morning, Zosia worked pulling weeds in the kitchen garden at her father's home in Kyiv. Enjoying the warmth and smell of the earth, she stood up and stretched her back. Picking up her three-year-old daughter Brigitte, so light like a bird, Zosia swayed, singing, "Keezalah, Meezala, Meizeleh, kootchi, kootchi, koo." Brigitte's giggles buoyed Zosia's heart, helping her forget for a moment her lost career as a dancer with the Kyiv Opera and her lost love. Prince Orlov left her when she became pregnant and he discovered her name was not the Russian one she danced under — Svetlana, but one too Jewish for him to accept.

Zosia named her daughter after the French ballerina, Brigitte Donadieu, the most beautiful dancer she'd ever watched perform. Few believed the story Zosia's father concocted for his customers at the grain house and for the rabbi; Zosia's husband was conscripted into the army. She heard the gossip. That she was a whore, like all women who danced on stage. The baby, though she had dark eyes and hair, looked like a Gentile. Zosia stopped dancing after Brigitte was born and her father kept her and Brigitte in his care. She was grateful, but it was not the life she wanted.

Zosia put Brigitte down and returned to pulling weeds. A few moments later, Brigitte began to cry.

"What is it, *Mameleh*?"

Brigitte sat stroking a dead kitten lying under the beans, weeping as if she understood death. The kitten looked like Zosia's Ketzele, her beloved pet she'd had growing up. Zosia's mother had not wanted her only child to be lonely and let her keep the kitten as long as she locked it away when the rabbi came to call. Cats were unclean.

"We will pray the kitten goes to *Olam Haba*, the world to come. Rabbi says this can never be so for a cat, but he is wrong."

Zosia showed Brigitte how to cover her eyes and say the Shema. "*Shema Yisrael. Adonai Eloheinu. Adonai echad.*"

Zosia thought of the letter she'd received from Prince Orlov requesting to meet Brigitte. Her father wanted her to go to him. Perhaps the kitten was a sign, she thought, of what would happen to her daughter if she stayed in Kyiv, in this house, in this garden.

Zosia wore her finest navy cloak, red scarf, and red boots to meet the prince. She bought Brigitte a new coat embroidered in red on the yoke, and shiny black shoes.

At the arranged hour, Zosia and Brigitte arrived at the St. Sophia Cathedral. They sat on a bench across the street from the bell tower to wait. A carriage arrived, and a woman in her fifties got out, walking with a pronounced limp.

"You are Svetlana?" the woman asked Zosia.

Zosia nodded, holding tight to Brigitte who had her fingers in her mouth and kept bending over to look at her shiny shoes.

"Prince Orlov sent me for the baby."

Zosia fought with the carriage driver, kicking him, and scratching at his arms when he pulled Brigitte away from her. Brigitte and Zosia both screamed in a fury of desperation.

"Stop this," Madame Blontskev intervened, putting her hand up. She took Brigitte from the man, putting her back into Zosia's arms. "Prince Orlov will have this baby, but I promise she will be cared for. I grant you a few moments to say goodbye."

Zosia could feel Brigitte's heart pounding. She looked at the bell tower, silent at the moment, the gateway to the St. Sophia Cathedral. She had never heard of a Jew finding refuge in a cathedral but she had to try. She ran, clutching her daughter.

She made it inside the cathedral, but the curious looks of the few people inside told the driver who had chased her exactly where they were. He snaked his hand around her waist and picked her up, carrying her all the way back to the carriage where he ripped Brigitte from Zosia's arms and handed the girl to Madame.

"No, please," Zosia pleaded, holding onto the driver's coat, using all her strength to stop him from taking her daughter away.

"I will let you say goodbye, but do not try that again," Madame said sternly to Zosia and motioned for the driver to again give the baby back to her mother.

Zosia held Brigitte so tight Brigitte could scarcely breathe. Zosia's words jumbled with her tears and kisses. "*Mameleh*, never forget how we danced together. When you dance, I will be with you. I will find you."

Brigitte, her face beat red, glistening with snot, cried pitifully, loudly, terrified.

When the driver snatched Brigitte a final time, Brigitte fought him like a demon, kicking and biting, even landing a blow with her shiny new black shoes right in his scrotum. He cried out in pain and fury, tossing her onto the floor of the carriage. Madame climbed in behind her. The driver leapt onto his seat, and in a moment the carriage began to move.

"Mama." Brigitte pounded at the carriage door, then tried climbing out the window. Madame held her by the back of her coat.

Zosia ran alongside the carriage. She lunged towards the door, her hand outstretched for the latch, catching hold of it for a moment, then tripping on a cobblestone. She fell, the wheel of the carriage rolling over her neck, breaking it.

Brigitte's piercing scream frightened the horses who whinnied and reared, then took off at a gallop, the driver fighting for control.

Madame Blontskev looked out the back window at Zosia lying motionless, her scarf fluttering away, her hair wild. She pulled the distraught baby into her lap. "Quiet, little ballerina," she said, her voice shaking. "You are safe now from the evil witch, Baba Yaga."

CHAPTER 1

St. Petersburg, 1874

"This is how you, Vera, came to be a Legher." Nina gathered the children around her on their beds in the small room. With Nikolai and Brigitte's trundle bed pulled out, the door to the room could not be opened fully. Nina held eight-year-old Vera on her lap and combed through her light brown hair with long, elegant fingers. "I sat beside the window one night in the springtime, though it was still chilly, mind you. I opened the window to catch the fresh breeze and smell the scent of earth and new leaves and flower blossoms."

Vera looked up at her mother, her mouth opened slightly, mesmerized by this account of herself. Brigitte felt a tug inside, a pain of longing that made her want to cry. She put her thumb in her mouth.

"I had the window open only a moment before a beautiful swan came flapping into this very room. I was astonished and jumped." Nina pulled Vera back with her in mock surprise. "Before my very eyes, the swan transformed into a beautiful maiden. In her hands, she held a large golden egg. Inside, she told me, was a princess who was so beautiful that Baba Yaga had tried to put a spell upon her so that she could never find her true mother."

Brigitte cried out at the name of Baba Yaga.

Nina looked at Brigitte and said, "Baba Yaga is an evil witch who flies around in a mortar and uses the pestle like an oar to steer. Her house stands on chicken legs. Whenever she wants to go, the house gets up and moves, so it is hard to find her. She captures little children and eats them. Those who manage to escape have a hard time finding their way home."

"Did I escape from Baba Yaga?" Brigitte asked.

Vera swatted at her. "This is my story."

Nina scolded, "Hush, Brigitte. This is Vera's story." Nina smiled at Vera. "The beautiful maiden was also a witch, a good and powerful one. She protected beautiful things, so she countered Baba Yaga's spells and put the princess into the egg to protect her until she could be delivered to her mother. To me." Nina hugged Vera to her. "So, you are especially safe from all harm because of the Maiden Witch."

Another night it was Evgenia's turn to sit in Nina's lap. She was just a year younger than Vera but already as tall.

"Evgenia, we found in the tsar's Summer Garden," Nina began the story. "At first, we thought perhaps it was a flower growing in the wrong place. For certainly the Summer Garden is the finest garden in all the world with so many fragrant and precious flowers growing there that do not grow in any other garden. But this flower was in a wooded area, left a little wild on purpose. Your father noticed first the movement under the leaf, but it was I who folded the leaf back, and there you were, no bigger than a rosebud with the most delicate features and the sweetest of smiles. We knew right away you had been placed there for us to find by Leshachikha, the wife of Leshy, the woodland spirit who protects the animals of the forest. Leshachikha hid you under a leaf and she, oh, so stealthily, made sure to move the leaf so your father would see you. We fell in love with your beauty and brought you home with us, our own little daughter."

Brigitte thought about this. Would it be better to come in an egg or a flower, she wondered? Looking at her sisters, there was nothing all that golden about Vera, and certainly, Evgenia no longer resembled the delicate flower.

When it was Nikolai's turn, he asked to tell his own story. Nikolai was the only boy then, two years younger than Evgenia and a year older than Brigitte.

"I remember holding onto the fur of a great bear," Nikolai said with great bravado. "But he wasn't really a bear. It was the tsarevich, enchanted by Baba Yaga."

Nina nodded and smiling said, "Oh yes, the tsar's son. And what happened next, Yolya?" Yolya was Nikolai's nickname.

Brigitte imagined Nikolai with his brave face and his hands wrapped around the bear's neck. "Were you afraid?" she asked him.

Nina hushed her with a frown that made Brigitte want to cry.

"I wasn't afraid because I was the son of the tsar, but a spell had been put on me, as had been put upon my brother."

Nina interrupted him. "The bear, who was really the tsarevich, took pity on you and decided that you should grow up in a home where you would become a great dancer. So, he wandered all around the world looking into the windows of all the great theaters until he found the best danseur, Gustave Legher, and his wife, the ballerina, Nina." Nina put Nikolai's hands together so he could clap, and Vera and Evgenia clapped and cheered. Brigitte laughed and clapped her hands. Then Nina said, "And while we were preparing to go out onto stage one night, the bear tucked Nikolai into my ballet slipper."

Nina squeezed Nikolai and laughed.

Finally, one night, Nina brought Brigitte up to her lap. She was now four years old and she'd mostly forgotten Zosia's face.

"Would you like to hear the story of how you came to be a Legher?" Nina said.

"Why should she have a story, Mama?" Vera said.

"Papa brought her home from school," Evgenia protested and was silenced by a wag of Nina's finger.

Nikolai rose to Brigitte's defense and he hit Vera and Evgenia on the arms, causing them to cry out. Nina ordered them to be silent. Then her voice grew soft and she hugged Brigitte and kissed the top of her head.

"This is Brigitte's story," Nina began. "It was an especially cold summer. We knew it would be a hard long winter if we had to throw an extra blanket on the bed before September. Poor Nikolai would shiver in the trundle bed all alone. One night Papa whispered to me that he wished we had another child who might help keep Nikolai warm."

Brigitte looked at Nikolai and he grinned at her.

"Papa saw something flying about, and at first, thought it was a moth, but it was a sylphide, a winged fairy. And because fairies are such light little things and find the cold difficult, especially in the late summer when they have not yet gone into their trees or underground for the winter, it was fluttering near you girls for warmth. The sylphide heard Papa's wish. The very next day, Papa went to teach his classes at the Imperial Ballet School. He again saw something flying about mistaking it for a moth. Papa heard singing and realized it was the sylphide. She told him to be on the lookout for a child, a sylphide child, who needed a warm place to call home, and a family to teach her to be a human and a dancer."

"Where did he find me?" Brigitte asked, her excitement growing. "Was I in your slipper? Under a leaf?"

"You were in the great ballerina Marfa Muravieva's tiara, as she gave a private performance for the tsar and the tsarina. Papa was partnering her and right as she did an *arabesque*, Papa caught a flash of sparkling light. There you were, peaking out of the jewels. Marfa did not even know you were there and was startled when Papa asked her to lean down so he could take you in his arms. He explained to everyone about the sylphide, and Marfa was so kind that she reached up to the top of her head, and you stepped so gracefully into the palm of her hand. Well, when Papa saw how elegantly you walked, he knew for certain you were the fairy child the sylphide had spoken of, and that you were destined to be a great dancer. The tsar and tsarina applauded, and the tsar declared that you would one day dance for him. That you were very special."

Vera and Evgenia gathered closer to Nina as she finished Brigitte's story begging and whining for their stories to be told again. Brigitte allowed herself to be pushed aside by the older girls. She climbed into the trundle under the blankets, thinking about the sparkling light. It seemed to her she could remember it happening, although vaguely. Nikolai jumped into the bed beside her and she turned towards him and snuggled close.

"You are supposed to keep me warm," he said as he itched his nose. "But you don't. You are more snow maiden than sylphide."

Brigitte felt the iciness of her hands and put them between her legs to warm them. "I guess I should have been a bear cub." She let out a quiet, "Roar!" He roared back and soon they were giggling and clawing at one another until Nina hushed them and turned down the gas lantern.

ST. PETERSBURG, SEPTEMBER 1876

On the morning of six-year-old Brigitte's departure to board at the Imperial Ballet School, Nikolai put a blue-colored stone into her hand, the one he'd found near the Summer Palace. "For luck. I wish it were me going," he said. He hugged her, cried a little, then whispered into her ear so their sisters would not hear and tease them. "Baba Yaga does not eat children big enough to go to school." Nikolai pulled back and bravely squared his shoulders. His furrowed brow and pinched mouth told her he lied and was worried for her.

"Who will scare her off if you are not there?" Brigitte said, her lip quivering, as it had all morning.

"How long before Nikolai can go to school with us?" Brigitte asked Gustave as they walked to the streetcar. He held Brigitte's hand and with the other carried her cardboard suitcase. Gustave wore his trousers tight to show off his leg muscles. His narrow face seemed too small for his broad smile.

"He can audition next year when he is eight."

"Why can't he go now?"

"He is not old enough."

"He is older than me."

"*You* are special." Gustave twirled her around in a circle.

Vera and Evgenia, wearing matching green coats and giant bows in their light brown hair, skipped ahead. They were also starting a new term but needed no suitcase since they were not boarding at the school like Brigitte.

Butterflies in Brigitte's stomach made the ride on the streetcar to Nevsky Prospekt uncomfortable. She sat on Gustave's lap, resting her head on his chest, pressing her face into his coat so she wouldn't cry. If she cried, her sisters would tease her.

When the streetcar stopped, Gustave put Brigitte down, straighten her straw hat, and took her hand. They entered the musical rabble of horses, carriages, and crowds that was St. Petersburg's main thoroughfare, Nevsky Prospekt.

"That's the wrong way. We will be late and get into trouble," Vera complained.

"The first time a ballerina comes to Theater Street, she should properly greet Tsarina Catherine. Going in the back door without showing respect is bad luck."

Leaving Nevsky Prospekt, they entered a small park square. Trees and flowers lined the walkway, and at the center, a statue of a majestic woman holding a scepter and a wreath. Below her, a fountain splashed a counter-melody to the noise of Nevsky Prospekt.

Gustave spoke to the statue as if he were performing for her. "Tsarina Catherine, may I present the next prima ballerina absoluta, Brigitte Gustoevna Legher." He bowed deeply. Brigitte followed, and curtsied, as Mama had taught her.

Vera scoffed. "So stupid."

"You are tempting the muses to leave you," Gustave warned her.

"When do we meet the real tsarina?" Brigitte said. Gustave laughed and took her hand again, leading them out of Ostrovskovo Square.

"No tsarina wants to meet you," Evgenia said.

"If you work very hard, and are fortunate, one day you will dance here." Gustave swept his arm up towards the buttery yellow building, gold in the morning sun. "The Alexandrinsky Theater." He pointed to statues on either side of a row of white columns. "The muses, Melpomene and Thalia." He dropped the suitcase and picked Brigitte up. "And up there, Apollo riding his chariot." She felt like Apollo might roll off the building and crush them.

When Gustave and Nina left in the late afternoons to go to work, they mentioned the Alexandrinsky, but what Brigitte imagined was a room like Gustave's dance studio in their apartment where he gave Brigitte and Nikolai their lessons, and where the tsar and tsarina sat on wooden boxes.

"This is where your life begins." Gustave put her down, holding her hand and twirling her again. Brigitte felt giddy from the attention.

"Come on, Papa," Vera demanded.

Flanking the street behind the Alexandrinsky Theater, two yellow buildings stood as mirror images of one another. Vera raced up the five broad steps leading into one of the buildings. She reached the tall wooden door, and using both hands, tugged the door open, and slipped inside, letting the door swing shut behind her. Evgenia did not have Vera's strength and waited for Gustave.

Inside, Vera and Evgenia stepped into a river of girls moving down the corridor pausing to hang their coats, before going up a broad set of stairs.

Brigitte held Gustave's hand tighter, fearful tears pooled in her eyes.

"This way," Gustave said. "You are in a special class." He led her down the wide hall past large, framed portraits of men and women dressed in costumes, staring down at her like Mama's icons of the saints.

Gustave opened a door into a spacious room with scuffed wood floors and no furniture but a piano and a single chair. Dust sparkled in the air swirling to the muffled, echoing sound of little girls sniveling.

"Brigitte Gustoevna, this is Miss Nadeah." Gustave gave the blonde woman the same deferential bow he'd given Tsarina Catherine.

"Hello little dancer," Miss Nadeah said. "You are very pretty." Miss Nadeah's blue eyes could freeze the Fontanka River.

"Sit there next to Darya." She pointed to a girl with a tear-stained face. Gustave kissed Brigitte's cheek. "Be brave."

She clung to him, whispering, "If I don't like it here may I go home to dance with Nikolai? I promise to work harder in our lessons."

"You'll like this better, my prima ballerina." He patted her head.

Miss Nadeah led her to the girl named Darya, who looked at Brigitte as if she were a stupid baby, the same way Vera and Evgenia did.

The girls squirmed, pulling at the strings of their ballet slippers. Brigitte looked up at the high ceiling of the classroom. They reminded her of church. Brigitte sat down and held very still as Mama had taught her to behave during mass. Brigitte had stayed vigilant in the huge church watchful for Baba Yaga, knowing she might fly in through the huge doors, over the heads of the mothers, and snatch their babies, then soar up to where the bells rang and out into the grey sky.

Her attention fell on a portrait of a ballerina wearing a tiara. It reminded her of the circles of gold around the saints' heads in Mama's icons.

"Do you think she is pretty, Brigitte?" Miss Nadeah asked as she walked over to the portrait. "That is Marfa Muravieva. She was a student here when she was young."

Brigitte's stomach leapt. She jumped up, determined to find Gustave and insist he bring her home so she could tell Mama about seeing Marfa's portrait. Miss Nadeah hurried to her before she got to the door.

"One day you might become as famous as Marfa," Miss Nadeah said. Brigitte heard her coming up from behind.

Darya asked, "Did she sleep here at night?"

"She did sleep here. Maybe, Darya, you will sleep in Marfa's bed."

Miss Nadeah picked Brigitte up and carried her back to her spot. "Stay there until you are dismissed."

Brigitte glanced back at the portrait. Marfa's smile seemed gentler than Saint Bridget's, to whom Mama taught she should pray for help. "I want to go home," she silently pleaded to the saint in the tiara who had been her first safe place. "I want Mama. Keep Baba Yaga away, and Miss Nadeah."

"In all the school, you girls are the most special," Miss Nadeah said, coming to sit on a chair in front of them. "You have been chosen for many reasons to be in this class. No other class like this exists. Should you all do well, and work very hard, you will excel far beyond the other dancers. You will be prima ballerinas, perhaps even prima ballerina absoluta. Do you know what that means?"

Darya shook her head first, and the rest followed, except for Brigitte, who did know because Vera and Evgenia talked about it all the time. She raised her hand.

Miss Nadeah called on her. "A ballerina who is the best in all the world."

"Correct. Because you are starting so young, you will be prima ballerina absoluta." Miss Nadeah sat back.

"You are not like the other students here. You are better. Ballet is being woven into you. Ballet will shine through you in ways that older girls will never be able to attain because they began to study when they were already too old. But not you. You girls are destined to be the best."

"Let's begin," Miss Nadeah said. One by one she showed them how to stand tall, shoulders back. Brigitte knew all of this already from Gustave's daily lessons. She felt proud, and relieved, she alone did not need her stance corrected.

Once they were posed, Miss Nadeah said, "You have been given the honor to begin your studies at the Imperial Ballet School at a young age. Some think you are too young. You will prove them wrong. You must work hard to show you belong here. Those of you who do not measure up will be thrown out." Miss Nadeah sneered and mimed throwing something over her shoulder. "You will disappoint all of Russia and disgrace your families."

The girls stood like statues. Mama and Papa disappointed? Vera warned her that once she failed at dancing, their parents would no longer want her. "They will feed you to the witch," Evgenia said. "She will crunch your bones."

At the end of their first lesson, Miss Nadeah introduced them to the governess in charge of their care, a severe-looking woman with dark circles under her eyes. "You are to be escorted everywhere. Never are you to be out wandering the halls without a governess."

As the governess led them up a staircase, Brigitte peaked over the ornate black iron railing to the floors below, so far down, then upwards as the stairs wound so far up. The governess spoke rapidly, one rule after another, echoing in the staircase; sharp words as indistinguishable as single drops in a driving rain. Brigitte sought out the hand of the little girl next to her, squeezing tightly. The girl squeezed back. They were taken up another floor, down a hallway, past more portraits of men and women, to the very last room on the right. Five beds and a single tall dresser were arranged around the walls. Lying on the bed under the lone window was her suitcase and a neatly folded pile of clothing, a blue serge dress, a white apron, a black apron, tights, and shoes.

The governess watched as the girls changed into blue dresses, then led them to the dining room. At one end were two round tables, a sideboard with a samovar, and a tray of glasses.

"You five are to eat before everyone else, and be well away from here before the regular students come in," the governess said. "This is your table." She pulled out a chair. "Brigitte, you are here." One by one, the girls were placed. "Do not move to any other seat."

A wide door opened and a woman wearing an apron came in carrying a tray with steaming bowls smelling of chicken fat. "There is no dessert here," the governess said, as though they were already in trouble and being punished.

At the end of the day, lying in bed, Brigitte listened to sniffling, until it seemed the others had all fallen asleep. Without Nikolai's arms around her in their trundle bed, his warmth, and the smell of his hair, she stayed wide awake. Her mind whirled with rules and the labyrinth of hallways and stairs. If she woke up to pee in the middle of the night, a chamber pot was across the room. Each morning one of them would be assigned to empty it. Mama always took care of that. Unfamiliar sounds surrounded her; footsteps out in the hallway, wind rattling the glass pane. The persistent thoughts of Baba Yaga tortured her. Images of the witch flying in her mortar, her narrow eyes squinting, and in her hands, the pestle she used to tap, tap on the window. She would not pass up an easy feast of five lonely children.

The door opened. Brigitte squinted her eyes so it would appear she slept, but when there was no further sound, she sat up. The door was closed. She had been certain she'd heard it open. It was a heavy door, and she'd heard the latch make noise before.

Light from the window puddled near the door. It began to move, coming along the two beds opposite hers. Brigitte looked out the window to see if it was the shadow of Baba Yaga. Darkness. Nothing. The cloud of light reached the last bed and came towards Darya; Brigitte's bed would be next. The cloud formed into a woman with a white gown, a face with blurred features, a mouth giving the impression of concern, sadness, love. The apparition floated to the end of her bed. She felt familiar. An old comfort, like a remembered lullaby, a recurring dream. She mingled with and then melted Brigitte's terror.

Again, the sound of the door opening, then closing, a definite click, as it latched shut. The room fell into darkness. Brigitte pulled the covers over her head and made her plan. When Gustave came to the school in the morning, she would tell him what she'd seen, and he would rescue her. But she did not see him the next day, nor for many days until she could not count them anymore.

CHAPTER 2

St. Petersburg, April 1877

A routine developed for the little girls in Miss Nadeah's Infant Class. After a simple breakfast of kasha, a warm porridge, they went to Miss Nadeah's room for instruction.

One morning the girls were seated on the floor, their tulle skirts bunched around small waists, their cold feet in pink ballet slippers.

"Today, we go on a walk. You will see children your age. You will see how you are different from them." Miss Nadeah said, looking at Brigitte, who sat up straighter. Miss Nadeah's words were accompanied by a slight smile. "You girls have long legs. You have small heads, long necks." Miss Nadeah shifted slightly; her own neck seemed to grow longer.

Brigitte studied Miss Nadeah's features and like pictures in a book, with each reading, the story became more familiar. When Miss Nadeah smiled, it did not mean she was happy. When she tilted her head, it meant, pay attention or be punished. When Miss Nadeah's cheeks were sucked in as though she had a lozenge in her mouth, that meant she was angry.

"Come here, Brigitte." She held out her hand. Brigitte sprang up. Miss Nadeah put her arm around Brigitte's waist, giving her an affectionate squeeze. "Look at your friend. At her long legs." Brigitte bent over to look at her legs. "Today, I want you to look at other girls. Some have long torsos. Some are very fat. Wider than they are tall." She spread her arms wide to the side.

"Do you see how long Brigitte's neck is? The lovely shape of her head?" She pulled Brigitte's dark curls back, piling them atop her head. "Today, you will see girls with short necks and odd-shaped faces and heads." Miss Nadeah held Brigitte's hand, motioning for her to take a step away. "These are graceful, long arms."

"Monkey arms," Brigitte said, giggling. The other girls laughed, too. Gustave praised her monkey arms many times. Miss Nadeah smiled indulgently, but her eyes were serious.

That afternoon, Miss Nadeah instructed the girls to line up and hold hands. Over-dressed in her uniform blue wool coat, Brigitte's neck itched, but she didn't dare let go of the hands of Marianna ahead of her and Darya behind her. She felt lucky Darya had chosen to hold her hand.

They reached a sprawling market square with vendors in booths, canvas awnings over simple wooden tables, and shelves filled with vegetables, pots, knives, and trinkets of every kind.

As the girls walked along the edge of the commotion, Miss Nadeah stopped them, pointing to a peasant child of about eight years of age. "You there," she commanded. "Come to me." The girl hesitated a moment, then obeyed. "See the shape of this peasant girl's body? She looks heavy, square, like an elephant. We can safely assume from the look of her that her legs are fat." The child looked down at her legs hidden underneath her skirt and tears welled in her eyes. Miss Nadeah dismissed her with a wave of the hand and, with another wave, motioned them forward to another child, older, perhaps ten. Miss Nadeah placed her hand squarely on the child's chest and ordered, "Halt!" She moved in front of the girl and turned her around so all the little dancers could see her. "Take off the bonnet." When the girl did not immediately comply, Miss Nadeah pulled at the ribbon under the girl's chin, sweeping the offending hat from her head. "Do you see the shape? She is all cheeks, but flat on top. Not rounded at all." The girl scowled and snatched her bonnet. Miss Nadeah beckoned the girls onward.

As they reached the edge of the market and approached the wooden bridge crossing the Fontanka Canal, Miss Nadeah pointed. A group of children, dressed alike in clothing that Mama would reject as cleaning rags, were tossing pebbles into the water. Miss Nadeah pointed to a girl with a withered arm and misshaped face. Her teeth protruded through her smile. Her eyes were sightless.

The girl's friends handed her pebbles, which she tossed into the canal. They all twittered with pleasure making sure the imperfect girl did not go empty-handed, coming to her again and again pouring stones into her outstretched hands.

"Brigitte! Where are you going? You have dropped Darya's hand." Miss Nadeah grabbed her arm.

Brigitte had wanted to touch the girl's face. She looked up at Miss Nadeah, expecting to find an understanding deeper than her own as to what might compel her to get closer to the girl, but Miss Nadeah looked furious.

"Never go near them. That girl is a Jew. Jews carry disease." She placed Brigitte's hand back into Darya's and returned to the head of the line.

"My father says Princess Aurora Demidova has a fat face," Darya said and laughed.

"There are a few in the aristocracy who are misshapen, but you are never to comment upon them. That would be very rude. If you offend, you will never dance again. You'll be turned out onto the streets to become ugly like the children you saw today."

Brigitte thought of Vera with one ear higher than the other. Mama braided her hair in two plaits in front of her ears to hide them. Evgenia did not have a long neck.

Miss Nadeah continued assessing the defects of strangers for the whole of the walk until the little ballerinas felt as though they walked amongst another species entirely.

"Others are jealous of you." Miss Nadeah said as they walked back to school. "They will want you to eat too much so you get fat. If you do, you will be expelled from school, your families won't want you back, and you'll be turned out onto the streets because you became hideous like the children you saw today."

Try as hard as she might, Brigitte could not stop the tears.

CHAPTER 3

St. Petersburg, February 1883

At thirteen, Brigitte had been a boarding student at the Imperial Ballet School for seven years. She danced with girls two years older, who ignored her, except for Julija, who had the bed next to hers.

As she was leaving mathematics class, Brigitte was surprised to find Gustave outside the door. Usually, Gustave only sought her out to tell her there was a new little Legher. Baby Sergei had been born the year before she'd started school. There had been four more children since. The last time Gustave came to find her in class had been the end of the last spring term when he gave her the sad news that her three-month-old sister had died. Brigitte had barely registered the baby's birth since she saw her family only on holidays and rare weekends. Still, it had been a sad shock; the whole family had been more subdued the whole summer.

"What is it, Papa?" Her heart was in her throat.

"Good news." His eyes danced. "Master Christian Johansson has invited you to study with him. He has never invited one so young. This is a great honor for the whole family. He takes so few students."

Her palms began to sweat. Johansson taught the *Classique de Perfection*, the class for the prima ballerinas and premier danseurs. Students from the ballet school, at times, were allowed to quietly sit on the balcony to observe, which Brigitte did at every opportunity. A thin man in his mid-sixties with good posture, Master Johansson's reputation as an uncompromising perfectionist drew the best dancers. He carried his violin in a black case and a sturdy black walking stick with a silver ball on the top. Raised in Sweden, his accent made him sometimes difficult to understand. It was said Master Johansson had eyes in the back of his head and could see through the body to the spine.

Brigitte had been able to get by in some classes, such as Lev Ivanov's, a talented choreographer, responsible for some of the greatest ballets the Imperial Theater had ever produced, but a terrible teacher. He simply didn't care, and his students knew this and took advantage.

"If Master Johansson thinks you are worthy of his time, he may even take you on for private instruction." Gustave grew serious. "You start today. Do not eat on your break. You want to be light."

Looking up into Gustave's proud face, Brigitte squeezed her throat shut. He wrapped his arms around her. Rarely was she touched, except for correction. Even Nikolai, who would grab her for impromptu dances when she was home, had mostly ignored her over the summer, spending more time with Sergei.

"What if I'm not good enough? They will not send me down to a lower class. They send those who fail away." Brigitte could hardly catch her breath.

Gustave held her for only a moment, then pushed her back to arms-length. "Pull yourself together. You have two hours. Get a cup of tea and sit by the window. Take deep breaths, as you would before performing." He turned her away with a nudge. "Go."

As she walked alone to the dining room, Brigitte felt as though her feet would not stay on the ground, a vaguely familiar sensation of flying and being swept away, of motion sickness.

Just before the class, Gustave found Brigitte in a sitting room the girls used for study and offered to escort her. "I want to be there when you walk in. The memory will keep me warm in my retirement."

Brigitte held his hand, drawing strength from him. Gustave opened the door for her and to her horror, the class was already in session. She turned to Gustave, but he acted as if he didn't notice this terrible breach.

Inside the class, eight girls held an *arabesque*; their forward hands on the barre, balancing on their left legs, the other arm and leg extended behind them. The master inspected each girl, moving among them, lifting a leg higher, repositioning a foot by tapping the girl's toes with his stick, extending an arm.

"There," Gustave whispered to Brigitte, pointing. "There is room for you at the end. Remember, head high." She did a fast tiptoe to the open space. By the time she'd turned around, Gustave had disappeared. The other dancers wore their toe shoes and she had only her slippers. Already she could feel Master Johansson's glare on her back, so she took a position, as Gustave had first taught her, finding a point in the imaginary audience. Then drawing the power from the center of the earth up through her leg, out through her fingers and her head, reaching up to God above and the audience, she rose onto her toes.

The girl in front seemed to Brigitte to be leaning too far forward. Johansson confirmed her assessment when he approached the dancer, pulling her shoulders. His eyes flashed over toward Brigitte. They were dark and piercing as if they could search her thoughts, and rearrange them. Any pettiness, weakness, or vulnerability had already been exposed. A single glance in her direction and he'd shed her of her skin.

She lowered her eyes to the floor and began to wobble, the lifted leg suddenly heavy. She wasn't sure she could hold it up, but there was no way she could lower it before he instructed them. She'd had no warmup. Her first class would be a disaster. Defeated in the first moment, her heart began to break.

Johansson skipped her in his assessments. Turning from the girls, he lifted his violin to his chin. "Legs lower, then lift, to the quarter, half, three-quarters...in *penchée*." He counted them in and began to play.

She concentrated, listening to the new music, and Johansson's Swedish-accented voice as he repeated, "Lift, and higher and higher ... down."

Her leg felt tight, heavy. Glancing at the master teacher, he seemed to be peering at her over the bow of his violin, his brow knit, his eyes looking into all her inadequacies. She did not know how to hide from him, so she decided to smile and kept smiling, hoping soon she could relax, so she might again become plastic, flexible.

The first week, Master Johansson said nothing to her, though he watched her with intensity. Normally Johansson played his violin for his classes, but Fridays a pianist came. The class moved through all the dance sequences with fewer interruptions so that they could practice continuity.

Five minutes into a dance, Master Johansson erupted. "B. Legher! Not for one more minute will I abide this on your face."

The piano fell silent. Everyone froze. Brigitte's face grew hot. She reached up to her cheeks and felt around. Turning to the girl next to her she asked, "Do I have something on my face?" The girl shook her head, but looked down at the floor, not wanting to be caught in the storm.

Johansson approached Brigitte like a dark cloud, his lips drawn into a thin line. He pointed to his own face. "A smile?" he scoffed.

Confused, words escaped into a black hole in her mind. A flashing sequence of memories of her teachers from Miss Nadeah to the ineffective Lev Ivanov telling her to smile, smile! "Smile for the audience, smile!" She must have been concentrating too hard and forgot her smile. Doing her best to push past her emotions, she managed a weak curvature of her lips and was rewarded with a sharp slap across her face.

"Do not," Johansson hissed at her, "smile." Pinning her with his stare, he said in a loud voice. "Piano, play last five measures."

The pianist, a bored woman in her middle years, and no longer impressed by howling teachers, played the slow, heavy melody.

"Listen." Johansson lifted Brigitte's chin so she would have to look him in the eye. "Hear emotion in music."

She heard the blood pounding in her ears.

"Enough," he yelled at the pianist. The room fell silent, except for the hissing of the heat registers. "Anything happy in music?" he asked.

The music sounded the same as all the other practice pieces she'd been dancing to for seven years. He stared. "If you cannot hear music, react with appropriate emotion, you are automaton. Not ballerina." Each word pierced her skin. "Do not smile when music is lament."

He sat on the wooden chair and leaned on his stick. "Performer performs. Performer smile. Ballerinas speak language of dance. Ballerinas reveal secrets of soul. Composer, musician. All speak language of soul, use sound. Painter use color. Performers?" Johansson's shoulders relaxed. "Performer use only smile. Waiter smile. Whore, she smile. Simple bag of tricks. Dancer, she use movement."

He tapped his stick three times. The girls collectively inhaled, preparing to move into the next dance sequence. "B. Legher, answer question."

"Yes, sir," she said, horrified at how meek her voice sounded.

"Will you be performer or ballerina?"

She did not hesitate. "A ballerina, Master."

"Then no smile unless music feel happy." He spread his lips wide, his teeth showing, his eyes twinkling. "When audience give you ovation because you break heart, then smile."

CHAPTER 4

St. Petersburg, September 1884

At the start of her eighth year in the Imperial Ballet School, Master Johansson stopped Brigitte after class by tapping her shoulder with his stick. "Start tomorrow, you partner with Rodian Petrov."

Rodian was notorious in the school for eavesdropping and tattling.

She took a deep breath. "A question, Master Johansson."

"Ja, B. Legher?"

"If I do not like dancing with Rodian Petrov," she paused, not sure how to proceed. "I mean, I have heard he is...."

Johansson's eyes sparked. His lips twitched. "What is question?"

"Might I partner with my brother, Nikolai, instead?"

Johansson frowned. "Petrov is, how do say in Russian? In Sweden, we say he is *hedge*."

Brigitte shook her head, not understanding.

"In Russian, you say a horse's ass, a *mudak*?"

Startled at his coarse language, she giggled, covering her mouth with her hand. "Then I can dance with Nikolai?"

"No. Rodian Petrov."

She lost her resolve and her tongue, giving him a consenting nod.

"Next fall he will be at Imperial Ballet, tormenting Tsar's finest. This, if he excel in partnering you."

Brigitte tried another tact. "But Master, shouldn't a senior partner with him? I am not good enough."

"You partner with Petrov. Others wish it so. I make it so."

He gently took her chin in his hand, lifting her face to look him in the eye. "You from Miss Nadeah's Infant Klasse, subject unnatural manipulations to growing body, which I never approve. You will suffer more than dancer who begin older age. For you survive, you must believe dance worth pain." He took away his hand. "Many quit. Your sister, Vera und Evgenia, already give up, ja?"

Brigitte nodded, feeling a pang of disloyalty. Vera had blamed Brigitte, saying it was impossible to be compared to the "special one" all the time. Brigitte embraced the pain of the exercise and manipulation. If she could feel something in her body, then she could believe what she was told, that she was special.

"How many in infant klasse?"

"Five." Her chest constricted as she thought of the girls, of Darya, Marianna.

"How many still in skoola?"

She squeezed her throat shut, closing off her emotions. "I am the only one."

"Tell me name. Where are now?"

She swallowed, trying to dislodge the grief. She never allowed herself to think of her first friends, but Johansson stared at her, expecting an honest answer. Despite herself, the words came from the place deep inside where she kept secrets. "Olga left first. Her family took her to Moscow. Marianna died from fever. Polina drank poison after she was expelled for not progressing. Darya grew too tall and ate too much. I don't know where she is now. Vlada went down onto the floor and curled up into a ball. No one could get her to stop crying. She lives in an asylum."

"Surviving to finish skoola, very difficult. Even more difficult, survive long career."

The pianist for the next class opened the door, saw the seriousness of the conversation, and excused herself.

With urgency and passion in his voice, Johansson continued. "You stay small. If Petrov or any danseur cannot lift, then is over. This hard truth. Many career cut short for girl cannot stay away from cake. Eat only enough to dansa, keep strong." Despite the smile on his face, his eyes held a dark warning.

That night, lying on her narrow bed, listening to the soft snoring, Brigitte thought more about Vlada and the Infant Class. She remembered the afternoon the little girls, at eight years old, learned to put their hair up into a neat bun. Vlada and Brigitte were paired with an eighth-year student, who talked fast while brushing Brigitte's hair. "Put the pins in your mouth, so they are handy. Don't swallow." She showed them how to pull their hair up into a ponytail, separate it into two and wind each half around, then described the placement of pins like the face of a clock, noon, three, six, and nine. "This will never fall out," she declared when she finished, playfully shaking Brigitte's head. When the lesson concluded, she hugged them, kissing their cheeks. "We will dance together at the Alexandrinsky Theater one day," she said.

Vlada had a secret; one that twisted her inside out, and dropped her onto the floor, and into madness. As Brigitte brushed Vlada's hair to practice their buns, Vlada described what happened in the balcony above the dance room where balletomanes could observe the class. Two men took interest in Vlada, inviting her to come up after class finished.

"I thought they wanted to tell me how well I danced." They promised to promote me, even over older girls, for student roles. They were old with rancid breath." Vlada stopped speaking. Tears brimmed in her eyes.

Brigitte slowed her brushing but did not stop.

"They made me do things. Things women do with men."

Vlada reached for Brigitte's free hand, squeezing it hard. She gasped for air. "They said if I spoke of what happened, I would be expelled. They said it was my fault for being so pretty." Her hands shook. "They asked me if I enjoyed it." Vlada looked up at the ceiling, a look of fury driving the tears from her eyes. "I want to be ugly."

Brigitte thought about what made Vlada different, made her someone who could be attacked by the balletomanes. If she could pinpoint what made her different, then she would know how to keep herself safe. She did not think Vlada was that beautiful, or particularly talented. That Vlada ended up in the asylum was the only thing Brigitte could land upon to make her prey to such men. She had some weakness that men like that could see. Brigitte never wanted to be that vulnerable.

Rodian had an array of facial expressions, all of them reminding her of the villains from an illustrated fairytale book. His eyes were small and wide-set. He waxed his sandy-colored hair. His lips were thin and colorless, his fingers, boney and menacing.

They had been working under Johansson's watchful eye for a full fourteen days when Rodian pushed her to her limit. She had been the first to the studio and began her warm-up at the barre. She hadn't heard him come in, though she suspected he purposely came in quietly to see if he might catch her unawares.

"You are too loose in your spine," he'd said standing directly behind her, speaking into her ear. She'd startled, turning into him so that her nose bumped his chest. "You are clumsy, too."

She could not back away because of the barre. "Move," she demanded.

He came closer, causing her to lean back against the barre and look up into his face. Her anger flashed in her solar plexus. She slapped him.

He moved then, rubbing his cheek, his eyes narrowed to slits. "You will regret that."

"You are impertinent," she said, leaving the barre, and going to the middle of the room. Where was Johansson? Or a governess? When a teacher couldn't be in the room, they always sent in a governess to chaperone.

"You do not know your place," Rodian said.

"I know it better than you do. I hear what is said about you. How they move you from class to class because they cannot stand your arrogance. I do not see how you will ever have a career with the Imperial Theater if everyone already hates you."

"I hear things, too. I know that I am your only hope of advancement past a lifetime of dancing with the *corps de ballet*, forever an entry-level dancer, relegated to the back row."

"If you are my only hope, I am lost already."

"You are a failure in a class born out of failure. I heard a group of balletomanes made a bet to see if great dancers could be made from children if they start young enough, even though they have no talent. That question has been answered. The answer is no."

Brigitte stomped her foot as if to lunge at him. Rodian took a step back. She had never heard that rumor before and wondered whom she could trust to ask if it were true.

Master Johansson came into the room followed by Madame Blontskev, who greeted them with a dismissive shake of her head. She limped slowly to the piano, lit a cigarette, and put it burning in the glass bowl on the piano lid.

"Fighting?" Johansson planted himself on a chair. "Fail to harmonize, both fail." The silence that followed filled Brigitte's ears with the sound of her boiling blood.

"Of course, Master Johansson," Rodian said with a modest smile. "I did not intend to upset Brigitte. It was all a joke. She misunderstood." He made a show of bowing to her before saying, "I apologize if you did not realize it was all in good fun."

Aching to slap him again, she clasped her hands together.

Johansson nodded, leaned on his stick, and said, "We begin."

For the rest of the hour, the two settled uneasily into the dance steps Johansson choreographed. She felt the strength in Rodian's body; the solid muscles that flexed when he easily lifted her into the air. She couldn't help but smile. He lifted her as though she were a bird holding lightness in her bones; in her strong muscles.

After they finished the last *pas de deux*, Johansson struck the floor with his stick and said, "Bravo, Brava. Ja, Ja! A perfect pair. Work ahead. But is all there, if you want badly enough."

Rodian rolled his eyes.

"What Mr. Peterov?" Johansson asked him, resting on his stick.

Brigitte noticed that Madame Blontskev also watched the young man, an unmistakable scowl on her face. Behind Rodian's insolence, his clear blue eyes held contempt and some of the fear Brigitte had seen when she struck him. Four years separated them, plus five inches in height and at least thirty pounds. Yet, she couldn't mistake the fear, for it dwelled in the eye of so many of the young dancers. He needed a haircut. Someone would be insisting that he see to that soon.

"I prefer a girl with better technique. She will make me a laughing stock."

She waited for Johansson to put him in his place.

"Nevertheless, she is for you." He sounded bored.

"She will destroy any chance I have. This time is vital for me. I must insist you bring me a more worthy partner."

"You have remark, B. Legher?" He made no effort to hide his annoyance with them both.

She shook her head. Putting her hands across her stomach, feeling queasy and hungry. *He has it backward. He is not up to my talent. He will bring me down.* She kept these words behind clenched teeth.

Master Johansson dismissed them and left the room. Rodian followed.

"Little Brigitte." Brigitte seldom heard Madame speak, and only to the teachers, never to students. "*Corps de ballet, coryphée,* third soloist, second soloist and first soloist, ballerina, prima ballerina, and prima ballerina absoluta. Tell me, little *vorobey,* what do you hope to be when you reach the pinnacle of your dance career? *Corps de ballet* or a prima ballerina absoluta?"

A trick question, but she did not know Madame Blontskev well enough to take the risk of answering incorrectly. "I would be happy to just dance, Madame, even if it were in the *corps de ballet.*"

Brigitte sat to take off her pointe shoes.

Madame lit a cigarette. "Ballet is who you are. Why do you have such small dreams?" She frowned. "Tell me, who is prima ballerina absoluta right now?"

"No one has ever been good enough for the title."

"Why then, is there such a rank? Why not just end with prima ballerina?"

Brigitte shrugged.

"So that even the very best have something to reach for," Madame said tenderly. "If Master Johansson thinks Rodian will make a good partner for you, trust his judgment. He has earned his reputation. Prima ballerinas seek his advice. You are fortunate to have his attention. I concede it may be painful for you to dance with such a selfish, complaining boy. If you make him feel important, he will become something you can take advantage of."

Madame Blontskev took her time standing, a flicker of pain flashing across her face. "You do not know this, but I have a say in who studies here. I had a hand in your coming to this school." Madame Blontskev raised her eyebrow. "I did not choose Rodian. No one asked my opinion then, but I will give it now to you." She smiled like a conspirator. "He is a fair danseur. Perhaps he has the potential to be good. He is selfish, which is dangerous in a danseur. But he wants only to be a soloist. You might take a lesson from him. He thinks he should be premier danseur. Believe you should be prima ballerina."

"Rodian thinks I am worthless. Master Johansson did not defend me. I know that I have a sponsor who wants me to be here, whether I have talent or not. No one has ever told me who. Do you know? Is that why Rodian is here, too?" Brigitte took a deep breath, hoping Madame would answer.

"Your understanding of the situation is not quite accurate," Madame said. "You are here because you are supposed to be here. Do not be distracted with pettiness concerning Rodian or any other passing danseur. If you need something to worry you, worry about your thoughts. What you think of yourself is more powerful than what anyone else thinks. If you believe you are only good for *corps de ballet*, you will be. Worry about that." Madame Blontskev gathered her bag, stubbed out the cigarette. "I think you are still a good bet."

Two weeks later, Brigitte was alone with Johansson at the finish of their private lesson. She was fastening the top three buttons on her white canvas shoes when he called her over to where he sat, wiping his violin with a soft cloth. "Stand straight for me. Best posture, straight back, head high, neck long, chest out."

What he asked, she did. She stood waiting to hear what would be corrected.

"Brava," he said. "Breathe in."

She took a few long, slow breaths, in, out.

"Ja, good. Feel body. Pay attention to your breath entering, leaving."

This confused her, for how did one pay attention to such a thing, but she did as told, realizing that the air was cold in her nose when she inhaled.

"Now, feel your body in this room, taking space."

She looked at Johansson. For feeling her body in a room, she needed more guidance.

"Feel how you are not standing here in this room, but you are a part of room. Now you know the room will continue to exist without you in it, but for this moment, you are in room."

As he spoke, it seemed the room became bigger, some trick of the mind he played on her.

"You, you body, you mind, parts make what teach in skoola. Picture of my idea. Of ideas of other teachers. You become a part of my mind. I become a part of you mind." He reached up from where he sat, tapping her forehead. "You mind holds my words, become you ideas, ideas now way you move, dance." Master Johansson tugged at her arm hanging loose at her side, turning her around in a circle. "You are strong, beautiful, talented."

"I feel the air is cold when I breathe."

He laughed mirthfully. "You young." He shook his head and pursed his lips together. Then said seriously, "When you on stage as soloist, you feel more than *pirouette, rallentando*. You *be* perfect turnout. Feel part of space on stage. Become part audience, balletomanes. Become aware. Feel room. Feel sound of my word inside you body." He tapped her chest.

She lost focus on her posture. "May I ask a question, Master Johansson?"

"Ja."

"What does that mean?"

He laughed. "Not something learn. You experience. Not show, then mimic. You discover. Only great dancers ever do. You go from class to class, place to place, enter café, walk on street, notice. How world move around? Person walk through you? No. Maybe push aside. Fish swim in sea, water move around. Monkey swing in trees, move leaf. Move bird. Color fly into sky. Notice."

She nodded to please him. She understood none of it.

He stood and put his violin into its case. "I watch you. You six-year-old in Infant *Klasse*. Many year watching." He closed the case. "Most impressive, though, when you dance with Rodian. You alive with tension. You feeling for him with whole being. He is leaf in tree you swing through. You see he goes where he need go, even when he does not know he end up there.

"In *corps de ballet*, you trust other too much, or you not care so much, not sure which. You lost inside skin. Forget come out until music stops."

"You can see that?" she asked, astonished he made such a long study of her.

"I see. When you worry, hold hand like this." He demonstrated for her. "Like pray." He tipped his palms up and open.

"I do not know how to pray."

"With body you pray. Become aware prayer."

He picked up the violin case and took his stick leaning against the piano. "Do not bother with trying. Just notice. Then you realize already doing."

After he left, she looked in the mirror, holding her hands as he had demonstrated. They looked strange. How could that be something she did without knowing it? What else did her body do without her being aware? How else could she find command over herself? Over every finger, every toe, every thought?

Brigitte thought that they had attained perfection when they danced the *pas de deux* from *Le Sylphide* for Tsar Alexander III in the school's theater, but Rodian berated her for moving on him so he had to chase after her. Knowing she never had to dance with him again, she felt no need to tell him that if she hadn't forced him to come after her, he would have been off by four beats. She was counting on him failing in the Imperial Ballet and being long gone by the time she graduated.

After the performance, the graduates dined with the Imperial family. Tradition dictated that Brigitte not attend the dinner, since she would not formally graduate until she was eighteen, four more years away. She stood, along with three other curious girls, behind the curtains between the small school theater and a dining room set up for a special banquet, to peek at the Imperial family. Brigitte had seen the tsar and tsarina only from a distance before when she'd danced student roles for the Imperial ballet at the Alexandrinsky Theater. Up close, the family appeared more human than she expected. She thought that they should radiate holiness like the saints in Nina's icons. The tsarina barely touched her food. The tsar spilled gravy on the tablecloth. Tsarevich Nicholas, handsome as he was at eighteen, was not very tall, and he seemed to be shy. She compared him to Nikolai, who did radiate confidence; the contrast struck Brigitte. These were not gods in human form. They were just people with power. Brigitte quickly banished the thought as dangerous.

When Tsar Alexander rose to leave, all the students stood and bowed. Brigitte quickly abandoned her hiding place hoping to get out of sight before the family reached the door. The others were faster than Brigitte, and the last one pushed the curtain back towards her so that it wrapped around Brigitte's leg, forcing her to stop and get untangled. She freed herself, then looked up to see Tsar Alexander watching her with a wry smile. She made a deep curtsey, her face hot.

As she rose, Tsar Alexander said, "You dance beautifully, Mlle. Legher. Perhaps I enjoyed your performance the most."

His smile shined on her, capturing Brigitte completely. She felt for the first time what it meant to be seen by a host from Heaven.

"Be the glory and adornment of our ballet," he commanded her. "Dance for Mother Russia."

"I will, your Imperial Majesty."

Tsarina Maria Feodorovna held out her hand, and Brigitte kissed it as protocol demanded. "It seemed you truly did have wings."

Brigitte's legs grew weak. She held onto the curtain as the rest of the royal family acknowledged her with kind words and praise. Not one frowned at her for breaches of etiquette, being where she should not be, dressed in her school uniform instead of evening wear.

That night, in the darkness of the dormitory, she lay awake on her bed, hearing again the tsar's command, his words a calling. Before meeting the tsar, she had danced for Gustave, to make him proud. To please her teachers. She danced to keep her home. She danced to ensure herself a future with the Imperial Theater. Now she knew she must dance for something larger. For Mother Russia, and the great father, Tsar Alexander III.

CHAPTER 5

St. Petersburg, September 1888

After Brigitte graduated, the Imperial Ballet hired her as a *coryphée*. She used her first wages to rent a room close to the Mariinsky, another of the grand stages used by the Imperial Theater for opera, orchestra, and ballet performances.

She savored the walk to the theater in the morning, enjoying being outdoors. The adventure of walking beside strange men and women, of looking at the displays in the shop windows, and feeling free to stop for a moment if she wanted to, without being rushed by a governess, was early morning bliss. The Imperial Theater provided carriage rides for their dancers to ensure there were no excuses for being late to rehearsals and performances, and again in the evenings to keep them healthy and safe. St. Petersburg in the dark was thick with thieves and drunks. Not yet impressed by the dangers, she preferred to walk.

So far she had only a small part in a divertissement, so it was with excitement that Brigitte arrived for rehearsals for her first full ballet, *Fiametta*, on a bright Monday morning in mid-September. Hearing that the casting list had been posted on the board next to the regisseur general's office, she went straight to see.

The regisseur, a man named Lubik Stonich, was short, mustached, and often red in the face from the frustration of being disregarded while trying to enforce the rules. He stood in his office doorway explaining to Rodian why he was being fined for an infraction. Rodian argued bitterly. Brigitte ignored them and ran her finger down the list looking for her name. *Coryphée*, first cast, meaning she would be dancing in the performance with the ballet's premier artists. In the *corps de ballet*, the group dances, her name was paired with Rodian.

"Excuse me," she tapped Lubik Stonich on the shoulder. "Is there a way to have this casting list altered? Change in partners?"

Stonich was nearly as short as Brigitte. She looked him in the eye. His expression answered her question. If ever she had seen someone dumbfounded, it was Stonich.

"You would like to be able to dictate whom you dance with?" he asked. "Are you a prima ballerina?" Stonich asked. "You probably want Pavel Gerdt to partner with you. Why not ask Master Petipa? See what he says."

"I'd prefer not to partner with you, either," Rodian snarled before walking away.

"Come back here!" Stonich yelled. "I'm not done with you."

"I wish I were," Brigitte said under her breath.

In the dressing room, the other ballerinas were talking about a party they had attended that weekend. Alayna, with dark hair and a scar across her chin, came over to a chair next to the one where Brigitte sat. Alayna took Brigitte's tights out of her hands, putting her toe into the leg. "You want to make friends to survive here, sweet thing," Alayna said.

"Those are mine," Brigitte said. "Give them back."

"I will trade you." Alayna tossed hers into Brigitte's lap. They were filthy, full of holes.

"Please." Brigitte could not afford to get a new pair of tights. She barely made her rent. "My parents gave those to me."

The other dancers laughed, then ignored her as they finished dressing and left.

Her choices were simple. Either go bare-legged or wear the filthy tights. One had to be used to offensive odors to live in St. Petersburg, and spend time around sweating bodies, but to wear someone else's grime and stink nauseated her.

On the stage, Marius Petipa, the elegant Frenchman who had held the position of ballet master for nearly twenty years, signaled the start of rehearsal by saying something indecipherable. Brigitte took her place in the front of the *corps de ballet* dancers, including Alayna.

"She thinks she's so special starting as *coryphée*," Alayna said.

"Look at her bare legs," someone else said, and there was snickering. Shame bloomed in her gut like a weedy flower.

Marius Petipa spoke very little Russian, though he had lived in St. Petersburg long enough to have learned. In the ballet, French sufficed. Russians loved the sound of French, more, it seemed, than they loved Russian. Many of the aristocratic children were taught French as their first language. In school, French was mandatory. Petipa's instructions were not lost on her until he tried to mix in his rudimentary Russian. "Me on you. You on me," Petipa said tapping his chest.

"Where soloist?" he called to the cast. "King Akdar, Princess Niriti?"

The prima ballerina, Elena Cornalba came out and stood next to Master Petipa.

"*Bien, bien,*" he clapped. "*Coryphées, pas de quarto* third act."

Rodian came and held out his hand to escort her to their place as called out by the master. Petipa quieted for a moment, glancing at her legs, his nose wrinkling. The cast had put most of their attention on the master, so when he went silent, they followed the direction of his gaze. The gasps and tittering made Brigitte want to sprout wings and fly up into the rafters.

The moment passed when Petipa turned away and called for the spirits of the earth. After two hours of working through the choreography, the dancers were all dismissed.

"Do not ever embarrass me again by having to dance with a woman with no tights."

"Alayna took mine." As she spoke, she searched out the quickly emptying stage for the *corps de ballet* dancers and spotted Alayna sitting on a chair talking with her friends. "I cannot afford another pair. I certainly cannot afford to supply someone like her with tights anytime she wants mine."

Rodian groaned. "You will not last the year." He pulled her behind him as he marched over to Alayna. In a single movement, he pulled the chair out from under her, dumping her onto the floor. She yelped.

"While you are down there," Rodian said, his voice flat, his words calculated. "Take off those tights."

Alayna rolled over onto her knees about to rise when he put his foot on her shoulder, holding her down.

"They are mine, you *zasranec.* I have a protector who will kill you."

Rodian's laugh sounded as though he were in the role of an operatic villain, so evil that Alayna stopped struggling to rise and instead tried to look at him. Rodian took his foot off Alayna's shoulder, helping her to stand. Then he slapped her across the face, causing her to lose her balance and fall sideways into her friends. "The tights," he demanded.

Petipa had not yet left the stage; neither had the prima ballerina Elena or Pavel Gerdt who had the role of King Akadar. Lubok, too, was on the stage with a notebook standing beside Petipa, pencil at the ready to receive the master's rehearsal schedule. None paid any attention. Brigitte expected someone to reprimand Rodian. No one cared. When she was not quick enough, Rodian reached down for the chair she'd been sitting upon, righted it, and shoved her down. Then he pulled off a ballet slipper, ripping the ribbons. "Do you want me to take them off for you?"

Alayna's expression suddenly changed from defiance to defeat. Shaking her head, she untied her other shoe.

"You *wed'mas* are to stay away from Brigitte. Bother her again, I will see that the punishment is severe."

Alayna put the tights into his outstretched hand. He threw the tights at Brigitte. "Never come onto this stage with bare legs again," he bellowed.

Brigitte decided to skip the light meal she'd brought with her, an apple still edible though it was shriveled, and a piece of black bread, when she felt a touch on her arm.

"I'm sorry about Alayna stealing your tights." It was Elena Cornalba. Elena had come to Russia from Italy and won the admiration of the balletomanes, though some felt her foreignness tainted the ballet. She had arrived as a prima ballerina. Her grace intimidated Brigitte, and she'd never seen a woman with such long eyelashes.

"Oh!" Brigitte stammered. "I am not sure what to do about her."

"I admire your courage walking out on stage as you did. Get your things. You can share my dressing room tonight. By tomorrow the *corps* girls will have someone else to pick on, but for tonight, while they lick their wounds, come with me."

Relief flooded through Brigitte's body. "Thank you."

"I will help you with your hair. I have time if we start early." Elena seemed excited, reminding Brigitte of the older student at the ballet school who taught the Infant Class how to put their hair up in perfect buns. She'd left the ballet to marry after her first year.

"Why are you being so kind?"

Elena led the way past the regisseur's office and to the stairs that took them up to where the premier ballerinas' and danseurs' dressing rooms were. "Not everyone here is horrid."

The prima ballerina had a soft hand; the bristles of her brush felt heavenly on Brigitte's scalp. Fashioning a simple bun, Elena said, "Madame Vazeem is hosting a party tonight. You should come with me." She pushed in the last two pins.

Brigitte laughed. "I cannot go to that. I am only a *coryphée*."

"Certainly, you may." Elena took out her costume from the wardrobe. "There are often *corps de ballet* girls there and you are better than them."

Brigitte's forearms tingled at the prospect of attending an elegant affair, but she was also terrified. Besides the dinner with Tsar Alexander and his family at graduation, where he again told her she'd been his favorite, and to dance for Russia, she'd never been to a fancy social event. "I have nothing to wear."

"After the performance, come here. We will dress together. The food is delicious. I am so hungry after dancing."

"I've only my day dress and street shoes," Brigitte protested. "Thank you for your kindness, but no."

On stage, Elena appeared youthful, her body fluid and graceful. Up close, her face was lined with age, and she winced in pain when she stood up. Rummaging through her wardrobe she said, "You would look lovely in violet, I think, or..." Sorting through more gowns, she said, "Light blue? Which do you like?" Hanging them both on the door of the wardrobe, Elena moved off to the side to look at them, then chose the violet, bringing it over to hold up against Brigitte's skin.

"I dare not wear one of your dresses."

Elena smoothed the silky fabric. "Is it not exquisite?"

"The décolleté is rather low."

Elena looked at Brigitte's chest, then down at her own more generous bosom. "Be brave." She hung the dress back up. "Have you had a lover, yet? Forgive me for being forward, but when men see you in that gown, they will want to make love to you. Are you prepared for that?"

Brigitte's cheeks grew hot. "At school, I could not even speak to my brother without a matron scolding us."

Elena took off her clothes. She seemed vulnerable. "Nothing to fear of the men at the party tonight. Most are harmless. I thought the way that Petrov came to your aid this afternoon, perhaps you were lovers."

"I hate him. He is vile, and a terrible danseur."

Moving over to the dressing table, Elena sat down and looked at herself in the mirror. "Alayna may have had it coming, but to hit a woman like that is coarse."

"I thought no one noticed." Brigitte watched Elena apply her makeup, interested in her technique.

"Not intervening was by choice. Spats happen every day. You have been here for how long? Two, three weeks? Such a baby. Meat for wolves. I want to wrap you in a blanket and put you in a cradle."

"Why would Rodian help me? We are sworn enemies. I hope I haven't caused any trouble for you with Alayna."

"She cannot harm me in the least. If she tried, she knows she'd be out on the street. She and the others need to see you in the same light. Becoming soloist, or prima ballerina is about choices. Ones that keep you safe, that get you the best roles. If Pavel Gerdt and Marius Petipa did not intervene to help her, it was because there was nothing to gain by doing so. Best to leave the little squabbles to those squabbling, or that is all you end up doing, breaking up fights."

"It was that way at school, too."

Elena raised her brow, looking at Brigitte in the mirror. "You are one of the prim ones, I take it? No lovers. No fighting in class?"

For two hours they dressed, nibbled on oranges sent from Italy, and talked. Brigitte felt she'd found a friend, and let down her guard. Elena would be in Russia for the rest of the year as a guest artist before returning home. She told Brigitte of the different world stages she'd adorned, the intrigues in ballet companies, and how she managed to avoid most of it. Her life seemed a dream.

Elena took the stage before Brigitte, but she invited her to stay in the dressing room until her cue, and to return after the performance. As Brigitte sipped on warm tea in a delicate cup, she looked around the room. A blue velvet fainting couch, a side table with wilting flowers in a crystal vase, and the soft, floral smells of one who has their clothing cared for. She thought she might enjoy a life with rooms like this one.

Reluctantly, she left the sanctuary for her ten minutes on stage in the second act. Elena would spend much of the three-hour program in front of the audience. She'd watched prima ballerinas all her life, but never had a private conversation with one. Rather than return to the dressing room, she stood in the shadows of the wings and watched Elena Cornalba dance. Elena had a refinement that surpassed most Russian ballerinas; her popularity was well-earned. But she did not possess anything by way of talent that Brigitte could not work hard to attain, except for being Italian. From that shadowy place looking out into the gaslights of the stage, she felt a rising hope. She promised Tsar Alexander. How much better for Mother Russia if her prima ballerinas were Russian, not Italian?

Elena dressed Brigitte as if she were a doll, making Brigitte uncomfortable. When the violet dress had been buttoned up, the neckline quickly altered by Elena's personal maid, she had Brigitte step away so she could look her over.

"You will create a stir." Reaching into her jewel box on the dressing table, she brought out a brooch, a graceful bird with amethyst eyes and diamond wings. She pinned it onto the back of the dress, tightening the bust some more.

Brigitte thought of the balletomanes who had molested Vlada, wondering if those same men might be at Madame Vazeem's party. The décolletage on the gown was indecently low. "What should I do if there is trouble? I have no experience," she confessed.

Elena pulled Brigitte's gown this way and that, securing tiny folds with two more brooches in the shapes of birds, adding even more elegance to the ensemble. "If a man invites you to his home, tell him to be patient. There are plenty of the *corps* girls waiting for crumbs, just as with ballet roles, but you will seem more enticing, and you will have a say when you are ready to accept the attention of one of them. If a man wants purity, he will be willing to wait, and to pay."

She looked at herself in the mirror. Elena had applied her makeup for her with a light hand, making her eyes look mysterious and her lips wet. She'd never worn makeup that hadn't been meant for the stage.

"I don't know anything about men… that way."

"*Bella* ballerina, men are eager teachers." She returned to the jewel case, selected a pair of amethyst earrings and a matching necklace, put them on Brigitte, and stood back, looking satisfied with how she dressed her live doll.

"I think we are ready." Elena picked up her fur coat, then stopped. "I neglected the coat for you."

"I can rush from carriage to door," Brigitte said.

"It is freezing." Opening the wardrobe once more, Elena took out a sable fur and helped Brigitte slip into it. Stroking the softness, Brigitte thought she would never want to take it off, especially at the party where all the men would see more of her than she'd ever shown before.

"This coat is worth more than you. I want it back first thing in the morning. The gown is worthless to me after tonight. But the coat is different. It is from a man I could adore if he were willing to leave Russia." Elena turned to go but Brigitte stopped her with a hand on her elbow. "What is it?"

"I do not know how to thank you."

"Tell me something," Elena said, her expression serious and sad. "Are you so prim? In your heart? Not just as you were required to behave at school."

The familiar nauseating flip in her stomach caught her by surprise. The image of being swept up by Baba Yaga and taken into the forest flashed before her. "I do not know what I am, yet," she declared.

"You are beautiful. Young, innocent, desirable. Find yourself a protector worth something while you have the power of youth. Things will happen for you, so long as you do not spill anything on that coat."

Madame Vazeem had taken the private dining room at the White and Black Restaurant for her party. Hugging the edges of the room, round tables were covered in white linen, black napkins, and black and white floral centerpieces. At the far end, an orchestra played. She recognized Riccardo Drigo, an Italian composer who captured the Russians' hearts, including hers. At least, she liked his music. He commanded the piano. Drigo nodded in Elena's direction. At one of the tables, to Brigitte's dismay, sat Rodian in the company of two *corps de ballet* dancers, both of whom had reputations for sloppy arm movements - and being tarts.

Elena's escort, a colonel, helped Brigitte to slip free of the fur, as she fought her urge to cling to the warmth and coverage. He had nuzzled Elena's neck in the carriage, while Elena laughed and whispered things to him. Brigitte had felt invisible.

Madame Vazeem floated towards them. The heavyset woman crooned, "Here she is, our prima ballerina, Elena, our Italian treasure."

Brigitte could not imagine bearing the weight of all the jewelry Madame wore. Her white gloves did little to disguise thick fingers, and neither did the gold rings.

"Arriving late. So charming." Madame Vazeem scolded Elena, embracing her and kissing her on each cheek. "Whom have you brought for me?"

"Promise me my share for her or I will take her out of here right now." Elena's demeanor shifted and she locked eyes with Madame Vazeem until Vazeem broke into a wide smile.

"Of course, Elena. You know I value your good taste." She turned her attention to Brigitte. "You must be a spectacular dancer," she said. "Colonel Kuznetsov, please, introduce us."

Elena's escort stepped forward, his braided cords swaying. "Brigitte Gustoevna Legher, daughter of Gustave Legher. Tsar Alexander declared her graduation performance from the Imperial Ballet School last spring to be his favorite." The Colonel smiled politely.

Madame Vazeem embraced her. Her hands moved up and down Brigitte's back and as she drew away, she brushed Brigitte's breasts. "You are lovely."

Madame Vazeem stood close to Brigitte, their bodies touching. Brigitte took a step back and bumped into Rodian. Madame Vazeem and Rodian greeted each other with stiff formality.

Taking Brigitte's arm, Madame Vazeem maneuvered her away from Elena.

"Delightful. Yes, there is someone you need to meet." Madame looked out over her guests and led Brigitte to where a group of five men stood arguing politics. The youngest had hair but was thinning on top. The oldest looked as if he might turn to dust within the hour. Two wore black tuxedos, and the other three formal military dress uniforms. Madame barged into their circle, bringing Brigitte with her.

"Look whom I have, gentlemen. A new dancer for you. Are you a soloist yet, dear?"

They turned their full attention upon her as a group. Two of the men licked their lips, flustering Brigitte. "*Coryphée*," she answered, her voice coming out as a whisper.

"Sorry," one of the military-dressed men said smiling. "Speak louder. You are a soloist?"

"No," Brigitte said, her mouth going dry.

"She is *coryphée*, Uncle," the youngest-looking man said, frowning. She appreciated his expression; far different from the other four who looked at her like hungry beasts.

"Brigitte Gustoevna Legher," Madame introduced her. "You will find her most amusing." With that, she disappeared, leaving Brigitte alone.

She discovered that she was not expected to say anything. Any inquiry directed towards her would be answered in assumption by another, followed by guffaws. Then they began to touch her. One rested his hand on her elbow, as he leaned in to look more closely at her necklace. She felt a hand on her bottom and turned to dislodge it. The oldest had a devilish grin. Another put his arm around her waist, pulling her close. "She smells divine."

Brigitte looked for Elena, desperate for help with how to handle the unwelcome attention.

"Excuse me," Rodian appeared beside her. "Brigitte, come. Dinner is served at our table." He did not wait for permission, but freed Brigitte's hand from the grasp of the men and led her off.

"I do not wish to be your dinner partner," she hissed in protest.

He spoke into her ear, "You will most likely be Madame Vazeem's highest earner this evening, but I have a mind to foil her scheme, at least this one time."

Rodian held her chair for her at the table. She sat, only to avoid embarrassment.

"There you are," Madame Vazeem said, the honey in her voice again, but the look she gave to Rodian was lethal. "I have a gentleman who would like to make your acquaintance." She held her hand out towards Brigitte, motioning for her to stand. "Come, come," she said.

"Excuse me, Madame, Brigitte is famished. The plates are beginning to arrive." Rodian stepped between them, gesturing towards the waiters who were now descending upon the dining room with overloaded trays.

Madame Vazeem was not easily put off. "There is a place beside General Makarov. You will enjoy him, Brigitte. Perhaps he will recite you one of his poems."

Rodian did not budge. "She has promised to sup with me. You will forgive me if I hold her to that promise, but you can see, she is quite the loveliest woman here tonight, besides yourself, of course," he smiled showing his teeth.

Madame showed her teeth as well. "An introduction will take but a moment." She waved at a man leaning against the wall by the front door, who quickly headed in their direction.

Rodian stepped aside, allowing Madame to propel Brigitte out of her chair. Madame murmured to Rodian, "My man here will break your legs if you interfere."

Madame deposited Brigitte in the chair next to a man with a fat cigar in his mouth, a wreath of smoke circling his head that matched his hairline. The General put his hand on her thigh; his table mate claimed the other. She tried to excuse herself but found that they held her down with caresses.

She had not been at the table more than a few minutes before Rodian appeared again, pulling her chair away. This time, no words were exchanged. He simply escorted her directly out of the dining room and requested her fur.

She allowed him to help her into it, and as they were leaving through the front door, she could hear Elena calling after her. "I should say good night." Brigitte turned, but Rodian held her by the elbow and kept moving.

He pushed her into a carriage and jumped in behind her. The driver, one of the thousands of Vankas in St. Petersburg, wore the uniform heavy blue coat and beaver hat. He shut the door and leapt to his seat, already clicking to his horses.

Brigitte felt like she'd just danced a full ballet, breathless and spent. Sensations, the hands, the leering, being pushed and tugged, ignored, and the center of attention; Elena Cornalba's kindness followed by her abandonment, and Rodian coming to her rescue yet again. She'd never experienced men like these balletomanes. Perhaps they were harmless and not like the men who molested Darya. She did not know. She did know that she hated the very sight of Rodian and now she was trapped in a carriage with him.

"I should slap you," she said. "Are all dinner parties like this?"

He answered, "The sooner you understand about Madame Vazeem's dinner parties, the better. Simply stated, she is a trader in flesh. If the sums being offered to her this evening for exclusive rights to you are any indication of your potential of pleasing the balletomanes and rising to the top, you may yet have a career ahead of you, B. Legher."

She thought about this for a moment, adding it like a collection of stones in a bowl filling with the cacophony of the day's events. "How is it she would earn money from me? Are you saying she was selling me like a prostitute? Ridiculous. I think I would know if that were the case."

"Are you so naïve? You walked through the door of the White and Black in that gown, spilling over, as it were," he gestured towards her chest. "You are the merchandise."

There were times in learning new choreography when the master named the movements, *rallentando ronde jambe*, rather than demonstrating. Brigitte always faltered until she could see the dance. The whole night felt like being told the choreography without seeing it.

"All those men there were looking for...sex? They are the aristocrats."

He laughed. "They are swine. Swine with money and the protection of their titles. If any other man in St. Petersburg acted in that manner, he would be flogged."

Brigitte felt sick.

Rodian looked out the window. "Where do you live?"

She hesitated to tell him, but at the moment, what choice did she have? "Near the Mariinsky." She gave him her address and Rodian stopped the driver, instructing him to see her safely home, paid him, then stepped off the carriage closing the door and saying goodnight.

Pulling the collar of the fur coat up tighter around her neck, she settled back into the quiet of the seat, thankful to have the space all to herself. Sometimes she wished that no one would touch her, that she could lift off and fly without a partner. All her life she'd been stroked. Teachers would come at her body with their sticks, pushing and prodding, tapping curved shoulders, and lifting a heavy leg. Her head had been tilted for her. Only her breasts and the hidden space between her legs were not subject to touch.

Inhaling deeply the heavy scent of the Neva River, smoke from the fires that kept homes warm and fueled the factories, and the sweet acrid fumes of the city's sewers, she wondered about her choices. What choices did she have? What was hers to save, protect, or sell?

Play. Not play. Was it a game, she thought? Winners, losers, fortunes made. If she did not play, she stood to lose the chance at a protector — a balletomane who would take an interest in her, promote her to soloist, perhaps even prima ballerina one day. A protector who would keep her from becoming a quick meal for the wolves at Madame Vazeem's parties. If she did not play, she would belong only to herself; that was worth something.

It occurred to her that most of the prima ballerinas were somehow associated with a powerful balletomane. She was curious about her mysterious sponsor. A man, or a woman, she didn't know which, who paid her parents to keep a household for her, paid for her time at school. Where was that sponsor now? Would this not be the time for this person to step forward and become a protector? But there had been no more money for her. No acknowledgment at all that she was the only survivor of the Infant Class. Had her sponsor ever even watched her dance? Did they care about her? She wanted a dressing room where she could lock the door, like Elena Cornalba. And fur coats, jewelry, pretty gowns. What she wanted was a peaceful place she could go at all hours of the day and night and get lost in the solitude of her own body. A place with a room like Gustave had in their apartment, where he taught lessons, where she would sleep when she came home for visits. She wanted her own dance studio.

As the Vanka turned down her street, she recognized three women walking together. Two were *corps de ballet* dancers who had been with the Imperial Theater for a long time. One of them for fifteen years already. The other was a seamstress with the costume department, known for lying about measurements if a ballerina had put on a little weight, then letting costumes out, for a small fee.

This would be her in a few years without a protector. Living in a run-down apartment, wearing a worn-out coat.

At rehearsal the next afternoon, Rodian lifted her like an object, not a woman. As if she were a bunch of flowers to twirl, toss, and catch. This was the work, to be the bouquet.

When Petipa finished with them, she headed toward the dressing room.

Rodian stepped in front of her, looking angry. "I had a visitor this morning. Madame Vazeem brought along a man meant to intimidate me with his size and stupidity."

"What did she want?" She felt for Rodian. He did seem to be helping her. But she also wished a little that someone would beat him up.

"To let me know I am now *persona non grata*." He smiled wryly. "To threaten me with physical harm if I prevent her from acquiring you as one of her assets."

"Have you told the theater director? Is that not what the theater police are for?"

Rodian laughed, a nasty sound. "You are a stupid *wed'ma*. We may belong to the Tsar but he will not protect you if his friends wish to play rough."

Worse than his speaking the truth, she was now beholden to Rodian for the risk he had taken on her behalf. She wanted to understand the nuances of the game. "Why were you at Madame's party last night?"

"Why would I not be there? For the free meal and to supplement my income."

It gave her a shiver of repulsion, like watching a rat, its whiskers quivering, its nose taking in the smells.

"Were you an escort for the *corps de ballet* girls?"

He bowed his head and scratched his chin. His teeth glinted in the dim stage lights. "Not there to escort them, no. Not all balletomanes are looking for ballerinas. Some of them prefer danseurs."

Brigitte stifled a gasp. He could not mean what she thought he meant. Pushing the thought aside to consider later, she asked, "Why did you take me out? Am I in your debt?"

"No," he said forcefully, his arm sweeping down across his body as if to deflect a missile thrown at him. "You owe me nothing."

He turned and walked away, his head down and leading his body in a posture that Madame Nadeah would have frowned upon. Always, head up.

She went to the women's dressing room to retrieve Elena Cornalba's fur from her locker where she had roughly shoved it inside, feeling as though she had been treated worse by Elena who stood to profit from the bidding on Brigitte's body. At first, she indulged herself in feeling betrayed; by the middle of the night, lying in bed staring at the ceiling, she realized Rodian had bought her time to learn Madame's game. Being angry at Elena served nothing. Her debt to Elena for any kindness the day before had been paid in full. Now they were equal.

Knocking on Elena's dressing room door. Elena invited Brigitte in.

"Thank you for the coat".

Elena lounged on the fainting couch. She reached over to a side table covered with a red scarf where there was a glass of tea and a cigarette case beside a crystal ashtray, two cigarettes already crushed out. Elena opened the case. "Smoke? You left without saying goodnight. Did you meet anyone interesting?"

"Madame Vazeem interests me."

Elena sat up and took a sip of tea. "I began dance lessons when I was eight. As little girls, they put so much value on our purity. What's more precious that a pretty little girl in a white dress? One lecture after another on the importance of practice and form. Passion was not mentioned until we were fourteen or fifteen years old, and only about passion in dance. Then you learn that you have not been trained for the expression of beauty or the attainment of perfection of the body." Elena moved from the couch to her dressing table. She examined her face in the mirror. "Madame Vazeem's parties are brothels. Balletomanes, the customers. The ballet? Simply a storefront where we parade, show a little leg, some flesh, and what do we get in return? Protection — so we can continue to dance because they teach us as little girls to love ballet. They make us hungry for it. Crave it. Do anything for a moment on the stage. A ballet lasts three, maybe four hours. What we do for those hours steals our soul for all eternity."

She looked at Brigitte, then turned back to the mirror to powder her face. "Your ash is about to fall on the carpet."

Brigitte got up and crushed the cigarette in the overflowing ashtray on Elena's dressing table. "I want to know how to choose who may run his hands over my body. How do I get a protector who will see that I have a private dressing room as you do?" She opened the jewelry case beside it, running her fingers over the sparkling stones. "Your necklace, earrings, and brooches are in your coat pocket, by the way."

"Go see Madame. She is not an unreasonable woman."

After the evening performance, Brigitte had been one of the first to rush out the backstage door, wanting nothing more than to get home and take a bath. A few of the men from Madame Vazeem's party had sent notes inviting her out and she needed time to strategize. Several carriages were waiting, and she chose one of the smaller ones usually reserved for principals. She expected the driver to question her status and was relieved when he didn't. If you act as if you were important, you are treated that way. She pulled the curtains on the windows to give herself privacy. At least one other would need to ride with her before the driver would leave and she sighed with relief when the door opened after only a short wait. She recoiled when she saw that it was Rodian.

"Seems I am destined to run into you at every turn," she said sounding crueler than she intended.

"No dinner party for you this evening?" he asked, taking the seat opposite her. The carriage jerked and took up a steady, jostling movement.

"Not for you, either?"

He shrugged. "As I said, *persona non grata*."

She could smell his breath, not sweet but not unpleasant. He had danced hard. She smelled that too. When it felt awkward to hear only the clip-clopping of the horse's hooves on the cobblestones, Brigitte said, "If you were not a danseur, what would you be doing?"

"Why do you ask?" He crossed his arms and rested his head back against the seat.

"You hate ballet."

"What makes you say that?"

"There is something you wish you were doing instead of dancing."

He laughed gruffly. "Have you wanted to be a prima ballerina since you began in the Infant Class?"

"Yes. But you, you wanted something else."

He leaned forward, taking her hand that rested in her lap, holding it, even taking her mitten off and looking at her fingers, though it was dark. "How do you know this?"

"My hand is cold," she said, but she did not pull away. "I partner with you," she responded. "You cannot help but reveal some secrets. I do not know how else to explain. Maybe you know some of my secrets, too," she said laughing, hoping to ease the seriousness of the moment. She hadn't expected him to be honest. Truthfully, she meant to rile him.

"I wanted to be a horse officer. As a boy, we had horses at our dacha. My father lost it all. Went into debt for a time. Horses have always made more sense to me than people. The men in the military make more sense to me than men in ballet, than the balletomanes."

"Your secret is that you are in love with me," he said. "You wish that I would kiss you."

"No," she shook her head, pulling her hand away. "Quite the opposite. I have appreciated your coming to my rescue, but don't imagine I like you."

The carriage stopped. The Vanka opened the door and Rodian got out. They were at his apartment building.

"My landlady prepares my meals. Her husband brings up a tray. She is an excellent cook. I have good vodka, too." His expression was relaxed, hopeful. "Join me."

Curiosity drove her to accept the invitation.

They walked up three flights. He led her to the first door on the left; his windows would look over the Catherine Canal. Rodian unlocked the door with two separate locks using two keys.

She walked into a cozy sitting room, a fireplace at one end with a neat fire burning behind the grate, a table with two chairs near the fire, and behind, a sideboard with plates, cups, and a samovar, bubbling away.

"It is as if you just left," Brigitte said. "You have a servant?"

"No servant, but for not too much more money, the landlady does all this for me. Sets the fire, lights the samovar, and brings dinner. It should arrive shortly."

He held out his hand to take her coat. If this had been her apartment, she would leave her coat on until the steam heat came up from the boiler in the basement, but it was warm here and she gave it to him.

The room smelled like Rodian, dried sweat, musky.

There was a knock at the door. Rodian answered, returning the gruff hello, and a small, balding man came in carrying a tray loaded down with a tureen, a plate with slices of dark bread, and a bowl with preserved apples. When the landlord noticed her, he paused and looked as if he wanted to say something, but thought better of it.

"Am I to surmise he has not often found women here?" she asked after the landlord had gone. It delighted her to think that he may be as innocent a soul as she.

"Not women, no." He responded, moving about to set the table with bowls and cutlery. Taking from the sideboard the bottle of vodka, he filled two short clear glasses, handing one to her. "*Na radinu.* To the Motherland."

He ladled out the thick soup. The broth was rich with chunks of parsnip, beef, and carrots. She'd missed dinner the day before from Madame's party, and had only tea and toast that morning before ballet class, and a handful of walnuts before the evening's performance.

When she still had half a bowl left, he took it from her as if to assume she could eat no more. "You want to stay light enough for me to pick up," he said, putting the dishes on a tray and setting it outside his door in the hallway, presumably for the landlord to pick up later. He then poured them both a drink. "*Na radinu.*" He swallowed in one gulp.

"To the Motherland." Brigitte looked at the glass. She took a taste.

"Drink," Rodian cajoled. "You are not a true Russian if you only sip vodka."

She drank it all at once, as he had done, dribbling down her chin and spitting some back into the glass, choking.

He laughed.

Had she ever seen him smile not just with his vicious dog teeth, but like this, with his eyes? Friendly?

Rodian refilled her glass. "Try again," he said. "To the tsar."

"To the tsar," she toasted. She got half of the burning liquid down before coughing and shuddering.

He laughed heartily and for the first time, he didn't look bored or angry.

"I am going to meet Madame Vazeem on Wednesday," she said. "What do you think?" She hadn't intended to tell anyone.

Standing slowly, he went to the window and looked out. "So, you will be her whore?"

"If we can come to terms. Maybe."

"For two years I have attended Madame's soirées. In two years, I have not risen to soloist. Neither have I been fired by the regisseur. Does she help me? Does she keep me employed? I have no idea anymore."

Brigitte picked up the bottle and brought it over to him, making a gesture to refill his glass. He held it out for her and she poured, looking him in the eye, rather than watching the vodka. When the glass overflowed, he put his hand on hers to right the bottle. She did not pull away. "If this is the game, I want a share of the winnings," she said. She willed herself to stay near him, while a voice in her head screamed *fly away, run*. Her hand began to twitch.

Rodian pulled her to him and kissed her. She tried banishing the screaming woman. When that did not work, she left her body, watching passively, standing by the sideboard, intrigued by the way Rodian unbuttoned her blouse.

He picked her up and carried her to his bed, cold, unwelcoming. From outside of herself she watched his white ass, the dark hair, and the way he moved with his pants around his ankles.

When he rolled off her, she took a deep breath, relief at the lift of weight. He went into the other room, took the water pitcher, added some warm water from the samovar and poured it all into a basin, then washed. He poured more water onto a washcloth and brought it to her. "You are bleeding."

She looked down at the blanket, horrified to see her period had started, or perhaps she'd been hurt. It had been painful and thankfully hadn't lasted long. She took the washcloth. He went out, coming back with the water basin. "I'll leave you to clean up. Let me know if you need anything."

He closed the door, leaving her in the dark room. In the shadows she did her best to dress, folding the towel between her legs.

When she came out, he sat in a chair drinking from the bottle, the glass abandoned. "You deserve better," he said sadly. "I have thought so from the first I watched you dance."

"You hated me straight off, same as I hated you."

"No, I never hated you." He smiled, stood, and put his arms around her. She held still.

"You scared me witless. You are so perfect and talented. So serious and intense," he said.

Pieces of her came back, drawn by her curiosity about what he was saying. "You were scared? By me?"

"Of course, everyone at the school was intimidated by you. Of how perfect your technique is. Who could compete with you?"

The stars had been put out by heavy clouds. The first snow of the winter began. Rodian noticed and went to stand again by the window where his vodka glass had been left on the sill. "This snow will stay until spring, I think."

"Do you have a cigarette?" she asked.

He went to his coat on the hook by the door, took a case from the pocket, and extracted one cigarette. At the fireplace, he lit a stick from the open flame, used it to light the cigarette, and then brought it over to her.

She inhaled the smoke deep into her lungs, feeling herself becoming meeker, as if what they had done stole some of her legendary intensity.

"If I open a bottle of wine, would you have some?"

The wetness of the blood seeping between her legs made her uncomfortable. What she wanted was her room, her washbasin, her own bed. "I would like you to summon a carriage," she said lightly.

She felt as though he moved across the stage away from her. She didn't want to pull him closer. It had been intriguing to hear him talk intimately and to see his manhood fully engorged. When had she become so curious? In school, she had been partnered by boys who could not control themselves as they stood behind her for a lift. She felt their mortification and desire. His fierceness should have frightened her, but it didn't. Rather, what frightened her was what he might expect from her now. Thinking he despised her was easier than this.

She waited for him to speak, but he sat silent, the snow falling, the smoke from her cigarette a haze rising to the ceiling where all the warm air uselessly gathered.

She tossed the remains of her cigarette into the fireplace prompting Rodian to retrieve her coat from the rack by the door.

"Do you want me to see you home?" he offered.

"I doubt anyone will bother me on the night of winter's first snow. Molesters of young women stay near their fires." She had meant it as a joke, but his brow was furrowed and he looked uncertain what to do. "I prefer to walk alone," she said.

If Madame Vazeem had been surprised by Brigitte's request to speak with her, she did not let on. Her manservant answered the door and showed Brigitte to a sitting room just off the foyer with four upholstered chairs in soft florals set at a small round tea table. A fire crackled and popped in the grate and the room smelled of cinnamon and cloves. On the wall across from the fireplace hung two rows of framed portraits, ten in all, mostly women.

A clock on the mantel tracked the time she sat waiting. Forty-nine minutes. The time it took for the fire to die down. Finally, Madame came in with a flourish, as though the curtain were going up on a stage.

"My ungrateful guest," she greeted Brigitte, a sneering smile on her face. "I was so disappointed when you rushed out the other night." Madame Vazeem seated herself opposite Brigitte. "How noble of Rodian Petrov to claim you for himself." She laughed, which turned into a hacking cough until finally, she pulled out a handkerchief, spat into it then tucked it into her sleeve. "I hate winter in St. Petersburg. If it were not profitable to be here during the ballet season, I would leave for Crimea."

"I am here to talk about working for you," Brigitte interjected, feeling the longer she allowed Madame to speak, the more control she forfeited. "If I am to be sold in some manner, I want to choose to whom, and, I want a portion of the payment."

"What a curious young woman you are."

Brigitte clasped her hands tighter in her lap. "You may sell me to a balletomane, but he must be stable. Not like the animals at your market the other night. If I don't like the man you select, I will go home alone. I will play, but not be toyed with. I am only interested in being a mistress to a man that can further my career. I want solos and to be prima ballerina."

"And if I deny you? I have plenty of ballerinas now. Without me, you will stay in the *corps de ballet*. I might even decide to see to it that your contract is canceled."

"I doubt you have lasted this long in St. Petersburg by having many dancers fired."

Madame's eyes were cauldrons of boiling, black water. "If you expect to interest one of the men who attend my private dinners, you need to speak with more subtlety and elegance."

"I can speak as elegantly as anyone. At the moment I have no wish to be subtle. If you agree to my terms, you stand to earn whatever amount it is you earn from the balletomane for the purchase of his ballerina. If you have me fired, you lose me completely and make nothing." She paused, allowing the silence to grow uncomfortable.

A log fell in the fireplace. Madame looked towards the grate, then reached for the bell, ringing it. Still, neither said anything. When her servant appeared, Madame pointed to the grate. "It is getting chilly. Build up the flame." The manservant left and returned with two logs. "Bring some tea," Madame ordered.

"The lone survivor of the ill-fated Infant Class. I lost money when I wagered that at least two of you would make it to first soloists. Good to be finished with the whole thing near to the start, I suppose. It can take years to make first soloist. I have often speculated that it was your training with your father, Gustave, that gave you an advantage over the other girls. How did you survive?" Madame moved up in her seat, leaning closer to Brigitte, then reaching out and touching her cheek. "Lots of secrets around the whole affair that I have never managed to uncover, and I am quite good at uncovering secrets."

Brigitte moved away from Madame's touch and thought carefully about how to answer. "The Infant Class gave me a perfect turnout, Madame. I have survived because as long as I can remember I have been told that I am destined to be prima ballerina absoluta. I know this to be true and there is nothing that I will let stop me. Not you, not the balletomanes, not even the tsar."

"The tsar?" Madame leaned back, a wry smile on her face. "Well, you were the only racehorse with an anonymous owner."

It galled Brigitte to realize Madame might know more about her sponsor than she did but she resolved to give nothing of her ignorance away. She forged ahead. "Bring me a man who will promote me. If I do not like him, or he fails me, I will not hesitate to refuse him. That is the proposition."

The servant knocked once, opened the door, and brought in a tray. Brigitte could smell the fragrant tea and the sweetness of biscuits and jam. He poured for Madame first, then for Brigitte.

"Put a cake on Mlle. Legher's plate," Madame ordered. "The tarts are delicious."

"Just tea, thank you." Brigitte smiled. "I do not eat sweet things, lest I get fat."

Madame scowled, dismissing the servant with a curt wave. "No sugar in your tea?"

"Please Madame, put as much sugar and cream in your cup as you want. I drink my tea plain."

At this Madame began to laugh, a hearty guffaw that soon had her dabbing her eyes. Brigitte watched, bemused.

"Oh, dear child, what a time life is going to have with you." Still chuckling she added, "One day you will discover this cleverness of yours has been quite your undoing." Popping a pink cake into her mouth, she said, "We have an agreement."

"One more thing."

"I look forward to your one more thing." Madame wiped her fingers on a pink linen napkin.

"I do not have a proper wardrobe. I leave the number of gowns I'll need to your expertise. Also, a decent cloak." Brigitte snapped open her beaded purse and took out a folded piece of paper. "These are my measurements." She stood up, putting the paper on the tray. "I believe that is all. I can show myself out."

Madame put her teacup down, pushing herself up out of the deep chair with some effort. "You are going to be very amusing to watch," she said. "I have a couple of men in mind who might find you of interest. You can buy your own gowns, however." She pushed past Brigitte, into the foyer to a gilded side table with a marble top and three drawers below. Opening one, Madame took out a quill, a pot of ink, and a card. She scribbled something out and slid it into a creamy white envelope. "Take this to any of the shops in the Passages at Gostiny Dvor on Nevsky Prospekt. It will allow you to charge a gown to my account. One gown. One cloak. One necklace and earrings. One pair of shoes. The appropriate undergarments, of course. Something pleasing." Madame took another card. She wrote on it, saying, "Go to this address. Ask for Moksha. She knows secrets to avoid pregnancies. The men I will introduce you to are not the sort to be trapped with babies." Madame stopped writing for a moment and scrutinized Brigitte's face. "Your mother may have figured out how to have a successful career and more children than anyone can count, but rumor has it not all your siblings were hers." She signed her name to the note with a flourish, sealed the envelope, and pushed it towards Brigitte. Going to the door, she opened it. "I will give you a little time to secure all you need, but expect my invitation soon."

Brigitte, horrified by the mention of Nina, managed to curtsy and departed.

As soon as the door shut behind her, Brigitte heard Madame break into gales of laughter. She walked swiftly down the sidewalk and around the corner, leaned against the wall of the building, and vomited.

CHAPTER 6

St. Petersburg, January 1889

It had only taken attendance at one of Madame Vazeem's parties to kindle a flame. Recently retired from the Hussars, the horse guard responsible for security for the Imperial family, Colonel Alexandrovich had spent his career beside Tsar Alexander III from the time the tsar had been a young man. He spoke of his Imperial Majesty as a dear friend.

The dinner had been an intimate affair. Madame Vazeem placed Brigitte in the middle of the long table so that all might easily look upon her. By the end of the evening, she'd found herself seated on Colonel Alexandrovich's knee in Madame's salon. He regaled them with stories of his escapades with the Hussars and the tsar. Brigitte wondered if his tales were greatly exaggerated. She could not fathom putting herself at such risk.

He had taken her to his luxurious apartment near the Alexander Palace that evening and to his bed. His wife's presence was felt in the décor and framed photos.

The colonel was a slow lover, so different from her single experience with Rodian. His chest and pubis of grey hair unsettled her, as did the taste and feel of his teeth and tongue when he kissed her. Wet. His demonstration of passion seemed rather like an assault of an overly-friendly dog. She played the role of ingénue, allowing him to instruct her the art of lovemaking, though even in her vast inexperience, she knew he was not a good teacher.

A bracelet arrived for her in a wrapped velvet box delivered to the theater the night after their meeting. He invited her for a private dinner in his home a week later and presented her with a silver hair clip and matching earrings. After their third evening together, he fell asleep with his arms wrapped around her and in the morning showered her with more gifts, a gown for a dinner he wished her to attend with him, and jewels and shoes to match. Brigitte felt as though she were all set, as though she had boarded the train to her future and she need only watch as the scenery swished by outside the window.

After a rehearsal for *The Talisman*, at Petipa's request, Brigitte stayed while Petipa sat in the front row beside the composer, Pytor Tchaikovsky, a distinguished-looking man with intelligent eyes. The two together made a powerful pairing huddled in the vacant theater. While they did not immediately acknowledge her presence, Petipa finally asked her to perform a simple pas, a series of movements she felt she executed perfectly. Then he dismissed her.

The next day when she arrived, the regisseur, Stonich, gave her a notice informing her that she would be a part of a revival of *Swan Lake,* which had first premiered in 1877 in Moscow and had never been performed since.

Brigitte worked in the rehearsal hall with Lev Ivanov, her old teacher, who never taught her a single useful thing, who was doing the choreography of Tchaikovsky's music.

Pavel Gerdt partnered her. An expert in miming, he'd been her teacher at the ballet school. For 30 years he had commanded the hearts of the balletomanes and harsh critics who found it impossible to write anything about him but flattery. Now nearing 50, his appeal grew with each passing year. A strong square jaw, tender eyes, and a full head of hair gave him the air of a hero, a likable villain, a dignified king.

After they had worked for a full week, Petipa came in to observe, sitting silently on a wooden chair for a half hour before he stopped them just as Gerdt partnered Brigitte's pirouette from a *développé* to an *arabesque*. "Her you make too hard for," he said to Ivanov. "She can no do. I care not of orders from Directorate. To hell with. Get Olga. Olga does."

Tears pricked her eyes. One escaped down her cheek. She pleaded, "I will work harder."

Petipa and Ivanov looked at Pavel Gerdt who had one hand on Brigitte's waist and the other holding her hand. She felt as though she did not exist to them.

"Again then," was all the ballet master said, standing and walking out.

The two-hour rehearsal had been more of a choreography session. Ivanov could not seem to settle on any part of the dance. When they finished, Brigitte was exhausted, and she still had a performance ahead.

Ivanov and the pianist left. Brigitte sat to take off her pointe shoes.

"Do not fret, *Lastochka*," Pavel said. "If *Swan Lake* does not come to fruition, and I suspect it may not if experience serves me, there will be another ballet for you. You are talented, young, and beautiful. Your moment is waiting for you. Don't pin all your dreams on this ballet. You will make yourself weak with want and worry."

She struggled to compose herself. "Come," he said and took her in his arms, holding her tenderly. She began to sob, as though his voice called the emotion from her. He stroked her hair, saying, "*Lastochka*, it is a small moment in a grand life." His use of the endearment *lastochka*, little swallow, soothed her.

After a time, she pulled away, wiping her eyes with the back of her hand. He reached for a nearby towel, handing it to her. It smelled of his sweat, but she didn't care. She blew her nose.

"This is my role," she said defiant, angry. Tears welled up again.

"We all see your potential, even Petipa."

"Will Petipa replace me?"

Gerdt shrugged. "This is a big ballet. Expensive. To build it around an unknown? It is not unheard of. Marius is unhappy with Elena at the moment. Unhappy with *The Talisman*. He says he would rather the orchestra be on stage and the dancers in the pit," Pavel laughed. "But perhaps he will like how things are looking in another week. He will appreciate your beautiful swan."

She put her shoes into her bag. They were worn out, finished. She'd been slipping and could feel the loss of support. Sometime in the next day or two, she'd have to go to Liftshedt's on Nevsky Prospekt, the best place in St. Petersburg to get shoes custom-made. The Imperial Ballet bought their dancers shoes. Between the *Classique de Perfection,* private lessons, her practicing, rehearsals, and performances, she would go through nearly 100 pairs of shoes by the end of the year.

"I am not sure I am good enough." In her exhaustion, she was not certain she'd spoken aloud, or just thought it but it was something she thought every day.

"Each dance is made up of single steps. If you try to dance the whole ballet at once, it comes out all wrong. Relax. Enjoy yourself. Take each step as it comes."

Brigitte continued to dance for Ivanov through the week as he continuously altered his choreography. That Wednesday, Pytor Tchaikovsky came in to observe.

The piano accompanist was particularly anxious and fumbled the notes, glancing apologetically at the composer. Ivanov was thoroughly frustrated with the way the dance was coming together. Brigitte felt it was her failure.

Ivanov had ignored his students' mistakes as a teacher at the ballet school. He was not ignoring them now.

Tchaikovsky politely asked forgiveness for the intrusion and then quietly watched. After a time, he rose and left. The pianist played much better afterward.

The next day as she was on the floor stretching, waiting for the others, Pytor Tchaikovsky again came in. "Little Swan," he said. "I was told you were here. The young man I asked said you are always in here." Pytor chuckled. "Like me with a piano."

As he walked towards her, papers fell from his hands, scattering about the floor. Moving quickly, she retrieved them. "New music for Petipa," he said accepting the pages back. "He's not been satisfied with revisions."

She handed him the pages. "He is not satisfied with me, either," she said.

He went to the piano and played for her.

As if the music had bewitched her slippers, she seemed to know each note before it sounded. Her partner became the notes themselves, lightly swirling around her, twirling her, lifting an arm, a leg, bending her, coaxing the wings from her shoulders, bringing her to the other side of life, into death.

When at last he took his hands from the keys, she found herself on the floor, her arms extended, her legs tucked underneath her.

"You are a swan."

Somberly, he bowed his head, as he would to an audience. "Petipa intends to have someone else dance the swan."

She crumpled, wrapping her arms about herself.

He stood, taking up his music. "You may believe that your life is in the hands of Marius Petipa, and he is powerful. Whether or not this music is ever heard largely depends on him. Much I've composed no one has ever heard. It may seem to Petipa that his life is in the hands of the theater director, and the director's life in the hands of the balletomanes and the tsar. None of it is true. Our lives are our own. Ours and perhaps God's — I am still undecided." He leaned in closer to her. "I can speak to Master Petipa for you. Perhaps it will make a difference."

"Thank you," she said, her heart breaking.

"Dance for yourself first. That is how you keep your life your own."

A short time later, Ivanov returned for their rehearsal, never mentioning that she was to be replaced. At the end of the week, though, the announcement came — the ballet was scrapped. It was not only her being rejected, but Swan Lake altogether, Tchaikovsky's music, Ivanov's choreography, and Pavel Gerdt, too.

Heavy with disappointment, she put her shawl around her coat for extra warmth before leaving that day.

"Have I heard correctly?" Rodian's hand caught her shoulder. He wore an expression of disdain. "Madame Vazeem paired you with Colonel Alexandrovich?"

"Yes. And it is none of your business."

"Bottom of the page." Rodian handed her a newspaper. "Died in his sleep. Perhaps he was a good man," Rodian said scornfully. The story reported the death of Colonel Gizla Michael Alexandrovich.

She felt no grief. Handing Rodian his newspaper, she said, "A week ago, there seemed to be no time for sleep. Now I have no afternoon rehearsals and no evening engagements."

"I would be pleased to escort you to a good meal. You look as if you could use one."

"I do not want to get heavy."

"You are too light. When I lift you, I fear you will fly up into the rafters."

She scrutinized him. "You can buy me a meal but that is all. I need a new dress and it would be a misstep in my career to turn down free food."

"On second thought," Rodian hesitated. "I will leave you alone to grieve your loss."

CHAPTER 7

Lisiy Nos, February 1889

When Madame's next invitation came, Brigitte had been planning on going to the Leghers' to help Nina with preparations for the family's Maslenitsa celebration. Since she'd been in school, and only came home for the celebration days, Nina had never asked her to help before. She had been excited to spend time with her mother, but also looked forward to being with her family.

She could not refuse Madame, of course. Nikolai had been the one who had taken it hard when she told them she would miss the festivities. Nina had only shrugged, which hurt more than Nikolai telling her she was a stupid *wed'ma*.

The train took her north out of St. Petersburg through the countryside to Lisiy Nos, on her way to a dacha of one of the balletomanes hosting a weeklong party. She rode with Julija, a third soloist and a friend Brigitte felt she could trust. Madame arranged for both of them to be the adornments of a Maslenitsa celebration hosted by Count Leonid Verontsov. Julija had more experience with Madame's special social events, so Brigitte followed her lead.

Julija attracted gossip the way dirt few through open windows. She had a flirtatious habit of twirling a strand of her auburn hair, worn loose, except on stage, through her fingers. She talked nonstop as they rode along, revealing that Count Verontsov's wife, Raisa, was Madame Vazeem's cousin, and although Raisa had spent a fortune renovating the dacha, she refused to leave their winter home in Crimea until midsummer. Raisa, herself, had written Madame Vazeem asking her to host Maslenitsa at the dacha in her place.

"I think Raisa hopes Madame will find someone for her husband so he will leave her in peace, and she can do whatever she wants. That's how these aristocratic marriages work, you know," Julija said. "I've met Count Verontsov. I think maybe Raisa is the awful one. He is a good man. And lonely. You can always tell. Men have this look in their eye like they are confused."

As the deep forests clicked by, Brigitte tuned out Julija and her thoughts traveled back to the Leghers and the week-long spring festival of Maslenitsa. Beginning on the Monday before Lent, called Welcoming Day, each day of the week held something special. Gustave made up silly dances, always ending with their arms linked, the family prancing through the apartment going faster and faster until they collapsed in heaps of laughter. There were special songs they sang. There were special foods that Nina was going to show her how to make.

Julija nudged Brigitte with her elbow. "Count Verontsov admires you," she said. "He asked Madame to invite you."

The dacha befitted a man of Count Verontsov's high standing. His primary residence was in St. Petersburg, but along with his home in Crimea, he kept a house in Moscow, too. The grounds were left rustic with a broad lawn still covered in snow, bits of tall grass peeking through, and the forest thick all around them. There were eight bedrooms, not including the servants' quarters. Some of the guests, Julija said, also had dachas at Lisiy Nos. In all, there would be about twenty people hosted by Madame Vazeem and Count Verontsov throughout the week.

Brigitte and Julija had been assigned a bedroom in the attic. Brigitte looked out the window at the frozen river. She mentally practiced her smile, but she did not feel like smiling. She longed for home and the precious, fleeting opportunity to be with Nikolai and her family. She heard Johansson's voice admonishing her for smiling. What would the music be like this week, she wondered?

The moment they came down the stairs, a manservant put glasses of raspberry *nastoiki* into their hands. Brigitte took a sip, shuddering from the strong alcohol. "Maybe if Ivanov could come up with a *pas de deux* like that for you and Rodian, you would like Rodian better," Julija said pointing to an actress with the Imperial Theater, straddling the back of her wealthy patron, who had assumed the position of a horse on all fours. With sisterly resolve, the women clinked their glasses.

Julija spotted Count Verontsov across the room, looking out the window, and pulled Brigitte over to meet him.

"Leonid," she cooed. "Let me introduce you to Brigitte Gustoevna Legher."

Though it was Count Verontsov's party, from the dour look on his face, he did not seem in a celebratory mood. "Welcome," he said. "I have admired your dancing, Mlle. Legher. I do hope you find your time here enjoyable."

"I have never left St. Petersburg before. I am afraid my experience with forests like these around your dacha have all been from listening to fairytales. Do you know, Sir, if Baba Yaga's chicken house ever passed by? I would quite like to go roaming, but I wouldn't like to fall prey to her or the *Deathless Koschei*."

Leonid looked down at the floor and laughed. "From the fairytale of the warrior queen Marya Morevna?" he asked.

Julija winked at Brigitte, then made an excuse to slip away.

"Yes. It is my favorite," Brigitte said, hopeful that perhaps she would not have to feign interest in politics. "*Deathless Koschei* always scared my little brother Sergei. I told him he had nothing to worry about as long as he stayed away from dungeons."

Leonid said nothing in response and they fell into an awkward silence. He seemed suddenly nervous. She didn't want to ruin her chances of winning his attention so soon in the week, so she blurted out the first thing that came to her.

"Have you been polishing your boots?"

"What?" His brow knit together in puzzlement.

"Your hands, they are dark. Like the men who shine boots in the market."

A broad smile lit up his face. She put her hand to her mouth in astonishment at what a difference it made in his appearance. Some people were like that, almost ugly until they smiled and then, beautiful.

"I have been helping move the snow, hoping to get the ground ready for planting. A fortuneteller told my land manager that spring is coming early this year. There is great optimism for a fruitful year." He lowered his gaze to the floor. "I do not believe in fortunetellers. But since boyhood, mud is irresistible."

"Like walking by a celebration where everyone is dancing and so you want to dance, too?"

He nodded. "I guess so, yes. Though I doubt anyone else here at this celebration would care to put their hands into the loam. I find shoveling snow and dirt a pleasant distraction."

"From what are you wanting to be distracted? Certainly not festivals and all this gaiety?" She leaned into him, a flirty move she'd learned by watching Julija and other of Madame Vazeem's dancers, the ones with the nicest dresses.

"No, not festivals. From Russia."

"All of Russia or just the parts hidden in the dark forests?" She tilted her head, letting a curl fall onto her cheek.

Count Verontsov took the curl between his fingers and smoothed it back. "When you are not afraid of a little dirt, the forest is the best distraction of all."

Shrove Tuesday, as the day before Ash Wednesday was called, Julija and Brigitte squealed in delight when they returned to their room to discover two boxes labeled *House of Worth, 7 Rue de la Paix Paris*. Inside were evening gowns.

"I could dance for a decade and never earn enough to purchase a *Worth* gown," Julija said, stroking the creamy dark blue satin, her finger circling the stiff place where something had been spilled.

"They are stained," Brigitte said, puzzled and disappointed. "Here is a rip." She held up the sleeve, putting her hand through the armpit. The gowns were not new, nor did they fit particularly well, but still, even in their imperfection, the gowns were beautiful. They put them on, not wanting to offend their hosts, but were somewhat embarrassed.

Two long tables were set parallel to one another in the dining room. Pancakes were stacked high on platters, surrounded by boats of melted butter and dishes of meat, root vegetables, and dried fruit. All the guests were dressed beautifully, but the women's gowns, like their own, were stained, with snagged lace, twisted ribbons, and missing buttons. The men wore gala attire, but the material on the knees was shiny with wear; the shirts were dingy and grey. Perhaps they reserved their best garments for St. Petersburg, wearing their second-hand finery, in the way that Nina cleaned the house in old dresses.

When the first pancake flew across the table, hitting General Makarov, a fat, pink-faced man, squarely in the jaw, it took Brigitte completely by surprise, but she attributed it to too much vodka. The woman who threw the pancake, Olga Ivanova, the controversial wife of Governor General Cherkotav, was reviled by some, being a divorcee, but loved by others for her vivacious personality. Her eyes sparkling with mischief and drink, Olga stood and shouted, "Feast fight! You best have fun during Maslenitsa or you are doomed to grow old in loneliness and misery!"

Brigitte tried to duck out of the melée.

The esteemed Prince Dogorukov picked up a boat of butter and poured it down the front of Julija's gown, grabbed her, and kissed her full on the mouth. As if the hairy house spirits called the *Domovoi* were running amok, it became apparent there was nothing to do but join in. Soon Brigitte's hands were dripping with jelly and cream, her hair sticky with syrup.

Brigitte felt a hand reach around her and smash crumbled pancake between her breasts. The hand snaked down and squeezed. She turned, slapping the face of Olga Ivanova's husband, the Governor General, whose hair stuck up in every direction, his long mustache drooping with gravy. Brigitte froze with fear that she'd just assaulted a man of his standing. Leonid stepped in front of her, and slapped the Governor General as well, but with a pancake. The Governor General roared with laughter.

Later, when they were alone together, Leonid licked the skin of her neck. She pulled bits of caviar from his whiskers. "How is this a tradition? Throwing pancakes at each other?" The Leghers knew how to celebrate, but Brigitte could not fathom Nina wasting so much precious food.

"In the old days, there were fist fights. We have grown more civilized."

When she returned from Lisiy Nos, a change in casting was announced for the final ballet of the season. Leonid had used his influence on her behalf and she was to be a soloist.

On opening night, within moments after brushing blue shadow on her eyelid, she felt a burn, with little blisters appearing on her skin. Julija picked up the tin and sniffed it. "Hot pepper juice."

She helped Brigitte to the washbasin, splashing water on her eye. "You take someone's solo, they take your eye."

Alayna walked over. "You will need to let Lubok know if you are unable to see to perform." She lifted Brigitte's chin and looked into her eyes. "Hmmm, looks bad. I will let them know for you." She handed her a filthy towel from beside the basin. Brigitte took it and dried her face.

"You need not bother," Brigitte said. "I can dance."

"There is medicinal cream in the first aid box by the regisseur's office," Julija said.

Alayna glared at Brigitte. "Are you surprised you have enemies, B. Legher?"

"I am grateful to have you as a friend," Brigitte said to Julija when she returned with the cream.

Julija smiled. "Jealous people do horrid things. Remember when I was given the second soloist over Preobrojenska?"

"Olga would not do anything this vulgar."

"Oh, no one thought it could be Olga who had me evicted from my apartment, but I have no doubt."

"You never told me you were suspicious."

"I had paid the rent," Julija said with indignation.

Brigitte looked around the dressing room. Four long tables, each with mirrors lit by gaslights. Hairbrushes, clips, and combs littered the surfaces along with a rainbow of colors of grease paint. The other dancers in the room pretended to ignore her injured eye. She reached over for Julija's hand.

"This is safe makeup." She handed a white stick of grease paint to Brigitte. "Keep it hidden in your bag. Use it to tone down the redness."

Brigitte tested it on the back of her hand.

"A note for B. Legher," Lubok called out from the doorway."

One of the dancers snatched it from him and started to open the envelope but Julija, quick as a cat, grabbed it and slapped the woman hard. The other dancers laughed.

"For you," Julija said handing the envelope to Brigitte, ignoring the angry stare of the woman rubbing her cheek.

"It is an invitation from Leonid to dinner. A solo part and a protector. I think I got what I wanted."

Julija looked at Brigitte and smiled at her, then frowned. "That looks bad," she said and dabbed a bit more of the cream on Brigitte's eyelid.

CHAPTER 8

St. Petersburg, September 1901

What Brigitte loved most about the two-story row house on Krasnoameyskaya Street that Leonid gave to her was the large room just to the left of the foyer. A half-hour walk from the Alexandrinsky Theater, it had been the home of a merchant who bankrupted himself. Leonid did the man a favor, accepting the deed in exchange for payment of bad debt. He gave Brigitte the house as a gift to celebrate her thirteenth year with the Imperial Ballet, and their nearly thirteen years together, putting the deed in her name. The room, traditionally intended for entertaining guests and large gatherings, was to be her *Chambre de Joie*, her room of happiness. The wainscotting was painted white, and trimmed in gold. Above the walls were robin's egg blue, with decorative panels also trimmed in gold.

The house had two bedrooms and a washroom upstairs, and a parlor, dining room, and large kitchen on the main floor. Her home stood at the end of the row, giving her extra windows to the east, capturing the morning light.

Nina Legher arrived early one morning carrying a bucket of paste and rolls of paper, the gift of a duchess whose daughter had been a student of Gustave's. According to Gustave, the paper went out of fashion before the duchess had a chance to redecorate.

"Mama, why are we starting so early?" Brigitte said as they rolled out the drop cloths pilfered from the Mariinsky Theater's scenery shop, in the parlor at the front of the house. The wallpaper would brighten the room and make it feel cozier.

"I have raised ten children and danced at least four performances a week for decades. I have learned there is no such thing as an hour that is too early, nor too late, on any clock. There is only the moment at hand. This is the moment." "You are hosting dinner for the whole family tonight. We had best get busy."

Brigitte could not think of a time she'd been alone in a room with her mother. Homeownership it seemed, had won her Nina's attention.

They had put up two rows of paper and were finishing a third. "This paper is very pretty," Brigitte said.

"The duchess has good taste."

"Nikolai told me that Sergei spent the night with you last Thursday," Brigitte said. "Did something happen between him and Maria Petipa?"

"She locked him out of their apartment. What he sees in her escapes me. Eighteen years older than he is. It is indecent."

"The *corps de ballet* girls are all heartbroken," Brigitte laughed.

The Legher family spoke openly about Sergei as the most beautiful of them all with his dark blue eyes, long lashes, and light brown curls. His talent had also surpassed them all, including Brigitte and Nikolai.

When Sergei had been only seven years old, Gustave said he was touched by the angels, and he would be destined for great success. Or great tragedy. Brigitte wondered if the fear they all had for Sergei was what made them love him all the more. Such a boy. How could he not be destined for something tragic? Now, with Maria Petipa, the daughter of the ballet master, as Sergei's common-law wife, there had been many conversations between Nikolai and Brigitte about what a tragic pairing Sergei had made. Nikolai told her that even as a student dancer, Sergei would follow Maria around backstage and try to get her attention. Eventually, Sergei wore Maria down, and when he graduated and became a soloist straight out of school, she accepted his invitation to dinner.

"Did he say why she locked him out?" Brigitte asked Nina.

"Another woman. Who can blame him? You said so yourself that all the *corps de ballet* desires him. Women throw themselves at his feet. He is too young to be settled with such a woman."

"Maria has been kind to you and Papa, has she not? Is it just her age you object to? And to Sergei's being still such a child?"

Nina stopped working for a moment. "Kind?"

"She treats you with respect."

Nina stepped around Brigitte and picked up the paste brush. "She is a prissy one. When she walks into a room, it is as if the lights go dim. If her father were not the great Marius Petipa, she would have no place in the Imperial Ballet. She is sloppy with her technique, and a bore to watch. Sergei is wasting his life with her." She took a breath.

"She is a *wed'ma*," Nina used the insult, calling a woman a witch, which would have meant a slap on the mouth if Brigitte had said it when she was a girl.

Brigitte, her eyes wide, turned her head away from Nina and smiled. It wasn't that Nina never swore, but she had always tried to instill in her daughters the need to be the embodiment of grace and deportment. "She probably thinks you are a *wed'ma*, too," Brigitte said, then broke into giggles.

"That I do not doubt." Nina laughed with her. "According to Sergei, she has said as much. He cannot keep secrets. It is a weakness in him. Although, I can never get him to tell me what a young boy of twenty-six sees in a *wed'ma* over forty." Mama itched her nose smearing paste on her face.

Nina unrolled more of the paper. "Nikolai is caught in his own web. Another *wed'ma*, Olga Tchumakova. She's at his heels all the time. His health is not good. I worry."

"He requested a leave to take treatment in the Crimea," Brigitte said. "Did you know that? Mathilde Kschessinkska helped him get permission to travel. Being the former mistress of the tsarevich gives her great powers and Mathilde owes Nikolai for teaching her the 32 *fouettés*."

"32 *fouettés*," Mama spat. "First Pierina Legnani comes from Italy with her fancy trick, then Mathilde shows her up. Bah, who cares? I do not understand why such an artless skill should garner so much attention. Nikolai looks ridiculous teaching tricks, rather than technique."

Ballerina absoluta Mathilde Kschessinkska did not meet any standard for beauty. She had a snaggle tooth. Her facial structure, while delicate, was not extraordinary. Her legs, oft spoken of in pornographic tones, were too short and thick for a properly proportioned dancer. She did have lovely ankles, Brigitte conceded. It was rumored she had been Tsar Nicholas' mistress. "I would like that artless skill. Nikolai said he will show me, but he has yet to. Even if he does, I am not sure I can master it."

"Olga is not any better for Nikolai than Maria is for Sergei." Nina stretched her back muscles with a graceful arch. "It is a curse for a mother to watch her children choose poorly. I include you. This rich count of yours is a mistake."

Brigitte looked into Nina's eyes seeing something there on the verge of being said out loud. Then, in a blink, gone.

"I sometimes feel like I don't belong when you speak of your children."

"You feel that way because you boarded at school. Your sponsor is to blame for that insisting you be in the Infant Class and live at school. We could not have afforded that. You were more fortunate than the others."

"It is more than that," Brigitte persisted. "It is a feeling, like memories that are mine, but not mine."

"What memories?"

"I remember having new shiny black shoes. But how could that be? If I had them, surely, they would have been Vera's first."

"What are you hoping?" Nina said angrily. "I was not a good enough mother for you? Do you wish you were a fairy princess? Perhaps the daughter of a tsar? Despite the stories, the aristocracy does not give up their progeny. Is that the sort of mother you wish you had?"

"I did not mean it that way," Brigitte stammered. "Only things from the past I cannot explain... I meant no hurt. But you are all so fair. My hair is nearly black."

"Your father had family from Lapland. But maybe you prefer to think you come from serfs, or gypsies, and the Jews? You think I would take such filth into my home, to raise alongside my precious children?" She glared. "Is that what you make of your strange little memories? The dreams of a baby? I suppose you do not count the gift of being a dancer in a family of dancers, whose grandparents were dancers, makes you anything like your family? Do you only look at your hair and not your talent?"

"I am sorry, Mama. I did not mean..." Brigitte touched Nina's arm for reassurance, but Nina pulled away and frowned.

"Enough. We will finish before your father comes. You are Legher, not a damned sylphide. You are a grown woman, not a child living in fairytales."

They worked for another hour in silence and had nearly finished when there was a knock at the front door, followed by Gustave prancing into the room, bubbling with joy.

"I have been paid," he sang. He had a pouch, which he shook, the kopeks inside jangling. "Today, at least, we prosper." Gustave came towards Nina, took the sponge from her hand, and dropped it into the water bucket causing a splash. He danced her once about the room, released her, gathered up Brigitte, and waltzed with her. The room filled with his merriment.

"Today, we eat, drink, and dance." Clapping his hands, he set a rhythm, reaching out for Nina again, dancing with her, trying to kiss her, until she pushed him away.

"We will be pleased to eat, drink, and dance if you help us finish the papering," she ordered.

"I did not collect payments from the tight-fisted parents of my less-than-promising students, to come here and work." He pressed the pouch into Nina's hand, then spun on his heels, picked up the sponge, and wiped down the wallpaper. As he worked, he made up a song.

Rent, vodka, tomatoes, good dark bread.

"Gustave, you are creating a disaster," Nina protested, but laughed, dropping the pouch into her apron pocket.

Brigitte's heart grew lighter amid her parents' playfulness. She adored them and felt foolish for entertaining ideas of not belonging.

Finished with the papering, Gustave said, "A family dinner in your beautiful new house. A house! Imagine a Legher with a house."

The fact that the house came not from dancing on stage, but from the seduction of a married man, did not diminish Brigitte's joy from Gustave's pride.

"Vera, her sourpuss husband, Sergei and Maria, and the younger children are coming from the school. We will feast," he exclaimed.

In the kitchen, Nina dug into the basket Gustave brought. "You found a tomato?" She held it up in awe. "I have not seen a tomato for months. But it is too early."

"The Jewess with the corner stall. She grows them in a greenhouse here in St. Petersburg. Charges a small fortune."

"The woman in the market who cackles like Baba Yaga?" Nina made a face.

"Likely she has cast a spell to make them grow. Are they poisonous, do you think?" Gustave said and picked up the tomato and inhaled deeply, then crossed his eyes, clutching at his chest. A graceful stagger, a choreographed fall over the wooden chair; a perfect landing on the floor where he feigned distress, rising to his knees. "Help," he said, his voice strained. "A kiss to save me." He reached out towards them, then fell face-first onto the floor; a trick he had perfected to impress his children. How did he never break his nose? Laughing, both women kissed his hands. He took an exaggerated breath, as though he sucked sand into his lungs, then kneeling and taking the arm of each of them, he bid them rise. "I have taken all the poison from the tomato. By your fidelity, it has been transfigured into nourishment. Let's make a sauce."

Vera arrived first along with her husband who sat uselessly in a chair while the four of them sliced, boiled, and stirred all the bounty Gustave brought.

Gustave enjoyed feast preparations. He had a captive audience to listen to stories of his maternal grandfather, a restaurateur in Sweden, who had taught him to relish the performance of cooking. "Grandfather danced until his legs gave out. Then he sat on a high stool over the stove and cooked fried herring."

The front door opened, followed by the cacophony of Sergei, Maria, and the three youngest Legher children.

Sergei strolled into the kitchen. The family teased him about the magnetism of his deep blue eyes. Brigitte had long found them uncomfortable to look into because they made her forget he was her brother. Brigitte thought of Nina's admonishment earlier. Her question of what did Brigitte hope for? Of course, she wanted to feel certain she belonged to the Leghers. But a small part of her, a part that she felt such deep shame to even acknowledge, wished she weren't, and it all had to do with Sergei's eyes.

Gustave, with great flourish, opened the bottles of wine, pouring glasses for all, including the youngest, eight-year-old Lubov.

He raised his glass. "In the fall when the birds of St. Petersburg fly to the south, there is one proud, beautiful bird who says, 'No more being chased by the snow. I shall fly to the sun to be warm.' She flies until her wings catch fire. As a falling star, she returns to earth. Let us drink that we remember the virtue of cold weather."

Brigitte clinked glasses with Sergei, noticing a tear on his cheek. "What is this?"

"Every time Papa makes that toast, I am so sad for the bird." He looked intently at her and she felt lost in his pain.

CHAPTER 9

St. Petersburg, January 1902

Leonid had been fascinated by the new telephones and had one installed in her house. She accepted gratefully, as she accepted all his gifts. When he called, she prepared for him. She didn't resent the leash any more than she resented her lovely cage. The cage and the leash kept her safe, and more importantly, dancing solos.

Her telephone number, 4501, did not have the same fashion as Leonid's lower number, 213. Few people called her, so the summons of the querulous bells startled her every time they rang, particularly one evening when Leonid himself lay naked on her bed, looking at her with a satisfied smile. Brigitte had excused herself to the wash closet to rinse away the fluids of their lovemaking. The indoor plumbing impressed her much more than the telephone.

"I could answer that for you, *Lyubemaya*," Leonid said using his endearment for her. "But what if it is my wife?" he laughed.

She grabbed the linen towel, quickly dried herself, then ran down the steps to the foyer where the telephone stood on a neat little F. Meltzer table, a man's face in the hand-carved mahogany who seemed to be looking up at her with his mouth open. She covered her breast with her arm and lifted the mouthpiece.

"Listening to you."

Nikolai's voice burst through. "I'm at Bears Inn and I am coming straight away." Even with the odd static riding along with his words, there was a discernible difference in his tone.

"Is something wrong, Yolya?"

"Olga has done me the great favor of tossing my belongings upon the street. She saved me the trouble of packing. I need a place to stay. Someplace I am loved even as I'm a scoundrel."

She could hear a slur in his words; he'd been drinking. He drank as much as any other man, but when there was an end of a marriage, even a common-law one as Nikolai and Olga had for nearly ten years, drink could bring out the devil. Brigitte didn't like Olga but had not approved of Nikolai carrying on an affair with Olga's younger sister, Antonia. Gossip backstage had to be brutal for Olga, and as unworthy as she was of Nikolai, Brigitte pitied her sister-in-law for the pain he caused.

"Give me an hour to arrange things. It will take you that long to find a sledge to pull you through this new snow." She could hear Leonid moving around upstairs.

"I promise to be a perfect guest."

As she placed the mouthpiece back onto the switchhook of the telephone, Leonid came down the steps, partially dressed, carrying her dressing gown. "You must be chilled," he said kindly. "Who called?"

"Nikolai. He needs a place to stay. Romantic intrigue."

He helped her into the silk garment, pausing to admire her small breasts, then sighed. "I am grateful not to suffer such intrigue."

She touched his bare chest. "You take good care of me. I adore you." She adored that he wanted nothing more from her than devotion and the use of her body.

Nikolai carried a leather travel bag, its straps missing, replaced with coarse twine. He kissed her cheek, set his belongings on the stairs, then went directly to the new F. Metzler sofa with hand-carved flowers and vines. "In the event, I behave reprehensibly under the influence of vodka, I would like to make our mother proud of my good manners by offering you my gratitude for this rescue." Nikolai dropped to the sofa and planted his face into the cushion.

Brigitte had changed into a sensible flannel nightgown, wool stockings, and dressing gown. "How is Olga?"

He groaned. "You torture me. I recant my expression of thanks. She is magnificent. Glad tidings to all the world to be rid of me."

"You quarreled?"

He peered up at the wall. "You could call it that. The neighbors summoned the police. Dreadful people who share our wall. Noisy as an opera chorus. Olga was screeching in that awful manner of hers. They believed she was soon to be dispatched by violence and barged in. Olga adopted their attitude. So here I am." He rose to sit upright. Then he began to cry, ugly sobs shaking his body.

She had seen this before. Both Nikolai and Sergei had a flare for drama. She'd seen how it rewarded them, particularly with their mother.

Nina may have been more tender towards her boys when they burst into tears, but she taught all her children that tea was the quickest way to restore emotional equilibrium.

Nikolai composed himself, accepting the delicate teacup she held out to him, his hands trembling. In a moment the cup fell from his fingers spilling the tea over the rug.

She went for a towel. "I have no idea how to clean a rug. I am ridiculous."

"Neither of us is any good at domestic life. Olga said as much. She said all the Leghers are miscreants."

Brigitte put her hand on her heart and said sarcastically, "I have never been called a worse name."

He held up a finger. "I distinctly recall you telling me Miss Nadeah called you a hopeless fumble foot. You were crouched in the hallway sobbing your heart out."

"Horrible woman," she laughed.

He stood, holding the teacup. "Where do you keep vodka?"

"All consumed by the miscreant family Legher."

"What does Count Verontsov drink when he visits?" Nikolai looked desperate.

"You may stay here as long as you like, Yolya, but you must make yourself scarce when Leonid comes by. He has a proprietary advantage."

She followed Nikolai to the kitchen. He opened cupboard doors, one after the other. "It is a pity you never found love. Too late now, at your advanced age."

"Leonid loves me."

"You do not love him. And he is married."

"True," she said, rinsing out the teacup. "I am not old."

"31 is old for a woman."

"If you are here to assuage the sting of your failure by accentuating mine, then you can sleep on the street."

"The timelessness of your legs holds you in good stead," he said by way of making up. "The wolves come to see your legs."

"I have chicken legs like Baba Yaga's house."

He opened a cabinet nearest to the back door, crying out, "A miracle." He took a drink from the half-empty bottle before reaching for a glass on the shelf beside the sink.

"I think the former owner must have left it. Careful it is not poisonous."

"A toast?"

She accepted the glass he handed her. He took another, pouring a drink for himself.

"I drink to the comely chicken legs of Brigitte Gustoevna Legher."

She laughed.

"You are going to host a party tomorrow evening. Music, food, dancing, wine. Count Verontsov will pay."

"Take as many into the sinking boat with you as will fit? How Russian."

Nikolai spread the word about the party. Most came for the food, and to see Sergei and Nikolai. Some came to see what Brigitte's house looked like.

Brigitte invited Leonid to Nikolai's party. Leonid had raised a brow when she told him the location. He inquired of her, "Your house but not your party?"

Brigitte had felt ashamed then. "It is," she said. "But Nikolai is the one who wants it. To feel better about his marriage ending."

"He moves in with you and throws himself a party?" He seldom commented on her brothers, unless to say how well they danced.

"I could ask him to move out if you want me to," Brigitte offered, knowing Leonid never would ask her but might enjoy feeling he had that sort of power.

"It is your house. Whomever you wish to abide there with you is up to you." He took out his wallet and handed her money. "For the food," he said.

"Who needs an extra chair or bookshelf? We all wish we had a grand open space to dance." Julija shook back her long hair, then hooked arms with Brigitte. "Let's open up a dance school together."

Julija, motioned for Nikolai to come over with the bottle of wine. "Get Brigitte drunk so she does as I say."

"Why do we aspire to teach?" Nikolai asked jovially as he poured out the wine. "Our prima ballerina Mathilde Kschessinkska does not aspire to teach."

"No." Sergei joined them in the *Chambre de Joie*. "She has her sights on ruling Russia from her bedroom." His joke earned him hearty laughs and pats on the back.

Brigitte glanced at Leonid in the parlor enjoying the attention of three young dancers. If they could steal him away, perhaps he would buy them a house, too. She didn't mind. Two things she knew about Leonid; he enjoyed the attention, and he changed only when change became necessary. He had chosen her when he found it necessary to have a woman in his bed. His wife gave him four children, then moved into her own room, locking the door. Now that he'd solved the problem, he did not revisit the solution. She made sure he didn't feel the need to.

Julija said, "What does Mathilde have that we do not? We play by the rules, but none apply to her. Is it because she is so perfect? The prima ballerina absoluta?"

Antonia, Nikolai's sister-in-law and new love interest, stood just behind him, a hopeful look on her face. Nikolai ignored her, though she shadowed him everywhere. It made him seem cruel. For this reason, Brigitte hated her. Antonia said, "Nikolai told me when they danced in Moscow, Mathilde was a full measure behind."

If he'd been sober, Nikolai wouldn't have said what he did next. Not out of loyalty, but because, as they all knew, Mathilde had spies and could be a bit vindictive. "When she had made ten mistakes, I stopped counting. Afterward, she rushed off to be with Count Alexei. If it had been you, or me, or Brigitte, we would be thinking it time to go teach. Give up the stage. The truth is, we all have off nights. We all make mistakes. There is no such thing as a perfect performance. We know how to cover up so the audience, and if we are lucky, the dance master, misses our mishaps. If they do notice, we try to thrill them with the rest of the dance so they will not remember. Who remembers Mathilde's blunders? They remember only that she slept with the tsar."

Julija reached towards Sergei, drawing him into an embrace, her hair falling across his shoulders. Brigitte moved to stand beside Nikolai.

"I need more wine," Julija demanded. "What about Maria, Sergei? Is she perfect? Or does she not worry because of her age and status?" She stroked his arm.

 Sergei had come to the party alone. Maria attended few social events, complaining they bored her. He looked around as if making sure she had not slipped in unnoticed. "She worries all the more," he said softly, sincerely.

Julija grimaced, then smiled, tapping his arm she said, "Mathilde is not perfect, but if Nikolai had not taught her the secret trick to doing the *fouettés*, and she did not have her hand resting on the balls of the Imperial household, she would be much less impressive."

Nikolai chortled.

Julija reached over and poked his chest. "Why don't you teach the rest of us how to perform Perina Legnani's fancy tricks so we can tell Master Petipa to go to hell whenever we wish, and still have a stage to stand on? For me, I have to be perfect, or I am finished." Julija crossed the line from being gaily tipsy to slurring drunk. "Why do you not teach your sister the *fouettés*?" Julija battered Nikolai. "Does she offer nothing to further your career? She dances perfectly every time. Her technique is flawless. Teach her the *fouettés*."

Nikolai's eyes twinkled, bright from enjoyment and alcohol. He put his arm around Brigitte. "She knows I am at her service. You are correct, her technique is flawless. But not perfect."

Sergei spoke next. "Every one of you has made mistakes. You, Julija, Nikolai, Brigitte. Maria has faltered. Mathilde. Pavel Gerdt. Even our beautiful madman, Alfred Bekefy, has only mastered a pretense of perfection."

Alfred, often a companion to Nikolai and Sergei when they went gambling and cavorting, stood at the edge of the conversation. He nodded his head, and pulled at his mustache, grinning and blurry-eyed from drink.

"All of us have bobbled, dropped our arms too low, legs lifted too high," Sergei continued. "If the music is especially moving, we may feel we were perfect. It is an illusion. Perfection is impossible."

The room grew quiet. Several of the partygoers emptied their glasses, then looked down into them.

"Except for Nikolai," Brigitte proclaimed. "He is perfect. How could he now teach the *Classique de Perfection* if he did not know it firsthand?" There were murmurs of consent mixed with laughter.

Nikolai kissed her cheek and raised his glass. "You see, Sergei. It is as I have told you since we were boys competing for Father's approval. I am the perfect one."

"Indeed," Sergei raise his glass. "To the one perfect danseur."

Nikolai, still with his arm around her, leaned forward to refill Sergei's glass. He pulled her forward with him, pushing her into Sergei. She lost her balance and Sergei caught them both in an embrace. Her beloved brothers encircled her, Sergei kissing her cheek, then Nikolai's. The brothers laughed and in that precious moment, Brigitte felt her life was perfect.

CHAPTER 10

St. Petersburg January 1903

"He denied my doctor's note. Fined me three rubles for missing a performance," Brigitte complained to Julija as they applied their makeup for a matinee.

Vladimir Telyakovsky, Director of the Imperial Theaters, had promoted Rodian Petrov to Regisseur General.

"My feet were a bloody mess. The theater doctor threatens to have me fired for dancing on injured feet and Rodian fines me for not dancing. What am I to do?"

Brigitte's feet were frostbitten on a misadventure with Nikolai, Sergei, and Alfred Bekefy when they had gone ice skating one frigid afternoon. Brigitte had not reported the skating part to the theater doctor. Dancers were forbidden to take such risks with their bodies. Her feet were mostly healed but were numb, making her prone to injury.

She put on the enormous Russian kokoshnik headpiece, blue velvet and dripping with strung pearls and crystals, that was part of her costume. It tilted on her small head, covering her eyes. "This cannot be right," she said, exasperated.

Julija burst out laughing. "You took the wrong hat."

"This had my name on it," Brigitte said in disgust.

"There are twelve of us in that dance. Feliks made a mistake. Go fix it." Julija scolded. "You complain too much."

Costumes hung on racks in a room down the hallway. Rodian blocked the door, penning in the costumer, a small, pale-faced man with disheveled hair and limp mustache.

"You have until tomorrow to fix this," Rodian threatened.

Feliks shook both fists, trembling. "This is the approved color. It is not my fault that in the Director's progressive mind, he does not see the need for the set designer to first speak with the costumer before he paints the scenery."

Rodian noticed Brigitte, and his eyes narrowed. She took a deep breath and stood straighter.

"You should already be dressed, B. Legher. You will be fined if you hold up the curtain," Rodian said.

Her palms tingled with the desire to slap his face. "I need a different headdress. This one is too large."

"You will have to see who has yours," Feliks said irritably. "The new baby, Anna, has a big head. See if it is hers."

Brigitte started to walk away but Rodian grabbed her arms.

"Report to me if you do not find it," he said. "I am keeping a close account of mistakes in costuming."

"I do not have to abide this," said Feliks, throwing up his hands and pushing his way past them.

"B. Legher." Rodian leaned in closer to her. "You have not congratulated me on my promotion."

"Congratulations, *mudak*." She jerked free from his grip. "Shall I call you Major *Mudak*?"

"You should be kinder to me. I can do more for you now than your count. As regisseur, I influence casting." Touching her cheek, he grabbed her earring and tugged it, hissing, "You should be nicer to me."

"Petrov?"

Rodian reacted to Nikolai's voice by ripping the earring from Brigitte's earlobe. She yelped in pain, then punched his face with a closed fist. Blood gushed from his nose. Nikolai and Sergei, who was with him, stepped in and rushed Brigitte away before Rodian could do more than shout, *Wed'ma.*

Her next pay envelope was short five rubles she had been fined "for disruptive behavior." She shoved the money into her bag, and went on the hunt for Rodian, finding him sitting in the stalls watching Nikolai and Sergei working on stage.

"Five rubles?" she yelled. "You tear my ear, then have the nerve to fine me?"

"You were warned to be nicer." He rose, walking towards the aisle where she stood, fists on her hips.

Nikolai and Sergei stopped working and were paying close attention, willing, she knew, to serve as protectors.

"I demand you reinstate my full pay." She lifted her chin. As he came forward, she took a step to meet him, pressing her chest into his.

"Your request is refused." He clenched his jaw.

"Not a request. A demand."

"No," he said through his teeth.

"You will be sorry. You leave me no choice but to go over your stupid, balding, empty head."

Brigitte phoned Leonid.

"*Lyubemaya*, I will give you the five rubles."

"That is not the point. If Rodian believes he can treat me in this manner, he will do so again. He needs to know his place."

She heard Leonid sigh. "Have dinner with me and we will discuss it."

That evening at the Bears Inn, Brigitte beseeched Leonid again about Rodian. She had just finished saying that if her ear did not heal properly, the earrings he gave her would forever dangle at an odd angle. Leonid sighed, looking around the room.

The balalaika band tucked into the corner began to play the national anthem in honor of the tsar. She stood along with Leonid and the others, to show their loyalty.

"I am sorry to badger you so, my darling," Brigitte said. "I feel better by being in your company."

Leonid smiled at her and they began to sing along with the others. *God protect the tsar.*

A young man seated alone at the table next to theirs, seemingly a university student based on his suit coat, white shirt and no tie, did not stand, and continued reading his book. Even the waiters stopped serving to sing. The young man seemed in a world of his own.

Strong and majestic. Reign for glory, for our lorry! Reign to foe's fear, Orthodox tsar. God, protect the tsar!

"Stand, boy," a bloated man at a nearby table said gruffly. "Pay your allegiance." Throughout the entire song, the young man continued to read. The last note sounded, and the waiters resumed their service. The angry man reached into his pocket, brought out a pistol, and shot the student in the chest. The boy fell backward, tossing the book high in the air.

A woman screamed. Brigitte screamed. Leonid reached for her hand, pulling her out of her seat. Leonid dragged her towards the door. "Come quickly," he said.

Pandemonium erupted as the diners all rose to escape. Outside, there were no carriages to be hailed; the Vankas would not expect the diners to be finished for another hour. Leonid took off his coat and put it around Brigitte's shoulders, then guided her through the streets. He walked so fast, she had to trot to keep pace with him.

"Why would he shoot in a crowded restaurant? Is he deranged? Why would the man not stand? What if he were deaf? Perhaps he did not hear the music?" Her mind raced; she didn't notice Leonid's silence. "Do you think he is dead?"

The shooting of the young man felt like an intrusion into the safe world of the aristocracy. If she wasn't safe at the Bears Inn, then where?

Brigitte was shivering and her feet aching by the time they reached the back entrance to her kitchen. Leonid used her phone to call for a ride for himself. "My man is coming with the carriage and a coat for me. Go and get yourself a warm bath." He kissed her. "I apologize for the sad evening, *Lastochka.*"

By week's end, on the notice board by the regisseur's office, there was a full apology tacked at an odd angle, stating that Brigitte Gustoevna Legher had been erroneously fined.

CHAPTER 11

St. Petersburg, February 1903

The theater was nearly full for the premier of a new play featuring an actress from Moscow that was currently taking St. Petersburg by storm. Brigitte, Nikolai, Sergei, and Alfred Bekefy took their seats as part of the audience. They were not premium. Middle on the floor, rather than the prestigious box seat.

She heard whispers of, "It's the Leghers," and felt the thrill of being recognized.

"Brigitte, Come sit by me." Alfred grabbed her hand, but Nikolai held her in place, making her the rope in a game of tug-of-war.

In the comedic play, Brigitte landed on Alfred's lap. The woman sitting behind them, elderly and bejeweled, likely with a title, leaned forward, her hands on the back of Alfred's seat. "This is not the vaudeville."

Brigitte stood, embarrassed, trying to behave as daintily as a blooming rose by sitting next to Sergei.

"You must excuse us, Madame," Nikolai said seriously as he rose to accommodate Brigitte. "My brother and sister and I have not had time off for months. We are the Leghers. Perhaps you have seen Sergei when he partnered with Olga Preobrojenska in *Javotte* last spring?"

The woman sat back, putting her hand up to her collar.

"I did see his performance."

"Did it meet with your approval?" he asked, as though her opinion mattered.

Sergei put a fist up to his mouth, and cleared his throat, stifling a laugh. He dropped his head looking down at his lap. Brigitte glanced away, fearful that she might catch the giggles.

"It did. You and your brother are talented choreographers and danseurs."

Nikolai sighed with relief. Brigitte feared she would let out an unseemly guffaw.

"Mr. Bekefy, he does a passable job, too? Perhaps you saw him in *Don Quixote*? We all enjoy watching him," Nikolai went on, his eyes twinkling. Alfred flashed the woman his most charming smile and winked.

"I have often commented to others on Mr. Bekefy's fine dancing," she conceded.

"And our sister, Brigitte. Surely, you recall her solo in *Sleeping Beauty*, as the Lilac Fairy?"

Brigitte frowned. It has been her last big solo, and already much time had passed.

"I am aware of Mlle. Legher's triumphs on the stage. I was there the evening she danced with Rodian Petrov and they were given a ten-minute ovation."

Brigitte turned to look at the woman. "Gracious, that was several years ago," she said.

"Yes, well, I recall it as one of the most exciting moments I have ever experienced at the Mariinsky Theater. It moved me to tears, and I am seldom so moved." The woman conveyed this news with such a stern disposition that it would be hard to imagine her with a tear in her eye.

"I am humbled." Brigitte bowed her head.

"You are talented artists. But there is a proper place for drama. It is not the theater," the woman sniffed.

"We promise to behave," Nikolai said just as the lights dimmed.

Alfred leaned over and whispered, "It is good to know what we have been doing wrong all this time, bringing drama to the theater. Let's try to keep it in our lives from now on, shall we?"

When Nikolai snorted with laughter, several people admonished him to quiet down.

After the theater, the dandy trio of fools proceeded to the Bears Inn, getting drunk on *yorsh*, a mixed drink of beer and vodka. When they left at Brigitte's insistence, Alfred could barely walk. Nikolai, too, staggered. Sergei, singing of birds flying to the sun, was the soberest of the three men.

Alfred's apartment was close to the Bears Inn, but the four flights of steps proved daunting. They stopped frequently, to catch their breath from laughing. Alfred missed a step, landing face first onto Brigitte's bosom, as she had taken the lead, and was walking backward, pulling Alfred up, as the other two pushed him from behind.

"Am I dreaming?" he slurred. She shoved him away, a bit offended. "You are a bore, Mr. Bekefy. A gentleman does not get into this condition when he is in the company of a fine lady."

The three of them burst out laughing anew, wiping tears from their cheeks. "Brigitte is a lady?" Alfred said incredulously. "You two know about this?"

"She is our sister," Nikolai said. "And if we do not get you safely to your bed, I fear you will discover just how unladylike she can become."

"Bloodied the regisseur's nose." Sergei bragged. "Not a woman to cross."

Once inside the door, Sergei and Nikolai maneuvered Alfred out of his shoes and coat and under the bedcovers.

Sergei gently placed a pillow under Alfred's head, patting his hand. "Good night," he said sweetly. She had such affection for Sergei. She felt like crying with longing for that kind of tenderness to be shown to her. Sergei caught her watching him and smiled. It pierced her heart.

Nikolai stuffed one of Alfred's shoes in the back of the closet. "He will never find it," he laughed.

When at last they reached the street, a stiff wind hit them. Sergei lifted the collar of his coat and pulled his hat down lower over his ears. Then he reached for her, bringing her close to his side. "You must be freezing."

With a whistling wind as accompaniment, Nikolai sang a made-up song about the wretchedness of freezing to death, making them laugh as they walked along the well-lit street. She was cold, but she would willingly freeze to death if she could be in her brothers' orbit.

At the next block, a frantic woman dashed out the front door of an apartment building and ran straight into Nikolai. She wore only a white nightgown, her feet bare, the expression on her face one of pure terror.

"Excuse me," Nikolai said after she collided with him.

She said nothing but looked upward.

Brigitte followed her gaze up to the third-floor window. A man. His bedclothes fluttered rapidly like the broken wings of a bird. He crashed at Brigitte's feet with the sound of crunching bone and sinew. Blood from his head splattered across the pavement. His arm and leg were under him at unnatural angles. His eyes were open, searching, his mouth moving. Then without thinking she knelt to him. A terrible, long scream came from the woman as Nikolai tried to turn her away from the dying man.

The man grasped Brigitte's hand, strong at first, but quickly weakening as his life ebbed away. "*Shema Yisreal.*" His words were filled with air, blood bubbling at his lips.

"*Shema Yisrael. Adonai Eloheinu. Adonai Echad,*" Brigitte replied remembering the blessing. The man's eyes closed, the strength in his grip faded.

She was lifted by Nikolai and Sergei together, from the sidewalk and pulled to the shadow of the alley. A shot rang through the air and the woman's screaming stopped.

They did not stop running until they reached her block, going to the back alleyway, and into the house through the kitchen door.

Once inside, she started to turn on a light, but Sergei stopped her. "Best to be here in the dark. See if we were followed." His voice was calm. Nikolai sat at the table, breathing heavily.

"That is twice now I have had to run home after witnessing a murder. I hate this city."

Sergei fumbled in the dark to find three glasses for vodka.

"What were you doing speaking Yiddish to a dead Jew?" Nikolai said, anger raw in his voice. "I thought you had forgotten it all."

"What?"

"You may have finally marked yourself." Nikolai's words were sharp, cutting. "We may all pay a price for your stupidity."

"What did I do?"

"You spoke Yiddish to the dead man."

"It is not Yiddish. It is…I guess Swedish? The man said it. I said it back. Mama taught us when the kitten died in the garden."

"Mama did not teach those words to you or to any of us. Mama never knew Swedish. Papa's family was Swedish. Not Mama's."

"Our cat, Ketzele. She had three kittens. I found one dead in the garden. You remember Ketzele. Maybe Sergei won't but…" Brigitte's confusion mounted.

"We never had a kitten or a garden for that matter."

"Did you see it was the police on the balcony? From how the man was dressed, they were Jews," Sergei said. "The police executed them."

Brigitte's hand shook, the vodka in her glass splashing out. "I did not notice," she said.

"I saw them as they aimed to shoot the woman screaming in my ear." Nikolai rose, taking the bottle from Sergei. "We stumbled across the police cleaning up the streets. If they heard you saying what no Orthodox woman would say, it is a matter of time before we go under their broom as well." He drank from the bottle, then went to the window, looking out into the alleyway.

"What did you say?" Sergei asked her.

"*Shema Yisreal,*" she answered, and then for the first time thought about it. "I do not know what it means. Something Mama taught us."

"She did not teach me. Nikolai? You know Yiddish?"

"I know the language she spoke that used to get me beatings until she stopped." Nikolai went to the door and tested the handle, though he had latched it. "She is a damn Jew, Sergei. Whenever she said her damn Jew words, Mama would beat me because it made her stop. And now you say them in front of the police?" he shouted.

She wanted Nikolai to turn back into her tender and kind brother. "You are drunk."

Sergei pulled out another chair, guiding Nikolai to sit, taking the bottle from his hand, and setting it aside. "Why would you say Brigitte is a Jew?"

"She is not our sister, Sergei. You would not know this because, by the time you were born, the rest of us knew to keep our mouths shut."

"Is this a joke? Like the horrid joke that you played on Alfred hiding his shoe. You are awful tonight." Brigitte's voice trembled with anger.

Nikolai folded over the table cradling his head in his hands. "I do not know what words you said to that man, but I have heard them before. Always after you spoke, Mama spanked you, then me, and told you to speak Russian. How could you forget that?"

"I have forgotten nothing," Brigitte shouted.

"No? We have never had a garden or a cat."

"Shhh," Sergei put his finger to his lips. "No sense drawing any ears to the door." He looked nervously at the window. "Nikolai, what is all this?"

"I have wondered sometimes if you had no memories of before you came to us," Nikolai said, his voice softer.

"What are you talking about?" Sergei said.

Nikolai took a deep breath. "She is not our sister. Our parents took her in."

"You are being serious?" Brigitte asked leaning forward to search his face for the twinkle in his eye. "You are hideous, Yolya. A man landed at my feet. I watched his spirit leave his body."

"A Jew, a dirty *abram*. He is nothing. Less than a dog. Which is what you were until you came to be a Legher," he said mournfully.

"But I am not a Jew."

Nikolai went again to the window. His words slurred. "Forget it. Nonsense is what it is." He turned back, leaning down to her, wobbling slightly, and kissed her on the forehead. "You are a Legher. I am a *mudak* and I am done for the night." He moved towards the doorway to the dining room.

Sergei halted his brother's exit. "You cannot say these things and then presume to leave."

Nikolai's shoulders drooped. "Have you never wondered that she is the only one in the family with dark eyes and hair? The only one to board at school?" He turned, looking at her. "Have you ever wondered why Vera and Evgenia never treated her like a sister? Or why Mama tied her feet to the bed to perfect her turnout but refused to do so for the rest of us? Jews are not allowed to live in St. Petersburg without a permit. She could be arrested. Our parents would have to answer questions. Who knows how that would go? Evgenia and Vera, we were fed the horror stories. To this day we dare not speak of it, even to each other."

"I would know if I were Jewish. What a preposterous tale of lies."

"I wish it were," he whispered. "You will always be my sister. Nothing can alter that."

He took her face in his hands, the smell of the vodka strong on his breath. "You will always be a Legher. Forget this. I am sorry. I will happily confess to telling lies. I am a miserable drunk."

But she knew. His story was true. She felt it in her bones. She knew she was not Legher. Had always known. But Jewish? She felt sick to her core. "If this is true, I am no better than the people executed tonight."

Sergei rushed to her side. "No, you are not like them. You have only ever been a Legher, Russian Orthodox."

Sergei's angelic eyes were so different from Nikolai's. "I am not your sister," she said to him.

Nikolai grabbed the vodka bottle again. "*Pizdets*! I have no idea how to sweep up this mess." Sitting heavily on the chair across the table from Brigitte, he filled his mouth with the liquor and held it there, swishing, then swallowed.

Sergei asked, "Who else knows?"

Nikolai shook his head. "Besides Mama, Papa, Vera, and Evgenia, I don't know. Vera and Evgenia worry they too are foundlings. I never thought that, though. I look too much like Papa. We all kept the secret. I kept it by forgetting it. I suggest that this is what we all do. Forget the whole thing. Really, what has changed?" He lifted the bottle to drink but it slipped from his hand, crashing to the wood floor. The shards of glass scattered sparks into the shadows of the near-black room.

In the morning when she came downstairs, Nikolai sat at the table in the dining room, the samovar noisily boiling at the center of the table. Her whole life she had been looking at his face, imagining the likeness to her own. Despite his grey pallor and bloodshot eyes, she thought his face handsome. Noticing his features in a new light, she realized she did not look anything at all like him.

He reached for a cup by the samovar, filling it with tea. "If you feel anything like I do, you will need this."

She thanked him, watching his expression, trying to assess the new terrain of their relationship.

"Sergei left a short time ago. Off to another of those infernal meetings with the other rabble-rousers."

Brigitte sat down and took a sip of the tea. In using the formal dining room for his morning ritual of breakfast when he stayed with her, Nikolai acted as if there were servants to wash up, dirtying more dishes than necessary. But it made her house feel like a home.

Nikolai excused himself to the kitchen, returning with a plate of rolls and taking his seat at the head of the table. He put a roll on a plate for her, then pushed the butter dish in her direction. "Excellent butter. Exceptionally sweet. I borrowed it from Duchess Dogorukov."

"How does one manage to borrow butter?"

He grinned devilishly. "With the help of a good laundress to remove the grease stains from one's pockets."

Others had cajoled her to eat when she wasn't hungry. Leonid treated her lack of appetite as some kind of personal slight. But for Nikolai, though her stomach was sour from imbibing the night before, she ate a bit of the roll and the butter he *borrowed*. She needed to make him happy.

"It's good?"

She nodded.

"It's whipped with honey."

They sat in silence for a few moments. Brigitte knew she needed to say something, but she had no idea what.

"There is something I should say," Nikolai spoke first.

Her cheeks began to burn. She held her breath.

"It is this business of Sergei. Changes are coming," Nikolai continued. "I am the first to acknowledge that nothing stays the same forever. But there is a time, a place, for change."

"What I am getting at, is…If anyone, including Sergei, invites you to one of these meetings, or asks you to join in a strike, stay away from them. Especially Sergei. It is a matter of time before they are thrown out of the ballet. If they are lucky, they will be able to leave Russia. Dance in Paris or Italy. If they are lucky, they will avoid prison. But you," he paused. "Petrov is waiting for you to make a mistake. He will want to destroy you. No little tricks, or fines or power plays. Your whole career will be over. Sergei does not understand. He is not a stupid man, but he is being stupid."

"I am not worried about Rodian. Leonid is in his way."

"Count Verontsov may not be able to keep you safe much longer. Some of the things he has been saying privately have reached the wrong ears."

She felt as though electric shocks were prickling her ears and fingers. "Leonid is careful. He is a loyal servant of the tsar. No one, least of all Tsar Nicholas, would question Leonid's faithfulness." She pushed her plate to the center of the table. "Why should anyone question my spending time with Sergei? Even Rodian would have no suspicion of a sister spending time with her brother."

"You are a talented dancer," he said. "But neither of you understands this world. What happened last night, what we stumbled across, is something happening not only to the Jews but to anyone who challenges the tsar's rule."

She did not know how to respond without proving his point for him, that she had no idea about these dangers he seemed intent on warning her about.

"Do you know our beloved tsar is headed into a war with Japan?"

"Leonid tells me some things." She did not tell him how little she listened to what Leonid said.

"For now, people are enthusiastic about war. But wars bring hardship. You know little of real hardship."

"Leonid looks after…"

Nikolai interrupted her by hitting his flat hand on the table. "When was the last time you read a newspaper?"

"I dance. The stories I hear come from music and movement. I do not care about what the world is reading."

He reached for her hand, kissing it. "I envy you in your tower. If you wish to stay there, heed my caution. Sergei is rushing headlong into a net that will catch him up and destroy him. Do not follow."

"Then you stop him. He listens to you."

"Once he is convinced of something, there is no altering his version of the truth. He believes we should have more freedom to operate as an artistic troupe composed of individual artists. He is tired, he says, of being the tsar's trained monkey."

She studied the carpet, following the swirling pattern, a path back to things Sergei had said to her about his discontent with the Imperial Theaters; how they were run as a military installation rather than an artistic venue. At dinner the evening before he had told them that *grandes pirouettes* were nothing more than political propaganda for the failing monarchy. Nikolai had shushed him, looking around anxiously to see if anyone overheard.

Brigitte wished Nikolai would shush now. He didn't.

"Without strict rules and confinement, we spin out of control," he said, lecturing her. "I see this happening in Russia. We need the tsar, fool though he may be. And in the ballet, we need him to need us." Nikolai twisted his napkin. "I have tried to get Sergei to grasp the folly of these meetings. I do not disagree that Telyakovsky and Rodian treat us like chattel. The system itself is not at fault. Striking like common factory workers will not change the tsar's mind."

"Sergei is loved by the balletomanes, by Tsar Nicholas, who follows him with pride and admiration. Is that not enough?"

"The Imperial Theater tolerates a certain amount of petulance from its artists. But when really challenged, it becomes beneficial to make examples of those who defy the tsar, and the Imperial Theater. The impact is all the greater if that example is made of one thought to be untouchable, like Sergei."

A tremor rushed through her gut. She put her hand across her abdomen and pinched her skin.

"I do all I can to protect Sergei, and you, too." He smiled at her, calmer now. "These are my worries. Please don't fret." He stood, picking up his dishes. "But heed what I say. Do not attend any of the meetings Sergei promotes."

She shook her head. "I won't, Yolya. I will talk to Sergei about them. Perhaps he will listen to me."

Nikolai laughed, rattling the teacup. "If he does, then indeed the world has tilted, and we will all slide into the sea."

The room fell under a shadow, the sky darkening with clouds. Brigitte shivered. "I think I will exercise at home today. It looks like snow."

"Do you think I will be too hard on you in the *Classique de Perfection*, given my hangover and ill temper?" he teased. "I am no Johansson. But I have taught the class long enough now that you should have forgotten the sound of his booming stick."

She shook her head. "You have yet to be too hard on me. Perhaps if one day you were, I might still become prima ballerina."

After changing clothes, she sat on the floor in her *Chambre de Joie* with a new pair of pointe shoes and a hammer. She pounded the wooden block in the toe to soften it. Her hips hurt, pulling her thoughts to her turnout. Her hips had ached for almost four years now. From her earliest memories, Nina worked on Brigitte's feet and hips, as Gustave instructed.

As Nina had manipulated Brigitte's hips when she was four years old, she'd told her, "Do you know your father sleeps with his feet tied to the end of the bed so that they will turn out more? His feet can rotate so far back, he sometimes plays tricks by standing behind a curtain, appearing to be facing the other direction."

Brigitte had panicked. If she were tied to the bed, she'd be trapped if Baba Yaga came in through the window. Her muscles grew rigid.

"Relax, little one," Nina cooed.

"Why can't you do that to me?" asked Evgenia jealously as she watched Brigitte getting their mother's attention. "I want a perfect turnout. Why does Brigitte get to have a perfect turnout?"

"Brigitte may attain a beautiful turnout, but she will pay for it," Mama said. "It is not a price I wish for you to have to pay."

"She has to pay?" asked Evgenia looking confused. "Where will she get money?"

Mama laughed, pressing down with all her weight on the back of Brigitte's hips as Brigitte lay face down, her legs spread, feet touching. "Not a price like that, my darling. She may grow old with aches and pains."

Even though Mama's hands were gentle, the manipulations were painful and Brigitte squeezed her eyes shut, not daring to cry for the fear of drawing Baba Yaga through the window to the sound of a naughty child.

"I don't want you to do that to me after all," Evgenia agreed.

"I do not do this to harm you," Nina said to Brigitte. "Perhaps you will not have to pay such a high price."

A whimper escaped from Brigitte's throat. "I'll be good. Don't tie me up," she said.

The pain had not yet crippled her, but it never left her either. She wore it everywhere like a corset.

Lost in thought, she didn't hear Nikolai come in.

"You should come to class. I promise to work you extra hard."

"Not today. Tomorrow, okay?" She began pounding her slipper again.

"Brigitte." Nikolai kneeled, stilling her hand. "You are going too blindly through life. Last night was a reminder of that." He stood up to go. "I will be at the Bears Inn with Antonia tonight. I may not be home."

"You torture poor Olga, you know," she said.

"In matters of the heart, one cannot be held liable for pain caused."

CHAPTER 12

St. Petersburg, March 1903

On this sunny day, vendors, shoppers, carriages and horses, and now the new motorcars were attracted to St. Petersburg's main thoroughfare. The smell of horse dung, sweat and mildew hung heavy. She longed for the cool spring breeze that blew in from the sea. All of humanity was out, it seemed, hungry for light. Even the balloon man, normally seen only in the summer months, called out to the children who clamored for his red, blue and green balloons. The largest balloons were white with red roosters printed on them, promising good luck. Soldiers, in gold-trimmed hats, mixed with the crowds of peasants in colorful scarves and embroidered sheepskin coats, all weaving together forming a cacophonous fabric. The noise was deafening, disorienting.

Brigitte had a day off and shopping to do. Gostiny Dvor, her destination, had been the project of Empress Elizabeth who came up with the idea of a marketplace indoors and invited architects to submit designs. A central dome had been added to give shoppers the luxury of feeling they were out of doors in the winter. To get there, Brigitte first needed to get through the rabble on Nevsky Prospekt.

She felt a tug at her handbag. Holding tight to the brass chain, she yanked it hard, then clutched it to her chest. Turning, Brigitte came face to face with the would-be-thief, a thin, dirty man wearing a heavy tanned-hide coat opened to his *kosovorotka*, a peasant shirt embroidered in reds and blues and held closed with a coarse bit of twine tied around his waist. His smile exposed broken teeth and a deep scar around his mouth.

"Pardon me, Lady," the man said. "Share your wealth?"

She turned away, holding tight to her handbag as she eased it inside her cloak. The man put a hand on her shoulder, and though she walked as fast as she could through the crowd, he kept pace with her.

"I know you have more than you need, Lady," he insisted. "I got to feed my children."

She rushed toward a uniformed policeman.

"Lady," the would-be thief persisted, "Just a kopek. I know you have money in your purse."

"Leave me alone."

"I have no qualms following you home. Give me your bag now, or I take even more from you later. A whole lot more"

Her breath came jagged.

"Lady, I need money." He pulled her backward and groped for her purse, grabbing hold of the bag through her cloak. She screamed.

A moment later, the policeman accosted the thief, holding him in an arm lock and bending him to his knees.

Brigitte fled, but looked back, catching sight of blood flowing over the beggar's brow as the officer beat him with a stick.

Brigitte rushed through the first door she came to, Alekseev's Emporium. Catching her breath, the commingling of rose, lavender, and fresh paint confused her senses. The store had only recently opened.

"Madame?" A well-dressed clerk with a gardenia on his lapel approached. "Is there something I might do for you?"

Unlike the thief's hand, the clerk's was well-manicured. He spoke with a heavy French accent. "You look as though you have suffered an ordeal?"

She felt comforted by his starched collar and the impeccable silver-and-black-striped tie primly held with a ruby pin.

Taking her handbag from its hiding place inside her cloak she said, "A thief."

The sales clerk nodded, his lips forming a line of commiseration.

"The tsar needs to realize that our city is under siege by the *rit ef raf* pouring in from the countryside, free to move about from place to place. Sterner laws are needed, Madame. Until then, who is safe?"

She watched him speak, following the mustache that had been trimmed to reveal an oddly feminine, pink upper lip. "I am fine now," she said.

A rainbow of colored lights on the floor created by an enormous stained-glass window put Brigitte in mind of having entered a church. She did not feel fine at all, wanting only to quickly collect her wits and get herself home.

"Perhaps Madame would like a sampling of our newest perfume from A. Bertelli. From Milan, Madame. *Gran Parfum.*"

She turned to look out the long window of the front door. Clenching her teeth, she pushed the door open. The thief lay on the ground, unconscious, his blood splattered on the ground. Nearby, the policeman gestured to a fellow officer across the street to assist him.

She walked in the direction of the second officer, heading towards the statue of Tsarina Catherine, sitting on her throne in Ostrovskovo Square. Behind the square was the Alexandrinsky Theater and the ballet school, safe territory. Her world. When she reached the statue, she sat on a bench to catch her breath.

"Brigitte."

Looking up at the sound of her name, she groaned. Rodian stood in front of her.

"You look wretched.'

"I have just been accosted by a thief."

"Goodness."

Brigitte thought she detected genuine concern in his voice. He scrutinized her. "Your cloak is filthy."

"It will come clean."

He sat beside her, too close. She felt his breath on her cheek. "Is there someplace I might accompany you?"

She stood to get away from him. "I do not need anything you have to offer."

Rodian followed her out of the square, then thankfully stopped. She walked the final block toward the side entrance to Gostiny Dvor, where she planned to shop. There could not be anything worth this inauspicious adventure, just to peruse a few shops, she chided herself.

Two men passed by, one of them catching her attention with his powerful air. Their eyes met.

"I beg your pardon, Mademoiselle. You look extraordinarily like the ballerina Brigitte Gustoevna Legher." He touched her arm. "The theater is just there so I am wondering if you might be her?"

She stopped, taken by his strong features, his angular jaw, and his dark, dangerous eyes.

"We are not properly introduced. I'm unaccustomed to speaking with strange men on the street. You will forgive me."

The man gestured to his companion. "Introduce me to Mlle. Legher."

The man clicked his heels and said, "I present to you, Officer Andrei Dimivich."

Smiling broadly, Dimivich bowed. "A great honor to meet you. I am an admirer."

She shook her head and resumed walking. Officer Dimivich followed.

"I mean no offense. If you would favor me with an autograph?" He produced a small notebook and pencil from his coat pocket.

She stopped. His fur coat was open and his grey suit looked expensive. What did she have to fear from men of means? They were not like the filthy thieves. She took the pencil and paper, scribbled her name, then bid him a good day.

"Where are you going?" Officer Dimivich kept pace beside her. "I will accompany you."

"Andrei," the companion said. "We have business. No time for the ladies."

In contrast to Officer Dimivich, the companion was not so finely dressed. He looked very much like a civil servant. It seemed odd that he might be the one to direct the actions of his better fellow.

"Might you be heading to the Passages? Is that your direction?" Officer Dimivich said. "It is not every day a man has the opportunity to promenade with a great ballerina. Our appointment will wait."

"I am stopping here in one of the lady's shops," she said making an effort to be firm but kind. "Please accept the autograph as a sign of my appreciation for my audience, and pardon me."

"I have dreamt of your performance in *Fiametto*. Are you on your way to meet your brother, Sergei? I hear there are secret meetings he attends now to talk of striking."

She slowed her step, shocked by his question. "I know nothing of that."

She made it across the street and was about to reach the side door to Gostiny Dvor when the companion pulled on Dimivich's shoulder. "There she is," he said pointing.

"Until our next meeting," Dimivich smiled. The companion went ahead and Dimivich ran after him.

For a moment the traffic cleared. She saw Dimivich and the other man run up to a well-dressed woman, the actress from the play she'd attended with her brothers and Alfred. They each grabbed hold of her elbows, lifting her feet off the ground.

"You have no right!" The actress's face was red with rage. They knocked her hat off and her hair stuck out at wild angles. "Release me!" she said, twisting, and flailing to no effect. They carried her a short distance and pushed her into a waiting carriage, the curtains in the windows drawn. In a moment, carriages and pedestrians formed a beast that collectively swallowed the actress.

Brigitte realized with horror that they had been Akrona, the secret police. And they knew about Sergei's meetings.

"Noah's first act upon disembarking the ark was to plant a vineyard and get drunk. The longer I serve Mother Russia and our father, Tsar Nicholas, the more I understand Noah." Leonid stood naked by the frosted window, sipping a brandy. The bottle had been a gift he said, from Tsar Nicholas. The only light in the room came from a single candle on the dressing table, flickering and dancing, making visible the drafts.

Leonid had arrived unannounced late in the afternoon. The troubles brewing with Japan, and his endless travels, kept him away for long stretches.

The front door had opened while she sat on the floor in the *Chambre de Joie,* smoking and listening to the gramophone.

She called out to Nikolai, but it was Leonid who came to the door. The deep lines around his eyes gave him a look of weariness. His hunched shoulders and downturned mouth shocked Brigitte to realize that Leonid had become an old man.

She led him up the stairs to her bedroom. She could think of no other conversation to have. The sun fled the sky, leaving them alone in the shadow of her bedroom, as his passion for her and her body also escaped him. Brigitte recoiled at his feebleness and frustration, his heavy breaths, and aggravated groaning. When he pulled his weight off her, lying prone under the sheet, she felt relief and deep worry that she would lose him.

"War, Brigitte," he sighed, "steals our pleasure." He looked at the ceiling. She curled her body into his, caressing the plain of his chest, his skin flaccid. He sighed again.

She stilled her hand, unsure of this new territory, a field of dirt and weeds. She did not want to follow him to that lifeless landscape but felt obliged. His hand turned into a fist, exposing his rage. Leonid stared at the ceiling as if watching an exhausting vision there. She waited. "You live here in this lovely house, this lovely, ugly city. Every day you add to the beauty of the world with your dancing." His hand moved to caress her breast.

"Are we in any danger here in St. Petersburg? From the Japanese?" She regretted asking when she saw a shadow of sadness move across his face. "If the Japanese came very far across Russia, surely they would be torn to bits long before they reached St. Petersburg."

She shivered imagining what he was seeing instead of her face. "We will throw young men at the Japanese to be killed, thinking this will somehow slow them down."

When he stood at her door to leave, he said, "I am attending the ballet on Wednesday. Perhaps you will allow me to escort you to the Bears Inn afterward?" Leonid took her hand and put a ring on her middle finger. Sapphires and diamonds.

She smiled and kissed him. "I will dance my solo in the second act just for you." She knew she had done well. Leonid seemed calmer; some of the shadows lifted a little.

Closing the door, she turned the lock, lowering the gas light in the foyer. She turned on the kitchen light and pulled up a step stool, reaching for a bottle of vodka.

"It's not there," said a voice behind her.

Startled, she screamed.

Sergei sat at the table, the bottle and a full glass in front of him. She put her hand to her beating heart. "How long have you been here?"

He stood, offering his hand, guiding her down off the stool. "Long enough. He is a noisy one, isn't he?" Sergei did not smile. Brigitte dropped his hand and reached for his glass.

"It is unseemly to discuss Leonid with you unless you wish to answer questions about Maria. I could ask if you have noticed the ugly wrinkles on her neck?"

"So many misunderstand our marriage," he said sadly. "I see Maria in a way others cannot."

She hadn't expected him to defend her. "Some think Leonid is only a money purse with shoes." How dare he, she thought, come into her home uninvited and insult her. Nikolai had given him a key, but she had on the tip of her tongue a thought to ask for it back. "He treasures me," she said instead.

"I treasure you. You hurt me when you avoid me."

"When have I ever avoided you?" she said, puzzled by his mood.

"All the time. I think I must repulse you."

"I have only ever thought you were wonderful and handsome. Perhaps in our odd upbringing, you have misunderstood me?"

"Now you are no longer my sister. Do I still misunderstand you? Misunderstand the way you turn away from me and go to Nikolai when the three of us are in a room together?"

She started to tremble. His eyes were like the mesmerist who entertained at salons. She could not look away from him. "Nikolai is different from you. We are close. He could only ever be my brother. It is not like that with you. It is as if you were a baby I adored. And then one day, a man I never saw before."

His warmth drew her in. She looked up into his eyes seeing his youthfulness and virility, so different from Leonid. "I cannot have you coming here unannounced, Sergei."

Sergei kissed her forehead.

She tilted her head up to look at him. He leaned forward and kissed her once on the lips. For a long moment after the kiss, they stood in an embrace, searching for a reason to pull away. A long conversation with no words, only questions. She could feel his heartbeat and her own.

Then he lifted her into his arms and carried her up the stairs to her bedroom. The blankets were crumpled. "I can smell him on you," Sergei said in a low voice.

She did not know if this intrigued him or if he was jealous. He put her down on the bed. As she rolled away from him, he lifted her dressing gown. She felt his lips on her bottom, his breath on her spine. His hands held her arms and pulled her back towards him. The strength of a danseur's arms felt like home and heaven. She gave herself to the power of his body.

In the morning she woke early, before Sergei, and drew a hot bath, imagining that the heat would cleanse her of her sin, and save her from damnation. He is not my brother, she repeated in her thoughts. She scrubbed her skin, and when she heard the sound of Sergei waking and beginning to dress, she thought her heart might burst from longing and shame.

She took a pumice stone to the soles of her feet. Working against the calluses, Brigitte lingered on a dream of Sergei always in her bedroom, in the daylight, making companionable sounds. She gasped for breath, having traveled too far beyond her body in her dream; pulled back by the necessity of air and the pain in her feet.

"Brigitte?" Sergei called.

"What is it?" She could hear the false calm in her voice.

"We have time for tea before class. Shall I light the samovar?"

She worried about Nikolai who often came by in the mornings after he'd spent the night with Antonia, before catching the Imperial Theater's carriage with her. She searched for an excuse to explain Sergei's presence at the breakfast table.

As if he read her mind Sergei said, "If Nikolai comes in, I will say I stopped by this morning expecting this would be the most likely place to catch him."

Even though he could not see her, she nodded.

"Brigitte?"

"Tea sounds lovely." She splashed her face with water, determined to remember who she was, and the kind of life she lived. How useless to pity herself for what could never be hers. What of the actress snatched up by Dimivich in broad daylight? The earth opened and swallowed her whole. What had she done to be consumed like that? Had she been born to a Jewess? Had she committed a cardinal sin with her brother, who was not actually her brother? How foolish to dream, even for a moment of having a normal, open life with Sergei as her lover, knowing that what happened to the actress could easily happen to her. Who would come to her rescue? Leonid? Nicolai? Sergei? She could not say with any certainty that they would.

Sergei set a steaming cup in front of her at the dining table. She watched him, feeling decadent to stare openly, where for so long, she dared only steal a glance. He had found the black bread and buttered both sides generously with creamy butter.

"Are you hungry?" He said offering a slice.

She shook her head.

"I have not been so ravenous in quite some time." His smile gave away his thoughts.

"On the nights you do not appear at home, what do you tell Maria?" Sergei's smile disappeared.

"I tell her nothing. She does not ask."

Brigitte looked at her hands in her lap. "Last night... Sergei. I am so glad we went there together. But we can never go there again. "After all, we all know what happens when the swan and the prince go to that dark place in the woods. They leap into the lake to their deaths."

"I would leap for you, Brigitte," he said his voice sincere. His eyes were serious.

"You would leap for me?"

"Only when the evil magician has us at the edge. But yes, then I would leap."

CHAPTER 13

St. Petersburg, Late March 1903

One of Marius Petipa's many objections to the production of *The Magic Mirror* was the lack of rehearsal time. Petipa bellowed the accusations of conspiracies against him and every ear that heard his wailing knew Petipa spoke the truth. Vladimir Telyakovsky, Director of the Imperial Theaters, wanted Petipa to retire.

With all the tension swirling in the ballet, Brigitte dreaded her *pas de deux* with Rodian. She stayed out of the intrigue, sharing no opinions. When someone brought it up or pressed her, she'd say, "I am here to dance, even if it has to be with Rodian." The single dress rehearsal had gone well, but in an interview with the press, Petipa ridiculed the terrible sets and costumes.

Opening night, Brigitte started her stretches backstage, listening to Rodian grumble. His thinning hair had begun to go grey at the temples in the last months. His haughtiness was less that of a petulant schoolboy, becoming more the grumbling of an irritable old man. "I was there when Petipa congratulated Telyakovsky for choosing Alexandre Golovin's superb sets. A half an hour later, Petipa is speaking with the *Petersburg Gazette*."

Rodian gestured wildly, forcing the ballerina nearest him to duck, as he nearly backhanded her.

Sergei came into the warmup area and sat on the floor near her. "I look forward to watching you dance. I missed your rehearsal."

"You know I am dancing with him?" Brigitte nodded towards Rodian. "You won't drop me, will you, Rodian?"

"Nothing would give me greater pleasure than to throw you across the stage. But the performance must be first. I noticed in rehearsal you felt heavier." Rodian sneered.

Her stomach clenched. She hadn't eaten since early morning; it was nearing seven in the evening. She craved the emptiness for how it made her feel lighter; hunger gnawed at her, a comforting queasiness.

Pavel Gerdt had a reputation for freely giving praise when he felt it warranted. Dancing in the role of the king, he came to stand beside Sergei. "Top-rate addition to the choreography in the third act, S. Legher."

He said to Rodian, "Brigitte is light as a feather. When you lift her, try not to appear as though you are unloading freight from the docks."

Sergei chortled, covering his mouth with his hand.

"At least I do not need assistance to complete the lift," Rodian retorted.

"I am nearly sixty years old. You are hobbling in your thirties?" He winked at Brigitte. "If you must compare yourself to me at your age, Rodian, then at least be man enough to do what you can to see that your ballerina is not harmed by your weakness. I am sure Master Petipa would loan the same danseurs he has gifted to me to help you lift Brigitte." Pavel bowed to Brigitte and held out his hand. She accepted and a moment later found herself flying skyward. Pavel held her aloft only long enough to prove his point. "Light as a feather," he said jovially, setting her down. Sergei applauded.

She delighted to see the scowl on Rodian's face. Pavel walked away towards the other side of the stage, and Rodian went in the opposite direction towards his office.

"Maria asked me to invite guests to a dinner party she is hosting this evening."

Brigitte reached to massage a muscle spasm in her shoulder. "You are inviting me to sit at a table with Maria?"

Sergei stood before a full-length mirror set up for the performers to check themselves before taking the stage. He spoke to his reflection. "I think Nikolai will be there with Antonia."

"Leonid is here tonight. I could invite him. He wanted to go to the Bears Inn after the performance."

Sergei's eyes darkened.

She held his gaze in the mirror. An electric feeling caught her in its current, buzzing through her skin, to her spine. Sergei looked stricken. The current connected them, frightening her. She reached for his shoulder, just to touch him, and have his skin draw the crackling charge from her so she might be relieved of it, but the closer she drew, the more powerful the magnetism. Her ears began to ring. Sergei took her hand.

"Come with me," he said. They went through the stage door towards the sitting rooms where distinguished guests were sometimes tucked away between performances. He opened one of the large, heavily carved doors, pulling her inside. Both glanced around. The fireplace smoldered as though it had not been tended for hours. Large mahogany chairs were scattered. Likely, the last to occupy this room had been red-faced men discussing politics before the matinee.

Sergei took Brigitte into his arms, holding her close. He leaned in to kiss her, but she put up her hand. "Our makeup," she whispered. He pulled back.

"I do not understand what spell you have cast upon me," his voice husky.

"I feel it too. A spell cast upon us both."

The electric torture grew in its intensity. She whimpered with the pain. Sergei flinched, his mouth held in a pout of confusion and desire. She did not know if she should give herself to him or run for her life. "Are we possessed by demons?" she asked.

"We are cursed," Sergei said. "It is our sin." His hands began to slide over her costume, lifting the skirt and seeking her warm center. She pushed him back and away. The current broke and she felt a sudden chill in the room.

"Brigitte?"

"I did not expect this," she said.

"Are you angry with me?" Sergei came after her; she moved away from him, two opposed magnets. He stopped.

"We have a performance."

She recognized that running from Sergei may be overly dramatic, but the intensity of the connection was too much. Sergei took her hand. She pulled away and made for the door.

Reaching back stage, she struggled to catch her breath before anyone noticed or questioned her exertion. At the table with pitchers of water, she poured a glass and began to calm down, feeling a return to the solidness of her body. Maria walked behind her. She had the role of Pavel Gerdt's queen. Her indifference to Brigitte, whom she completely ignored, felt newly deserved.

The curtain went up late. Brigitte had a brief solo as a zephyr, a warm wind, but that wouldn't happen until the middle of the act. She had no idea what delayed the curtain but knew with Tsar Nicholas in his box, it would not go unnoticed. Rodian should be held responsible, but with his closeness to Telyakovsky, he'd become untouchable. Petipa would bear the brunt. Petipa sat pouting on a wooden folding chair in the wings.

The orchestra played the overture; the lights came up with the curtain, illuminating the set designer Aleksandr Golovin's controversial scenery. At first, the tittering could not be heard over the musicians, but then it turned into hearty guffaws. Brigitte's stomach tightened. She looked toward Petipa; his expression was unchanged. Rodian smirked by the manager's podium to the left of the stage.

Once the dancing began, the laughter died down. Brigitte withdrew to the hallway outside the dressing rooms where it was quiet. She could stretch, stay limber, and get her feet back on the ground before she needed to go on stage. Muffled voices caught her attention. One of the voices belonged to Sergei and came from Maria's dressing room. Then she heard Nikolai pleading.

"Gather yourself," he said. "Use this argument in your dancing."

"If you knew my heart, Yolya, you would call me a *Deathless Koschei*."

Nikolai said, "You are, indeed, a scoundrel, but hardly a *Koschei*."

"Maria despises me." The sound of a strangled cry burned Brigitte's ears. "I cannot bear to lose her," Sergei sobbed.

"Maria is devoted to you. She gets upset sometimes with what you put her through. She will come around even before we pour out the first glass of vodka tonight. You will see."

Brigitte burned with shame and guilt, and jealousy.

"I have sinned, Yolya. I am damned to hell."

Now afraid that Sergei was a breath away from confession, Brigitte knocked on the door. She opened it. Sergei looked terrible. "I heard your voices." She pinned a look of warning on Sergei. "Has something happened?"

Nikolai came over, putting his arm around her. "Our brother is in love with his wife and they had a spat. Tell us, Sergei, what did you say or do to make Maria so angry?"

Sergei shook his head and went to the mirror.

"You should be out there. Your cue is coming up." She hoped Nikolai wouldn't notice that her voice sounded shaky.

Sergei dabbed a powder puff around his face and under his eyes, ran his hands through his hair, then grabbed his hat pushing it onto his head. Without another word, he walked out.

Nikolai looked concerned for a moment, then brightened. "All is well again. There is nothing wrong in this world that a cue to dance cannot fix."

Brigitte asked, "Did you hear the laughter when the curtain went up?"

He followed her out the door. "The terrible sets. Mathilde arranged for her sycophants to be especially expressive this evening. She is upset with Petipa for not giving a speech at her father's retirement benefit last month."

"But Petipa was sick. He had no voice to speak with."

They neared the wings. "Mathilde thinks he faked his illness. Besides, it is to her advantage to keep us all aware of the power she wields. Were it me, I would do the same."

"You would not, Yolya. You do not lower yourself to intrigue." She placed her hand on his arm. "Did Sergei tell you anything about his fight with Maria?"

"No. It is the pressures of this rebellious group he is associating with. Too much talk of artistic freedom. Anyway, I look forward to witnessing the spectacle of tonight's performance."

"Is that why you are here?"

"I would not miss this one. I hate secondhand gossip."

The lust for gossip and Sergei's big mouth, Brigitte thought, is what she had to fear the most.

At the end of the night, Leonid came backstage to congratulate her and say he did not feel well but would see her home if she wanted. Turning the key in the lock of her front door, it surprised her that it was already opened.

Nikolai stood in the hallway, his hand on the doorknob. "Brilliant disaster," he said with great excitement.

Inside she unwrapped her muffler. Nikolai danced around her swaying his hips back and forth.

"The whole ballet or only my *pas de deux* with Rodian?" She felt annoyed and tired.

"The *pas* was perfect, to be honest. I know it irritates you to hear that when you dance with him." He smiled. "No, no, the whole ballet. The sets. The costumes. Even the choreography." She sat on the foyer bench. Nikolai gracefully dropped to one knee, helping her remove her boots.

"I thought you would be at Maria's party. Honor Master Petipa and all of that."

Nikolai frowned. "Our dear sister-in-law invited both Antonia and Olga. I thought it would be a good night to catch up on some reading." He dropped her boots and bounced up. "You hungry? I pilfered fruit from Maria's gift basket."

He had a little picnic set up in the parlor, inviting her to sit on the sofa cushions he'd tossed to the floor. "Of all the directors the Imperial Theater has ever had, Telyakovsky is the most disastrous. A viper, untrained in the arts and hell-bent on destruction." Nikolai held a piece of the prianiki, their mother's gingerbread she made especially for him, and a cigarette, which he'd not gotten around to lighting. "Telyakovsky uses Rodian to keep us ill at ease."

"Telyakovsky chose his minion well. Rodian had the nerve to tell Mathilde she is getting fat. He must be very secure with Telyakovsky, to dare say that. Today he told me I am fat. I hate him."

Nikolai grew serious. "You are not fat. You need to eat more."

She laughed. "No one would be able to lift me." It was as tiresome to hear a command to eat more, as to hear she was getting fat.

"Don't be angry," he said. "But there are danseurs who worry they will break you in two because you appear so fragile. They fear partnering with you. A ballerina must be strong."

"You mean fat?" she said bitterly.

"There is a difference between strong and fat. Anna Pavlova is slight, but she is strong."

"I am strong," she argued. "Probably stronger than Anna Pavlova, but you favor her over me?"

Nikolai nodded. "She will be prima ballerina absoluta one day. She will make Sergei and I a huge success when she dances for us in our ballet next month."

Brigitte suppressed the desire to clobber him, showing him how strong she could be. "You and Sergei care about nothing but the choreography of your stupid *Fairy Doll* and Pavlova. I'm growing weary of both."

"Her hands," Nikolai said ignoring Brigitte. "I could weep with the movement of her hands." His eyes were almost glassy.

What Nikolai said was true. Anna Pavlova did have something special, unteachable, inherent. She could work harder than Anna, spend more hours at the barre - *had* worked harder, and would never gain what Anna had in abundance. This knowledge made her stomach hurt.

The ringing telephone startled them both. Nikolai stood first to go answer. "Count Verontsov is going to spoil our little party. Too bad."

"It cannot be him," Brigitte said. "He only now has left me at my door."

Nikolai picked up the mouthpiece. "Mama? Yes, right away. Cover up. Stay warm. I am coming. Brigitte, too."

"What is wrong?" She asked in alarm, grateful to Leonid who had a telephone installed in Nina's apartment, as her health had begun to fail.

Nikolai ignored her question, continuing his conversation on the phone. "I will ring the doctor. He may even reach you before we do. He can let himself in. We will have a carriage sent for Evgenia."

"Mama needs the doctor?"

"Sergei, too, Mama." Nikolai hung up, turning toward her. "She is asking for us." With calm sternness, he commanded, "Get your coat."

She followed Nikolai up the narrow staircase through the dingy smell of mold and dust to the second floor of Nina's apartment building. He opened the unlocked door. Brigitte stood a moment on the threshold. Three years earlier Gustave Legher had gone without complaint in the middle of the night, discovered by Nina in the morning as an empty vessel, his eyes closed and a blissful smile on his lips. For them all, the light had dimmed in the apartment. The rooms were quieter, void of his voice. She tightened her resolve and followed Nikolai in.

Sergei stood from his chair at the kitchen table and came straight to Brigitte, taking her hands in his and searching her eyes. "She is dying," he said.

The doctor was putting on his coat and cleared his throat. "In my experience," he said firmly, "a patient with your mother's symptoms has at most a day."

Evgenia came in next. "Hello," she said. "Brigitte. I have not seen you in a long time. You look haggard." She went to Sergei and they hugged and kissed. Evgenia did the same with Nikolai.

The doctor repeated his prognosis, causing Evgenia to gasp and fall into a chair by the hearth. "Are we really to lose our mother?" she said.

The wall beside the closed door to Nina's room was covered in framed pictures of the Legher children at various ages, all dressed in costumes. Nikolai was represented most, then Sergei. Brigitte looked at them, wishing for more time here. Not just in the future, but in her childhood. For more moments sitting on Nina's lap, having her hair brushed, listening to the fairytales of how they had each come to be a Legher. Her resentment towards the other children filled her closed heart. She was grateful for the distraction of the angry fire inside of her, illuminating the blackness coming with Nina's impending death.

"We should go in," Nikolai said.

Brigitte hesitated only a moment before she pushed the door to Nina's room open. The smell caught her off guard. Nina always prided herself on her fastidiousness. Brigitte blamed the smell on Evgenia who had been charged with Nina's care after Gustave died.

Mama slept. Even in the dim light, her skin looked pale and yellow. The quilt on her bed could not hide the bloated belly formed by a tumor.

"We need to get her clean," Brigitte admonished Evgenia. Moving in sync they began to collect what they would need. Brigitte put a kettle on the stove to heat. Evgenia went to the linen cupboard.

The doctor excused himself after giving Nikolai a bottle of heroin with instructions on its administration. "It is meant primarily for coughs, but we've found it relieves pain more effectively than morphine," the doctor said. "Crush the tablets into warm water. Try to keep her quiet."

Sergei and Nikolai gently lifted Nina from her bed while Brigitte and Evgenia changed the sheets. The men left the room so the sisters could bathe Nina and dress her in a clean nightgown. She had awakened during the commotion but was too weak to help or protest.

"Evgenia," Nina whispered. "Let me talk alone with Brigitte." Both sisters were surprised. Evgenia looked hurt.

On Nina's dressing table, arranged amongst the tortoise shell brush and comb, the jewelry box, Brigitte found her perfume atomizer and spritzed a few times around the bed.

"All clean," Brigitte declared, coming to sit on the small blue slipper chair beside the bed. She reached for Nina's hand.

"I do not so much sleep now as practice for eternal rest." Nina smiled weakly.

"Practicing?"

"I close my eyes, feeling myself beginning to lift up and away. It is an effort to stay."

Brigitte opened the drawer to the nightstand where she knew her mother kept handkerchiefs. She took one, pale pink, embroidered on the corner with flowers. Nina seemed to have an endless supply of handkerchiefs, needing them in the raising of all her children. As Brigitte held the linen, she could not recall her mother wiping a single tear for her amongst all the tears of all the children. Grief and anger tightened in her chest.

Nina pointed to a book on a nearby stool. Tolstoy's fairytales. "Do you want me to read to you?" She opened the book to where an envelope marked the story of *Marya Morevna.*

Nina's eyes closed again. Practicing, Brigitte thought. The Legher children were raised to always be practicing. She closed the book, putting it on the nightstand.

Like the little sprites and fairies in the tales, her memories sprung out of the dark forest of her mind, cavorting over the bedclothes, reminding Brigitte of herself as a tiny child climbing up into the bed where Nina and Gustave cuddled together, trying to find a place for herself there and being scolded and sent out of the room. Gustave's deep voice, angry at being disturbed. Twice when she'd come into their room, they had not sent her away but slept on, as she found deep comfort between them and their quiet resting. The times she'd been shooed away, she'd snatched up the book of Tolstoy's fairytales and sit beside the fading embers of the fire in the kitchen. Unable yet to read, she looked at the pictures depicting heroic tsareviches and the wicked Baba Yaga flying in her mortar, steering with the pestle.

Nina's labored breathing made Brigitte lightheaded, as she wanted to breathe for her.

Brigitte thought of the fairytale that Nina made up for her. How she had been a sylphide that stepped out of a ballerina's tiara. She could remember so clearly the sensation from her earliest childhood of flying and had believed with absolute certainty that she had once had wings and somehow lost them. Now the story broke her heart. Where had she come from? Not the fairytale version; the real story. Watching Nina dying felt like watching an unread novel smoldering in an ashy fire.

She left Nina to sleep, going back to the kitchen where Evgenia had set out tea and the very last of Nina's prianiki. Evgenia wanted to know what had been said, what she'd been left out of. With nothing to tell, Brigitte allowed the red flower of bitterness to bloom in her heart, giving Evgenia a pitying glance, happy to see her sister's face shade over with fear.

"It is snowing," Sergei announced. The flakes blew against the glass as if trying to come inside and cover them with the weight of sorrow.

"So, we wait now?" Evgenia asked Nikolai, frustration thick in her words. "I need to get home to my family."

"I will get word to you if you should come back. Sergei will see you home." Sergei stood, coming to stand beside Brigitte.

"No need for you to go out in the cold." Evgenia put on her coat and bolted out the door without saying goodbye.

Nikolai went to lie down in Gustave's dance studio. Sergei went to sit with Nina.

Brigitte tucked into the bed that Evgenia and Vera had shared, with her and Nikolai's trundle underneath. She'd been so young when she left this room to go to school, the pain still oddly fresh as she recalled the first nights in the dorm, a cot all by herself.

When more children were born, Brigitte slept on a pallet in Gustave's studio when she came home on holidays and summer breaks. Nina rolled it out each night, making such a fuss, Brigitte assumed it an honor to sleep on the hard floor on piles of colorful blankets.

When she returned to school after short visits home in those early years, the first night would always be the most difficult, her longing for her mother leaving her shaky and tearful with no one to comfort her.

Now she slept fitfully, dreaming of Gustave's soothing voice telling her to lift her arms without raising her shoulders. As she began to awaken, she realized it was not Gustave in the room, but Sergei. He sat on the bed and she reached for him. He held himself rigid. Then Brigitte remembered where they were, and what was happening.

"Mama?" She asked.

"She is resting." His voice trembled. "She took a little of the heroin the doctor left, with some water."

His body shook as he began to cry. Again, she reached for him, to comfort him but he stiffened and shook his head.

"I have been deceived," he said, his voice otherworldly, unrecognizable. "You deceived me and made me a wretched sinner." His eyes were tired, broken.

"What are you saying?"

"Mama told me the truth. She said Nikolai is wrong. He misunderstood all these years. It is all a treacherous lie. You led me into mortal sin. We are damned."

"What did you say to her?" She grabbed his arm, though he shrank away. She needed to hold fast to the pieces of her heart slipping from her, his love receding into the darkness of the room, a shadow chased to fiery spaces.

"I asked her who your parents are. I told her what Nikolai said." His nose began to run. Spittle glistened on his lips; his skin turned red and splotchy. She took Nina's handkerchief from her sleeve where she'd tucked it, handing it to him. He ignored her. "You are a Legher. My *sister*." Sergei contorted as though the word were a worm in his gut.

"She said it was a joke that you were like a changeling. Only a joke." Sergei moaned. "What we have done is disgusting. We are unclean." He ran to the empty chamber pot in the corner of the room and vomited.

She put her hand to her mouth.

Nikolai woke from his nap, finding them in a wretched state. Brigitte clutched a pillow. Sergei sat in the kitchen, his head in his hands. Alarmed, he asked Sergei if Nina had died. Sergei repeated his words about giving Nina the heroin.

"Mama told Sergei they did not take me in as a foundling. I'm a Legher, like you, like Sergei."

Nikolai smiled. "It is what she wanted to be true, dear sister." He motioned for her to rise. "Come sit beside her with me."

She tossed the pillow aside. "What is the truth, Nikolai?" she pleaded. "I feel in a short time I will never know."

Sergei sat in the kitchen unmoving, looking horrible; he had become the wretched being that Nina's words made him.

"We are going to sit with Mama. I do not think she has much longer," Nikolai said with profound tenderness.

The gaslight in Nina's room gave off a soft, warm glow. Just as they walked into the room, Nina jerked suddenly, flinging a leg over the side of the bed. Nikolai lifted the leg back. Brigitte covered her with the quilt.

"Help me, Yolya," Nina said. She did not open her eyes, nor appear to even be awake, but crying out in her sleep.

"She wants help," Brigitte said.

"She is lost to us. We can only watch."

Nina's body jerked again, flailing about, as though she fought demons. The coldness of death slid into the room. Brigitte looked to the dark corners expecting to see glowing red eyes, the open maw of a shadowy form. Nina's leg flew out from under the quilt again. Together they tucked her back in.

"Help me," she said, this time so quietly that had they not been beside her, they would not have heard.

The scene repeated several times until Brigitte thought she could bear to watch no longer. Nikolai sat on the slipper chair in the quiet between the skirmishes with the Angel of Death, his face wet with tears.

Nina lay still, barely breathing. Brigitte's mind wandered away from the room, back to the time Nina sat with the older children in a photographer's studio. The photographer, often employed by those in the theater, had been unused to children and had frightened them all with his orders and shouts as he arranged them around their mother. Gustave held Brigitte in his arms and made jokes for the children so they would sit still.

Gustave had put Brigitte down on a chair and instructed that a picture be taken for her father. She'd only been four years old, but there had been something different about the way he said *father*. Mama interjected, "A picture of Brigitte just for *you*, Gustave."

"Yes, of course," he'd laughed but his expression was odd.

She knew this look, though. She'd learned it in the study of her mother and father's faces. He gave this look when he tried to convince her of something she knew to be untrue, like the time he told her to tell Mama he had no money. She knew he did. They had come back from a special outing for just the two of them to the fountain in the Alexandrovsky Garden. He had met a friend, a man with a big mustache. The man had given her a doll.

Few of her father's friends paid attention to her. This man had commented on how bright her eyes were, just like her mother's. Nina's eyes were blue, and her own, dark brown. She thought she could see the similarity and it made her happy. The man had given Gustave a leather purse, which he opened there in the park. She could hear the clinking of coins.

Nina rose suddenly, her eyes still closed. Blood poured from her mouth. Nikolai sprang up. "Get towels and a basin, quickly," he ordered.

She raced into the kitchen. Sergei lifted his head from the table. "What?"

"She's bleeding. Get linens from the cabinet."

He bolted from the chair. Brigitte grabbed the bowl Nina used to make the prianiki, then rushed back to her room. Nikolai held the quilt to Nina's mouth trying to catch the fountain of blood, wiping her mouth. "She is choking," he said reaching for the bowl; holding it under her chin, as it filled with his mother's blood.

"Oh, dear God," Sergei said.

Brigitte snatched a towel from him, wiping splatters from Nina's face. Blood began to pour from her nose. "She's not breathing. She can't breathe," Nikolai said panicked. "She can't breathe."

"We've got to stop the bleeding," Brigitte said. "She's losing too much blood."

Sergei began to whimper, backing up to the wall. "Mama," he moaned, the man fleeing, leaving a small boy to watch his mother die.

The towel saturated; the bowl filled. Brigitte reached for another of the towels Sergei had dropped at the foot of the bed and handed it to Nikolai. He gave her the bowl. She rushed to the kitchen, pouring her mother's life force out, amazed at how it stained the white porcelain sink. She grabbed another smaller bowl. How many eggs had Nina beaten in this bowl?

When the big bowl filled, Brigitte handed Nikolai the smaller one, going again a second time, and pouring it out into the sink. In the bedroom, they switched again. Brigitte used a fresh towel to clean Mama's face, as Nikolai held the bowl.

Then Nina was dead. The skin on her face, white as snow, made her glow in the early morning light. Brigitte looked out the window, astonished that the night began its struggle with the dawn. Snow piled up on the sill as the heavy flakes fell from the sky.

CHAPTER 14

St. Petersburg, April 1903

Sergei stopped speaking to Brigitte entirely. Nikolai did not exactly avoid her, but he came and went, leaving only a teacup in the sink, his shoes by the front door, and dirty clothes in a bag waiting for the laundress to pick up, letting her know he still used her home as his own. She ached for Sergei. But she missed Nikolai.

One day after taking Nikolai's *Classique de Perfection*, he came up to her as she dried off with a towel. "Your legs are stiff with no plasticity."

She didn't feel stiff. When she did not reply, he looked pained, then rushed on to say, "I've given your solo in *The Fairy Doll* to Agrippa Vaganova. You are not ready for it."

She stood frozen for a moment, then said, "Agrippa is tall, ugly, and with the charisma of a turnip."

"Technically, she is superb," Nikolai countered.

The Fairy Doll had been a gift from Telyakovsky to the Legher Brothers, their first ballet as producers; a gesture meant as a clear signal to Petipa, his time was over. There would be only one performance held at the theater in the Hermitage, the tsar's winter palace, and only for the tsar's family and honored guests.

"After the performance, if you like," Nikolai offered as compensation, "I could help you with exercises to loosen you up."

"You gave my solo to Vaganova?"

Before Nikolai could respond, Sergei came into the room. After Nina's death, he'd quit coming to the *Classique de Perfection*. Nikolai excused himself to speak to Sergei. After a few moments, he waved at her, giving her a weak smile as he turned to leave with Sergei.

She yelled at Nikolai to stop, rushing to the door, and pulling both by the arm back inside. Neither could look her in the eye.

"You put Nikolai up to this," she screamed at Sergei.

"It is best." Sergei's face turned red.

"Please do not be upset. It is how things are in the ballet. You know that. This ballet must be the best. Perfect," Nikolai said touching her shoulder.

"Perfect? I am not perfect enough for your ballet?"

"No." Sergei's shoulders drew back and he dropped his hands to his sides looking as though he might take off in a leap at any moment, waiting only for the cue.

"How could you do this?"

"For the good of the ballet, try to understand," Nikolai said. "Sergei and I have our reputations, our whole futures at stake. If Telyakovsky is happy, we have the chance of a lifetime."

"To be the next Marius Petipa?"

"Yes," Sergei answered.

"At least we will be in line for his throne," Nikolai said.

"If I thought that you were replacing me with Vaganova because I was not perfect enough for you, Nikolai, I would have to hate you." The word "hate" tasted vile in her mouth. "I think it is Sergei who must be rid of me."

A shadow crossed Nikolai's face. "You only need a little more time to work. I will give you some exercises. I promise, once we are made the new ballet masters, you will have solos. This is too important. Sergei, tell her."

"We should go, Nikolai." Sergei opened the door.

Brigitte thought of the strength in Sergei's hands, the gentleness in his eyes, the kindness and love that had been hers. She could never hate him, or Nikolai. How could she hate Nikolai, who had never for a moment been cruel to her or disloyal to Sergei? She loved him all the more for his love of Sergei.

"I will be happy to work on your exercises," she said. She went to Sergei and whispered in his ear, "What Mama told you is not true. I feel it. It is a lie that is making you do this to me."

Sergei turned and walked away, Nikolai following apologetically behind him.

The night *The Fairy of the Dolls* opened, Brigitte attended with Leonid. Wanting Sergei to notice her, she chose a light pink-mousseline gown, the velvet bodice trimmed with gold. White tulle embroidered with gold beads and small pearls floated around the hem held in place by dark pink silk roses.

"*Lyubemaya*, for you." Leonid held out a jewel box. Inside was a brooch, half the size of her palm, a gold swan with diamond wings and eyes. He kissed her, then took the brooch and fastened it to the black velvet choker at her neck, the one he liked, he said, for the way it made her neck look so long.

He kissed her skin just under the brooch. His breathing changed, growing lustful. He kissed her again. All her careful preparations were about to be undone, as would the back of her dress. They would be late for the ballet. She hated to miss even a moment of *The Fairy of the Dolls*. But this was business. She followed him to her bedroom.

The 250 people attending the ballet were there at the invitation of the tsar and tsarina. Brigitte never felt comfortable walking into a theater through the front doors. For a small theater, it held unmatched grandeur. The red-velvet seats were set in a semi-circle amid coral-colored marble columns and white marble statues of Apollo and the Nine Muses.

They arrived in time for the call to take their places in the sixth, and last, row, aisle seats. *The Fairy of the Dolls* was last on the program, which meant it promised to be the most entertaining. Leonid seemed happy; his smile eased the tightness in her chest.

A man wearing an equal number of medals and ribbons on his jacket as Leonid did, firmly shook Leonid's hand.

"Too much drama in opera and plays. Do we not find enough of it in our own lives?" Leonid joked as an excuse for being late.

The man complimented Leonid. "I hear this Trans-Siberian railroad will open within the year. You are accomplishing great things for Russia. All the more impressive with this mess going on in Japan."

As the lights dimmed, she imagined the preparations happening in the wings. Sergei and Nikolai dressed in costume, shaking out their limbs, and rolling their heads to loosen tight muscles.

She distracted herself by looking at the opulence of the jewels and gowns worn by the women nearest to her, sparkling even in the dim lighting.

"She is his mistress," Brigitte heard whispered loudly in the row ahead of theirs, a conversation between two women. From behind, and from the dull color and style of their hair, Brigitte judged harshly, they were wives who drove their husbands to find mistresses.

When Leonid brought her out in public, she overheard the names women used to talk about her. "Trollop" and "tart". If Leonid heard, he never said. She didn't complain or speak of how the relief of reaching the quiet sanctity of her home at the end of such nights far surpassed the relief of the curtain dropping on a horrible performance.

Leonid gained power by flouting social conventions, unfettered by limits lesser men contended with; he dared to flaunt his mistress. In the esteem of his colleagues, he was envied. She participated, knowing what he gained, losing pieces of herself in the transaction.

The gentleman next to her slid his hand to her thigh. She turned to look at him, but her attention went directly to the man's companion, a sour-faced crone. Before Brigitte could suggest the man remove the offending hand, Leonid leaned over her.

"Count Rumyansev," he greeted him. "It is a great honor to see you here this evening."

The two men spoke briefly. When the conversation naturally concluded, Leonid looked at her with pride. She knew, while he perhaps felt a deep fondness for her after all their years together, he still only saw her as a possession, purchased for his enjoyment and prestige.

From the moment the curtain went up, the audience adored the Legher Brothers and their ballet. They cheered for Mathilde and Anna Pavlova. They even warmly received Agrippa Vaganova, though Brigitte knew she could have made more of the solo. In the end, it was Nikolai and Sergei, as the harlequins competing in a most comedic manner for the attention of Mathilde, as the Fairy Doll, who stole the show. Leonid guffawed along with the crowd. Brigitte dared not breathe for fear she would lose hold of herself and become a spectacle.

Her brothers had left her behind. She knew it was impossible to ever catch up to them. Sergei danced, happy, buoyant.

Sitting next to Leonid, Count Rumyansev's hand occasionally stroking her leg, she felt utterly alone, abandoned, not just by Nina's death, but by

Nina's dying words to Sergei; by Sergei's demand that she be banished, by Nikolai choosing Sergei over her.

At the end of the evening, Leonid saw her to her front door. He had already bedded her once; that would be the unspoken reason he didn't come in.

She hung up her gown and changed into a thin slip. In her *Chambre de Joie*, she did not bother with music. That would only be a distraction from the chiding voices in her head, pointing out every humiliation she'd ever suffered. She needed to fight them. Every single one. She tried to throw them high above her head as she danced. She moved her legs reminding herself of how strong they were, how beautifully they held her up, carrying her from one corner of the room to the other. The room ran the entire length of the house allowing her space for *grande* emotion, *grande* expression. She leapt, falling to the floor, rolling into a small ball, then expanding from the ball, blooming, only to be covered with a heavy grey curtain. Futilely, she tore at the fabric with her nails. Panting, she curled into herself, eyes closed to it all. A slim comfort and lessening of her grief came from her exhaustion.

Nikolai made a noisy entrance, singing, "*Dark eyes, passionate eyes, burning, and splendid eyes. How I love you, how I fear you. Verily I espied you in an ill-starred moment.*"

She sat up, waking from a dream or falling into one, she wasn't certain which. Nikolai swayed; his left arm half caught in the sleeve of his coat. He dropped down next to her. Reaching over, she helped pull off the heavy overcoat. He gave an exaggerated look of the love-struck harlequin and finished his song.

"*I am not sad. I am not sorrowful. My fate is soothing to me. All that is of the best in life, God has given us. As a sacrifice, I have given up to the fiery eyes.*" He pulled a bottle of champagne from the inside of his morning coat. Missing a cork and half its contents, the bottle had sloshed, staining Nikolai's vest.

"A triumph," he slurred. Holding up the bottle, toasting himself, he drank and passed the bottle to her.

She took it and held it, not feeling like celebrating. "You were brilliant, Yolya."

He looked at her astonished, his mouth slack with shock. "You were there? That's wonderful."

"Leonid took me."

"He is a fine one." He took the bottle back, holding it up. "A salute to Count Verontsov who is a fine one." He drank and handed her the bottle.

"I am celebrating because tomorrow I will be shipped off to Siberia. You will never hear from me again."

She saw a flash of fear in his eyes just before he closed them.

"Has something happened?"

"I have offended."

"Whom have you offended?"

"Tsar Nicholas." He hiccupped. "Should not matter too much to offend the tsar, right? A nobody. A dancer. A harlequin." Nikolai grew serious, looking at her intently. "The trouble with our tsar, he does not take so seriously the important issues of Russia, but he does take great interest in the faux pas of insignificant men like myself."

"Yolya, what have you done?"

Nikolai leaned his shoulder against the wall and peered into her face. "*The Fairy Doll* is a triumph. Telyakovsky came up to Sergei and shook his hand. He is replacing the great Marius Petipa. Sergei and I will be the new ballet masters. Telyakovsky is giving us the position. We feel like the Angels of Death, Sergei and I. knowing our triumph is Petipa's end. But perhaps even in this dark hour, someone is writing out the order of my execution." Nikolai put down the bottle. He clapped his hands together and held them clasped. "It is the top for us. We have reached the very top of the mountain."

"So why do you think you are now going to Siberia? You are impossible when you drink." He and Sergei may have made it to the mountain, but they left her in the foothills. She wanted to slap him. Her feet hurt all the more because they were cold. Her whole body ached. She needed sleep.

"It is all spoiled. Sergei and I will be arrested and sent to prison. We will dance for thieves and murderers."

"Has something happened or are you being a fool?"

"*The Fairy Doll* was a triumph," he said again, smiling sadly. "It happened in our excitement."

"What happened?"

"The tsar had a banquet laid out for all of us, including the actors and the singers. We performed last. The good bits went to the fat opera singers and the fat actors. When we finally went to sup, all that was left were bits of lettuce, bread crumbs." He hung his head in a gesture of defeat. "In a moment of bravado, because we were a triumph, the new ballet masters..." Nikolai took a drink from the bottle and let out a silent burp. "I declared that the tsar's feast was unworthy of my company. I would treat them all to a real dinner."

"You said that out loud?"

He put the bottle down, then rolled over onto all fours. "We danced perfectly. You know that is impossible, right? Everyone danced perfectly."

"Who heard? Who was there?"

"I did not take attendance. That rapscallion Petrov had a horrible grin on his face."

"He would like to be ballet master," she said flatly.

"Telyakovsky knows he does not have the talent to do more than what he does now, spy on us. He is a brainless parrot who writes out Petipa's ballets and the stupid things we say when we think we are triumphant."

On his knees, Nikolai reached for the champagne bottle. "We went to Cubats. Splendid place."

"Did you see anyone there who would report you?"

"They were all there. Bekefy. He could not help but boast how I was a better host than the tsar. He began to drink the moment he left the stage." As though reminded, he picked up the bottle, taking a sip. "He is going to Siberia, too. He was excited. We were all excited. *The Fairy Doll* was a triumph." He hoisted the bottle in a salute.

She bit her lip. "How could you be so insulting? To the Tsar. To me. You banished me from your stupid ballet. How could you put yourself in such danger?"

He looked down, frowning.

"I would hate you if I could." She did not want him to be exiled to Siberia. Being exiled in the comfort and luxury of her own home felt terrible. How much worse to be cold and hungry? She could not bring herself to serve him with the same sorrows he'd given to her.

"Talk to Mathilde."

"Mathilde?" he smiled. "She was a triumph as the *Fairy Doll*. Telyakovsky offered us the position of ballet masters." Nikolai paused, furrowing his brow. "Did I say that already?"

"Yes."

"Telyakovsky said, 'Masters Legher One and Two, in one week, I want to receive your intentions for the next ballet.' Just like that." Nikolai's face crumpled; he began to cry, deep silent sobs. "What I hoped for, worked for. We worked for, Sergei and me. Gone now. I will be dead in a week."

"Talk to Mathilde. She will smooth things over with the tsar. She adores you."

"She adores her goat," he said sniffling. "Some people she finds more useful than others." He paused. "No, I take that back. There are a few she seems to genuinely care for." He grew introspective for a moment. Wiping his face with the back of his hand, he said with excitement, "Did you notice Sergei's *grand jeté developpé*? Fantastic."

Brigitte sighed and stood, stretching her back. "He was a triumph."

"I hear what they said." Nikolai lay on his side, hugging the champagne bottle. "Sergei is the handsome one. The better dancer. His choreography is more inventive. Telyakovsky treats him as though he were the tsarevich himself."

Brigitte's feet throbbed. She shivered.

"Some say, 'Legher One must hate Legher Two.' But there is no hating Sergei." He laughed, holding the bottle aloft, rising to his elbow as if the bottle lifted him. "To Sergei, the triumphant new ballet master of the Imperial Ballet. He will not be sent away to Siberia, thank God." He drank and handed the bottle to her. She took a sip.

"He is still there at Cubats, celebrating. No idea how Maria will get him home." Grinning, rolling onto his hands and knees again, he used the wall to support himself as he stood up. "We need another bottle of champagne."

"If you were not finished celebrating, Yolya, why did you leave before your party ended?"

He tilted his head as though she puzzled him. "Are you shaking?"

"I'm freezing."

"Your nightgown is soaking wet. You look as though you've been caught in the rain. Were you dancing?"

She let out an exasperated laugh. "I do nothing else in this room."

"But it's three in the morning."

"It is four now."

"What could you possibly accomplish by dancing in the middle of the night after a performance?" He leaned his shoulder against the wall.

"You gave my role to Agrippa."

He swayed back. "Have they come for me yet? Check the street. The police should be here soon to arrest me. I want to be very drunk and not remember a bit of it."

She wanted to punch him. Instead, she pushed him out of the way.

"I will cast you in the next ballet. I am the new ballet master. I can do that now."

"You could do it before," she said, as she stormed up the staircase and retreated into her bedroom. She pulled off her nightgown, grabbing a thick flannel nightgown that covered her head to foot.

Nikolai knocked on her door. "Can I come in?"

"No. You threw me out of your ballet."

"I didn't throw you out, Sergei did. Be angry with him. He is not going to Siberia. I am."

"You both did. It was not just Sergei."

She opened the door quickly. He ducked his head covering his face with his forearms as though expecting her to come out fighting. His flinching and weakness made her feel suddenly bloodthirsty. "You betrayed me. You turned your back on me."

"Sergei said it would be too upsetting to work with you around. He says all he can think about when he looks at you is the blood of our mother on your hands."

She pushed past him again, going down the stairs. "You wore her blood, too."

"He is brokenhearted. An artist. I give him his way when it is important to him."

He had followed behind her, colliding with her when she stopped at the bottom of the staircase and turned around. "You should leave here, Nikolai. You and Sergei are not my brothers. You have never really been family to me. Not really. I am not Legher. I should thank you for waking me up to who I am. Who I am not."

"Why are you so upset?" Nikolai asked as if she were a ballerina absoluta throwing a temper tantrum.

"You are a triumph. You and Sergei. The amazing Legher Brothers. I am the dancer who is not good enough."

She went to the parlor and sat on the divan, tucking her feet up underneath her gown

"I do not like when you are angry. Any other woman can be mad at me. I do not care. But for you to despise me, that is worse than being sent to Siberia." Nikolai sat next to her, leaning against her shoulder. "You ruin my great happiness in this evening's triumph. Celebrate with me. I will get more champagne. We will toast to all the Leghers living and dead, who danced for the tsar. There is a bottle I left by the door when I came in. Drink with me, before I am executed."

"You need to find another place to live, Nikolai," she said, tilting her face away from him. "You are not my brother. It is no longer decent for you to live here."

He sighed. "Some evenings you just cannot get drunk enough." He stood, heading for the foyer, returning a moment later with the champagne. Swaying and fumbling, he popped off the cork. She braced herself in case he fell on top of her. "Sergei is not like you and me." The cork exploded hitting the ceiling, then the wall behind her. He put his mouth over the foaming bubbles. Licking his lips, he continued. "He has weaknesses. No, that is not the right word."

Brigitte knew what Nikolai meant to say.

"He is not a good Russian, in control of his emotions. You are a good Russian. I am a good Russian. Sergei is not a good Russian." Nikolai slurred, putting his hand on her shoulder to steady himself as he lowered down beside her. He held out the green bottle for her to take. From the label, she knew it was expensive. Had he bought it when he bought dinner for his *triumphant* troupe? "If I thought that he could finish the ballet with you there, I would not have agreed to replace you with Agrippa." When Brigitte refused the bottle, he put it down on the side table.

"You should move in with Antonia. She has not yet learned how disloyal you are."

He shook his head.

"Let Sergei give you a bed."

Nikolai laughed. "I doubt I could hold my suitcase over the threshold before Maria called the authorities. You are the only one who harbors me."

"Rent your own apartment. You are ballet master with plenty of money."

"That would be too lonely. I prefer it here."

She began to shiver more violently. Had the heat gone off entirely? Her body ached from the deep chill, making her even more sad and tired. She stood and went upstairs to her room without another word to Nikolai, and crawled into bed. The linens were cold.

He pushed open her door. He held a bottle of something darker than champagne. Tucked into his arm were two small glasses. "Cognac. Mathilde introduced me to a Frenchman this evening. He gifted to me this bottle as a congratulation. From the man's vineyard, or so he made claim. Inside this bottle is the summer sun. When you drink a glass, you get warm."

He put the bottle on her dressing table along with the glasses, then opened it.

"I do not want your congratulatory cognac. Do you ever think of what I want?"

"I am thinking of you at this moment. You are shivering. Once you get warm, you will be less depressing. These minutes with you may be my last ones as a free man. Listening to you sulk is not how I want to spend what little time I have left."

He filled both glasses, drank his in one gulp, and poured himself another, before handing Brigitte the other glass. "To the Leghers."

"Think of something else. I am not a Legher."

"What name is on your contract with the Imperial Ballet? Does it not say Brigitte Gustoevna Legher?"

She took the glass from him and drank the cognac, burning her throat. She coughed. "I was not born with that name."

"Better to be a despicable Legher, sister to the triumphant Legher Brothers, than a dirty Jew." He gave her his most charming smile. The one he used to reward the ballerinas when they performed well in his *Classique de Perfection*. The one he used to control dancers like dogs trained with meat scraps.

"I can no longer trust you. I am nothing to you but a bed in a house where you can put your suitcase over the threshold." She put her face into her pillow.

"You are more than that. You are the one drinking with me on the night of my triumph and demise." He took her glass from her hand, and a moment later nudged her, holding it out, refilled. Overfilled. Some spilled onto the bedcovers. He giggled like a child. His eyes were moist and bright. "All those hours we spent shaping our turnouts." He drank. "No one had a better turnout than Father. Unnatural. Admittedly a bit disgusting, but undeniably remarkable."

"I am not Legher. Not good enough for the Leghers."

He waved his hand holding the glass; cognac sprayed across her bed. "That is enough of that. Stop pitying yourself. Do you think you are special to have no mother or father? If I were to toss this bottle out the window of a moving carriage on Nevsky Prospekt it would bounce off ten orphans before shattering on the stones. Now I am an orphan, too." He sat at the foot of her bed. "We are alive. I am not yet on a train to Siberia, and *The Fairy of the Dolls* was a triumph."

Nikolai crawled up beside her, laying his head on her pillow, facing her. "You feel bad because you did not dance in our ballet. So what? Now the ballet is over. The night ended. The draymen will soon fill the streets selling their rags. The sun will peek in at us here to see if we are alive or dead. Our mother is dead. I am not yet on a train to Siberia. I have some ideas to make you more plastic. Enough talk of betrayal. You may not have been born Legher, but now you are nothing else." He closed his eyes. "I believe I have had enough to drink."

She watched him fall asleep beside her, the feel of him reminding her of the safest moments in her childhood when they were tucked in together in the trundle bed beneath Vera and Evgenia's big bed.

"Tomorrow, Yolya," she whispered. "Talk to Mathilde. She will keep you safe."

CHAPTER 15

St. Petersburg, January 1904

Rehearsal for *The Romance of the Rosebud and Butterfly* had not been going well. The hardest on the cast and crew were all the long breaks while Petipa conferred with Nikolai, who was spared punishment for insulting the tsar, thanks to Mathilde. In the past, Petipa managed rehearsal time expertly. Now the troupe moped around. Everyone stayed close to the stage, unsure if they might be called back after their part had been rehearsed.

Brigitte sat on the floor in the wings, the soles of her feet pressed together. She dreamed of leaving St. Petersburg and going to Moscow, Paris, or even New York City. She imagined going to the Settlement of the Pale in the south, the one legal place for Jews to live in Russia. A muscle in her thigh began to twitch.

If she left rehearsal early, would Rodian notice? One of his tasks was to officially dismiss them. Anyone leaving before then had their pay docked.

She heard Director Telyakovsky's voice down the hall; her plans of escape evaporated. Normally the director spoke softly so if she could hear him, she knew he meant to be heard. Rodian walked beside him. Telyakovsky had still not managed to force Petipa into retirement, though his efforts had turned some balletomanes against him and earned him negative press.

"There are just too many old ballerinas in this company. Even ten years on stage is too long for some of these hags." Telyakovsky carried with him a clipboard, thick with pages. "Nothing more unappealing than watching dried-up *wed'mas* hobbling on weak ankles, nursing old injuries. Sickening."

Rodian had let it be known that Petipa had composed a list for Telyakovsky of dancers past their prime. All, but the girls who were fresh from Ballet School, were anxious. At the age of 33, Brigitte knew she fell into the category of a "dried-up *wed'ma.*" Maria was older and still commanded prime roles. Nina had danced into her early fifties.

Telyakovsky stopped next to her and looked down. She felt like an errant child who escaped from the nursery rather than an old woman.

"You are in Petipa's *Rosebud*?" Telyakovsky asked her.

"The violet," she said, warily.

"You *were* the violet," Telyakovsky said.

"Petrov, did Petipa cast B. Legher?"

"N. Legher and J. Kchessinsky," Rodian responded. He ran his fingers through his slicked-back oily hair leaving comb lines.

"Is she on Petipa's list?" Telyakovsky asked.

Before Rodian could answer, Mathilde spoke, appearing from out of nowhere. "Petipa's list." Her voice held disdain. "Congratulations Director, on your expert rumor-mongering." When she spoke, both Rodian and Brigitte were startled, but not Telyakovsky. He was too much of a military man to jump.

Mathilde put her right hand on Telyakovsky's arm and leaned towards him so he could kiss her cheek. He obliged.

"Have you decided about my benefit?" Mathilde asked Telyakovsky.

After twenty years of service, every principal dancer was entitled to a benefit whereby all the box office proceeds for that one night would be given to them for their retirement. Mathilde had only been dancing for twelve. When she requested a benefit, Telyakovsky had turned her down outright. She had appealed to a higher court.

"February the fourth," Telyakovsky answered curtly. "Unless that is too soon for you. Then we could schedule it for February the fourth, eight years from now."

Mathilde smiled, victorious.

"*The Romance of the Rosebud* is February fourth," Brigitte said. The three looked down at her, their faces blank as if she'd come in on the wrong cue.

Telyakovsky guided Mathilde down the hall, "Come. We can speak in your dressing room."

Nikolai and Sergei were on stage with Maria; Nikolai held up her arm, and Sergei kneeled to shift her foot.

"Look at the tsar's box, then just below it. That is where your index finger should be pointing," Nikolai said to Maria. "The rest of your body will be in the correct line. Find that point."

Brigitte thought of Gustave teaching her and Nikolai to point at the icon of the Blessed Virgin hanging on the wall in the dance studio of their apartment. She always imagined hearing the voice of the Holy Mother whispering to her, "Poor darling." The whispered words made her feel pitied for never being perfect; pity from the highest. As she got older, she tried to change her focal point, finding she couldn't without losing her balance. Gustave would shout in frustration, "Find your point." The Holy Mother would whisper, "Poor darling."

Sergei glanced at her, no more than a shift of his eyes. If she had blinked, she would have missed it. Her chest hurt, a muscle spasm, or a heart attack?

If she fell unconscious, she would know it was a heart attack. Deep breaths hurt; she took several small shallow breaths.

"Are you satisfied, Master Petipa?" Nikolai shouted out to the stalls where the old master sat, slumped in the front row. He repeated himself twice before then saying, "Rodian will post the next rehearsal schedule."

"Petrov," Petipa said in disgust as he pushed himself up in his seat. Brigitte looked back to where Rodian had been, to see if he returned from the private meeting in Mathilde's dressing room, pen in hand, wetting the tip with his tongue, always ready to record the steps of a ballet or someone's self-incriminating words.

"Petrov is *Deathless Koschei.*" Petipa pulled on his long white beard. "He to me lies."

Nikolai commented to Brigitte a few times in the past months that Petipa had been showing up for rehearsals when there were none and missing others. He hadn't been sure if it was Rodian giving him the wrong schedule, as Petipa claimed, or if Petipa had lost the faculty to keep track of time.

Turning to the wings, Nikolai called out, "Someone have Petrov officially conclude this rehearsal."

Rodian appeared with his clipboard and Maria confronted him. "Did you hear Nikolai? Do not dare dock our salaries for leaving."

Rodian mumbled something. No one asked him to repeat himself.

"You seemed unhappy with your dancing today," Nikolai said, walking off the stage towards Brigitte.

What could she say? That Sergei's indifference towards her, his proximity, made it impossible to hear the music?

"Ride home with me," he requested.

A knot had been steadily tightening in her stomach and she thought if she were to throw up or die of a heart attack, she would prefer privacy.

"Sergei," Nikolai called, motioning to him.

Sergei shook his head.

"For God's sake, he goes too far." Nikolai stomped his foot. "Sergei, come, now."

Sergei walked away, pulling Maria with him. Nikolai called again but Sergei disappeared down the hallway.

"Is this to punish you or vex me?" Nikolai complained. "I wish you would reconcile." He threw up his hands. "Meet me at the door. I need to speak to Sergei."

Two days later, Rodian pinned a new rehearsal schedule to the board next to his office door. A dozen dancers waited for the posting, including Brigitte. Rodian stood in the doorway to his office, avoiding looking at them, but smirking.

Besides the rehearsal schedule, was a notice stating in all capital letters, "PERFORMING OUTSIDE OF THE IMPERIAL THEATERS WITHOUT WRITTEN PERMISSION IS PROHIBITED. - V.A. Telyakovsky."

She had already been engaged to join a small troupe, touring south for two months. While not a new policy, the Imperial Theaters controlled nearly every aspect of its members' lives, they had allowed touring as long as notice had been given. Brigitte needed the distraction that performing outside St. Petersburg promised. She needed to get away from Sergei; to feel her heart beat normally. She wanted the better roles that the small traveling troupe brought her.

She further scanned the schedule to see when *The Romance of the Rosebud and Butterfly* would have its last rehearsal. In Rodian's neat handwriting was a notice that due to the outbreak of war with Japan, the performance and all future performances at the Hermitage Theater were canceled. She noted that Mathilde's Benefit performance was still slated to go on.

"No Violet for you, B. Legher," Rodian said.

"War with Japan?"

Rodian shrugged. "Do you think your Violet is more important than Mother Russia?"

Others were beginning to murmur about the notice of cancellation and the policy reminder.

"Why is Mathilde's benefit not canceled then?" Brigitte asked.

"Because she is not planning to dance at the Hermitage, the home of the tsar and the Imperial family, and they are not expected to be in attendance at her benefit. By the way, you have been fined three rubles this week." He had picked up a new affectation in the time he'd become regisseur, a sneer.

She thought through the entire week beginning with the *Classique de Perfection* on Monday morning but came up with nothing she had done. Before she asked him, Rodian explained.

"You did not sign your name below the schedule verifying you have seen it." He leaned forward, pointing out the door towards the postings where there was a mostly blank sheet of paper with a pencil hanging by a string attached to a nail on the wall. Rodian's signature was the only one.

"Something new you failed to notify any of us about."

"You are not the only one being fined. If you had been paying attention, you would have heard me explaining the new policy. Ignorance is no excuse. Three rubles."

The knot in her stomach tightened. She hardly noticed.

Leonid invited Brigitte to attend a dinner at Cubats in honor of Mathilde following her benefit. He paid for her to have a new gown made, designed by a young costumer who had impressed St. Petersburg's most finely dressed with her daring, and perhaps most important, attention-grabbing creations.

Brigitte's gown was made of water silk in a delicate shade of light blue. With her dark hair and the emeralds Leonid gave to celebrate the anniversary of their meeting, Brigitte looked ethereal. As she came out of her dressing room, Mathilde was walking by and glanced at her twice. Brigitte knew then just how stunning she looked in the gown.

Outside of Maria's dressing room, Sergei leaned against the wall, his arms crossed. When he saw her, he put his hand to his throat, a familiar tenderness in his eyes. She had been about to say something to him when Maria emerged from her room, dressed to go nowhere but home, looking as though when she arrived there, vases might be smashed, dishes thrown.

"Let's go, Sergei," she said. He followed Maria without looking back.

The office of the Chief of Police for the Imperial Theaters was co-opted as a smoking room for the balletomanes. Leonid waited for Brigitte there. When she came in, she noticed the chief sat in a corner chair, as his desk had been appropriated by a duke. The group of men wore their military finery, ribbons and chords, metals and emblems adorning their chests and shoulders. As she stepped through the doorway, the men stood. She offered each her gloved hand, and each, one after another, kissed it.

Leonid looked as though he owned the prized pony at the race. "You are magnificent," he told her as he escorted her from the theater to where his driver waited. Leonid looked more exhausted than she'd ever seen him. As if he might even be ill.

In the carriage to Cubats, she said, "If you would rather return to my house, Leonid, I would not mind."

"I will not be deprived of the opportunity to be the envy of every man." He smiled and she realized his teeth had all turned brown.

"Is everything all right?" she said.

"*Lyubemaya*, the tsar is asking for advice about this war. Then, he ignores it."

"Does he not trust you anymore?"

Leonid sighed. "Our tsar would have made an excellent mail clerk. As emperor he has many failings."

Brigitte gasped at his candor. They were in a private car and with the loud motor, the driver hearing Leonid's words seemed unlikely.

He turned to her. "You are not a spy, are you?"

She shook her head, unsure if he joked, but sensed no humor. "I would be sent to Siberia for failure if the tsar chose me as a spy."

Satisfied, Leonid sat back. "He surrounds himself with incompetence. I question why he keeps me around. Perhaps I, too, am now incompetent?"

"You are not," she protested. "What of the railroad? How is it you could have a hand in building the longest railroad in all the world if you are incompetent?"

"Indeed." He pulled her close to him. "If I did not relish observing the jealousy of my fellows as they ogle your beauty, I should take you up on your offer to go home." He took a deep breath.

Mathilde's party spilled out from the private dining room into the main restaurant. There were no empty tables. She glided from person to person accepting congratulations and tokens of appreciation. Mathilde made animated short speeches of thanks as she worked the room, saying of her pending retirement. "I do not like being owned by any other than myself."

As few could step outside on a clear night when the moon was full and not look up, so few could resist the gravitational pull of Mathilde.

Leonid sat against the wall, champagne glass in hand, surrounded by several men engaging in animated conversation. Brigitte decided not to intrude and began to stroll about, feeling untethered.

A loud argument broke out at one table. A large man, highly decorated, with a shaved head and a pure white horseshoe mustache, raised his voice to his table mate, an equally decorated younger man.

"We are defeated. The war games were played in the 80s and 90s. You were not there. Probably the reports have been hidden away. But it is a known fact there are not enough troops." The man had not only a red face but a red scalp. He looked like a blood blister. The younger man stood to confront him, silently drumming his fingers on the white linen cloth.

The older man said, "Tsar Nicholas has been fully informed. His advisors have given him all that a reasonable man would need to wait for engaging in an unwinnable war."

A hush fell over the room as they listened to the treasonous talk. The younger man looked around, then took his seat and the argument quieted down. Partygoers picked up their din of conversations.

Mathilde's brother Joseph, looking elegant with a red rosebud on his lapel, waved at Brigitte as he made his way through the crowd. When he reached her, he kissed her hand and said, "Did you see the notice posted on the board?"

"The reminder that we need permission to tour?"

Joseph nodded his head.

"Strange the Director feels the need to start enforcing that rule and requiring written permission."

"Not strange at all." Joseph shook his head. "We must remain beholden to and controlled by the tsarist regime. If we can earn a better living dancing on other stages, the tsar might lose his propaganda puppets. When we are reliant upon the tsar's goodwill, our interest lies in behaving as his loyal playthings."

"This seems to be the night for voicing opinions about our great father and risking arrest," Brigitte tried to sound lighthearted.

"You cannot give a man his freedom, then ask him to be your slave." Joseph took out a cigarette, tapping it against a silver case. "Even God has had little success with free will. Yet, the church fills with the oppressed."

Brigitte said, "I am already contracted to tour."

"Why do you suppose Mathilde is retiring early? To be free to do as she pleases. To dance where she likes and not have to go begging to a man who knows nothing of the arts. Groveling to Telyakovsky, hoping he will grant her permission to change her damned panniers."

Brigitte looked around, hoping no one paid attention to them. She understood Leonid's unease better now when he asked her in the car if she might be a spy. She wished to distance herself from Joseph.

He paused, then apologized. "You must excuse me," he said. "My wife tells me I am passionate and frustrated and that makes for a dull conversationalist. But Mathilde is wise to use her position to free herself from the shackles of the Imperial Theater," he rushed on. "She will come back often as a guest artist. Dance on the Imperial stages, but not live under Telyakovsky's thumb."

Brigitte sighed. "I am not Mathilde. What if Telyakovsky denies my request to tour?"

Joseph leaned in close to Brigitte's left ear. "Organize. Just like the other workers in St. Petersburg. Strike if we have to. Force Telyakovsky to see us as artists, not as, as..." She felt his hot, angry words on her neck and she wanted to put her hand up to protect herself. "As common peasants and Jews." He waved a hand, his fingers clenched into a fist. "Soon there will be pogroms against artists. We are dangerous to the tsar. Read your history.

When an emperor fears the loss of power, the first to go are artists. They censor us, control us."

Brigitte saw Sergei watching her, and beside him, the theater police chief, also looking in their direction. Leonid sat not far from Sergei, and he, too, had his eyes upon her.

"I want another drink." She held up a near-empty wine glass.

"I have good news for you," he said, his demeanor changing from revolutionary to gentleman. "I've been hired as dance master for your tour. The matter of permission is already resolved."

"Mathilde sorted it out?"

"She is a magical creature in possession of great powers. A *wed'ma*. She sends her requests out to Tsarskoe Selo, where the tsar is in residence, and..." he mimed waving a wand. "All is well."

"So, I will have Telyakovsky's permission to tour?"

"The entire troupe, with me as your leader." He took her glass and finished the last swallow.

"That is good news. Thank you. "

"Thank Mathilde."

Posters began to appear on the sides of buildings championing the war. In one, monkeys, yellow and slit-eyed, were running away from a giant white fist. Brigitte mentioned it to Leonid as they lounged in her bed. He sighed.

"I do not want to talk of war." He sounded weary.

"Is it true we cannot win?" she asked. He sat with his feet in her lap while she rubbed them. She doubted his feet could hurt more than hers. But ballerinas complaining about sore feet was far worse treason than old men complaining about war.

Leonid asked. "Did the monkeys on a billboard say that?"

"The man at Mathilde's benefit dinner who shouted about war games did. What is that? War games?"

Leonid's shoulders fell in an exasperated breath. "You need not worry. The war will not come this far. You can believe in your tsar and think of him as the father who protects you from the enemies of Russia." Leonid spoke with undisguised hostility.

He wriggled his toes. She tried to think of another way to ask about the war games because she was curious. She always thought of their relationship as a game she had mastered. She tilted her head coyly to the side. "About the war games."

"The military uses games to determine outcomes. The man you heard shouting at Mathilde's dinner spoke of classified information. He drank too excess and said too much. Something we all need to be careful of doing these days." Leonid fell silent.

He leaned up to look at her, his eyes wide and angry. She held her breath, waiting for him to speak, not sure if he might be having a heart attack. As if she had a gun pointed at him, he slowly extracted himself from her hands, rising from the bed.

"What did they use to get to you? I doubt it is a love of your country. Did they tell you that you would never dance again? Do they hold some dark secret over you?"

"Are you all right?"

"You were correct to say you make a terrible spy. A woman with no idea what I do and little understanding of what is happening in the world around her unless it occurs inside a theater or a bedroom. Now you wish to know about classified war games?"

Leonid reached for his shoes. He seemed agile enough to Brigitte and not in imminent danger of collapsing. She'd heard stories in the dressing room of old men dying in their mistress's beds.

"I have done everything for you, Brigitte." He pulled on his trousers. "I gave you this house. Dresses. Jewels. I took you to the Hermitage Theater to show the world you were more than a common prostitute. You deserved that. I thought you deserved it all."

"You have treated me with nothing but kindness." Her concern for his health melted as a new fire of worry ignited.

He put his shoes on without his stockings. "I am famed for recognizing the liars. Colleagues. Friends. I have warned them to not trust women. Finally, my turn to be the fool." He reached for his shirt hanging on the back of the chair. "I pity you having to tell whomever it is you report to, that you have nothing. That you will never get anything. These men get angry, Brigitte. They look at little birds like you and break their wings."

"What did I do?" She'd fallen into a confusing nightmare.

"The idiocy of these men thinking you are smart enough to be a spy for them. Forget Japan. Russian buffoons will destroy us first." He stood at the door, wiped his nose, and looked hard at her. "I have loved you, so I leave you in peace in this house. My last gift is to not wrap my hands around your neck. Goodbye, Brigitte Gustoevna."

"You think I am a spy," she laughed. "Leonid, please. I am no spy. No one has asked me to spy on you."

She sprang off the bed, half-dressed, chasing after him. "You are mistaken. Please. It was just one question about something I was curious about. How did I know anything was secret? The man shouted across a crowded room."

He walked down the stairs to the foyer where he grabbed his coat and hat. She reached for him.

"Oh my God, you don't believe me? I am no spy. I should not have bothered you with war talk. I know better. I don't care about war talk. You tell me that war will never touch me. I believe you. I trust you."

She tried to hold him, to convince him of his mistake, but he pushed her hard, tumbling her backward. She banged her head against the wall and gasped. He'd never, in all their years, touched her in anger.

She sobbed, " I would never betray you. I need you. You are my protector. I love you, too. I know you love me. Please, stop this."

His jaw was set. He reached for the doorknob. "I pity you."

A blast of cold air came at her through the open door. He walked down to the street, waving at his driver sitting in his car.

She crawled to the threshold. "Leonid!" she shouted, fear gripping her. The wind carried her voice away. Her loose hair whipped her face. "Please, Leonid."

He got in his car and a moment later was gone.

CHAPTER 16

St. Petersburg, Fall, 1904

The tour with Joseph Kchessinsky's troupe ended early for Brigitte. Desperate for the money, now that Leonid cut off her allowance and returned her pleading letters unopened, she tried to cope with the deplorable conditions. Mainly, the food on the tour was inedible. Meat especially. Greasy, rich, undercooked, spicy. When offered a rancid plate of head cheese, she fled the table. Joseph, as dance master, gave her the plum solos. In every way, he took care of her, as well as the entire troupe. But choosing between hunger and queasiness, Brigitte chose her old friend, hunger. When she fainted on stage, Joseph telegraphed Nikolai, who arrived by train.

Taking Nikolai aside, Joseph tattled, thinking she was out of earshot. "She tells me she has eaten, but our stage manager finds her food hidden under tables."

On the train together, Nikolai said little beyond small talk and unimportant gossip. At dinnertime, he brought out a simple meal from his bag, black bread, jam, and an orange. She ate every bite, tears streaming down her cheeks. Nikolai's only comment came in the form of a single raised eyebrow.

At first, Telyakovsky did not want to allow her to dance at all, complaining that she looked skeletal. He feared gossip that Tsar Nicholas starved his dancers. Nikolai managed to convince him to let her into the *corps de ballet*.

On the first day of rehearsal, Sergei's jaw dropped when she walked on stage. Not until that moment, seeing herself through Sergei's eyes, did she realize the full impact of not eating enough. Her emotions were unpredictable. Dull one moment, weeping the next.

Even simple warm-up exercises required concentration. But once the dance began, vitality returned to her body. Afterward, she felt drained. With Nikolai's encouragement, she gained six pounds in a month. By September, she began to feel much better. Stronger. And angrier.

When a *coryphée* attempted suicide, thus ending her dance career, Nikolai's seized the opportunity, making sure the position went to Brigitte. She knew better than to hope for first, second, or even third soloist. But at least she would be dancing above the *corps de ballet*, with better pay.

Opening night arrived but without the usual excitement. Whispers of the war from overheard conversations dampened everyone's mood. The theater felt different without Marius Petipa, and without Leonid waiting with a bouquet. Pavel Gerdt, with his unflappable good nature, had finally retired, too.

A *corps de ballet* ballerina sat at the long makeup table, her voice high and anxious, like the screeching of a violin. "Students marched with signs, shouting at us. We were terrified."

Ignoring her, Brigitte slipped off her street shoes and pulled her dress up over her head. Feliks came in. Women in various states of nakedness paid no attention to him. He handed her a navy blue tutu.

"What's this?"

"S. Legher says you are dancing the duchesses tonight. Urikova is out. You are in."

Her breath caught. "Sergei chose me?"

"Don't get excited. He still despises you. No great secret. No one has figured out why though." Feliks pulled at a loose string on the tutu. Whipping out a small scissor from a pouch he wore at his waist, he clipped it off. "He is punishing Urikova by replacing her with someone he hates. Sending a message. He's not saying he likes you."

She winced.

"I look sickly in navy. Find out if I can wear something else?" She pushed away the tutu.

"No one looks good in navy." He looked irritated and bored.

"Give me the damn tutu." She snatched it, walking out of the dressing room in her shift and stocking feet, on the hunt for Sergei.

He sat together with Nikolai and Rodian, just outside of Rodian's office.

"Put on a dressing gown," Rodian growled.

Ignoring him, she said to Sergei, "I look sickly in the navy. I am wearing a different tutu for the duchess solo." She waited, counting silently. He had ten seconds to say something, then she'd leave. *One, two, three.*

"Fine." His voice was barely audible.

The three men returned to their conversation. Nikolai winked at her.

She found Feliks in the costume room. "You got your way? N. Legher has been on everyone to be nice to you." He looked at the blue tutu. "No one looks good in this."

They settled on emerald green. She put it on while he averted his eyes by looking up at the ceiling. The costume hung on her. He took thread from his pouch and a needle out of his sleeve. "So, I've heard that you owe your luck to Rodian." He ran the thread through his teeth and bit it off. "He gave you the part, not Sergei."

Feliks enjoyed watching the fallout from intrigues, but he seldom played the game himself. She wondered if he had begun to dabble.

"You know, Telyakovsky will be in the audience tonight. You will disappoint him since you've not rehearsed."

Feliks was right. She had only danced alongside Urikova, as a support, while she learned the choreography. Brigitte reminded herself that the solo was not difficult. "You can talk all night, Feliks. I know dancing a solo is always preferable to being stuck in the *corps de ballet*." She moved as she spoke and he pricked her with the needle. "Ouch," she said.

"If you don't want to get hurt, don't move," he advised.

Brigitte sat at the makeup table lining her eyes when Rodian pulled up a chair next to her. "Green is good. You look beautiful," he said.

Her guard went up.

Rodian rested his elbows on his thighs. His eyes looked tired. "We have been enemies for so long, Brigitte. " He knit his brows. "There is much I regret."

She wished his dancing were as good as his acting. "It surprises me you even know this word, *regret*. Can you spell it? Maybe you are more familiar with the word, *malice*."

He looked as though she'd hit him. For a moment, she felt regret.

"I deserve your disdain. Deserve it all, and more." He put his hand on her forearm and she lowered her hand to the table. "I have a chance right now to do something for you. I would like to, as a way of apologizing, if you will allow."

A memory flashed of a much younger Rodian, standing by the window in his apartment. Perhaps it had been a brief moment, but she had seen this side of him before.

Rodian continued. "I find myself in a position of power with Telyakovsky. He tells me his private thoughts. He likes you, but he is not sure he can trust you. He wonders if you hold the same radical ideas as Sergei."

"I do not know anything about any of that."

He nodded. "I told the director as much. One of the reasons he gave you Urikova's role is that she is causing trouble. With dancers he can trust, the Imperial Ballet can become strong again. Telyakovsky is working to restore the Ballet to what it once was, a symbol to the Russian people of Russian culture, strength, and beauty. Telyakovsky needs to have happy dancers, not troublemakers. If you dance well tonight and then demonstrate your loyalty to the tsar and Telyakovsky, I know for a fact, you will see your career rise to a level you have always wanted. Telyakovsky rewards loyalty.

"Since our school days together, I have known your dreams. Let me help you. I want to make up for all the times I should have helped and did not. To acknowledge the truth of what everyone says, you make me look like a better dancer than I am." He paused. His voice had grown husky. "Let me make amends."

Despite herself, she softened a little. "What is it?"

"Tsar Nicholas is not expected tonight. During the curtain call, after you curtsy to the tsar's box, curtsy to Telyakovsky to show that you support him."

"That is all?" She slid her arm away from his hand. "Just a curtsy?"

"The ballet is fickle. You wait and wait, then one day, it is your turn. A simple thing happens, and all your dreams come true."

She turned back to the mirror, picking up the rouge and a brush.

"Will you do it, then?"

"I will keep it in mind."

"When you are ballerina absoluta, I hope you can finally forgive me. All I wanted from our very first dance, is to be your friend." His eyes were sincere.

The sound of the audience's jeering echoed in her head like a pounding headache. She could not think about what happened after she curtsied to Telyakovsky. Her mind closed. Not forgetting. Forgetting was to not remember. She remembered everything. She knew what had happened. Instead of applause, she had been booed.

She fled the theater as soon as the curtain dropped, throwing her coat over the emerald green tutu, and rushing out a side door to avoid the gauntlet of angry people waiting to pelt her with insults. Until then, she'd not realized that those in the theater were no longer mostly the wealthy aristocrats holding subscriptions, but now, were also rebels clambering for change. The ideas that Sergei and Joseph were talking about were not limited to backstage griping.

She'd never been booed before. Someone in the audience shouted, "Do you dance for us, or Telyakovsky?" Fighting humiliation, she wished she had screamed, "I dance for Russia."

The carriage driver seemed to know her shame and despise her. The world hated her. She could not think of it. Inside her bedroom, despite the chill, she took off her costume, went naked to her basin, and vomited.

Wrapped in her covers, she slept fitfully, waking when Nikolai come in. He nudged her over and sat down. She thought a moment of her nakedness under the blankets, but this was Nikolai, not Sergei. What did it matter?

"I was worried for you." He laid down, rolling towards her, wrapping his arm around her, and resting his head on a part of her pillow. "You danced perfectly."

"They hate me."

"Not your dancing." He kissed the side of her head. "Telyakovsky came looking for you. He wants you to be prima ballerina in the next ballet. Is this what you hoped for?"

She had no answer.

"I say good for you. But be careful. You have lifted your head with a war going on. Heads are lost that way."

She didn't understand his meaning; could not think about the balletomanes, or whoever they were, the insults, the booing echoing in her ears.

"Sergei is furious. He thinks you did this to hurt him. I explained that you do foolish things." He laughed.

The tears came, streaming down her cheeks remembering Sergei's face contorted in hatred. Telyakovsky was his enemy. "I would take it back if I could."

"All is not lost. Your career has taken a giant leap forward. You will win over the true balletomanes by dancing as you did tonight."

"Sergei hates me."

"He does not hate you. He is unreasonable." Nikolai's voice soothed her. He could say anything, she would feel comforted, such was her hunger. Her great friend, her brother. Her only protector now.

"Urikova will return for tomorrow's performance. Take the day off. Stay home. Rest. Let this blow over. People have short memories. You are prima ballerina now."

Brigitte received invitations to brunches, salons, and private affairs wanting her to dance. Telyakovsky sent her a letter as well. He thanked her for her gesture and predicted the influx of invitations. He listed which ones she should accept; the consequences of refusal were not explicit, but she understood what he meant when he said, "All eyes are upon you. It would be a pity should you blink and stumble."

Telyakovsky accompanied her to a soirée hosted by a baroness, introducing her to the guests as the next Mathilde Kschessinkska. She heard tittering from the back of the room, scoffing at the presumption. Brigitte danced, nibbled at the buffet to prove she would not get too thin again and left as soon as Telyakovsky turned his back.

Nikolai sat in the foyer of her house, waiting with her gown draped over his arm.

"Where have you been?" he asked.

"Selling my soul. Why are you holding my dress?"

"Sergei says he wishes to meet us for dinner. We are almost late."

"Sergei?" Her heart leapt.

Nikolai handed her the dress, taking her coat in exchange. "He seemed happier than he has been since Mama died. He will say he is sorry. You will say where you were. Then I will once again know all there is worth knowing."

The maître'd led them into the dining room. Sergei rose from the table, ignoring Nikolai and embracing Brigitte. His scent, clean soap, and hair tonic filled her senses, making her dizzy.

"We need to speak privately," he whispered. He held out her chair.

"I am disappointed," Nikolai said after they had settled in. He lifted an empty glass. " No standing in the middle as you two argue it out? No wine thrown across the table? This is quite a letdown." He waved the waiter over. "We will start with champagne. Soon we will have to have an invitation to a palace to find a glass we can afford."

Sergei took Brigitte's hand. "I am sorry." For the rest of his apology, he spoke silently with his eyes.

"Sergei is no longer upset. Brigitte has had a change in luck," Nikolai said to the waiter. "I am, of course, still miserable in an unpleasant marriage with my ex-mistress and mostly living with my sister. But tonight, we drink to the Leghers, N., S., and B." His light mood elevated them all.

Through dinner, Nikolai told family stories. Legher Legends, he called them.

At one point, Sergei stood, excusing himself. He'd thought he'd seen a friend from the Pavlovsky Guards who owed him money from a card game. When he returned several minutes later, he said the man had fled at the sight of him.

"Do you recall the time we climbed the tree at the Alexandrovsky Gardens? Sergei fell into the bushes."

"Father was speaking with Prince Orlov. Yes, I recall," Sergei said. "Orlov dropped his white gloves in the mud rushing over to catch me. I believe he lost a button and ripped his trousers wresting me out of those bushes."

They laughed.

"I never heard that story." Brigitte had been at school for these Legends, making her feel lonely.

Nikolai covered her hand with his. Sergei reached out for her other hand. "You missed our best mischief, being a boarder at school. But you were spared our punishments."

"Were you hurt in the fall?" She pulled her hands away from them both.

"He bounced like a ball. Papa swore us to secrecy. You know what they say the best way is to keep a secret," he said.

"By forgetting?" she said.

"You keep it." He tipped his chin down towards the table, touching his lips with the tip of his first finger. "Shhhh."

"I did bounce like the rubber ball Prince Orlov gave us. I understand better now why he was there with gifts." He looked at Brigitte.

Her throat constricted. "I had fun as a boarder, too."

Brigitte touched her finger to the corner of her eye as if a spec of something were bothering her. She did not like this game of family memories. She tried to remember a happy time at school to compete. "There was a time the older girls came into the dormitory to show us how to put our hair up into a proper French knot."

They looked expectantly at her for more to the story. She smoothed the napkin on her lap.

The waiter arrived with a bottle of champagne. Nikolai clapped his hands. "What is this? We have not finished the first bottle."

"For Mlle. Legher, courtesy of Officer Dimivich." The waiter held the bottle out for Nikolai's approval.

"The spoils of war roll in," Nikolai said.

The name sounded familiar to Brigitte, but until the waiter pointed the man out, she couldn't place him. The Akrona policeman who had arrested the actress on Nevsky Prospekt. No one ever did hear from her again. More disconcerting had been the seeming lack of curiosity amongst the Directorate and her fellow actors.

Dimivich stood along the wall and bowed to her. She felt obligated to wave, though having the attention of the Akrona did not bode well. As soon as she acknowledged him, he approached the table.

Nikolai stood to shake his hand. "You honor Brigitte. Her brothers also enjoy your kind gesture," he said jovially.

"I still have your autograph," Dimivich said taking his hand from Nikolai, ignoring him.

"You are kind. Thank you," she allowed him to take her hand and kiss it. She could feel the tip of his tongue flick out and lick her.

"You are the ballerina to watch this season. I assure you, Mlle. Legher, I will be watching." His dark eyes flashed a warning. She withdrew her hand, putting it in her lap.

"How do you know this?" Sergei asked defensively. "Nothing has been announced."

Dimivich's eyes sparked; the face of a murderer. "How, indeed?" He glared at Sergei. Then to Brigitte, he said, "I am hopeful you will allow me to visit you backstage after your next triumph. To congratulate you of course."

She saw his leer and felt the danger of him. "No. But thank you for the champagne." She smiled, hoping he would hear her refusal, but not be offended.

It didn't work. His jaw tightened, and the lines between his eyes furrowed in anger. "Have a pleasant evening," he said.

Once he'd left the table, Sergei said, "He strikes me as rather forward."

Nikolai drained his glass. The attentive waiter appeared and taking the bottle that Dimivich gifted her, poured more for him.

Her glass was empty, but when the waiter moved to fill it, she waved him off.

Nikolai licked his lips, "I assure you this champagne is not cheap or poisoned. It is delicious."

She glanced at Dimivich. He was looking at her.

She whispered. "Why would Akrona be interested in me?"

"He is Akrona?" Both Sergei and Nikolai turned and looked at Dimivich again.

"Perhaps because of what you did the other night," Sergei said, sounding hurt. "You know how I feel about Telyakovsky. Were you wanting to punish me?"

Nikolai put a hand on her back to steady her.

Turning to Sergei she said, " I did a stupid thing. It did not seem like much at the time. I had no idea the reaction waiting for me. If I thought it would hurt you, Sergei..." her voice trailed off.

He shook his head. "Forget it. I am finished with these divides." He drank his champagne, allowing the waiter to fill his glass from Dimivich's bottle.

Again, the waiter gestured to her. This time she nodded holding up her glass. "I guess it is fine."

Sergei toasted, "To the Leghers. To Brigitte."

"To me," she said, trying to be glad but unable to brush away her uneasiness.

"Is that Antonia over there?" Sergei asked, nodding in the direction of the arched doorway.

"Oh my," Nikolai grimaced. "She will insist on joining us. Perhaps she is here with a new lover," he said hopefully. "Excuse me."

Sergei did not waste a moment once Nickolai had gone. "Nikolai will go home with Antonia tonight. I am certain of it. May I take you home?"

"I have never closed my door to you." She ached to curl into his arms.

As predicted, Nikolai came back to the table expressing regret for leaving.

Brigitte and Sergei walked in an electric silence back to her house, their hands brushing, touching, but never clasping.

Once they were inside, even before taking off their coats, they embraced. He finally stepped back and asked for a cup of tea. "Maybe with a splash of something stronger in it?"

They settled in the kitchen, Sergei pulling out a chair for her, then sitting down beside her.

"I found a letter," he said excitedly, taking a breath and exhaling audibly. "When Mama died..." he paused. "I spoke to her before she became incoherent. She insisted that you were my sister." He looked down at his hands. "I told her about us and that if it were her wish, I would divorce Maria and marry you." He looked away towards the window. "I confessed my truest feelings." He took her hands, running his finger over her knuckles. "I am ashamed now that I burdened her as she was trying to leave this life. How she fought to stay. She did not battle death because she feared death. She battled until she knew you and I would be safe."

The memory of Nina's thrashing and pleading crashed over Brigitte like a wave. She couldn't stop her tears.

"She asked if I had told anyone. I assured her, not even Nikolai suspected. I thought it important for her to go knowing that by bringing you into our home, she ensured my happiness. I did not expect her reaction, her anger. How could I have expected anything else? She said we were sinners, and pleaded with me to repent for my soul's sake. Her last words. I wish I had been strong enough to defy her, to defy those words, defy God." His hands were trembling as they held hers. "I regret hurting you."

All the shame she had buried escaped. Her face burned.

"I took Mama's book of fairytales from her room after she died. I can hear her voice, the words she used to point out details in the illustrations. It has been on my shelf all this time, untouched, until yesterday."

"Vera wanted that book. She accused me of taking it."

Sergei kept on "I opened it to *Marya Morevna*."

"One of my favorites," Brigitte murmured.

"Mama always started that story saying to us younger children, 'This is Brigitte's favorite.'"

She could almost feel Nina's hand on her head, stroking her hair as she told the story of Marya, the Warrior Queen who defeated the *Deathless Koschei*.

"At that story I found an envelope addressed to Mama from Madame Blontskev."

"She played piano for Johansson. She called me *little vorobey*. She called Rodian, a *mudak*." Brigitte smiled. "I liked her."

"Madame Blontskev wrote about Prince Ivan Alexandrovich Orlov. He was your father."

Her heart lost its steady beat. Sergei grasped her hand tighter.

"You did not know, did you?" He stood and went to the cabinet where Nikolai hid the vodka. "Cognac. That will do." She looked at the amber liquid. Sergei pulled his chair around so he sat directly in front of her.

He reached into his coat pocket, bringing out the letter. "I will read for you. She writes of your mother. Are you ready?" he asked. "Sip first?"

"Do I want to hear any of it?"

He leaned forward, kissing her gently on the mouth. Then, began with a strong voice.

As he read about Prince Orlov, she remembered a man with a deep, sonorous voice who brought her bags of candies. He visited the school, as balletomanes often did, sitting with Petipa, or Johansson in the balcony.

"Dear Madame Legher," Sergei read. "I have held a secret at the expense of your family for too long. My time on earth is short. I wish to make amends before I die. I did not realize how the years would slip by, the weight of the secret upon on soul growing heavier each year." Sergei paused and licked his lips, then continued to read through to the end.

"I was a close companion and friend of Prince Orlov. My career as a dancer ended with an injury. It was Prince Orlov that arranged for my employment with the school. He confided in me that he had fallen in love with a dancer he met while traveling to Kyiv. He claimed at the time he did not know her to be of the Jews. He said she used sorcery on him. Her name was Svetlana and when he spoke of her, I could hear she still held him in her spell. To that tryst was born a child.

"Prince Orlov became convinced that children instructed in ballet at an earlier age would become the best in the world. He conceived of the Infant Class and convinced Christian Johansson and Marius Petipa to create one at the ballet school. Many balletomanes participated in a wager around the success or failure of the Infant Class. There was much intrigue in certain circles about the experiment. The prince wanted to have a hand in choosing the children. Brigitte was his first choice.

"Prince Orlov asked me to travel to Kyiv where Brigitte lived with her mother. From there I was to bring her to your husband so she could begin instruction with him right away. Prince Orlov said Svetlana was the most graceful dancer he had ever seen and he was convinced that the child, if trained early and properly from the best in the world, would be prima ballerina absoluta for all of Russia. I believe the mother, Svetlana, is now dead from an accident. Prince Orlov said you had many children close in age and thus another would not raise suspicion. He wanted it hidden that Brigitte bore Jewish blood, for her sake.

"I believe that Prince Orlov confided in no one else but me about the child's lineage. He swore me to secrecy, fearing the child would suffer unfairly because of her mother. I owed Prince Orlov for all he did for me, so agreed.

"I have never whispered a word of Brigitte Gustoevna Legher's history until the composition of this letter. As I leave this world, I need to reconcile with God for the sin of bringing a Jewish child into an Orthodox household. I pray for God's forgiveness. I pray for your forgiveness, too."

Sergei put the letter on the table. Brigitte stared at it.

"We are not siblings," he said brightly.

"Madame Blontskev called me little *vorobey*," Brigitte said. "But she thought I was wretched. Mama and Papa thought the same thing, didn't they?" She felt herself disappearing into Svetlana's wickedness. Was it a spell, those words she still remembered? *Shema Yisreal.* What did it even mean?

Evil swirled about her, filling the room with witches cackling, and screeching. Sergei's voice blended dissonantly with the sound of a thousand devils, the sound of the names of Svetlana, and Orlov.

A memory, shiny black shoes, a little embroidered coat, tears that were not hers. Baba Yaga lifting her into the Mortar, the vessel she steered with the pestle. The feeling of being swept away, flying, dying. The swooshing sound in her ears, the beat of her heart and hooves, the devils prodding her, touching her, taking her shoes and coat.

"Brigitte?" Nikolai said.

She had not heard him come in. "You are here?" He seemed to be in a dream.

Sergei stood by the sink. " She has been catatonic for ten minutes. I thought you were staying with Antonia tonight."

"We quarreled."

"My mother's name was Svetlana."

Nikolai looked at Sergei, then at her. "How do you know this?"

"I found a letter in Mama's book," Sergei explained. "Yesterday, I found it. I just read it to her."

Nikolai's expression clouded, like watching a storm approach from the bay. The gaslights flickered. "What possessed you? You should have burned that damned letter." Nikolai's voice matched the sound of the wind howling outside.

"I thought she should know. About Prince Orlov," Sergei said weakly.

"Do you know how hard our parents worked to keep a protective blanket around her? And you pull it off?"

Sergei shifted his shoulders back, a defiant look coming over his face. "You were the first to blurt out that she is a Jew. If Mama wanted to keep the secret, why keep the letter?"

Brigitte felt a chill hearing again the word Jew, her identity, her truth. What did she know of Jews?

"I do not know why Mama kept the letter," Nikolai said. "But we three of us must forget about it. If Petipa knew, he is forgetful now in his dotage. Johansson is dead, as is Madame Blontskev. Prince Orlov is dead. Mama and Papa are gone. Only we know. Let us forget. Give me the letter." Nikolai took a match from his pocket, striking it, the smell of sulfur soothing her. He dropped the burning letter in a blue glass bowl, black soot rising, devils swirling, fading. Relief came as a rush through her body and she moaned.

Nikolai showed her the ashes, a small flame licking the last words. "We will never discuss this again." His authority comforted her.

"You did not get to read the letter," she said.

"Mama showed it to me a long time ago. No one else, including Papa. Prince Orlov was still living. She asked me to approach him for more money."

"You knew all this?" Sergei said.

"Mama felt we had been underpaid. You too, Brigitte. You should never have had to sell yourself to Count Verontsov for a dress and shoes. Not when your father was a prince. She wrote a letter and I delivered it to him."

"Did he threaten you with jail?" Sergei asked.

Nikolai smiled gravely. "He thanked me, all the Leghers, for looking after you. He said, Brigitte, that the greatest tragedy of his life had been not knowing you well."

"When was this?" she asked.

"Some years ago."

"And my mother? Svetlana?"

"She is nothing. Think of her as the means by which you traveled into the world. She is long dead and not the mother who raised you. Not the one who taught you to dance, Brigitte. To dance. Nina and Gustave gave you ballet. Forget her. It will be as before." He took out his flask. "See, as before," he smiled tipping it upside down. Not a drop came out. "Nothing. Empty. All as before."

Sergei laughed, sounding like a boy. Brigitte suddenly feared him. Nikolai proved he could keep secrets, but Sergei? His emotions clouded his reasoning. What might he confess to Maria someday, thinking he was in an intimate moment?

Never mind, she thought. Sergei belonged to her again and they were no longer damned to hell.

CHAPTER 17

St. Petersburg, January 22, 1905

She'd heard about the strikes, and calls for revolution. At dinner parties she attended, hoping to find a new protector, it seemed all the bejeweled, and well-coifed could think of to discuss was the growing unrest. The conversations, like dark shadows, filled the corners of rooms. Words. Nothing real. She did not dwell in shadows. Sergei lit the way.

The ballet *Caprice de Papillion,* a benefit performance for the prima ballerina, Olga Preobrojenska, had been sold out for weeks. Brigitte arrived early for the Sunday evening performance, managing to have her makeup and hair nearly finished before the rest of the dancers started arriving. With pins in her mouth, tucking them one by one into her hair, her thoughts wandered to Sergei, his strong body, his tender kisses. How he seemed able to entangle himself around her until she could not tell where she ended, where he began. She felt lonely knowing he was away for a month on tour with Nikolai.

A wave of dancers arrived in a cacophony of frantic voices. Brigitte went out into the hallway, curious about the noise. Some of the women wept. A few of the men, too. A man named Lubochek, a danseur whom Brigitte had partnered with several times, collapsed to the floor, shaking.

"What is this?" Brigitte asked Julija, who had just come in, looking pale and frightened.

"It has happened," she said quietly, taking off her coat. "Revolution. All these threats back and forth. The endless pushing and shoving. There was blood spilled today. People were gunned down in the street. The tsar's hands are stained forever. Mother Russia will never again know peace with him as our leader."

Brigitte gasped. "Come get ready in my dressing room and tell me more," she invited Julija.

"Father Gapon led a peaceful march of women this morning and Tsar Nicholas ordered his soldiers to fire on them. Thousands died. A little girl, climbing upon the statue to see better was flung into the air by a volley of bullets." Julija's mouth pinched into a tight line. "How did you not notice anything when you came in tonight?"

Brigitte shook her head. Russians exaggerated. A thousand dead would turn out to be one or two. "Who is Father Gapon?" Brigitte asked.

Julija shot Brigitte a look that said she was stupid. She'd seen Julija give that look to many women in the years they had been friends, but never as fiercely as now or to her.

"He organized the workers. They were bringing a petition to the tsar asking for better conditions, for an end to this war. Good Orthodox Christians, thousands of them, came together to ask Tsar Nicholas to help them. He had them shot."

The two of them went together to stretch and warm up in the wings. Rodian came by comforting a dancer. Julija leaned towards Brigitte. "Her brother is missing," she said. "He was there when the shooting started. No one knows where he is. Lubochek, is very close to him, too. They were classmates." Julija leaned even closer and whispered. "And lovers."

Rodian, looking panicked, led the young dancer to a chair. Brigitte recognized Rodian's expression as the one he wore when he didn't know what to do. She watched for this look when they danced together, just as she listened to the tempo of the music. If the conductor went faster or slower than in rehearsals or previous performances, she needed to stay sharp and prepared. Watching Rodian was like that, and it saved them from his mistakes.

Five minutes before curtain, four dancers were missing. News of a demonstration at the Alexandrinsky Theater interrupting a performance had them all rattled. Rodian wrung his hands. He had no instruction from a higher authority to hold the curtain.

"I just heard the Mikhailovsky Theater closed early. There will be an angry mob on their way here," someone said. "To tear down the tsar's puppet show."

The orchestra began to warm up. Rodian moved among the fidgeting dancers. "We go out on stage like always. If the world is crumbling, do we not have even more reason to dance?" he said, his voice full of unsteady conviction.

Brigitte heard a stifled scoff. A few people nodded. Rodian went to the dancer whose brother was missing and patted her shoulder. She shrugged him off.

Brigitte wondered if she were to find out that Nikolai or Sergei were missing, perhaps dead, could she still dance? She knew the answer. Always. That is where she could find them again. In the music. Besides, her brothers were safe in Paris.

The curtain rose to a half-empty theater despite being sold out. The audience coughed and whispered throughout the ballet and by the final curtain call, most of the seats were abandoned.

"Vera Trefalova is having a dinner party," Mathilde said to Brigitte. She'd been in the audience and come backstage to congratulate Olga.

Brigitte wanted only to go home. But if you needed new ballet slippers, you go to Liftshedt's. If you need a new protector, you go to Mathilde's parties. Mathilde had driven Madame Vazeem into retirement and taken over her game.

"Will there be anyone good for me?" Brigitte asked.

Mathilde adjusted an earring. "You and I are similar. Businesswomen." Her eyes went over Brigitte's body. For a moment she felt as if she were back in school standing half-naked before her teachers while they weighed and measured her.

"I admire you," Mathilde said, her words a spider's silk thread. "I admire Vera Trefalova, and Olga, who was not given proper tribute here tonight. Vera is hosting the party. Of course, you cannot expect to have the same big catch you had as a girl. Count Verontsov was a big fish. That you held him on the line for so long speaks well of you. What happened? No one told me."

Brigitte ignored her question, and instead inspected the skirt of her costume for stains.

Mathilde's eyes twinkled more brightly than her diamond necklace. "The merchant class is not so bad. They have money to spend. Makes up for their lack of pedigree. I find they are more dependable, if not as lucrative. Their gratitude is endearing." She tilted her head, a flirtatious affectation. "We will ride together in my carriage. " She started to walk away but stopped. "I nearly forgot. There is a gown for you in your dressing room."

"You have a gown for me?"

"Not from me. An admirer. He is looking forward to making your acquaintance."

Brigitte could feel the thread winding around her, spinning about her arms, pinning them to her sides. She knew there was still time. She could go home. Have a cup of tea and go to bed. Instead, she went to change into the dress. Owning a house was expensive. She had bills to pay.

She would not have chosen the geranium pink gown. Few women could pull off such a bright color. The label sewn into the collar said *Paul Poiret*, an expensive designer. It fit as if Feliks had sown it onto her body. What Brigitte's admirer wanted to buy was easy access to her breasts. The plunging décolleté' of the bodice told Brigitte what awaited her. Never mind the rioting hordes. The danger she faced would be seated at Vera's table.

Then she knew. Feliks gave her measurements to Mathilde. Brigitte realized that Mathilde's ménage á trios with her two archduke lovers, and her affair with the tsar, had given her power, but Mathilde had cultivated that power into something lucrative by knowing how to sell women to men.

"I worry about Nicholas," Mathilde sounded melancholy as they rode together. "These peasants stand about, lazy and derelict, thinking we have had our good fortune handed to us. These ignorant peasants come to St. Petersburg thinking to escape their filth. It will never be better for them because they bring their misery along in their luggage. The ones running amok tonight are the worst of them. They have no ideology. Not like Father Gapon, who at least thought he was helping the less fortunate."

"Why are we not going home to the safety of our beds?" Brigitte said.

In a smooth voice, Mathilde said, "A woman alone in bed is never safe."

They rode in silence then, hearing occasional shouts, and gunfire. The Vanka hollered to them to hold tight, as the carriage sped up, tipping to the left as they took a corner. Brigitte tumbled to the floor.

"Are you all right?" Mathilde offered her hand.

"It is fine now," the Vanka said in a strong, loud voice, as the carriage slowed. "Drunkards are no match for the horses."

Brigitte gracelessly got up, smoothing out her coat, and straightening her hat.

"His name is Vassili Poyarkov," Mathilde told her.

Brigitte gasped. "Poyarkov? He is vile."

The memory of Poyarkov making a spectacle of himself at Cubats set her teeth on edge. A large man with a big head and bloodshot eyes, he'd been drunk and came to sit at her table. As he held her hand longer than was polite, he vomited on the white tablecloth, splattering her gown and their dinner. The maître'd and two waiters had dragged him away.

"He will keep you in that little house of yours. Poyarkov has money. He likes you. I am doing you a favor."

"But what has he given you that you are so persistent to deliver me when doing so may get us both killed?"

Mathilde laughed. "Enough that he has an invitation to a dinner where I must look at his hideous face." She peaked through the curtain. "Nearly there," she said. "There is much in it for you, too."

Their host, the ballerina Vera Trefalova, fully embraced the Art Nouveau movement in decorating her drawing room. The last time Brigitte attended a party at Vera's apartment, the decor had been much more classical, gilded. Vera was doing well financially.

She greeted Mathilde with kisses. "Miserable night. Half the guests rang to say they aren't coming. She grabbed Brigitte's elbow and escorted her to Poyarkov. "I would like to introduce you to Vassili."

Self-consciously, Brigitte reached for the thin strap of her gown, lifting it on her shoulder.

Poyarkov took her hand. "I am a great admirer of yours." His accent reminded her that French and Russian were not his first languages. He spoke in a village dialect, making him sound boorish.

Vera and Mathilde smiled at one another. Brigitte knew that Vera could hear the sound of coins falling into her purse, too. What had this man paid? What might Brigitte get from him?

Poyarkov did not attempt to look anywhere but at Brigitte's breasts. The coolness of the air on her bare flesh reminded her of how exposed they were.

"You like the dress?" He guided her towards a settee with a carving in the dark wood of a swan with a long neck twisted, as though it had just been wrung.

"Thank you," she said. "From Paris I noticed."

His eyes brightened. He began to speak of himself, his business, and of America, where he said he intended to travel. Within minutes she realized he would do all the work of conversing; she would not have to think of a single clever thing to say, nor give him any false compliment. She thought about the inevitable conclusion of the evening. A tear rolled down her cheek. She had trouble controlling them since going on tour and letting hunger make her fragile. She hated the weakness that tears exposed. Discretely she wiped them away. Poyarkov said nothing; he wasn't looking at her face.

Sitting at Vera's table with Poyarkov, she felt sick watching him eat. His teeth were yellow. The whites of his eyes were yellow, too. His nose was purple and pockmarked. Giving her time to Poyarkov was business, wasn't it? She would sell; he would buy. Did she want to sell at his price? A dress that she hated as an earnest payment did not speak well of the arrangement.

"If the strikers are to get a shorter workday at the same rate of pay, I shall go out of business," Poyarkov complained.

"You'll be out of business if your workers all starve to death," said a prince or count from Germany. Wilhelm, Hans? Brigitte hadn't been paying attention to Vera's introduction.

"Nonsense." Poyarkov's gruff voice made her want to put her hands over her ears. "They eat plenty. Father Gapon exaggerates the food shortages for political gains. The workers want me to pay them to not work. It is ludicrous. I suppose I should operate the machinery in my factory, then invite them to sup with me when I have finished. You are like the *Norodnik* populist intellectuals who feel sorry for the worker. Feel sorry for the hard-working man paying them and getting nothing."

"Of course, I feel for them," the German said. "They are dying around you. You refuse to look down and see."

It seemed the tightly closed drapes could not keep out the night. A steady rumble of shouting and gunfire sounded like an approaching thunderstorm.

"Do not fall prey to the propaganda of the revolutionaries. I invite you to visit my factories. To the factories of my colleagues. Look for yourself to see if there are corpses. I assure you, there are not."

"What of your policies against Jews? The Pogroms?" said Alexander Ropoff. Vera said in introducing him that Ropoff had gained some renown for an invention that had impressed Tsar Nicholas. Brigitte remembered his name because he had greeted her respectfully, and his eyes were intelligent.

"Bad business to employ the Jews. If that were not the case, it wouldn't matter to me one way or another. Trouble follows them. That is bad for business." Poyarkov's eyes followed the dinner plate being set before him by Vera's houseman. The server's eyes flashed for a moment, then the flame vanished.

Ropoff said, "I have three students, all Jews, who are the brightest of the lot. I am ordered to fail them, so they may be expelled. These men have much to contribute to Russia. I refused." He spoke with an inner calmness, yet his hand resting on the table shook. "Never mind, they tell me. The tsar favors me, so my insolence is overlooked. But I am ordered not to interfere. What do you make of this, Mr. Poyarkov?"

Ropoff seemed the type of man to seldom smile. Judging by the cut of his jacket, Vera did not include him to liven the party, and he had little wealth. Brigitte wondered what Vera stood to gain by this teacher's presence.

"If it is advice you seek," Poyarkov said, "I suggest you approach the problem as one of economics. Is the cost of complying with the wishes of your employer worth the cost of losing the potential of these young men?"

Poyarkov leaned forward, putting his hand upon her thigh, slipping into her lap, and groping for her pubic bone. She felt the color rise in her face.

"Excuse me," she said standing. The men rose. "Your powder room is where?" she asked Vera.

Vera pointed towards the doorway.

Suddenly, there was a loud crash, the sound of glass shattering. Shouting, and screaming rent the air. Mathilde stood and rushed to the window, peeking out the curtain. "They are right below us. Twenty or more."

"Death to the tsar." The chanting of angry voices grew louder. "Death to the tsar."

"I think they mean to loot the ground-floor apartment," Mathilde reported.

"Thieves," Vera hissed.

Brigitte put her hand to her breast. "Are we in danger?" She looked at Ropoff, the one man who seemed trustworthy.

"I doubt they have the will to climb three flights of stairs," Poyarkov said. He took a bite of the fish soaking in dill sauce. "Come away from there, Mathilde. They will see the light. Let them have their spoils. Soldiers will be here soon and shoot them all dead."

As though he had predictive powers, gunshots rang out, followed by more screams. The clomping of horses' hooves mingled with the scattering sounds of men running for their lives. Poyarkov laughed.

"Look again, Mathilde," he said his fork loaded with fish. "How many did they get?"

Mathilde peeked behind the curtain of the window. She cried out, stepping back, her face ash white.

Vera rang the little crystal bell beside her. The servant appeared, looking nervous.

"Pour the brandy," she instructed. "Use the large goblets."

Brigitte could no longer stand and watch Poyarkov eat. She excused herself again and went through the open double doors to the lounge to sit on the couch with the broken-necked swan.

"You are anxious to leave," Ropoff said following her. She looked through to the dining room. Poyarkov lifted his fork to his lips, even as he continued to converse with the others.

"I am anxious to feel safe," she said. "Is your wife somewhere safe tonight, Dr. Ropoff?"

Ignoring her question, he said, "It is my understanding that Mr. Poyarkov is taken with you, Mlle. Legher. I have no desire to impinge upon his plans, but should you need help in getting home, I will speak to him for you."

She found his offer both chivalrous and demeaning. "Do you attend the ballet?"

"Never."

"Dr. Ropoff prefers standing out in the rain," Mathilde said, leaving the window and joining them. "He listens to the sound of lighting."

"You mean thunder?" Brigitte said.

"I'm an electrical engineer," he said.

There were more shots and shouts. Mathilde turned to look at the windows as if she expected something to fly through.

Dr. Ropoff continued. "One day we will be able to predict thunderstorms. You have no idea how many people lightning kills each year."

Vera came after them. "It is too small of a party to be breaking up," Vera said. "Come back and have a brandy."

Reluctantly, Brigitte followed them back to the table and sat down. More shouting and gunshots outside. The young actress seated across from Brigitte fidgeted with her sparkling necklace. Brigitte compared herself to this younger, yet worn-looking girl. The man next to her was a friend of Leonid's. Every time she had seen him at a social event, he wore the same disapproving look. The actress did not seem to have the power to change his expression.

A rapping at the door caused them all to jump, except for Poyarkov.

"Should I answer?" Vera asked Mathilde.

"It may be a guest arrived late," Mathilde conceded.

"No guest would venture through the mayhem below," Ropoff stated.

An argument broke out amongst the men over opening the door.

"It is looters," the actress said, her jewelry flashing as she trembled.

Poyarkov stood, and threw his napkin on the floor. "I'll see to it, Vera. God knows your houseboy is not man enough."

Poyarkov went through the lounge to the foyer. The rapping grew louder. All eleven of the remaining guests stood, going to the doorway to watch.

"State your name and business," Poyarkov roared, one hand on the doorknob, the other on the lock. "Louder, man. I cannot hear you," he shouted. Then swearing, he opened the door.

Three rough men burst thru the door, pushing Poyarkov aside. One raised a pistol and without hesitation, shot Poyarkov in the chest. The actress screamed, then fainted, falling to the floor with no one rushing to catch her.

Brigitte stood behind them all, closest to the dining room window. In the confusion of the moment, she slid behind the same curtain that had concealed Mathilde when she'd looked out before.

"Everything into these bags," an intruder said. Silver clinked; the women whimpered. The men protested. A gun fired. A body thudded to the floor. The actress, revived, began to sob, pleading, "Dear God, dear God." Brigitte stood utterly still, imagining if she looked, she would turn into a pillar of salt.

"We could hold them for ransom," a man with a thick accent said.

"We take what we can and leave," another responded with an authoritative tone that identified him as the leader. "Kill them all."

Another shot, a woman screamed, and a body thudded to the floor. A long moment of silence. The horror strangled in Brigitte's throat. Then more shots, more cries. Furniture moving and toppling. The sharp slap of fists meeting flesh.

She barely breathed, holding her clenched fist to her mouth. How long the struggle lasted, a moment, an hour? It was Mathilde, blood splattered across her gown, who pulled the curtain away.

"It is safe. You can come out," she said. "Dr. Ropoff is calling for his car."

Vera's beautiful table lay in ruins, adorned now with broken plates and glasses and the pummeled and semi-conscious body of one of the criminals. Vera stood over him with a candlestick, her face contorted. Then she smashed his skull. He jerked. She raised the candlestick again. Dr. Ropoff came, easing the gilded weapon away.

"We will carry him out to the street," he said, waving to the other men, the German, and two others. Each grabbed a limb. They slid him off the table. A serving bowl fell to the floor spilling out the dried figs that rolled into a pool of blood.

"Why not the window?" suggested the German, who held the criminal's leg. "It would save my back."

Vera rushed to throw back the curtain and opened the balcony doors.

The gentlemen easily carried the small man to the balcony. His face was crushed, whitish jags of broken teeth exposed through his cut lips. One eye squinted up at her through the slit of his lid. She saw in him for a moment something kindred. A man doomed.

The criminal did not make a sound as he was flung over the railing.

"There's my car," Ropoff said looking down. "Let's be quick."

Vera offered not a single word of farewell. Her manservant, holding a tray, had begun to collect the broken dishes. The pieces rattled together as his hands shook. The actress lay gracelessly in a heap behind a chair, her necklace gone.

"The two other rascals ran for it once I got the pistol," Ropoff said to Brigitte. "Foolish of him to shoot women first. Wasted the shots." Brigitte saw now the body of the other woman, her blue gown ruined by her blood, her hands covering her face.

Ropoff ordered Mathilde and Brigitte to put on their coats. The three of them had to step over Poyarkov's body to get out the door.

"So, this is a revolution," Mathilde said. "I cannot say I care for it."

They saw Mathilde home first. When the car began to move again with just Brigitte and Ropoff, he reached for her and kissed her, an angry kiss that tapped the river of fear inside her. She kissed him back.

CHAPTER 18

St. Petersburg, Late February 1905

A brief sentence in one of the newspapers mentioned the death of merchant Vassili Poyarkov but nothing of the fate of the young actress.

Alexander Ropoff never contacted her. She did not search for him. In the silences, there was room to pretend none of it had happened. When Sergei and Nikolai returned from their tour, she told them only that it had been a difficult performance with most of the audience leaving and Olga Preobrojenska having a disappointing benefit. She kept the night secret, not out of shame, but because her mind closed itself to all thoughts of the night. If Sergei or Nikolai heard anything from Mathilde or Vera, neither said so.

After what was being called "Bloody Sunday," the city began to reassemble itself, flesh growing over a wound. New panes of glass went up in the storefronts. Bullets were dug out of the buildings, the holes patched and repainted. Winter ended. Spring chased the last of the snow from the ground, washing away the blood.

Brigitte spent time with a balletomane, Dr. Betz, a neighbor and acquaintance of Leonid's. Dr. Betz, a decade younger than Leonid, had red hair and splotchy skin. He acted like a spoiled child and he bored her by taking her out to dinner, then leaving her alone at the table for a good part of the evening while he greeted friends. They returned to her house, and she entertained him as expected. Brigitte left him asleep in her bed, snoring and drooling, a sight that had been charming on Leonid, and especially on Sergei, but grotesque with Dr. Betz.

In the kitchen, she lit the samovar for a footbath, pouring boiling water into a small washtub and adding herbs to soothe her feet. She heard a key turning in the lock of the front door. She'd told Nikolai she would have a guest and advised him to sleep at Antonia's, but perhaps he'd had too much to drink and forgotten. Drying her feet, she slid into her slippers and went to the parlor to chase Nikolai away before he woke Dr. Betz.

"Sergei?" She whispered. "What are you doing here?"

"I only have a short time," he said.

"Shhh," she said, going to him. Brigitte pointed up the stairs, and then at Dr. Betz's frock coat. Sergei looked disappointed.

"Leonid?"

She pulled him to the kitchen where Dr. Betz would be less likely to hear.

"I cannot abide the prison Maria holds me in," he said, wilting into the chair she had just vacated, kicking the tub. Water sloshed onto the floor. "With you I am free." He reached for her, pulling her onto his lap. "Let's go to Paris. The Parisians love a good scandal. We could be together out in the open. Buy a cottage with a rose garden. You will give me the sons Maria is too old to have. I will teach them to dance, as Papa taught us. People will flock to see us on stage together, dancing. The scandalous Leghers. Run away with me." He smiled, his eyes brimming with tears. "Please."

That she could smell the roses irritated her. The cottage had a whitewashed chimney and along the short fence surrounding the garden, a neatly trimmed path. Even the toddling boys in their little military uniforms came vividly to mind. Brigitte stood, moving away from Sergei.

"Come to me tomorrow night. Go now," she said.

"I am ready to escape my life. All of it. Maria. The Mariinsky Theater. The Imperial Ballet. The tsar. Russia. St. Petersburg. The Neva. The cold and nights and endless days. Come with me."

"Your voice, Sergei," she said in a hushed tone. "It carries." Brigitte pointed up toward the ceiling imagining Dr. Betz stirring.

"These secrets we keep, they are no good. I am ready to tell Maria, to tell Nikolai." He tried to hold her, but she twisted away.

"Do you wish me dead? You are the great Sergei Legher. You will be forgiven everything. But I will be shunned. This love of ours is a formidable sin. Even if the truth were known, that we share no blood, I will be looked upon with disgust."

"Once people know your father was a prince, it will be different for you. You might even be entitled to his legacy. You could dance just for the love of dancing, not because you need the money."

"Your fairytale is dangerous. Svetlana was no princess. Women like her get killed every day. I may not pay attention to the plight of the workers who marched with Father Gapon. Maybe they are all wretched and ungrateful. I know Jews are killed just for being Jews. No one likes them. No one cares what happens to them."

He smiled as though she were an errant child. The smile that came just before it turned into a grimace.

"I will protect you," Sergei said, grasping her shoulders in a firm grip. "There are many artists in St. Petersburg who are Jewish. You exaggerate their plight. The St. Petersburg Music Conservatory was founded by a Jew and half the students are Jewish."

Brigitte scowled. She had listened to hundreds of discussions over the years at dinners, balls and salons about the number of Jewish musicians in St. Petersburg.

"I can't pretend to know what it is like to be a Jewish musician, but I imagine they all are waiting for the time the music stops. Just as I now wait. You want to rush me like Odette to the edge of the lake?"

He looked up at the ceiling as if he'd heard something. She listened, anxious that they had woken up the doctor.

"I will come tomorrow." He caught her, kissed her, then left out the kitchen door.

As promised though, he appeared at her bedroom door the next evening, as she sat at her dressing table sorting through old cosmetics and jewelry. He held out a basket with food. "From the Bears Inn," he said brightly. "You do not cook or eat and I am hungry." He turned and went back out saying, "I'll put it in the oven to warm the pelmeni."

Light filtered in through the windows, though it was nearly nine o'clock. She'd always loved the White Nights in the summer, but a part of her felt exposed. She opened a tiny jar of lip rouge, the surface dried and cracked. The color was bright pink. She dropped it in the leather waste can.

Sergei appeared again at her door, his mood, buoyant, playful. She craved playfulness from him. "You are what I am hungry for." He came behind her and stroked her cheek, his hand traveling down her neck and slipping under her décolletage, cupping her breast, rolling his finger around her nipple. She leaned into him.

Sergei pulled her up from the chair, turning her to face him. His kiss held a violent urgency, the tenderness of before gone. She allowed him to push her to the bed, pull at her clothes, and force her legs open.

"You love me," he said. "You have missed me." He shoved himself deeper until she cried out in pain. "You like that, don't you?"

She closed her eyes and thought about the mending waiting for her in a pile at the bottom of the wardrobe. How she needed yellow thread to reattach a button. She thought of the music for barre exercises. How the little tunes came back to her at the oddest of times. So loud was it in her head now, she bit her lip to keep from humming.

Sergei rolled off, bounding out of bed in an acrobatic movement. "I am famished." He rushed naked across the hall to Nikolai's room, returning wearing his brother's silk bathrobe. "Wait right here," he said excitedly, then disappeared out the door.

She straightened her clothes and returned to her dressing table and the task of sorting, picking up a pearl necklace. The clasp had given way and several of the pearls were missing. She could not recall where the necklace had come from. Probably Leonid. The roundness of the beads felt good in her hands. She'd sell them. The money would get her through the summer since she did not intend to go out on tour again.

Her feet hurt more than ever. If she couldn't eat, as had happened before on tour, she would grow weak. She feared she would not be able to dance in the fall. She needed the summer to heal.

Sergei returned with a wooden serving tray, two plates of meat dumplings, potatoes, and a bottle of wine.

The wine had been delivered that morning, a whole case, a gift from Dr. Betz. He'd been disappointed that all she could offer him to drink the night before had been Nikolai's hidden and half-empty bottle of vodka. Not the good Smirnoff vodka, but the cheap one that the guards drank when they played cards and took Nikolai's money.

Dr. Betz included a note thanking her for the evening, asking her to accept the wine as a token of his gratitude. She knew the wine meant he intended to visit her again, and when he did, he would drink her gift. She preferred money.

Sergei put the tray on a chair, took his plate, and climbed under the covers, spilling a dumpling on the blanket.

"The White Nights." She looked out the window. "The light at this time of night is soft, like being in a dream, romantic, but sad, too."

She left the pearls in the blue bowl on her dressing table and crawled up onto her bed. Sergei's smile broke her heart. With his fork, she pierced a potato, bringing it up to his mouth, drawing it across his lips, and feeding him.

"Are you hungry?" he said, pointing to the second plate on the tray. "It is very good." Brigitte could tell his interest was in food, not her. She leaned against the upholstered headboard. "The waiter at the Bears Inn said the head chef is leaving soon. He's a Jew and may be losing his permit to live in the city. The owner of the Bears Inn is trying to fix it. The waiter thought perhaps it was one of the restaurant's rivals making trouble. The chef's food is practically the only thing I've ever seen you eat. You may starve if he goes."

She let him feed her a meat dumpling. "Their food is very good." She swallowed her sadness.

"We could go to New York City," he said. "I wonder if the sun stays up all night in New York?"

"I imagine it would."

He put his plate on the covers and rubbed his hands together. "We could disappear. Take what we can carry. Leave the rest for others to plunder." His eyes gleamed. "I have enough money for passage on a ship. We could start our own company."

"In New York City?" She laughed. "Who would come to see us dance? They want someone like Isadora Duncan prattling about naked. No need to go to school to learn to do that."

"I thought you admired Duncan?"

"I admired the fact that she gets away with such technically devoid dancing and tours the world." She pulled at a loose thread on her sleeve. "We have our lives here. No one needs to know. I feel closer to you sharing this secret." She smiled, hoping he'd agree.

He looked thoughtful and for a moment she relaxed.

"You hate St. Petersburg. Most of the year you are frozen. When have I touched you that you were not like ice? We could go where no one cares who we are. Where you will be warm."

Even now her feet were cold and aching.

"Come with me to a place where we can dance together. Brigitte, I am dying here." Sergei rose to his knees. "I want to marry you. Become my wife?" He took her hands.

"You are already married," she said.

"We are divorcing. Maria is angry with me all the time."

Tearing her hands away, she slapped him hard across the face. "Damn you," she cursed him. She sprang off the bed, and grabbed his plate, flinging it at him. "You are my death, Sergei!" she screamed. "You expect me to smile while you plot to kill me?"

He brushed the potatoes and sauce off Nikolai's robe as he got up. Grabbing her wrist and holding it in a painful vice, he pushed her backward pinning her against the wall with his body. He wiped sauce off his face with his free left hand.

"You wound me," he said, his voice gruff.

"You are hurting me," she complained. He released her wrist but held her trapped with both of his hands now posted against the wall on either side of her.

"Go home to your wife. You want to marry me? You may as well say you want to see my corpse floating in the Fontanka."

"If you are so fearful, how can you not see this as a chance to escape danger? See the paradise I am showing you." A tear streamed down his cheek. "Russia is driving us mad. Let's escape this vile country, a *Deathless Koschei* stealing our souls."

She struggled. "Let me go. Get out."

He did not budge. "Stages are waiting for us. New music."

"Sergei."

"You do love me, don't you?"

"It is you who does not love me," she cried.

"Do you love me?"

"Yes, Sergei, I love you. But I will not die for you."

"Then live for me." He stepped back. She rushed to the other side of the room, putting space between them.

"Love me, Brigitte. Live with me. Be with me. We could go soon. Anywhere you want to go."

"This is my life. My house. My *Chambre de Joie*. My clothes, my gramophone. You cannot give me those things. Maria has all the money. You have gambled yours away playing cards. Maria complains about it to everyone backstage. You don't have money for passage anywhere. How would I start in a new company with girls half my age? Would you have me give up my pension? No, Sergei. Go live in your rotting fantasy where you have no home, no stage, nothing but secrets you can share with people you do not know, who do not understand your language, nor care about you. Go home."

"I will not leave." He went to the bed and picked up his plate, putting it back on the tray, and taking it and the soiled blanket downstairs. He returned to the bedroom, went into her wardrobe, looking through her things until he found an exercise dress. "Put it on," he said, handing her a pair of her pointe shoes.

He left again going across the hall to Nikolai's room. "Are you changing?" he called out after a few minutes.

She looked at the dress' stained armpits, the hem torn from a time she'd caught her foot. Pulling at the tear, she ripped off the bottom. She found a pair of tights, equally as worn, and put them on.

Sergei came in wearing a pair of Nikolai's pants and his dance shoes. "Play Tchaikovsky on your gramophone. He makes you happy. Like the light during the White Nights. Romantic, soft. A little sad."

Was this how he mended arguments with Maria, she wondered?

In the *Chambre de Joie*, the music poured forth filling the space. Sergei held out a hand beckoning her. The extension of her arm, as it moved towards him, mesmerized her, watching the will of her body separate from the will of her mind. Sergei wound her into his embrace, then gently pushed her away into a *pirouette*. The conversation changed. No longer did they stare at different futures, trying to explain with words what they saw. They spoke in a shared language of the present moment.

Sergei and Nikolai left on tour. Brigitte spent the summer resting. Nikolai gave her some of his private students for extra income. But by September, she was dismayed that her feet were no better.

When his tour finished, Sergei returned to St. Petersburg, rushing directly from the train station, satchel in hand, to her house.

"I have found a place for us to live," he said excitedly. "On the outskirts of Paris. A cottage."

Anger bit at her heart, all the more painful for its tenderness towards him. She pushed him away.

He stayed single-minded. "I have seen our lives, our future. I am excited for it to begin. Let us go tonight." He took her hands and swung them as a schoolgirl might with her playmate. "Only your fear holds us back."

She slid her hands away, turning her back on him. "Telyakovsky has given me a first soloist role. A good one. Rehearsals start in a few days. I will be relieved to return to the routine of classes and performances." She felt him behind her, his body, their breathing slowing together. "There will be a Duma soon, they say, as soon as the tsar approves it. You will notice how life is getting better, especially on the streets. The war is ending."

Sergei put his hand on her shoulder and kissed the top of her head. "I wanted to see you first before I go home."

"Does she know what train you are on?"

"Of course. She keeps track of things like that. I have no freedom with her. There will be no new freedom in the Imperial Ballet. None with Maria. None on the stage. And here, too. You hide inside the cage, the door wide open, and you cower. If I want to be with you, I too must live in the cage."

She hated his words. "It is not I, Sergei, who confines us."

"What if you are Jewish? What if we were raised as siblings?"

She brushed away an angry tear. "Can we just be together safe in our private world? Safe here? Free here?"

He kissed her lips, a quiet and gentle brush, and then turned and went through the house and out the front door.

When rehearsals began, the tension at the Mariinsky Theater reached a pitch beyond her experience, even surpassing Marius Petipa's last days and Bloody Sunday. Two or three dancers huddled in every corner, whispering, glancing about nervously. Rodian thrived on the discord, sneaking about eavesdropping.

She decided the best strategy would be to keep quiet and work hard. Telyakovsky gave her a prestigious solo. Rodian had not yet instructed her, but she expected he would again tell her to bow to the director. She'd already made up her mind that she would, even if the balletomanes booed and jeered.

Michael Folkine, Nikolai's former student, and - because he often disagreed with Nikolai - his greatest disappointment, choreographed her solo. Amidst the dark mood of the theater, Folkine shone as a rising star.

The first rehearsal took place on a sodden day, with everyone shaking out umbrellas and hanging coats over heaters to dry.

Folkine had a way about him that confused her. His dance style, like a foreigner with an accent, was hard to understand. His heavy features, eyes, nose, and mouth belied his slight but muscular frame. Looking at his countenance one did not expect he could lift off so high into flight across the stage.

"Stop!" Folkine yelled at her midway through her pirouette. He stood directly in front of her. "Sway." He put his hands on her hips, then moved her back and forth. "Not so rigid. Fluid. You need to be more plastic. Like a reed in the breeze. Sway."

She remembered Isadora Duncan. Her flailing about influenced Michael. Only he called it "swaying," not flailing. She feared Folkine would make her look like a fool. Dancing in this artless way was a betrayal of all Gustave had taught her. A betrayal of Petipa and Johansson and Lev Ivanov. Bowing to Telyakovsky had cost her half her admirers. Dancing as

Folkine wanted would cost her the rest. She could always wear a shorter tutu, she thought.

She complied. She would sway in rehearsals to keep the peace and in her performances, she'd dance her way. Folkine would not have a long career with the Imperial Ballet if he insisted too much on Russian ballerinas imitating untrained novelties from America.

Folkine released his hold. "Yes, lovely. So beautiful," he said, his large droopy eyes, shining upon her, catching her off guard. She could not remember the last time a choreographer had thought her dancing lovely.

Sergei came into the room quietly. When the pianist started, Brigitte rushed to her mark. She danced, keenly aware of Sergei watching her. When the music stopped, she looked first to Sergei, before Folkine. Sergei's eyes were bright with excitement. Her joy in pleasing him gave way to confusion. If Sergei had scowled, she could understand why. Dance grew more complex all the time.

At the end of rehearsal, Sergei handed her a towel to dry off. "The trees are turning. Come for a walk." Her life was lived so much inside, in the dark. The thought of sunshine was irresistible. Brigitte nodded.

She linked her arm through Sergei's as they strolled along the canal toward Nicholas Cathedral, the Sailors' Church. Sunlight reflected off the five gold spires and onion domes. The blue church held the hope of color, of clear skies and light, even on the darkest of days. They walked past the four-story bell tower with its gilded spire and into the gardens of St. Nicholas Square. The foliage had changed to oranges, yellows, and reds, tinting the waters of the canal that captured the fallen leaves, bearing them away on its persistent current. A leaf slowly drifted down in front of them. Sergei captured it midair.

"I went to the ballet schools in Paris," Sergei said. He twirled the leaf in his hand. "We have so much more to offer than anything I saw." His words were pictographs from a future he'd visited, where all turned out well. "Would you like to sit?" he said as they passed a bench underneath an old Linden tree. Brigitte shook her head.

She reached up and pulled off one gold leaf from a low branch, and next to it, a leaf still holding on to green. She held them to her nose, smelling summer and fall. "If we left, how would you tell Maria?"

"I confess," he said, "I have no idea." His eyes misted. "It is not that I love her, as I am in love with you. But we have a bond. Something with no convention."

"Perhaps, you cannot leave her?"

He shook his head. "I can leave. I should have left years ago, but until there became you and me, nothing has made it worthwhile."

"I am worthwhile?"

He dropped the leaf he'd captured, letting it flutter to the ground, then moved to kiss her. She stepped back putting a hand against his chest. "Sergei," she cried out. Then whispered, "we are in full view."

He looked about, his face reflecting horror with himself. "It is difficult to hide your soul every single moment of every day. I am weary. I find the mask slipping more frequently. It scares me."

She dropped her leaves. "Let's take our time. Be careful. Maybe we will find a way to wake up in your dream."

That night as she lay awake listening to the heavy wind and rain, she thought of the leaves. By morning many would be ripped off the trees and washed away in the canals. Her mind drifted towards possibilities. In her imagination, she went room by room through her house filling a travel bag. She added up the rubles from selling her jewelry, then subtracted the price of train tickets, and lodging.

She imagined Sergei's strong arms around her, his physical strength, and the strength he gained from her belief in him. How many children would they have? Two. Two boys. She saw them in her imagination standing at the barre with their father, their young, thin arms already defined, as Nikolai and Sergei's had been. They danced around the Christmas tree. They danced before bedtime. They danced out fairytales. As she drifted to sleep it was with the names of her sons on her lips, Gustave Sergeevich and Nikolai Sergeevich.

CHAPTER 19

St. Petersburg, October 1905

Though the war with Japan ended on September 5th, troubles in Russia did not. Nikolaevsky Railroad workers threatened to strike. The stores and stalls were bare from stockpiling and hoarding. The lights in the streets were unreliable, and dark nights scared off audiences.

In a ridiculous attempt to infiltrate the ballet, two Akrona agents joined as danseurs. One of the men constantly badgered for advice on how to land a soloist role. He'd had only basic ballet training, so was relegated to peeking out from behind the scenery. The other agent was a better dancer, but only when he was sober. Brigitte found the men comforting, providing proof that though the Directorate was watching them, they were wholly incompetent.

Walking the streets of St. Petersburg became an act of courage. Strangers pleaded for food, money and help, hurling curses when she did not open her handbag. Crowds gathered around speakers decrying the Tsar. Every brick, flag, and statue buzzed with fear and anger.

The ballet's audiences were vocal, too, making the performers all the more nervous. New rumors sprang up daily of protests and plans to demonstrate in the theaters.

Nikolai rode with Brigitte in the car that the Imperial Theater sent for them each day. Sometimes Sergei came over early in the morning to join them. If she rode with her eyes closed as she sat between the two, she could block out the unrest in the city. Often she did just that.

"The artists in the *Queen of Spades* are striking today," Nikolai said one morning as the car passed a group of men, two of them holding a banner calling for revolution. "The tsar issued something called the October Manifesto. I hear it promises more civil liberties. I pray to God this means these insane rioters will all calm down."

Brigitte listened, wishing Sergei and Nikolai spoke of the weather, or fairytales, anything but politics and revolutionaries.

"The Directorate has been laughing at the artists all along. Theaters should be closed until the tsar and police can guarantee the safety of everyone on stage. Someone yelled "Down with the autocracy!" during a play at the Mariinsky the other night and an actress went into hysterics and spilled the tea she was drinking all over her costume." Sergei fidgeted with his hands. "The Directorate refuses to shut down. We are put out there to make people believe that all is in hand. 'See,' the Directorate says, 'The tsar has control. Go to the theater and watch the ballet.' We are passive puppets being put in danger so the tsar and the Directorate of the Imperial Theaters can pretend." He nudged Brigitte. "Do you feel like all is well?"

She looked at Nikolai. Sergei clucked his tongue in disgust. "I do not believe you have a brain in your head," he said.

She stared at her hands folded in her lap, thinking back to her school days when Miss Nadeah commanded them to be still, hands folded where she could see them. All the girls would sit quietly, models of decorum and acquiescence. Docile. No threat to anyone, thus safe from attack.

At the Alexandrinsky Theater, they entered through the stage door where a young man from the opera chorus shoved a pamphlet into Sergei's hands.

Sergei read it over. "It is a caution to close the theater. That there is to be a demonstration."

"What do we do, Nikolai?" She grabbed a hold of his arm. "Should we leave?"

Rodian came up behind them. "Leave and you will be fired." He looked exhilarated by the opportunity to spread panic. "You forfeit your pensions, your rights to perform anywhere in the city, or in all of Russia."

Maria Petipa rushed to Sergei, kissing his cheek. "The dancers are going on strike," she said. "We are striking, Sergei." With no makeup, she looked wrinkled and old.

"Rodian locked my dressing room door. He says I am not performing in the matinee today. He says those of us who talked of striking are being replaced for the matinee performance. You should check your dressing room." She glared at Rodian, who glared back at her.

Sergei put a protective arm around Maria. Joseph Kchessinsky came in through the stage doors. Maria rushed off to talk to him.

"There will be no performance this afternoon," Sergei declared angrily.

"Like hell, there won't be," Rodian retorted. "Already there are students from the ballet school on their way here to take over for any cast member disloyal to the tsar. They are in costume and ready to perform."

Sergei's mouth dropped. Nikolai pushed him away from Rodian and towards the stairs to the dressing rooms. Brigitte followed, feeling safer with Nikolai.

"Let the students perform," Sergei spat.

Joseph Kchessinsky came up behind them. "We are gathering in the large rehearsal hall to strategize, Sergei. Now." He put a hand on Sergei's shoulder. "The time has come. We need you with us."

Nikolai gripped Sergei's arm. "Wait to see what happens," he advised.

"We need everyone," Joseph said looking at Brigitte. She owed him a debt for failing him on tour, and he was calling it in.

Shamed, Brigitte hung her head, turning away. Sergei shook off Nikolai, going with Joseph.

"So, do we dance?" she said.

Nikolai nodded, handing Brigitte a key. "Use my dressing room. Get your costume, go there, and change. I will be there shortly. Rodian, and Telyakovsky, if he is man enough to show up, will see we are here, willing, and ready to go on. No fault will be found with us."

"And Sergei?" she said.

Nikolai ran his hand over his scalp. "I'll try to pull him away."

She took the key. The costume room was unlocked but one of the theater police guarded the door while Rodian prowled, seeming to be everywhere. She felt his eyes. Dancers prepared for the ballet portion of the opera. Singers warmed their voices in the hallways.

"Telyakovsky is on his way to Peterhof Palace to speak with Minister Fredericksz," Rodian shouted. "He does not have the authority himself to shut down the theaters. Only the Minister can do that. In the meantime, either you go on, or the ballet students will. If that happens, Telyakovsky will see that you are banned from performing for life." There was a timbre of doubt in Rodian's voice, though his words were defiant.

Once she had her costume, she ducked inside Nikolai and Sergei's dressing room and locked the door. The outside world did not belong backstage. She resented the revolutionaries, the Japanese, the men shouting in the streets, Rodian Petrov. Sergei wanted this chaos, so she resented him, too. They agitated for changes. But changes for the worse. Who did not know this? No one alive in Russia could believe anything but misery lay ahead.

She put on her tutu and a short time later there were three sharp raps on the door. She let Nikolai in; Sergei was with him. Their faces told her they'd been arguing.

"To not attend this meeting is cowardly and traitorous." Sergei shoved the dressing-table chair out of his way. "Brigitte, you owe it to Joseph to be there."

"She will not go."

"For me, she will go." Sergei looked at her through the dressing table mirror. Nikolai looked from Sergei to Brigitte. Nikolai pushed Sergei down into the chair, throwing his costume at his head.

Sergei's eyes were crazed. She felt the floor could slide away any moment leaving them dangling over hell.

"There is something you should know, Nikolai," Sergei said, his voice strong. "About Brigitte and me."

Brigitte threw her pointe shoe at his head, hitting him. "No," she yelled. "What are you doing?"

"I want him to go with us. If he is to come, he must know why."

Nikolai pulled up a chair. "Go where? Why?" Nikolai sounded so much like Gustave.

"Yolya, Brigitte, and I are in love."

She leapt at him, wanting to shred his tongue with her nails. Sergei caught her, holding her wrists in a vice. "Who will you tell next? Who will you give me up to?" She cried out.

"Nikolai loves us."

She wriggled away from him, throwing herself into the corner and covering her face.

"Once this strike is over and the directorate has granted us more liberties, we are leaving for Paris. We will be married there."

"Who are you two?" Nikolai said, his voice barely above a whisper, all the muscles in his face drawn tight.

Crawling on her hands and knees she went to Nikolai laying her head in his lap. He lifted her face and looked into her eyes. "Who are you?"

"Brigitte is not Legher. Her mother is a long-dead Jewess. Her father is a prince. She is not our sister." Sergei sounded bright, as though he had come up with a way to win at playing cards.

"I fear for you both."

"We are in love." Sergei came to Brigitte and stroked her hair. Nikolai looked at him as though he'd become the *Deathless Koschei*. She wished Sergei would shut up so she could talk to Nikolai. Make it all sound less horrible.

"If you breathe a word of this to anyone, Sergei, you two will be shunned. You may end up in jail. How could put Brigitte into this kind of danger? You will not be safe here. Not anywhere. Not in Paris, not in the furthest reaches of China. The world is cruel to sinners. You might paint the picture differently, but there is only one way the world will paint a picture of you and that is as incestuous abominations." He shivered in disgust. Nikolai pushed her off. "As for you," he said standing. "I have forgiven and overlooked your stupidity because you are my sister. But this suicidal infatuation? It is immoral."

There was a knock on the door. They froze.

"Twenty minutes to curtain," Rodian called. In their silence, they heard his footsteps moving away from the door.

Panic flooded her veins. What had he heard?

Nikolai stood, reaching for his costume hanging on the back of the wardrobe door. "Leave," he ordered her. "You have your own dressing room. Get out."

Her makeup ruined by tears, Brigitte silently picked up her pointe shoe from where it had landed after hitting Sergei and went towards the door. Sergei rushed to stop her, holding her in a desperate embrace.

"Forget Nikolai," he said. "Don't let him make you afraid. Otherwise, we are lost."

"I am afraid of you, Sergei," she whispered. "You have murdered me. All *is* lost." She kissed his lips, feeling the warmth in them. Then walked away, her skin electric with his betrayal.

Finding a dark corner behind the scenery, tucked in behind the ropes and sandbags, she sat, her limbs frozen. Too frozen to stretch or prepare to dance. Too frozen to put on her pointe shoe; she held it to her chest. When Rodian announced to the few people in the audience that the opera matinee had been canceled, she came out of hiding. As she walked to Nikolai and Sergei's dressing room, where she'd left her clothes, she overheard the whispers that too many artists, singers, and dancers had refused to perform.

The Legher brothers' dressing room was empty. On the dressing table and floor were droplets of blood. A fight. She gathered her clothes.

As she walked by the women's dressing room, the door wide open, she noticed eight women in various stages of undress talking. "My mother was killed by the tsar's soldiers," said Lubov, a woman less than two years away from being able to retire and collect her pension. She had been a loyal member of the *corps de ballet* her entire adult life. "Mama went to see the march with Father Gapon. My nephew, Vasya, went with her. He is young. In gymnasium, his third year. He wants to be a doctor." A sad smile shaded her voice. "He is always practicing on the family, telling us what to do for a cough or sore foot." She cleared her throat. "He could not save Mama, though. Her body was too heavy for him to carry, so Vasya dragged her for sixteen blocks. I think about that when I walk through St. Petersburg. Mama's blood spilled out on the street."

Most of the women had their heads down looking pensive, like ghosts. Ghosts surrounded Brigitte. Lubov's mother, Nina and Gustave, Svetlana, Prince Orlov. Watching. Judging.

"When Vasya got her home, my father collapsed. He acts now as if all is well, but I hardly recognize him, like the apple that has dried up. In some ways, he seems more dead than Mama." Lubov wiped away a tear with her sleeve. "I will be at the meeting Joseph Kchessinsky is organizing. I will strike if that is what they decide. I cannot live here anymore the way it is, under a tsar who shoots at old women who have always been loyal. If we fail and I am sacked, I will leave Russia for good."

"Who will look after your father if you go?" one said.

"We all go. My brother, his wife, Vasya. My father."

In the morning, Brigitte went to the *Classique de Perfection* alone. Nikolai had not come home the night before. Joseph Kchessinsky hovered by the door, and put his arm out, blocking her way. "I have a petition," he said. "It is our statement to the Minister and the Director of the Imperial Theaters making demands. Our manifesto." Joseph looked energized by his convictions. He held out a clipboard. "Will you sign?"

She shook her head.

Three others came in behind her. Wasting no more time on her, Joseph handed the petition to the first woman, barely twenty, who had recently begun to change shape. Her flat chest filled out and her hips were rounder. She would not last another year in the ballet. Like Brigitte, she shook her head. "I can't," she said. "I am already on notice. If I sign, I may as well go back out the door and never return."

Joseph offered the petition to the next woman, Olga, who gave the young dancer a disgusted grimace. Olga had been with the Imperial Ballet for ten years, and though she had fine technique, her temper kept her from soloing, and ironically, from getting fired. Brigitte admired her gift for terrifying Rodian to the point that he avoided her. It seemed she backed down at the right moments, but never really surrendered. She signed with a flourish and handed the petition to the man beside her. He bit his lip, shifting from foot to foot. Finally, he signed and passed the document back to Joseph.

As Joseph held the petition down at an angle, Brigitte could see. Sergei's signature was near the top. Folkine's slopping scrawl was just above Anna Pavlova's, whose signature looked like a knight on a horse riding into battle, with the 'l' in 'Pavlova' as the lance.

"There is a meeting tonight in the rehearsal hall. A delegation is to be selected from amongst us to present this petition to Director Telyakovsky." Joseph spoke as though he were on stage. "Put aside individual interests for the good of all. We do not ask for martyrs, but for strength in numbers." He stepped against the wall and allowed the dancers to walk by.

Brigitte took her place at the barre. Nikolai came in, never looking in her direction. The young dancer with the newly-rounding body asked Nikolai tearfully, "What should we do about this meeting? About the petition? I don't want to be on the wrong side?"

Nikolai waved her off with his graceful, stubby fingers. "Take all cares and worries to the barre," he said.

Brigitte's muscles were tight as fists. In an ordinary class, Nikolai would comment on her rigid movements.

He called out their exercises, his French as lyrical as his hands. She had to shut her eyes to hear him. She moved to the left instead of to the right, bumping into the dancer beside her. Nikolai said nothing. When she opened her eyes, she saw Julija at the other end of the barre appearing distressed. Then she realized, they all were. Everyone except for Nikolai was falling to pieces, holding for dear life, onto the barre.

After class, she went to the board outside of Rodian's office to see if there was any word about the closing of the Imperial Theaters. Had Telyakovsky gone to the minister to plead on behalf of the artists? Others had the same idea. A group had assembled.

"The theaters in Moscow are curtained," someone standing behind her said. "But we are still to go on tomorrow night?" There was a crescendo of murmurs. "What about rehearsals?"

"We can show up, but if S. Legher and M. Folkine are not there, will they get student ballet masters from the school to fill in?"

"Joseph is right. We can't all be let go. There are not enough dancers in the school to replace us. Look at what is happening now with Rimsky Korsakov. He resisted, lost his post and there is so much protest he will have to be reinstated."

"That is all over the question of the Jews," someone said. "Too many Jewish students at the Music Conservatory. Different issues altogether."

"But it's not," another said. "What is happening is that we are seeing how powerful we can be as artists if we stick together. I am going to the meeting tonight. To not go is to be more worried about your career than about the welfare of all your fellow dancers. That is not Russian."

They all spoke at once then, arguing with each other from the same side. Without Nikolai or Leonid to advise her, she had to figure out for herself what to do. A hundred times she changed her mind, but in the end, not being able to find a ride home, and not wanting to walk with all the streetlamps out, she went to the meeting, finding a seat in the back row.

Peter Milchalov, a dancer of unusual height, which impaired his ability to partner, led the proceedings. His facial features were angular and severe, softened by shoulder-length blonde hair. After calling the meeting to order, he invited Sergei to read the *Declaration of Intent* that would be sent by the elected delegation to Telyakovsky.

Sergei cleared his throat. "We are organizing ourselves to secure freedom of association and an improvement in our economic situation. We can no longer tolerate intimidation from the administration, that is, the Directorate." As he read many of the dancers whistled and clapped. Some repeated back Sergei's words. "Not tolerate intimidation."

"If there ensues any manner of repression on the part of the administration concerning our resolution, we have in mind ways and means to struggle against this arbitrariness."

The men and women in the seats around her stood cheering, halting the meeting for several minutes. Peter Milchalov stood beside Sergei, clapping along with the crowd, both men sharing an expression of resolve.

Rodian pushed his way to the front coming to stand next to Sergei. "Should you choose, in your state of madness, to present that piece of rubbish and filth to the Directorate, you shall find yourself locked out of the Imperial Theaters. Locked out of every stage in Russia." The crowd booed him. Undaunted, he raised his voice. "You delude yourself with notions of self-importance, all of you. It is your duty to Russia to show...to PROVE to the people that the tsar has things under control."

"He has nothing under control!" a man shouted back.

"You are Telyakovsky's sweet boy," another said.

Rodian looked small and weak next to Sergei and Peter, but he persisted. "I warn you, everyone in this room. If you sign the petition, you spit in the face of the tsar. You will be punished for treason."

Peter motioned to a powerfully built young danseur in his early twenties, who nodded and came forward to grip Rodian's shoulder. Rodian shook him off. The surly youth tried again, only this time he pushed Rodian.

For a moment it appeared Rodian would lose his balance, but he steadied himself, putting his arms up in defense, to keep the younger man at bay. "I will see you all arrested. You think you are irreplaceable? You will disappear. In a short time, no one will remember your names."

The youth pulled at Rodian's shirt, untucking it from his trousers. Joseph Kchessinsky stepped forward towards them. Rodian lunged, swinging at Joseph with his fist.

Joseph leaned to one side, reaching out at the same time, catching Rodian, as he lost his balance. Propping him back up on his feet, Joseph shoved Rodian into Sergei, who held Rodian's arms as the young dancer punched him hard in the face. Rodian dropped. The room fell silent.

Brigitte willed him to rise. She hated him; hated him all the more now for making her take pity on him.

When he stood, he was bleeding from a cut under his eye. The young dancer pushed him towards the door. Rodian squared his shoulders defiantly but walked up the aisle. As he passed, he looked into Brigitte's eyes flooding her with his anger and humiliation.

Brigitte ducked out of the meeting shortly after, watching not to run into Rodian, and walked straight home.

The next afternoon when she arrived for the matinee performance the theater police stood by the door. A group of five women just ahead of her were barred entrance. As they turned to leave. Brigitte asked them what was happening.

"We signed the petition," one said, her face contorted by anger.

The policeman waved Brigitte inside. She went to Nikolai and Sergei's dressing room first, hoping to find Nikolai. Maria Petipa came out of the room, slamming the door shut. Despite the heavy makeup and painted-on smile, Maria looked livid. "You Leghers," she said through clenched teeth. "I hate you all." She slapped Brigitte hard across the face. For a woman who barely acknowledged Brigitte's existence, the slap felt like something she'd wanted to do for a long time. Maria stormed away, a cloud of foul language polluting the hallway.

Brigitte panicked. She jumped when Rodian walked by, his eye purple and swollen shut. He shoved a piece of paper at her, a flyer warning of the consequences of signing the petition.

Behind Rodian, a matron from the school tapped his shoulder, then pointed to the cluster of terrified boys and girls. "For some, this is their first time performing," she said.

Rodian looked them over with his one good eye. "The curtain can go up now." To the students, he said, "Be proud. You are in service to the tsar. Your loyalty shall be rewarded."

Sergei came out of his dressing room, his head down, sullen. She'd seen his name on the petition. How had he gotten past the police?

"Hello." He kissed her chastely on the cheek. His eyes were dull. "This is all so pointless."

He went back into his dressing room. She followed, nudging her way inside before he could shut the door.

"Where is Nikolai?" she said.

Sergei shrugged. Going to him, she intended to wrap her arms around him wanting to love the light back into his eyes; tell him she would find a way to forgive his betrayal, but he thwarted her with a wall of despair.

"Answer one question," he said, his voice dissonant. "Will you leave with me on the train tonight?"

"The railroad is on strike. There are no trains."

He went to the makeup table.

"How did you get past the police? I saw your name on the petition."

"I removed my name," he said. "I signed an oath of loyalty to the tsar and Telyakovsky."

He sat down, picked up a small brush, and swirled it in white face paint. "Maria threatened to leave me if I didn't take my name off the petition," Sergei reported in a flat tone. "I told her I had a lover. That I used your home for secret trysts." Sergei unbuttoned his white shirt and took it off. His undershirt was crisp and clean. Moving to the sink, he splashed water on his face. She handed him a stained towel.

"It surprises me," he said. "She seems to have no interest in who this lover is." Reaching into the wardrobe, he took out his costume. Tights, pantaloons, a velvet jacket with a gold belt. "Rodian came over to the apartment this morning. He knocked on the door not more than three minutes after Maria left for the theater without me."

Sergei stood holding his clothes. "There are certain people you never imagine finding at your door. I let him in. I even gave him a cup of black tea."

Brigitte's mouth went dry.

"He said he had heard an old rumor that Prince Orlov was your father and was interested to know it was true. He was especially intrigued to learn more about your mother. I guess he overheard something I said." Sergei draped the costume over the back of his chair. "He offered me a bargain." Taking a clothes brush, the bristles worn and facing every which direction, he began to attend to the velvet jacket.

"If I were to desist in my leadership role promoting the petition and a dancers' strike." Sergei paused mid-stroke as if he were listening again to the exact words Rodian used. "To desist as leader of the dissonant faction within the Imperial Ballet, which has become a thorn in the side of the Directorate, and if I were to sign an oath of loyalty to the tsar and the Imperial Theaters, he would see to it that no one ever learned your matronage." Sergei sniffed. "He threw in the added incentive that not only would he not ruin Nikolai's career, but he would see to it that he becomes first ballet master. To continue to practice his art, is how he put it."

Brigitte put her hand over her mouth.

"There was one more condition." Sergei resumed brushing. A button came off and pinged as it bounced to the floor. "After we close the *Queen of Spades*, I will be permitted one final ballet. Telyakovsky will choose which one. I am then to resign my position. If I ever perform at any of the private theaters, Nikolai will be immediately dismissed, but with his pension. A generous concession. And," Sergei dropped the brush. "You will be revealed to be a Jewess whore." He threw the brush, hitting the wall.

She could not go to him. Something cold surrounded him, something icy and evil claimed his soul and beckoned menacingly for hers. He'd been broken by the devil. He had become the *Deathless Koschei*.

"I took my name from the petition. Joseph wept. He said it would be the end of him, too, if I deserted the cause. Anna Pavlova called me a traitor. But I signed Rodian's oath."

She put her hand on the knob, turning it.

"I have two pairs of shoes. I had planned on going to Liftshed's to order more. Enough to get me through the fall. Now, two are enough. There is not much dancing in this opera. One more ballet. That will finish them off."

She fled. The clock next to Rodian's office door said only forty minutes before curtain. She went to her dressing room to put on her costume, then down to the wings to warm up with the others dancing the divertissements between acts of the opera.

"Tsar Nicholas signed the manifesto at the Peterhof Palace." Word was spreading quickly. "There are celebrations out in the streets." The dancers were in a frenzy as if they were fish in a pond being fed breadcrumbs. "He is allowing a Duma to be elected."

"We can travel now without having to get permission?" The dancers were giddy and anxious. Brigitte felt as though ants were crawling under her skin, but listening to the talk distracted her from trying to sort out what the future might hold now that Rodian knew her secrets.

"The strikes will end. Trains will run. Food will be brought into the city."

A woman burst into tears. "It is over? The dancers' strike, too? Can we please not hear any more about that?"

"The war with Japan is over. The revolution is over. The people win."

She would go home and pack a bag. If the railroad strike had ended, in the morning she and Sergei could get on the train. What choice did she have but to leave now that Rodian knew?

The idea of life away from St. Petersburg, from Nikolai, alone with Sergei, who was no longer the man she thought she loved, horrified her. If Sergei could still dance in Paris or London, he might become himself again.

The stage manager called for places. Brigitte lifted onto her toes, wincing at the pain in her feet. Her heart felt too small for the space in her chest, beating harshly as if it could break down a door. Filled with fear and dread, she made up her mind. After the opera matinee, she would tell Sergei that she was ready to leave, even if it meant walking over the border into Finland. He could wear out his shoes on the way.

She listened as the orchestra began to play the national anthem, *God Save the Tsar*. The audience sang over the orchestra, sharp boos and whistles cutting through the melody. Tradition dictated the anthem be played three times in a row. By the middle of the second chorus shouting and jeering drowned out the singers.

In the wings, the performers were restless. "I am not going out there," declared the soprano.

"Someone should tell the conductor to stop. If he gets to the third chorus, there will be a riot."

"Down with autocracy!" The shouting became chanting, countering the anthem. Voices joined in from the other side of the stage from the opera chorus, adding to the volume and intensity.

A woman screamed, the sound like the shriek of Baba Yaga flying over the heads of the aristocracy.

"They're leaving!" the stage manager yelled. "Great disaster! Someone just fell over their seat."

More screaming from the women in the audience, the music only barely audible as it entered the final chorus. The theater police who had barred entrance at the stage door rushed past them, yelling at the manager to open the curtain.

The performers in the wings surged forward to see what was happening. A man in the front row was drawing a decorative saber from his uniform.

"Does he think this is a battle?" said the baritone.

Chairs overturned as the men fought for the exits. The orchestra stopped, the musicians pouring onto the stage trying to protect their precious instruments from the spillover of the panicked audience.

A heavy red-haired man stood by the exit nearest the stage, holding a chair up over his head. Brigitte recognized Dr. Betz. He bellowed, "Right, you revolutionaries, come to me. I'll reduce you to splinters! You ungrateful swine!"

Theater police tackled him from behind, holding his arms down. "I am helping you," he hollered, his face scarlet. "I'm ridding the theater of these traitors!" The police pulled him by his boots through the exit.

More police swarmed in and began to restore order. In the end, twenty-five people remained in their seats. As one voice, the remaining audience insisted the orchestra return to play *God Save the Tsar* fully, all three choruses. The conductor, with no one of higher authority than the stage manager to instruct him on what to do, ordered the musicians back to their stands where they made several noticeable mistakes. When the last note sounded, the curtain closed. The stage manager shouted the announcement that there would be no further performances that afternoon or evening.

The streets were crowded and chaotic, but Brigitte made it home safely. She shut her door and locked it. Not bothering to shed her coat, she went straight to the *Chambre de Joie*. A form moved in the shadows. Brigitte screamed. Nikolai grabbed her by the shoulders, shaking her, then slapped her face. Her throat closed; she couldn't get a deep breath. Putting her hands up to her neck, she backed away from him.

"Nikolai."

He pivoted on his heel and turned his back. "He is my brother. You were my sister. You are nothing now. I came here to get my things and tell you there is no place for you in the *Classique de Perfection*."

She noticed his satchel next to a small wooden crate filled with vodka bottles and the Frenchman's cognac. He must have had bottles hidden all over the house.

She followed him. "Forgive me. Forgive us."

"I forgive Sergei. He cannot help himself. He is an artist. That keeps him from thinking clearly. But you." He looked down at her as though he looked at the vilest of insects. "What did you hope to gain by destroying Sergei? Have you hated the Leghers so much all these years that you would seek to ruin our name?"

His contempt felt powerful enough to stop her beating heart. "I... we... Please, Yolya."

"If I ever find you have further interfered with Sergei, I will see that you are thrown out of the Ballet. You will never find a protector powerful enough to keep you safe from me." He picked up the satchel and tucked the crate under his arm. A moment later the front door slammed.

Curling into a ball on the cold, wood floor, she squeezed her eyes shut. The darkness could not blind her to the way Nikolai had looked at her. Grief rode over her as a dark horse, rearing and screaming, pummeling her body. What had been caught in her throat escaped now, a wailing sound, shocking and wild. She put her hands over her ears to shut the sound out.

Leaves hit the windows as the wind danced in a frenzy, a ghoulish host come to wake her in the morning. She'd slept on the floor. The cold stirred her, carrying her to her new life. Her whole body ached, her feet most of all. For a full minute she held still, adjusting to the pain, then, resolved, she went to dress and pack a bag.

The streets were quiet. Shattered glass and empty bottles glistened in the golden light of morning. The wind stole her scarf and she stopped to pick it up where it fell behind her, rewinding the crimson wool around her neck, and tying it in a thick knot.

The walk to Sergei's took an hour. As she came to each intersection, she hoped she'd be able to wave down a carriage or car, but there were none. When she climbed the stairs to his apartment, she no longer had any doubts. She'd deal with Maria if she had to, but hoped she was away. Sergei would be happy. She would show him her satchel filled with all of her prized possessions and most basic needs, light enough for her to carry to Finland. The words had been composing themselves on her walk. "I love you. You need to dance. Let's go to Paris."

She reached Sergei's door, squared her shoulders, and knocked. It shocked her when Nikolai answered. He looked broken.

"Yolya?" she held her hand out. He slapped it away.

"Who is here?" Maria's voice was lower by an octave.

Nikolai stepped out into the hallway, shutting the door. "I asked you to leave Sergei alone," he said accusingly.

"I know, but..." She squared her shoulders again ready for the confrontation. This was Nikolai, her brother. Her best friend. Her ally. Not Rodian or some other bully. Nikolai. "I am here for Sergei. We are leaving." She said it out loud, and for a moment, her resolve vanished. She sounded silly. But too late, she thought. "Get out of my way."

He looked from her towards a dim, dust-covered window at the end of the hall. "He is dead." His lip began to quiver. In a flood of horrible words, he went on. "He came home last night drunk. He and Maria argued. She locked him out of the bedroom. Early this morning she found him. He cut his throat with a razor." Wiping his mouth with the back of his shaking hand, Nikolai began to weep.

"No, oh please, no." Faltering, she leaned against the wall.

Nikolai looked at her, his face wet, ugly. "You are not welcome at his funeral. I forbid it. You stole him from me. I will keep your murderous secret, but not from any regard for you. I do it for Sergei. To preserve his honor. You have none. GO. This is a place for family only. You are not family. If I could tear from you the name Gustoevna Legher..." His voice broke with emotion. "Go!" he ordered; the word fierce, violent.

She held up her hand in response to block the blow of the words. Sergei dead? "Can I see him?"

Nikolai took a step towards her, his head leading the way like a charging bull. She flattened her body against the wall. "No. Only family."

Holding tight to her bag, Brigitte backed slowly down the stairs and out into the wild wind with flying gold and red leaves swirling around her.

CHAPTER 20

St. Petersburg November 1905

Two weeks after Sergei's suicide, Telyakovsky named Nikolai second dance master in partnership with ballerina Evgenia Sokolova. The position of first dance master remained unfilled. That same day, Joseph Kchessinsky punched Rodian. Within the hour, a notice was posted on the board announcing Joseph's resignation from the Imperial Theaters, forfeiting his pension.

Rodian came out of his office holding a white cloth to his lip. He looked at her, his eyes traveling down her body making her feel violated. "You can thank me for the solo in the divertissement." In one sentence he managed to combine a sneer, a warning, and an invitation.

"Thank you," she said with lackluster sarcasm. She had no strength to hold up make-believe shields and swords. She hated him and wished him dead, and wished Sergei alive.

"I do not think you meant that." He stepped around her as she tried to move away from the noticeboard blocking her way. "You might show more gratitude. How did you show Leonid Verontsov gratitude when he helped you to get solos?" Rodian ran his hand lightly down her arm.

Brigitte froze.

"There are things I know about you," Rodian said. "I see you know what I am talking about." He took her hand, pulled her into his office, and shut the door. Before she could fight him, he used his foot to sweep behind her ankles, knocking her off balance. She tumbled back into his chair. Rodian leaned over her, one hand on each arm of the chair trapping her. He licked his lips, "Any of the young dancers are mine if I want them. They are like you were, looking to become prima ballerina before they are twenty." His breath was hot on her face. "They believe I can make them prima ballerinas. Mathilde convinces them that rich men can make them prima ballerinas. I have been puzzled why all of you women are too stupid to realize that Mathilde is the only prima ballerina, and she had to sleep with Tsar Nicholas, and two of his relatives. But there are many reasons a woman gives herself to a man. Let me tell you one."

She tried to get up but he forced her down. She tried again. Rodian shoved her and stepped between her legs spreading them with his knees. He leaned his entire body against hers, paralyzing her.

"I will tell your secrets. That you bedded your brother. Why should I be the only one who knows what a vile creature you are? The church will excommunicate you. But what do you care about the church? You are a Jewish whore from the Pale."

She gasped, and though she knew this was coming, it still shocked her. He lifted off of her. His words held her down more effectively than his body. "I do have something that makes me of value to you." He leaned against his desk. "At my bidding, you will come. Do you understand?"

The room grew smaller, Rodian taller, his hands and fingers stretched into claws, his teeth fangs. He grinned like a wolf. "I've heard since our school days you make me look good. Some might find that maddening. After all, it is the danseur who should be the one to make the ballerina look good, not the other way around."

On his desk were scissors and a letter opener. She'd been putting up with him for so long, he'd stopped being any real threat. But he'd never had such a sharp sword before.

"I have the power to see you dance more solos." He touched her cheek. "Perhaps I cannot buy you a house, but I can keep you alive."

He touched her cheek and she flinched, turning away from him.

"Go change for rehearsal." He opened the door; cool air rushed in. Rodian stepped out of her way and she ran from the room, grabbed her coat and bag from where she'd left them on a chair by the notice board, and went for the nearest exit.

The November air foretold snow any day, maybe even that evening. Nina described Father Winter as a powerful and angry wizard who punished humans until defeated by gentle Spring. Brigitte pulled on her coat, then fished her cigarette case from her bag. With shaking hands, she tried to strike a match on the side of the theater building.

Michael Folkine skipped up the steps. He stopped, took the match from her, struck it once, put the cigarette between his lips, and lit it.

She thanked him but could not look him in the eye.

"Sorry about your brother," he said. "I know he felt as though he let us all down taking his name off the petition. I wish I could tell this to him, but I want you to know, I never saw it that way."

She wished he would shut up and walk away.

"There are those who are angry, ones who have been forced out, but everyone agrees that it wasn't worth Sergei's life. I'm sorry he took it so hard."

Michael helped himself to a cigarette from her case and a match. She didn't want him there, talking to her about Sergei. Words formulated themselves but they couldn't get organized enough to blurt out to him that he should go the hell away.

"Some people think that with the tsar's Manifesto, we won the revolution. That is not how it is. I have watched you. I know you are cunning. One does not survive this long in ballet if they are not smart. Sergei wanted artistic freedom for you, too. For all of us. In his memory, you could help the fight, instead of letting yourself be controlled."

Brigitte felt weary to her bones with the threats of men. She had no idea how to deal with Rodian's threats. But she owed nothing to Michael Folkine. He had not been tossed out of the ballet yet because they still needed him, but his career would be short.

"You are choreographing my *pas de deux* with Rodian?" she said, her voice shaking from cold and emotion.

Folkine nodded.

"Can I ask you for a personal favor? Even though I am in no position now, nor will I ever be in a position to help you fight for artistic freedom, in Sergei's memory or anyone else's."

He looked at her as though she'd just become more interesting. "What is it?"

"Make him look like a fool."

Folkine's smile began and ended in his heavy-lidded eyes. He took another cigarette from her case, putting it in his pocket. "My pleasure."

Nikolai worked at the Alexandrinsky Theater, while she rehearsed at the Mariinsky. The framed publicity pictures of Sergei at the Mariinsky were removed. No one mentioned him, at least when she was around.

No amount of stretching at the barre could loosen her up, putting her in danger of injury. Rodian's touching her every day at rehearsals made it difficult to concentrate. Each night she scrubbed away his touch with a rough brush.

Folkine kept his word. Rodian struggled. At the end of their *pas de deux,* he could barely catch his breath. Telyakovsky asked Folkine to alter the choreography and he complied by putting in more difficult elements. To add to the sweetness, Folkine partnered with Brigitte during the first dress rehearsal, demonstrating the entire *pas de deux* for Rodian and the cast of dancers. For six minutes dancing with Folkine, she let go of her grief, her muscles became fluid, and her spirit began to rise. From that height, she remembered her wings. Then the music stopped.

Brigitte heard murmurs afterward of how much better the *pas* was without Rodian, assuaging her anger.

Opening night, Brigitte began her makeup. Lubov, the dancer whose mother had been killed on Bloody Sunday nearly a year ago, had not taken her father and left the country. She came into Brigitte's dressing room, her face sad, as it now always seemed to be, and handed Brigitte a note. "Rodian asked me to give this to you. I hope you are not forced to resign. He is a *mudak.*"

Reading the note, her stomach seized. He instructed her to join him at once in a small reception room at the back of the theater; a room seldom used because of its inadequate size and draftiness.

The hallway felt narrower and colder as she neared the room. As if the tall, heavy door wanted to protect her, it did not open easily.

Some events defy memory, defy the mind's ability to hold them for examination. She remembered after leaving Rodian, being in her dressing room putting on her makeup, wincing in pain at the bruising around her anus, each time she shifted even slightly in her seat. Her mind asked for a memory, an explanation of the pain; she had none. "Are you injured?" Lubov asked as Brigitte came to warm up in the wings. "You are limping."

She waved Lubov off, concentrating on walking normally through the burning.

Her music began. She glanced across the stage to the other side, a habit, making sure Rodian was there. Nikolai was at his side.

For a long moment, their eyes locked. She saw what she most wished to see. He cared for and missed her. A sob escaped. Nearby dancers looked concerned. She held her arm across her stomach. Nikolai did not look away. Through her tears, she dared not blink for fear of losing sight of him.

"Your cue, your cue," the stage manager whispered loudly, shoving her from behind.

She danced towards Rodian. He, towards her. Had her in his arms, turned her in a *pirouette*. She caught a flash of Nikolai, whose hands covered his mouth as if he witnessed something heartbreakingly terrible. She moved into an *arabesque*. Rodian lifted her, but she could feel him pushing her too far forward.

He let her go too quickly on the descent and she lost her balance, forgetting that she needed to be vigilant about him doing such things. She lunged sideways to steady herself but caught her foot on her calf. She landed on her cheek with a heavy thud, shattering a tooth, a cracking sound in her head as a bone broke. The collective intake of breath from the audience could be heard over the orchestra.

Brigitte lay still.

Rodian snatched her up and tried to twirl her back into motion. Not finding her bearings, she crumpled in a heap, blinded by the stage lights.

"Nikolai," she cried out. Rodian stood over her, his hands reaching out. She rolled over onto her knees, swatting him away. She lifted her head, seeking out Nikolai but he had gone.

The audience booed and heckled. She stood, looking out at them, at the bright lights for the last time. Then she limped off the stage, from the light into darkness, knowing her career as a ballerina had come to a humiliating end.

CHAPTER 21

Petrograd, December 1915

With the advent of war with Germany, Tsar Nicholas changed the name of St. Petersburg to Petrograd, a Russian name, not German. When Brigitte heard the news, she thought of Nikolai telling her, if he could, he would take from her the names Gustoevna and Legher. She would be simply Brigitte, as St. Petersburg now was simply Petrograd.

The name Petrograd dimmed the beauty of the city. Her home had undergone another kind of dimming. When Leonid died in 1910, his barrister gave Brigitte a bequest, a sum of money not part of his official estate. She'd accepted it as Leonid's apology for believing her to be a spy. The amount was enough to pay a carpenter to convert the second floor into an apartment. She would lose her beloved tub, but the rent would bring her security.

Her tenant, Mark Reznik moved in alone, but a short time later his daughter arrived with her two children, a teenage boy and a girl of seven. Brigitte overheard the boy threatening to join the revolutionaries, not worrying that his landlady might be an informant to the Akrona. She wished for the thousandth time that she still had her lovely bedroom and her bathtub. She hated using a chamber pot.

Following her morning routine, she put away her teacup, the plate of rusks, then tidied up the dining room, where she kept a narrow bed pushed against the wall. Mr. Reznik's voice carried down to her. The girl giggled. Heavy footsteps. Singing.

His hands had been the reason she'd let him have the apartment. They reminded her of Nikolai's hands; short, fat fingers full of incongruous gracefulness. At night he played the balalaika. She enjoyed listening. Her feet ached to move but the pain in them stopped her from such nostalgic frivolousness. She danced now only to demonstrate for her students.

Her ride would be by in half an hour. She sat at the kitchen table with nothing to do until then. "Strange for you to have a moment like this, isn't it?" Nikolai said to her, part of an ongoing conversation she had in her thoughts. He spoke loudest at night, but whenever she quieted, he slipped into her mind.

"My white mittens need mending." She spoke out loud.

"You will just get started and the car will arrive," he said.

A knock at the kitchen door interrupted the conversation. Mark Reznik held a basket; beside him stood the girl.

"Yes?" She said, her voice stern, a habit learned from hours each day chiding young dancers.

"Madame Legher." Reznik bowed, tapping the girl on the back, compelling her to make an awkward curtsy. "My daughter made cinnamon babka." He offered the basket.

Who knew what state their kitchen might be in? How was it possible she had an oven for baking? Mr. Reznik reached out with his hand, so like Nikolai's, took a hold of her, uncurled her fingers, and put the handle of the basket into her palm.

"I would like to inquire about ballet lessons for my granddaughter, Chana." He put his hands on the girl's shoulders. Most children would lower their eyes to the floor. Chana looked her in the eye, grinning. Her two front teeth were missing.

"I want to be a ballerina," she stated.

Brigitte wondered if the girl was precocious or ignorant.

"My daughter has been asking the going rate for a half-hour lesson. We could pay you in milk and vegetables."

Brigitte regarded the offer. It would save her shopping. She didn't like crowds.

"Come inside a moment. Let me look at her," she said. "Take off your coat."

Mr. Reznik ushered in his granddaughter. "No wonder we stay so warm upstairs. It is like summertime in here."

Brigitte scowled. He was built like a peasant, stout, tall and strong. Men like that never felt the cold, as she did.

Chana unbuttoned her orange felt coat, handing it to her grandfather. She stood straight.

"You are wearing too many clothes," Brigitte criticized. "If you are destined to be built anything like your grandfather, lessons will be a waste."

Chana kept grinning.

"Take off all your clothing, except your shift. Make haste. I have a car coming for me in twenty minutes."

Chana looked up at Mr. Reznik; he nodded.

Chana had long arms, a graceful curve to her back, and legs that potentially would remain longer than her torso. Nikolai whispered in Brigitte's head, "Monkey arms."

"Stand like this," Brigitte said, assuming first position, demonstrating a turnout.

Chana moved her bare feet into place. A perfect turnout. A shadow of Nikolai sat in the corner of the kitchen clapping his hands, ecstatic. Such natural turnouts always excited him. There would be no tying this girl's feet to the bedposts at night. Brigitte felt Chana's hips and inspected her toes.

"I tolerate no insolence," she said, arms crossed. "If you presume to speak without being spoken to, I shall ask you to leave and there will be no further lessons."

Mr. Reznik laughed. He indulged the child too much, thought Brigitte, expecting this would lead to Chana's failure.

"She may begin on Saturday."

Mr. Reznik shook his head. "Sabbath is Saturday."

She had not realized they were Jewish. "I only take private students on Saturdays," she stated.

"Chana rises early to sell milk for the dairyman. One day a week, her brother can do this for her. He found work at the Bears Inn but in the evenings." Mr. Reznik gestured as he spoke.

"I do my shopping on Tuesday mornings. Perhaps in addition to the milk and vegetables, your daughter would do this for me. I could see Chana at 7:30 Tuesday mornings this way." Brigitte applauded herself. She would much prefer teaching to being groped by crowds. The Jewish part troubled her, but they wouldn't be in the city without a permit.

Mr. Reznik rubbed his chin. "You will provide a list and the funds?"

"I tolerate no mistakes. If I say fresh black bread, I do not expect day-old rye."

"Yes, my daughter can do this. Then we have an agreement?" He held out his hand to shake. He had thick calluses on his fingertips. His skin was clean and smooth.

"What is it that you do?" she said without taking his hand. "Your trade?"

His eyes brightened. "I am a scribe. A *sofer stam*."

"I do not know what this is. *Sofer stam*?" she said.

"I write out the *Torah* and other sacred texts."

She nodded realizing that he was not simply a Jew, but devout. Noticeable to the authorities. She preferred Jews like herself, who kept it secret, and who attended the Orthodox Church for the Divine Liturgy, despite being beyond redemption, condemned to hell.

"I heard your grandson talking about revolution. The Black Hundred visit men like him with fire and murder." She waved at Chana. "Get dressed." To Mr. Reznik, she said, "Tell the boy... what is his name?"

"Zeev," Mr. Reznik said.

"Tell Zeev, that what I hear others can also hear. He should be careful with the lives of his family and the life of his landlady."

His hands were folded in front of him; he gave her a peaceful smile. "Hard to tell a young man anything," he said sadly. "But I will pass on your words of caution and pray they make an impression."

The car to Theater Street arrived at precisely 9:08 am. Two women, also living in the Admiralteysky District, shared the ride. The youngest, Innya, was a *coryphée* and Brigitte's former student. Innya kept them updated on the latest intrigues. The other, Madame Chikaskia, stout and stern, taught history. A dedicated monarchist, she carried the Black Hundred newspaper, the *Russkoye znamya*, outside of her bag in a show of her loyalty to the tsar.

Brigitte considered herself to be a monarchist, but Madame Chikaskia's talk of the pogroms advocated by the Black Hundred against the Jews made her fearful.

When Brigitte's dance career ended, she was given a position at the school, for which she was grateful to the tsar. For teaching seven hours each day, she received one meal, transportation to and from work, and a modest stipend that paid for most, but not all, of her living expenses. In addition, she'd received two-thirds of her pension from the Imperial Ballet. Having resigned three years short of the required twenty years of service, her pension had been forfeited. She'd heard that Rodian had a hand in an exception being made for her. Each time she received a payment, her bitter resentment towards him rose anew. He deserved no redemption.

Innya made room for Brigitte, as if she were a throw pillow on a divan, then leaned against her.

"There were several of them," Innya said to Madame Chikaskia. "Standing on the comer of Sadavaya Street. My companion pointed out that they were deserters. Their uniforms were worn to rags. The ones coming to Petrograd are ignorant peasants."

"Who is your companion these days?" said Madame Chikaskia.

"Someone," Innya said, a flounce in her tone. "Met him at a dinner party."

"One of Mathilde Kschessinkska's soirees," Madame Chikaskia sniffed.

"You are jealous." Innya returned Madame Chikaskia's haughtiness.

Brigitte saw a narrow smile on Madame's lips, an old woman enjoying secrets from her youth.

Innya continued, "My companion was so livid at the disloyalty to the tsar that if he had been carrying his gun, he would have executed them all right there where they stood."

Madame Chikaskia muttered something under her breath.

"Your brother married his former student," Innya said. "Natasha Vyborg. She is barely eighteen. How old is he? Sixty? The gossip is she tried to get into the Imperial Ballet, but she was not good enough. Master Legher quit. He started teaching her when she was nine. That's like marrying his daughter." She made a sour face. "Repulsive."

Brigitte heard Nikolai had divorced Antonia after she'd given him a daughter and failed to lose the weight she gained. But she had not heard of a new wife.

"There!" Innya exclaimed, pointing. "Deserters, by the statue."

The women looked out the window. A group of six men stood around the bronze-faced bust of M. Lomonosov, who looked as though the stench of the men offended him as he presided over the square named in his honor. The men wore ragged clothing. One sat holding his foot, wrapped in filthy cloth.

"Master Legher asked to teach at the school and was turned down," said Innya. "Too bad. Even though his wife dances poorly, he is a good teacher. He taught the *Classique de Perfection*. But you knew that." She laughed. "Have you met his new wife? They are going on tour soon. She is a terrible dancer. I've seen her. Have you seen her, Mlle. Legher?"

Madame Chikaskia clicked her tongue. "Innya, you are rude."

Innya sulked and got quiet.

The buttery yellow of the Imperial Ballet School clashed against the iron-grey sky like a colorfully-dressed woman at a solemn funeral. When the car stopped in front of the school, the driver came around to open the door. Madame Chikaskia fed a coin to his palm. She did this each day. Brigitte could not imagine parting with a single precious kopek unnecessarily.

Brigitte taught in a room with high ceilings and tall windows. In the darkness of the morning sky, she wished for more electric lamps, craving light. The piano sat in the corner like a loyal dog. Every day the pianists played the same melodies she heard as a student; each note rang in her ears as an unchanging annoyance.

A few moments before the girls arrived, a slight man, shorter even than Brigitte, came striding in, greeted her with a nod, put the thick book he carried with him on the piano bench, then sat. Mr. Mokorov did an adequate job but he did not use the pedals on the piano, not having the capability of reaching them. Every song sounded like a march.

Her room had a balcony accessed by a door on the next floor. Brigitte discouraged the perverted balletomanes claiming to be there just to observe, by calling attention to them. She had known promising dancers who were ruined by these men. There were no observers in the balcony that morning; one less detail to manage.

The little girls came in two groups, one arriving moments behind the other. She counted them. Two were missing.

"Where are Margareta and Olga?" she asked the girls who formed two neat rows.

Leyla answered without raising her hand, "Margareta has been taken to hospital. She has typhoid. Olga received news yesterday of her father's death in battle. Her mother came to collect her."

The information sifted through the air. Brigitte wished she could open a window to alleviate the stuffiness, but the chill would be unbearable.

"In the future, Leyla, you will ask permission to speak, or you will stand outside the door during class."

Leyla nodded, licking her lips nervously, assuring Brigitte the girl understood. "Yes, Mlle. Legher," she said meekly. "I ask your pardon."

Taking a hold of her walking stick, Brigitte thought again about Christian Johansson who once ruled this same classroom and taught her the merits of the stick. She wrapped her hand around the staff and cursed her beloved teacher, as she did every day, for pairing her with Rodian.

Striking the staff four times upon the floor, she set the tempo for exercises. Mr. Mokorov began to play. The piece sounded like a goat traipsing, no — marching, along a mountain pass. The ridiculous goats had skipped gracelessly for decades, never reaching the mountain meadow, always on the broken path, trying to get over the rickety bridge. Marching. The girls moved from the floor, marching towards the barre, spacing themselves with learned precision. With both hands on the barre, they began with *demi pliés*.

There were days when the sight of young bodies, the sound of marching goats, stirred a rage she struggled to contain. Using her stick, she tapped the feet of the girls who were not in a proper first position.

"You are a lazy one," she scolded the girl at the end of the row. The dancer beside her had an arch in her back. Brigitte used the stick to hit her shoulders. "Are you a peasant slouching in a ditch?

"Idiot child! Have you brains in your head at all? You obviously cannot count." The girl had failed to turn three rotations in a portion of a dance. Clunking the child over the head with the staff, she hit her harder than she'd intended. The girl would probably have a lump. "I've no time for stupid ballerinas. Learn the dance or leave school. There is no place here for those who do not keep up with the others. You have not done it right once."

The girls were sweating. Some looked as though they would soon break under the strain. These were the ones Brigitte determined to weed out as a kindness. Better they not waste their time only to fail when it truly mattered.

The oldest girl in the class, Leyla, who had so brazenly spoken before, had barely grown in the two years since her first assessment and admission to the school. Leyla's father abandoned the family shortly after her admittance. Her mother struggled to keep up with tuition. Her younger brother had gained entrance that fall. Word among the staff was he held potential. Brigitte did not see this in Leyla. Her head was too big for her body. Her natural turnout was not responding to exercises. Her eyes were light green, giving her a disquieting impish appearance. Unless the girl worked harder, even *corps de ballet* parts would be beyond her reach.

"Come to me," Brigitte beckoned to Leyla, a thrill of power rushing through her veins, seeing fear in the child's acidic eyes. Brigitte spoke words she grew up hearing. Terrorizing words meant for every girl in the room.

"You are not good enough to be here," she said her voice chillingly calm. "A mistake has been made. We hoped your body would grow differently, but it is a disappointment. There is no hope for you. Sometimes a dancer can overcome unfortunate legs with superb technique, but that takes discipline and determination. I see neither of these traits in you."

Brigitte waited, watched. What came next, she had seen hundreds of times. The first time, she was six. Miss Nadeah's class. She could feel it; the pulling thread of fear threatening to unravel the most carefully held composure. Even though the words came now from her own sharp tongue, they still made Brigitte want to cry. The tears, the quivering of the mouth and chin. Finally, Leyla covered her face with her hands.

"There will be a reassessment. The school director will contact your mother about your return home. Do you come from some faraway peasant village? That would explain the foppishness of your feet."

Leyla's shoulders shook. Brigitte trigged the earthquake, as intended. One of two things would happen next. The girl would run from the room or fall in a heap on the floor. Brigitte guessed Leyla to be a runner. The droppers, immobilized by shame, didn't cover their faces first.

When Leyla neither ran nor fell, Brigitte added a final insult. "Your face looks dreadful with those red blotches. No one wants to look at a dancer with such an ugly face."

The door was too heavy for Leyla to slam shut.

That evening, Brigitte sat in near darkness, listening to the gramophone, her records worn and scratched. In the shadows, she imagined Nikolai and Sergei seated at a small café table sipping vodka, the smoke from their cigarettes clouding their faces.

Nikolai said, "When they cry, we know they care."

Sergei had been more tender-hearted. "Give Leyla another year. What a growing body puts children through is torture. Think how you changed from a chubby mouse into a swan."

"I was never chubby," Brigitte protested. "What do you think of the Jewish girl?" she asked Nikolai. "Her turnout?"

"If she were to audition for the ballet school, the promise of her turnout would win her a place."

"You must not push her," Sergei said. "She has spirit. Let it get stronger before you shape it."

"Another Olga Preobrojenska." Brigitte said.

"Very difficult for a Jew to enter the Imperial Ballet School. Not impossible, right?" Nikolai winked. "Bring her to dance for me."

The record began to skip. Brigitte roused herself from the conversation.

That night, as she dozed, Nikolai returned behind her closed eyes. Her imaginary Nikolai sat on the foot of her bed, curls of smoke from his cigarette around his head. "I have heard you have a new lover, Yolya," she said.

He shrugged.

"Natasha Vyborg? A child."

He stood. She could feel the bed move.

"Did you need to resign in protest? Did you think they would beg you to stay and bring your child bride?"

He faded away, leaving her lonely.

CHAPTER 22

Petrograd, February 1916

Brigitte stood on a bridge in Yusupov Gardens at the skating pond watching the students in her charge. They needed an extra chaperone, it was a nice day, so she volunteered. One after another the young skaters fell, cracking their bodies, rolling into heaps upon one another like a pile of puppies. One fall on the head, or broken leg, and careers would end before they started. But the sun made the snow sparkle. What did she care of anyone's career?

Lost in the pain of her freezing feet, she was alarmed by a man putting his arms around her. She elbowed him hard in the ribs, but her small frame proved no match for his athletic body.

"Brigitte Gustoevna. If you had been someone else, this would be most uncomfortable." Alfred Bekefy's heavy-lidded eyes and thick brows belied his playful nature. He detested hats. His hair was still thick but had gone mostly grey. She accepted his kiss on the cheek.

"You're a reminder of the good days," she said, smiling.

He had been forced to resign from the ballet at the same time as Joseph Kchessinsky. Mathilde made sure Joseph kept his pension.

"I heard you showcase at Narodny Dom," she said hoping not to offend him by mentioning how far he'd fallen. The Narodny Dom, the People's Theater, offered performances for the uneducated and common.

"Glad for the work," he laughed. "Join me for tea?"

He'd lost two side teeth. To age? An unlucky fight? She motioned towards the frozen pond and the squealing children. "I must see these snow girls and boys back to school."

He furrowed his brows nearer together as if two caterpillars were about to collide on a branch.

"I am free for an early dinner. Before your performance? What time do you go on?"

"Cubats? Dannon's? Oh, wait. I am broke." His laugh rang out, becoming part of the sparkling light on the frosted birches. "I will be a loyal *Zhuchkas* with you and watch over your snow girls and boys."

Her affection for him reignited. "*Zhuchkas?*"

"The Little Snow Girl? Her loyal dog, *Zhuchkas?*"

Brigitte shook her head.

"The dog is driven off by the grandfather for allowing a fox to steal chickens, but redeemed by saving the Little Snow Girl from a bear and a wolf."

"A happy ending, Alfred? Is this a Russian fairytale? It must be French. English."

He guffawed, putting his arm around her shoulder. "Unusual, I know. My mother loved happy stories."

"She is not Russian then. Was the Little Snow Girl under an evil spell? She had a frozen heart?"

"My mother was French."

"I wonder if Nikolai knows that story?" she said out loud, though it had been a private thought. It took her aback when Alfred answered.

"He knows it. We have talked before about writing the libretto. Sergei's idea. He carried about a book of fairytales, scheming to turn them all into ballets." Alfred grew serious.

She could barely remember the last time someone had said Sergei's name.

"I think Nikolai looks for him each time he walks into a theater. Stupid thing to do at the Narodny Dom. Sergei would never have ended up there, as we have. He was better than all of us combined."

"You bring him back from the grave for me." Her voice shook. "I am grateful."

"What happened?" He asked so gently, for a brief moment, she felt tempted to tell him.

He removed his arm from around her shoulders. "Nikolai catches everything. Sick all the time. He battles back like a true Imperial soldier." Alfred chortled. "He is right as can be at the moment. Come and see for yourself."

"With Nikolai," she began, but tightness constricted her throat. She swallowed hard.

"Come see me dance. See Nikolai. You do not need to wear your best gown or a single jewel. Best if you dress like a peasant." He laughed heartily. "To have you there would make us all feel as though we have not lost so much."

"I had your niece in my class two years ago. She is quite promising."

He beamed with pride. "Destined for greatness."

"And your wife? She is well?" Brigitte said.

"I hear she is well and content with herself in Warsaw." His brows knit together. Besides his lovely dancing, his eyes and brows had translated far out into an audience a sense of excitement and drama, of joy.

Brigitte caught the less joyful and quite disdainful look another chaperone from the school pinned upon her, expecting help rounding up the students.

Taking a deep breath, Brigitte hollered in an authoritative voice, "Skates off and in line. We leave at once."

Alfred stared at her open-mouthed. Then he let out a jolly laugh. "A swan no more. You are a honking goose."

She scowled, clapping her hands toward the children. "If you are left behind, it will be more than dinner you miss."

"Only one of you needs to swallow your pride," he said.

"Pride? What is that? Thank you, but I must decline."

His expression remained hopeful. "Shall we meet again, soon? I will come to one of your student performances," he suggested.

"Your heart might break to see how pathetic these young ones are. Not like when we were at the school. I am afraid none of us teaching, myself included, are like Johansson or Nikolai." Brigitte looked at the children taking off their skates, a pain of disappointment spreading through her chest.

"A group of intellectuals is meeting at the apartment of a writer tonight. The discussions are lively. We could talk more. Free food."

"These days, I am fast asleep by ten."

"I will have you safe at home by midnight."

"What time?" she said, tempted.

"I'm finished after the first act. Where are you living? I could pick you up around nine." His brows arched in high hope.

Like a randy child rushing out an open door, words of agreement slipped out unbidden.

"This is not exactly the ball gown and diamond set you are used to. No need to brandish the glitter."

"I'll see you tonight." She watched him go, feeling a bit of her old self returning. Walking back to the school, she brought up the rear in the procession along the Fontanka Canal. The children pulled her along, as though she were tethered to them, each shadow a pull on her shoulders. Her legs tingled as she thought of running; going to dance at the Narodny Dom. Did she have more pride than Nikolai?

Despite Alfred's advice, she dressed carefully. Three years earlier she'd bought a red silk dress on a whim, having no place in mind to wear it. The price had been reasonable; a trifle compared to what Leonid paid for her gowns. She liked the elegance of the ivory bouillon lace around the deep V-lined collar and the cuffs. When she put it on, she felt her old power returning to her limbs. In the mirror, pinning up her hair, she noted that her skin had not wrinkled and faded like the faces of other women her age; her hair was still dark and thick, no traces of grey.

She selected a pair of calfskin boots lined with rabbit fur and trimmed in scalloped leather. They were worn a bit, but not too noticeably. Leonid had given her a beautiful diamond and opal necklace with a leaf design, perfectly matching the embroidery in the sash of the dress, but it was too dear. She left it hidden in a box and wore a strand of clear glass beads.

At nine o'clock, every hairpin in place, she went to wait near the door. Away from the heat in the kitchen, the coolness helped, as she did not want to stain the armpits of her dress from nervousness.

When Alfred had danced, the stage always came to life. Petipa had seldom cast him in serious roles. He danced the jesters, the buffoons. Smiling to herself, she could see him in her mind's eye tossing a bouquet meant for the ballerina, rolling forward on one shoulder; leaping high into the air, and catching the roses before they landed on the stage.

Alfred had instigated Nikolai and Sergei's gambling with the guardsmen. She wondered if he did that anymore, now that the soldiers were much younger. How many of those guardsmen were dead after fighting two wars?

Lost in her memories, one thought following another, with a start, she realized it was after ten.

At midnight she took her dress off, hanging it in the wardrobe. She rewound clean rags around the arms of the hanger so that the shoulders of the dress would not crease.

A tooth had started to hurt. Her eyes were heavy and itched. Her midday meal had been her last and her stomach growled. Climbing into her narrow cot, she pulled the heavy wool quilts up under her chin. "Go to sleep," she said out loud to herself.

Nikolai and Sergei appeared, this time sitting in the stalls at the theater, both dressed formally, wearing slick top hats. Sergei held a sketchpad in his lap, drawing busily. Nikolai watched his progress, but most of his attention was on the stage where Brigitte saw herself doing barre exercises.

"Shall I count for you?" Nikolai said. "You are not doing very well. No excitement at all."

"But, Yolya, they are just exercises. Since when have you expected something interesting from exercise?" She moved through a *passé dèveloppe.*

"That is the whole point," he said with an air of impatience. "If you do something with no interest, why do it?"

"To dance beautifully."

"You have passed over beautiful dancing, coming to this..." he yawned. "Boring repetition."

She tried to rethink how to be more interesting in her routine, but her legs would not obey. As though she had put on the shoes from the fairy tale that enchanted her feet so she could never stop dancing, the more she struggled, the faster she moved. Gustave admonished her to not clutch the barre, but she found herself doing so, her knuckles turning white. Her free hand began to flail, stiff and graceless.

Nikolai laughed, but when she looked at him, he laughed at Sergei's drawing, not at her. Sergei held up the caricature he'd drawn. It was of her as a honking goose.

MARCH 1916

Chana had long mahogany hair. Her brown eyes held intelligence and confidence. They were as penetrating as Leyla's eyes, but more comforting, as though by having the girl's attention, Brigitte again existed in a world that normally made her feel forgotten.

At seven years old, Chana was nearly as tall as Brigitte. Brigitte gave her one of her old dresses and a pair of tights. The classical lines of Chana's body and her elegant posture opposed the raggedy costume.

Often forgetting her manners and speaking without permission, Chana questioned everything. Twice Brigitte sent her home. Both times, she returned with a curt apology. Brigitte allowed her back, glad that she did not give up easily.

Brigitte took the basket of provisions Chana brought, noticing an extra jar. She held it up. Golden white cubes were laced with brown spices.

"Soused apples," Chana said. "From the last of the stored apples. Now we wait for more to grow." She went ahead of Brigitte to the *Chambre de Joie*. "I practiced every day this week," Chana bragged. "I can jump higher."

"We shall see," Brigitte said dismissively. She wondered where she practiced jumping in a two-room apartment shared by four people.

Constant footfalls and muffled voices from upstairs drowned out the music on the gramophone. She tried to ignore Zeev's angry shouting.

Chana kept her eyes on the mirror, correcting herself before Brigitte had a chance. Above her head, scuffling feet and then a crash. Brigitte jumped.

"Zeev is hoping *Dedushka* will give him money so he can go away," Chana said in the same tone of voice that she'd explained soused apples.

"What does your grandfather say?" Brigitte knew better than to ask the question, but she was curious about this strange Jewish family.

"For him to earn for himself. Zeev does not close his mouth to listen. That is what *Dedushka* says." She finished her barre on her left side, turning to face the right. "Our father went away and never came back. Mama says he must be dead. Zeev wants to go look for him."

Brigitte marveled at Chana's ability to speak so brazenly.

"*Dedushka* wishes Zeev would leave so that we could have peace, but he is afraid that if Zeev does leave, we will never see him again. Mama says it is a curse to have a son in these times."

Chana lost the rhythm for a moment. She paused, listened to the music, then resumed her exercise. "Are these bad times for sons?" Chana asked.

"I have no sons," Brigitte answered. She could not imagine there had ever been a good time in Russia to have a son or a daughter. Did her Jewish mother wish she'd lived in a better time for children?

How many children from the ballet school had she known who had been lost to illness or accident? The damp chill, vapors from the canals snaking through the neighborhoods looking for weak lungs?

"Where are you from, Chana?" Brigitte said.

"We lived in Kovno, in the Pale of Settlement. Everyone had to leave." She lifted her arm beautifully up over her head. "I had to leave my doll and her clothes. And two horses Zeev carved for me."

The Pale of Settlement. The only region in Russia where Jews were legally allowed to live. Where Brigitte's mother had been from. A deeply buried piece of her stirred at the incantation.

"Zeev says Germans are living in our apartment now and German girls are playing with my doll and they have broken the legs of the horses."

Brigitte adjusted Chana's arm, her hips. "You must hate the Germans," she said.

"Hate them?" Chana looked at herself in the mirror. "*Dedushka* says a little bit of hate gives us courage. Too much will cause us harm. He says it is like a small bit of arsenic can heal an infection, but too much will kill you."

How much arsenic she had taken over the years hating Rodian?

"You are letting your arm drop too low. Pay attention."

Chana lifted her arm. Another loud crash came from upstairs.

"Would Zeev harm anyone?" Brigitte asked.

Chana smiled. "*Dedushka* says Zeev believes he is an *Ivanshko Medvedka*, the Little Bear."

Nikolai's favorite fairytale was about Ivanshko, a strong man who had been raised by a bear sow. Nina told it, especially for him. At the end of the story, Ivanshko Medvedka killed the evil witch, Baba Yaga.

"*Dedushka* says Zeev thinks he is stronger than the giants."

When the record ended, the raised voices above their heads were clearer. "He must upset your mother."

"I am in trouble all the time. Not Zeev." She rolled her bottom lip into a pout. "If I say what I think, as Zeev does, I get hit. No one hits him."

Brigitte put on another record and commanded, "Walk." Chana moved on the diagonal toward Brigitte. "You are lifting your right foot too high. This is not a march. Be a beautiful ballerina; not an ugly soldier. A delicate woodland fairy."

Brigitte thought of Chana's family fleeing Kovno. "You are sinking too much into your *demi-plie*, lighter, lighter," she sang. "Don't trail your back foot. Walk forward on your feet. Walk, walk."

At the far wall, Chana turned.

"If you cannot walk like a ballerina, you cannot dance like a ballerina. Walking must come first. Learn to walk. You have not been practicing your walking."

Chana slowed down, taking each step carefully, no longer in a rhythm with the music.

"Did you see Germans when you were leaving Kovno?"

"Zeev said that Tsar Nicholas's cousin, Prince Nikolayevich made us leave, not the Germans. He said it is because we are Jews. The Christians could stay."

Brigitte bristled. "You should not tell people you are a Jew, Chana," she scolded, waving her back across the floor. "It is a bad thing to be Jew. Does your grandfather tell you that?"

Chana did not react as Brigitte had expected.

"*Dedushka* says we had to leave because Prince Nikolayevich thought we were helping the Germans win."

"*Epaulement*!" Brigitte shouted. "Where are your eyes? Are you looking at the floor or the audience? Nose in line with your elbow." She clapped her hands for emphasis.

"We rode on a train," she said as her gaze shifted up towards the window, squinting into the light. "It smelled bad. There were too many people all sitting on top of each other. Zeev made sure no one sat on me, though. He kept us safe. I did not see, but Zeev said an old woman died. She smelled bad."

With each step, Brigitte could see Chana's improvement. "Come back again," Brigitte said.

"Mama made us get off the train even though Zeev was mad and said it was too early. We walked then. We had to be tricky about it. We walked at night. Zeev stole clothes for us so we would look more like peasants, less like Jews. Mama said we couldn't speak Yiddish, but when she prayed to give thanks for finding a place to sleep or something to eat, she got to speak Yiddish. I was scolded every time I forgot."

The music changed to a faster tempo. "Now run. Watch your head. No bobbing up and down."

"It took a long time to get to *Dedushka's*." Chana ran around the outer parameter of the room. "Zeev said I walked too slow. My legs, too short."

"You have long legs. Dancer's legs."

Chana smiled.

"A dancer with short legs is no good," Brigitte continued. Chana became radiant. "One more time. Then to the center for *battement tendu à la seconde*."

She changed the record to one without scratches; her favorite and difficult to replace, so the one she played the least: Tchaikovsky's *Song of the Lark*.

Chana listened, her head nodding to the slow tempo, then she ran delicately around the room. Brigitte listened, thinking of Pytor Tchaikovsky. He had seen her. She could tell by the way his eyes followed her hands, her feet. She had watched him watching her. She saw him, too.

Reaching for a piece of chalk she kept near the gramophone, Brigitte stopped Chana. "You are not center." Brigitte drew a line on the floor. "Center," she pointed. "Once again. We are almost out of time for today."

"I like it here," Chana said as she stood on the line. "There was no one in Kovno to teach me ballet."

The shouting upstairs grew louder for a moment, a door slammed, then silence. Brigitte hoped that when the Akrona came to arrest Zeev, they would not take Chana; she was growing fond of the girl.

OCTOBER 1916

The sun made a poor effort of rising over Petrograd, not up to the battle with the heavy clouds and the steady haze of smoke from the factories. Stepping out into the cold, putrid air, Brigitte waited on her steps for the car. A notice had come from the Director of Imperial Theaters that transportation no longer would be provided. Madame Chikaskia had taken it upon herself to contract with the driver privately, and Innya and Brigitte split the fare.

Innya had failed to show up on their first day back riding together in September. Madame Chikaskia told Brigitte that Innya's father, a Jewish man, had been discovered without a permit to reside in Petrograd and been arrested, and the family ordered to leave the city. Innya's companion and protector, a merchant of the first class, failed to find her. "We both owe more." Madame Chikaskia said disgusted. For the past three days, though, despite being paid in advance, the driver had not shown up.

She waited fifteen minutes past the time for the car to arrive, then began walking. She would talk to Madame Chikaskia about another collaboration. In the meantime, the exercise would do her good.

Since the tsar had taken off for the front to command the army in its war with Germany, Petrograd felt neglected; the gilded and glorious statues and monuments tarnished and dirty, the onion domes covered in soot and ash, their bright colors dulled by the muted morning light. She walked with her arms hugging her body, her bag tucked inside her heavy wool coat. The pain in her feet, like a persistent headache, made her wish she'd waited. All the softness of the city seemed to have been lost with the name change; even the smooth cobblestones felt sharper through her boots.

She purposely ignored the city when she could, the beggars and ugly rabble. When she reached Zabalkansky Street, she lifted her head to carefully cross without being hit by an automobile, a horse, or a man.

Nikolai's distinctive gait caught her attention. She'd not laid eyes on him in years. He came towards her from the opposite direction. Held to her spot as if the pavers had taken possession of her boots, she became immobilized. Pedestrians flowed around her like water in a stream.

He advanced straight towards her, lifted his head, and jerked back.

He'd aged. His face longer, drawn, weathered, his eyes sinking into his head. His stern countenance broke her heart. He stood in front of her, looking like he couldn't make up his mind.

"Yolya," she said, her voice too quiet to be heard. Her legs weakened; she needed something to hold on to. Instinctively she reached out for his arm.

She'd spoken to Nikolai each day in her mind. This old stranger murdered him. This Nikolai had gone on with his life and forsaken her.

Nikolai tipped his hat, advanced a few steps away from her, then turned suddenly and came back to stand beside her. His mouth moved as he chewed on the words. "I cannot," he said finally.

Brigitte put her hand up to her mouth, dropping her bag from underneath her coat. Nikolai reached down, picking it up for her. She received it, so badly wanting to touch him, hold on to him; never let him go.

He shook his head sadly, "I cannot," he said. In an instant, he vanished, taken in by the rush of people fighting to cross Zabalkansky Street.

She stumbled to the steps of an apartment, sitting on the bottom stair. Something inside of her unraveled, crumbled like the civilizations that disappeared overnight. Pompeii buried in molten rock. So much time had gone by, how had she not seen the ruin before? She sat, grasping for what was her life before she crossed the street, not wanting to bear witness to the final destruction being wrought within her body.

A man wearing rags sat on the top step. He put his hand on her shoulder. She closed her eyes, holding her breath, willing him to have a knife to cut her heart out.

"I'm an old soldier," the man said. "I see nothing but death in my sleep and in the faces of those who pass me by. I returned from the war to my village. My house burned down. My family scattered beyond reach." He spoke in a deep bass, like the great singer, Feodor Chaliapin. "I hear the rasping voice of the Dark One like a scolding mother pulling at my ears."

He sat beside her. "For the past three months, I have been looking for my family. Looking for a place to sleep. Food to eat. Work. Looking, always looking." He smiled at her; his teeth rotted. "Do you know what I find?"

She shook her head.

"Kindness. I cannot understand this. Someone gives me a crust of bread. Someone slips a few kopeks into my hand." He lifted his pant leg, pointing. "These boots are nearly new. A woman said her son had been killed. He had no more use for them. She wept and handed them to me."

Brigitte imagined Chana's mother holding out Zeev's boots to this man. The weight of her world collapsing held her as his captive audience.

"Death gnaws my bones. My last breath is written. I doubt I will see the New Year. But each day my spirit is freed and fed by acts of kindness."

He stood to kneel in front of her. "Before I went to war, I had no kindness in me. As a soldier, I killed with no kindness in me. How is it now, blessings are given to me? I am filled every day. Filled by kindness." He put one hand upon each of her boots. "May I bless you?" he said.

She nodded, dumbstruck, amazed as her feet became warm, then hot. She stared at the man, open-mouthed. His eyes were closed, his lips moving in prayer. Her feet felt as though they were awash in sparks.

Then his hands flew away as a police officer struck him with his baton, beating him back. He held his hands up to deflect the blows, but the old soldier smiled. "You will have no more trouble with your feet. That is over. When you need to know the way, just follow where they take you."

"Get moving before I arrest you for vagrancy," the policeman said, lifting his baton.

"He is not bothering me," Brigitte protested but the policeman ignored her, hitting the soldier across the shoulders.

"Move!" the policeman shouted.

In a single moment, the old soldier disappeared.

She had missed her first class. She would be fined. Her students were unorganized and lazy. The girl, Leyla, went so far as to sit in the corner, refusing to dance. Brigitte scarcely noticed. Her mind flit and fled like a butterfly across thoughts of Nikolai and the old soldier. Finally, during the last twenty minutes of her last class of the day, she demonstrated to the girls a small bit of choreography she had been trying to teach them. She found herself dancing. Her whole body resounding with joy.

JANUARY 1917

Brigitte had been home a short time from work, having walked in the fading light, feeling unsafe. Snow melted from Mark Reznik's felt boots onto her kitchen floor. In the dim gaslight, his shadow filled the room. His massive fur coat reached past his knees, giving him the appearance of a great bear. "I'm unable to come up with all the rent."

"Are you asking that I give something for nothing? What do you propose?" She intended to sound harsh but something about the softness of Mr. Reznik's expression foiled her.

He brightened. "Yes, a proposal."

The money seemed the least of her concerns. She'd stopped worrying about how she would feed herself when she was no longer teaching, and begun to think only of how she would make it through the week. The old soldier taught her this, and she could not imagine living a long life anymore, not in such a world.

"I have never asked you to provide any proof of having a permit to live in Petrograd, as a Jewish man, but I am hearing more about Akrona appearing at all hours of the day to arrest and evict Jews here illegally. Is there a possibility of this happening to you?"

He smiled calmly. "I have a permit."

Looking up at the tall man pained her neck. "Come sit for tea."

He took the *ushanka* off his head. Underneath he wore a *yamaka*. "It is cold. Tea would warm us both."

He sat at the table. Icicles in his beard thawed, turning to water droplets he wiped away with his hand. "Some repairs are needed," Mr. Reznik said, his voice cordial. "I do carpentry. Painting. I do it all."

She filled a teacup from the samovar, placed it on a saucer, then slid it across the table towards him. "That would be interesting if I had the funds for paint," she said. Seldom did she have anyone at her table for tea. She enjoyed the feeling of a strong man in her kitchen. She stayed always on alert, ready for whatever might come next, day or night. Having him here allowed her a moment to relax. If the house caught fire, he would put it out. If a madman broke through the door, he would subdue him. While he drank tea, she relaxed.

The negotiations were a formality. She would teach Chana because of her perfect turnout. The same reason she'd let the Rezniks stay.

"The pipes could use repair. The gas lamps cleaning," he said as he poured the tea from his cup into the saucer, filling it to the top, then lifting the saucer in his large hands and gracefully sipping.

"I have two broken lamps."

"In the spring we could do more. Plant a garden in the rear yard. Reglaze the windows."

She pondered his suggestions. "I have no sugar for your tea. I imagine you are used to sweetness."

His eyes crinkled at the corners; He shook his head "Sugar. What fond memories I have of sugar."

"Would Zeev walk behind me in the evening when I return from the work?" she said.

He raised a brow. "Are you not delivered each evening in a car?"

"The tsar may still have sugar for his tea, but not cars for his teachers." As soon as she heard her words spoken aloud, she bit her lip. She lowered her head and glanced up to gauge his reaction. "I do not mind walking in the morning, though it is dark, the sun is not far behind me. The rabble-rousers have gone to bed. In the evening, I wish to feel safer."

He smiled. "Protection."

Brigitte nodded. "He must not walk with me. He is too much of a troublemaker. I should not like to find myself begging for food in Siberia for the crime of being mistaken for a conspirator."

His expression did not change as she spoke ill of his grandson.

"I would have him walk behind me, or across the street."

He filled his saucer once again from the teacup, drinking without spilling a drop. "Zeev works evenings as a waiter, but he does not leave for work until after you get home. Fridays, he must be home before sundown for Shabbat. What will you do then?"

"Walk more quickly."

He put the empty saucer down, placing the teacup in its center. "I have a friend, a gentile who owes me a debt. He lives nearby. He will walk on Fridays. Mikhail is strong and fierce-looking. I trust him."

"Then we have an agreement."

His entire face broke out into a smile, yet his eyes held sadness. Chana's eyes were the same. She wondered if all Jews had eyes that could not hide their sorrow. Alfred Bekefy had the exact opposite look. She knew he had suffered loss, but his eyes held no trace of it.

"Where were you born, Mr. Reznik?" she said. "I know nothing about you."

"In Vilna. My father was a doctor. He understood that grief can make a woman take to her bed. Drinking too much comes from a soul sickness. I learned much from him, including how to speak Russian." Looking sufficiently warmed up, Mr. Reznik worked his arms out of his coat, laying it over the back of his chair. He wore the dress of a Russian merchant, a well-tailored brown suit and tie. "He taught us that to survive in Russia, we must be prepared. He would say, 'We were slaves until, G-d be praised, he sent Moses to free our people. Now we are slaves to our fearful hearts. Feed the mind with knowledge, you will not be afraid. You will be free.'"

Brigitte tried to picture Mr. Reznik as a small boy but she could not see past his long, greying beard. "And your wife?"

"We all have sorrows. To know she is safe with G-d, freed from this world, comforts me. Tonya has been gone many years."

The sound of gunfire interrupted him. He stood, knocking over the chair burdened with the weight of his coat. He put his *Ushanka* back on his head, righted the chair, and grabbed his coat, in one swift motion.

"Lock the doors." He left through the back door. She locked it, then rushed to the front of the house.

Pulling the front window curtains closed, she peeked outside. In the middle of the street were three Cassock officers sitting astride their horses, wearing full-length dark-grey coats, and *papakhas* on their heads. A group of men stood before them, their hands up. Between the Cossacks and the men, lay a body. She looked for Zeev.

The Cossacks took turns shouting orders to drop their weapons and prepare to show their identification papers. The men hunched their shoulders, as though they could make themselves invisible.

One of the men made a run for it. A Cossack lifted his pistol in a smooth arc, shooting him in the back. The man dropped on the spot, motionless. Startled, Brigitte fell back.

Upstairs were muffled footfalls; the sound of Chana's mother, crying.

Another shot rang out. Then, shouting. Curiosity got the better of her. She peeked out from the corner of the window. Men scattered in all directions with the Cossacks shooting. Another man fell, as the rest escaped.

The sound of heavy boots running up the outside staircase to the Rezniks' apartment, then raised voices, and finally Mr. Reznik shushing them. The house, itself, felt as though it trembled with fear. Her newly hired protector brought danger to her doorstep.

The next evening, if Zeev kept the agreement to walk behind her, he also followed her order to be discrete. She never saw him. She let herself in the front door and locked it. She began to unbutton her coat when she heard a loud knock at the kitchen door. Leaving on her boots, she trailed melting snow through the parlor, the dining room, and into the kitchen.

Mr. Reznik pushed his way in the door, Chana in front of him. "Zeev has gone into hiding," he said, his voice urgent. "I have given him every kopek I have. *Baruch hashem,*" he said. "Thank G-d, Zeev is alive and not gunned down." Mr. Reznik pointed towards the front door, the street. "We are Jews, Madame Legher. Chana," he said. "She is not safe with us." He looked down at his granddaughter so lovingly. "She needs to be hidden until we can leave Petrograd. Leave Russia."

"Leave Russia?" Brigitte was shocked. "You are asking for me to conceal her? Here?"

Mr. Reznik nodded. "Pretend she is yours," he said. "Your daughter. Your niece. A foundling."

He told Chana to go sit in the other room until he called for her. Once the girl had closed the door to the kitchen, Mr. Reznik reached into his deep pocket and pulled out a bit of blue silk. Unwrapping the cloth, he held out a large brooch in the shape of a cross, inlaid with rubies. At the four corners were the double-headed eagles of the Romanov family, the Imperial insignia, gold, inlaid with diamonds. "It is the Order of the St. Alexander Nevsky," Mr. Reznik said.

He held it out for her to see, but she pushed his hand away. "Is this a valuable that one might assume is stolen?"

"It has been the most valuable possession in my family, besides our Torah, for over a hundred years."

"This medal was awarded?"

"To my great-great-grandfather. No one would believe that such a thing could wind up in a Jewish household. All these years passed from father to son with warnings. *The Guard of our Starvation* is the name my grandmother used." He wrapped it back up and pushed the bundle into her hands. "This is for Chana," he said. "If anything happens to the rest of the family, tell her when she is old enough, she should leave Russia. Sell it to buy herself a new life in a new country."

"Mr. Reznik," Brigitte said. "This is too serious for you to involve me." She handed back the dangerous treasure. "I am only your landlady." Her face flushed. "To presume I would care for one of your family members is absurd. You ask me to lie about who she is? And to leave the country? Have you no loyalty? No courage at all?" She expected he would at least have the humility to hang his head in shame. He surprised her.

"Madame Legher, it is not courage I lack, but the cold heart to see a young child harmed because of who she is. I am sorry to have troubled you. I made a mistake." He put the Order of St. Alexander Nevsky back in his pocket.

For the next three weeks, Chana did not come for lessons, nor did Mr. Reznik appear with rent. Brigitte heard their footsteps, but without Zeev's shouting, the noises were subdued. Each night, she tried to talk herself into going up the stairs outside her kitchen door to their apartment, demanding the rent and Chana's return to lessons. Then the samovar would boil. She would content herself with a cup of tea, not wanting to go out.

One morning she woke up to a house so cold she could see her breath. Shivering, she knocked on Mr. Reznik's door. His daughter answered. Brigitte had not been this close to her, and if Mr. Reznik had ever told her, she could not now recall the woman's name. Her face spoke of a young woman turned old by hardship and grief.

"I'm wondering if Mr. Reznik could help me to get the heat working," Brigitte said.

He came into view, Chana behind him. She saw their relief, realizing it was just her. Had they been expecting the Akrona? She'd seen no one but the family climb their stairs.

Chana's mother invited her inside what had once been Brigitte's bedroom, now used as a kitchen. A wood fire burned in a small brazier, a metal pipe ventilating the smoke out a boarded-up window. Despite their anxiousness, she felt a pang of longing for the comfort of living with family. Loneliness threatened to overwhelm her.

"Let me get my tools," Mr. Reznik said.

"You are welcome to wait here until the house is warmed," Chana's mother said, offering a chair near the stove. Brigitte accepted.

"I practice every day, Mlle. Legher," Chana said, coming to stand in front of Brigitte. She'd lost weight.

"You should resume your lessons." Brigitte's voice shook as she shivered.

Mr. Reznik put on his coat and grabbed his tools.

"I left the kitchen door unlocked," she said, not wanting to move from the warmth of the little stove. Mr. Reznik nodded.

"What is your name?" Brigitte asked. Chana's mother stood by the table in the place where Brigitte's dressing table had once been, cutting up bits of bread.

"Klara. We haven't much but…" Klara presented Brigitte with a small plate of breadcrumbs and a teaspoon of jam.

"I already had my morning tea, but your hospitality is appreciated." Klara handed the plate to Chana, who took it greedily.

"Have you heard from Zeev?" Brigitte said.

Klara turned her back to Brigitte, preparing another plate. "No. Nothing."

"I can show you what I've been practicing," Chana offered. She used the back of her chair as a barre and began her exercises.

Suddenly, Mr. Reznik appeared in the doorway that led to the hall and the room that used to be Nikolai's, red-faced and breathing hard. Brigitte was confused. She'd seen him leave the apartment. "The Akrona," he said in a loud whisper. "Chana, quickly." He waved for her.

"But how?" Brigitte said, open-mouthed.

Chana moved swiftly reaching for her coat and shoes. She went towards her grandfather. Klara snatched a large basket from underneath the table, handing it to him.

"Madame Legher, Chana requires a place to hide." He said it as a command.

"How?" she said.

"You will be less likely to get caught up in any of this if you are not here." Klara pulled her up by the hand, stepped behind her, and pushed Brigitte towards the door to the hallway. She followed him to what had once been her bathroom, now with a closet built against the far wall. The door to the closet stood open. The shelves held blankets and baskets, except for the bottom one. A large basket had been pulled out and sat in the middle of the floor. Inside the closet, the risers of the staircase were exposed. The carpenter had enclosed them when he had sealed off the second floor. Chana went down first, crawling into the closet, stepping into a hole in the floor to walk down the steps. Below, Chana crawled through a hole in the wall and disappeared into Brigitte's part of the house, into the *Chambre de Joie*.

Her home suddenly became like a strange dream where a hidden room is discovered.

Brigitte followed Chana, taking the basket that Klara handed her. Mr. Reznik closed the trap door. The only light in the old staircase came from below. She crouched to crawl through the wall, marveling that Mr. Reznik, large as he was, could fit. Once out into the room, she realized the opening was a panel in the wainscoting's trimmed squares, hiding the secret doorway.

Chana lifted the panel back into its place on the wall. Brigitte was amazed to hear a firm click as it closed.

"Who built this?" she said.

Chana answered by putting her finger to her lips, saying, "Shh." Taking the basket from Brigitte, Chana opened it, tossing a pair of her dance shoes onto the floor. She dragged the basket into the other room, hung her coat on the hook in the foyer, and put her street shoes on the mat next to Brigitte's boots. She rushed towards the chest of drawers in the dining room. Grabbing an armful of her clothes from the basket, she pushed them in on top of Brigitte's things. The last thing she pulled from the basket before stashing it away in a corner, was a doll. This she tossed, haphazardly, onto the sofa.

Brigitte picked up the little doll, not old, but well-loved. The Rezniks had prepared for this visit. Chana did her part expertly as if she had practiced.

She came to stand next to Brigitte, took her hand, and held it tightly. The room was still cold, but Brigitte knew that was not why Chana shook. Taking a blanket from the back of the sofa, she wrapped it around Chana.

"I'm to be called Anna. That is my Gentile name." Chana swallowed hard. "I am a niece belonging to your brother who died. *Dedushka* heard that you lost a brother."

"Sergei died long before you were born," Brigitte said.

Chana shivered but was undeterred. "Another one of your brothers, then," she said.

Brigitte stood and fetched Chana's coat, telling her to put it on. "It is time for me to leave for school. What did your grandfather tell you to do while I am at work?"

"He said I should follow you."

"I have not had my morning meal," Brigitte said. In the kitchen, she cut off a thick slice of bread and opened a jar of applesauce. Chana followed, wearing her coat. The Samovar hissed and bubbled, reminding Brigitte that she'd lit it before going up to see Mr. Reznik for help. "Tea?"

Chana nodded and sat down at the table. Glancing out the window, Brigitte saw two men climbing up the stairs to the Rezniks' apartment. They jumped when they heard the violent knocking on the door above them. Bursting into tears, Chana laid her head on the table. Brigitte came over and rubbed her back.

"I am to call you Aunt Brigitte," she whispered, her emotions making it difficult for her to speak. "If anything happens, I am not to go to them. Pretend it is the neighbors being arrested." She looked up at Brigitte. "Do you think they will be arrested?"

"Of course not. They will answer some questions. Then the men will leave them alone and you can go home."

The time passed for Brigitte to leave, but she was riveted by the shouts coming from upstairs. They heard Klara crying. Furniture being moved.

Brigitte seated herself at the table, taking Chana into her arms. She rocked her and sang her the song Nina sang to her children when they were tearful.

"Nannies three watch over you. Wind, sun, and eagle. The eagle flew home; the sun hid over the water; the wind, after three nights, comes racing to his mother."

If the Akrona had been watching, they would know she should be leaving now for work. "We must get going," Brigitte said. "Wash your face." Brigitte took a cloth from the shelf, wetted it with the water from the samovar. "Careful, it is hot. Put on your boots."

"I only have shoes," she said.

"No boots?"

Chana shook her head. "My feet are bigger."

"We will go get you boots. Put on your shoes, and then wait for me on the front steps."

With Chana outside, Brigitte collected her money from under the loose sill on the window next to her bed.

Upstairs the commotion continued, more shouting and crying. Brigitte cursed Zeev for what he wrought upon his family.

Outside she found Chana dancing. "Are your feet cold?" she said. Chana shook her head.

"I am practicing, Aunt Brigitte," she said, her voice cheerful, as if the Chana of just a few minutes ago was long gone. She hummed Tchaikovsky's *Song of the Lark*, slipping her hand into Brigitte's.

"You forgot your mittens, Chana," Brigitte said horrified. "We should go to get them."

For a moment Chana looked like a baby bird plucked too soon from her shell, but she calmed herself, and in a peculiar voice she said. "Anna, Aunt Brigitte. My name is Anna."

"Yes, Anna. Did you leave your mittens?"

"We gave them to our good neighbor, Auntie. He needed them before he went away."

Brigitte bit her lip, feeling trapped in a bizarre child's game of make-believe. "Chana, there is no one near us who can hear our conversation. You do not need to pretend."

"My good neighbor taught me that the more I am Anna, the more Anna I will be."

Brigitte could almost hear Mr. Reznik's voice coming from his granddaughter.

In the gallery above the dance studio, Chana rested her head on the railing, watching. The other girls ignored her so completely, Brigitte wondered if they didn't see her.

She prepared a story about a great-niece on Nina's side of the family hoping fewer people at the school remembered any details about the family. No one asked a single question, which relieved and troubled her.

After school they went to Gostiny Dvor for boots; Chana gawked at the salesman as he placed her foot inside a brand-new boot made of kid leather and lined with rabbit fur.

"How did that passageway into my apartment come to be?" Brigitte said to Chana, as they walked home.

Chana ran a few steps ahead and jumped into a snowdrift. "They are so warm," she said happily.

"Answer me."

Chana rejoined Brigitte on the sidewalk, again slipping her hand into Brigitte's. She had mittens pilfered from the school's lost-and-found. "Certain neighbors built it while you were away during the day. It took them no time at all. A certain beloved neighbor says, "If you are seen as a rat in the house, then it is prudent to have a hole to hide in."

They turned onto their street. There were lights in the upper-story windows. If the Akrona were watching for them, they were well hidden. Her thoughts shifted to the unresolved problem of her cold rooms. Once inside the house, she ordered Chana to light the samovar.

Chana left her boots and coat on, as it was still freezing. Brigitte made for the window sill to replace the money she still had. Chana screamed and came running.

"A man," she cried. A dark shadow loomed behind her.

"Good evening, Mlle. Legher," the man said as though he were the one who lived in her house. He turned up the gaslight in the parlor and became solid. She recognized him, but could not place from where? The Akrona were like that; faces frequently seen in public places. Another man sat on the sofa holding Chana's doll. He stood, bowing.

"We apologize for the intrusion," the second man said.

Chana wrapped her arms around Brigitte's waist burying her face. "You have terrified my niece and I," she scolded, finding courage by imagining she spoke to errant students. "I demand you leave at once."

The first Akrona officer took a step closer to them. "We have some questions first, concerning your tenants."

Bile rose in her throat. "Who are you?"

The man with the doll said, "I am Officer Sobetivich and this is Senior Lt. Dimivich."

Dimivich had thinning hair, an ungroomed mustache, and unruly eyebrows that dominated his forehead. She felt certain she'd met him before.

"I have influential friends. I should file a complaint about the way you have broken into my home. Count Leonid Verontsov, before his death, worked very closely with Tsar Nicholas. I am still close with many of his collogues."

"Who is the child?" Dimivich said.

"My niece. My brother travels frequently. His wife does not like children." She hesitated for only a moment. "Nikolai Legher."

"This is not your tenants' child?" Dimivich said menacingly.

"Nikolai's wife would like him to deny her. Anna's mother is dead."

Dimivich came towards her. He carried the mingled aromas of kerosene, wool, and the breath of a man with a sour stomach.

"Anna, go to the *Chambre de Joie*," she ordered. Chana whimpered but left the room. "The girl lives here. She knows nothing of her mother. I keep from her the details, and I do not intend to break my brother's confidence just because you bully your way into my home, waiting here in the dark, like thieves."

Sobetivich eyes were angry slits, his jaw tense.

"Legher?" Dimivich said softly. He smiled, coming closer. She backed up almost to the front door. "Nikolai Legher is brother to Sergei?"

She nodded not taking her eyes from him.

"You are Brigitte Gustoevna Legher." Dimivich said, smiling broadly.

She removed her scarf, setting it on the foyer table. She took off her gloves, set them on the scarf, then unbuttoned the first two buttons of her coat.

Dimivich said again, "Brigitte Gustoevna Legher." His face was bright, the furrow of his brow smoothed out across the wide plane of his forehead. "I used to go to the ballet just for you." His tone became consolatory. Sobetivich looked at him in confusion.

"Sergei Legher was a revolutionary," Sobetivich said still looking at Dimivich.

"Would it be possible for one of you to go down and get the boiler working? It is freezing," she said coming forward from the foyer, towards Sobetivich.

Dimivich halted her progress by putting his hand on her chest. "I miss watching you dance. Sobetivich, go down and see to the heat."

"I am not a repairman," he protested, but when Dimivich waved his hand towards the kitchen, Sobetivich let his shoulders sag.

"The cellar door is…" Brigitte said.

"I know where the door is," he spat. "I know every corner of your house, every hiding place." He watched her, his eyes squinting. Then he blinked, grunted, and descended to the basement.

She did not waste a moment, turning her body in a subtle twist that Madame Vazeem had taught her, becoming an open invitation. Dimivich responded by touching her cheek and sliding his finger to her ear.

"You have a beautiful face," he said.

"Tell me your first name again." She would have normally put her hand on top of his and caressed it, but her fingers were cold; she feared it would distract him. Instead, she put her hand on his chest and applied gentle pressure.

"Andrei." His breathing became shallow.

"Once it is warmer in here, Andrei," she said his name softly, "perhaps you can send your friend on his way. You would enjoy a private performance?" He slid his hand down to her shoulder in a caress. She tilted her head. "Powerful men have always been my favorite audience."

He made a low sound in his throat. "Can you still lift your leg as high as you did all those years ago?"

"High enough. If I have the right leverage." She'd answered similar questions years ago from similarly tempered men.

He licked his lips, leaning in. "You smell good."

"You seem familiar. Did you used to wait outside the stage door?"

"The meeting you are straining to remember was at the Bear's Inn. I bought you champagne." He took her hand, kissing it.

"I wish I remembered," she said. She did remember. Vividly. As she now remembered the sound of the actress calling for help on Nevsky Prospekt.

"I have never forgotten," he said. "First, we can go to your brother. He can take the girl. Then you show me how you still lift your leg so high." His cold hand snaked inside of her coat, moving through the layers of sweaters until he reached her bare skin.

She'd not had her breast touched in years; though it repelled her, she felt the return of her power. She'd given her body to disgusting men before. He squeezed her nipple hard, and she winced. Then, deciding she had given him enough of a taste of delights to come, she twisted away from him, clasping his hand to pull it out of her clothing. He did not let go but squeezed harder.

"You are hurting me," she said angrily. She held his wrist with both of her hands and he relinquished, a smile on his lips. "I will not dance for you," she said pouting. "You do not appeal to me."

"If you are telling the truth about the girl, and your brother claims her, then perhaps you will let me show you how appealing I can be?" He went to the sofa, picking up Chana's doll. "But if you are lying, trying to protect a stinking *zhidovka* baby," his mouth straightened into a smirk, "I doubt it will matter much to you if I am appealing. Nothing in your future will be appealing."

He came at her in a rush and grabbed her around the waist, kissing her roughly. "Of course," he said releasing her by pushing her backward. "You could tell me the truth now and save me the trouble of looking for your brother. We take the girl away and then you and I can become good friends. I could be your new protector. There are many dangers in Petrograd. I could keep you safe."

She steadied herself and smoothed her hair. "I am not a plaything any more, Andrei," she said. Brigitte walked into her parlor and sat on the sofa. She crossed her ankles. "Do you have a cigarette?"

"Hoping to calm your nerves?"

"Two men have broken into my home, threatened me, and threaten to take away my niece. One of those men is handsome and admires me. If you were a woman, would you be anxious?" She poked the tip of her tongue between her lips, another flirtation on which Madame Vazeem had given her instruction.

She took the cigarette he offered, allowing him to hold the lit match. "You are not as charming now as you were the last time we met."

Sobetivich returned to the room. "Fixed." He looked at Dimivich, then at Brigitte as though trying to read them.

She ran her hand over her breast, inhaling deeply, sighing aloud. Sobetivich would see a woman who had been treated like a lover. Perhaps a rift would divide the two men. The divide would be enough space for her to wriggle away.

"Go find Nikolai Legher. Bring him here," Dimivich ordered Sobetivich.

"You think I know where he is?" Sobetivich complained.

"Have you arrested my tenants for something?"

"The Rezniks have a permit to live in the city. But if it were me, I would throw them out on the street tonight."

Brigitte wanted to cry with relief. She held Sobetivich's gaze, trying to read his thoughts by the light in his eyes, as he was probably trying to do with her. "When you have spoken to Nikolai, you will want to get him away from his wife if you want him to speak truthfully."

"Where does he live?" Sobetivich said.

"I have no idea. Not since he married his child bride and left Anna with me. She dictates how he lives his life. A life that does not include me or Anna." Brigitte filled her words with the pain and hurt she'd felt since Nikolai had cut her off. Her voice broke, unintentionally, but she saw that it affected Dimivich and he believed her.

When they left, she allowed herself a single sob, a release of fear and disgust. Chana rushed into Brigitte's arms when the front door slammed shut.

Chana cried, "Are they going to kill me? Zeev said they would come and shoot us."

"Zeev is wrong," Brigitte said wiping a tear. She buttoned her coat back up. "We need to find Nikolai."

"Can I go upstairs first?"

"No. We must hurry. I'm not sure if I even know where he lives. I have heard rumors. If I am wrong, then it will take us a little longer to track him down."

They hesitated a moment at the door to see if the Akrona were watching. She checked the windows in the buildings across the street for prying eyes. At the first chance, she waved down a car for hire.

She gave the driver the address Bekefy had mentioned, and though the fare cost her dearly, they arrived within fifteen minutes.

 Getting out on the street, they stared up at the rundown building. She had no idea what floor, much less which apartment. Chana took the lead, opening the heavy door. "Look, Aunt Brigitte," she said. "There are names listed on a board."

Nikolai and Natasha Legher were on the fifth floor. Brigitte rushed up the stairs pulling Chana along. Out of breath, and with her heart pounding from the exercise, as well as fear of Nikolai's rejection, she knocked on his door. The woman who opened the door was tall and slim. She wore her hair short like a man and held a cigarette in one hand. Brigitte had never seen Natasha, except on posters. She expected her to be much prettier. This woman was young but quite plain.

"What do you want?" Natasha said, her voice unwelcoming.

"I am Brigitte Gustoevna Legher. I must speak to Nikolai." She looked around at the ramshackle room. Everything inside was old, patched, worn. Brigitte pushed her way inside.

"You cannot just barge in here," Natasha said grabbing at her.

"Is Nikolai here?" she said loudly. Before Natasha could answer, Nikolai came through a doorway and stopped to regard her.

"Hello, Yolya." Her legs began to shake, her heart hurting.

"Brigitte," he said. Pointing to Chana, "Who is this?"

Chana looked on the verge of tears, as if her resources for inner comfort were running out.

"This is Anna," she said. "We need your help. I am sorry to involve you but the Akrona, they are coming here to ask you about her."

"What do I know of her?"

"You must know everything about her. You must tell them she is your daughter. You must say she is your daughter with Svetlana Sharapova."

He frowned. Brigitte forged ahead. "They won't be able to corroborate the story because Svetlana is dead. From the rumors, she died in childbirth." Holding up his hands to stop her, Nikolai said, "Of all the preposterous things."

Natasha reached over to Chana, pulling her by the coat, her hands like vicious claws. "You two need to leave. Your sister is an insane woman, Nikolai. You said you had a good reason for not speaking to her. I see now for myself."

Brigitte moved to Chana's side, wrenching Natasha's hand off her sleeve. "The Akrona will send this little girl to her death if you do not tell them she is yours. Tell them you sent her to me because Natasha does not like children. I could offer her a more stable life since I do not travel. Tell them we do not speak, but the girl is yours. Please, Nikolai, you must do this to save her life, and now mine. If they learn I have lied to them, I will be arrested."

Natasha reached to grab Chana again.

"Leave her alone, Tasha," Nikolai intervened. "What trouble have you gotten into, Brigitte?"

"She has a perfect turnout, Yolya. So much talent and promise. She could be a prima ballerina absoluta, but not if she never gets to grow up." Brigitte pulled Chana around so she stood in front of her and held onto the girl's shoulders. "Show him your turnout," she ordered.

"Whose child is this?" he said, watching Chana's feet splay out.

"I cannot tell you. She sleeps in your room. You should see her dance." Brigitte held his gaze, and all her love for him rose inside.

How could she have let him push her away? He had been her strength, her protection, her champion. How had she survived without him? He stood before her as one just out of reach; one who could belong to her again or shatter her once more.

"You come here after all this time with a foundling I know nothing of, nor care about?" He turned his back and walked toward the window, the curtain dusty and torn.

"The girl's grandfather told the Akrona that she is my niece, that she is my brother's child. He knew I had a brother who died. He did not know that happened long before Anna's birth. That means she can only be yours. The Akrona came to my house tonight and they are coming here next."

He whirled around to look at her. Natasha cried, "The Akrona are coming?"

Nikolai's face was contorted with fury. "Was it not enough that you had a hand in Sergei's death? Now you want to see me in harm's way as well?"

She held her hands out to him. He stepped back. Determined, she went to him, wrapping her arms around him and holding him tightly. "I wish you no harm. I wish no one harm. I wish Sergei was still alive. That all of my crimes could be undone, and Sergei was not dead. I died with him. You know that is true. How else could you have found a way to live without me?" Her sobs threatened to choke her words but she could not stop. "Nikolai, help us. If you tell them I have lied, I will be arrested. Sergei would tell you to help me. You know he loved me. He loved me, Nikolai." She gasped for air. "And you loved him."

He brushed away a tear on his cheek.

"Tell me you will help us," she begged.

"He won't lie for you" Natasha snapped. "We have a show to do. You have to leave. How dare you upset him before a performance." She yanked Brigitte away from Nikolai.

Brigitte let herself be pushed towards the door. "Please. Gustave and Nina saved me. Help me save Anna. Be like Mama. Like Papa."

Natasha opened the door. "Out."

Brigitte's mind raced to what she could do next. All she could think of was to flee the city.

Chana's voice interrupted her planning. "It will be all right, Aunt Brigitte," she said softly. Chana approached Nikolai. "I'm Mlle. Legher's student. She teaches me, and all the time she is saying, 'If you were a student of my brother, Nikolai, he would lift your arm, like this." She lifted her arm and positioned her hands in a graceful wave. "When Mlle. Legher first evaluated me, I heard her saying to herself that you would find my turnout a good one. I think she did not even know she said it out loud. Now that I see you, I know that when I am in my lesson, you are there, too."

Nikolai looked at Chana as if she were a small animal given the miraculous ability to speak. "What is your name?" he said.

"To the Akrona, my name is Anna Nina Nickolaiyevna Legher."

"What is your real name?"

"It is best you do not know, Master Legher." She reached up on tiptoe and whispered in his ear. A smile broke across his face, and he laughed. Chana grinned.

"Tell me what our story is, Anna Nina Nickolaiyevna Legher," he said sitting down on a worn upholstered chair.

Chana stood in front of him, as Natasha shut the door in defeat. Chana said, "First of all, your wife does not like me very much. That is why I do not live with you."

His smile broadened. Brigitte put her hand to her mouth, pressing her lips against her teeth as though she could hold in her emotions, and relief washed over her.

"I'm eight years old. I was born on August 16, 1908. I am smart. I do not know my mother because she died when I was born. She was not your wife. Natasha doesn't like me."

Nikolai looked at Brigitte. "Clever to choose Svetlana. She had no family."

Brigitte nodded. "Yes, I know, and she was very pretty. You would have made a nice couple."

Natasha scoffed and left the room. Nikolai returned his full attention to Chana and she continued their story.

"Aunt Brigitte took me. She does not like your wife, so you two do not speak anymore." Chana finished and paused a moment, then hugged Nikolai. He patted her on the back.

"You will have to dance for me someday," he said.

"We should go," Brigitte said softly to Chana, holding out her hand. "We cannot be discovered here." She reached out to touch Nikolai but a shadow flashed across his face, and she let her hand fall. "Thank you," Brigitte said, her words thick in her throat.

At the door, Brigitte said, "The Akrona officers are imbeciles. I hope you will not be troubled by them." She leaned in towards him. "If one named Dimivich comes, tell him that I have syphilis, would you?"

He looked surprised. "Are you okay?"

She nodded and this time she did reach out to touch him; she stroked his cheek, grieving fully how empty her life had become since Sergei died.

He opened the door and she and Chana slipped out into the hallway. She took one more look at Nikolai before he closed the door.

Back on her own street, she could see a dim light through the closed curtains of the Rezniks' apartment. Chana asked to go there, but Brigitte shook her head. Once inside the kitchen, warm now that the boiler had been fixed, Brigitte and Chana did a thorough inspection to make certain there were no more uninvited guests.

Together they went from the kitchen to the dining room to the parlor and finally to the *Chambre de Joie*. Brigitte took the two straight-back chairs from the kitchen and shoved one under the knob of the front door and the other under the knob of the kitchen door. She did not know how Dimivich and Sobetivich had gotten inside earlier but hoped they wouldn't return while she was home.

She turned out all the lights and then told Chana to use the hidden passage to go up and see her family.

Holding vigil, Brigitte moved back and forth from the window in the front of her house to the kitchen window at the back, watching for movement, but there was none except for leaves and trash tossed about by the frigid wind. Her mind raced through all that had happened since the morning. Nikolai. How tired he looked. He hadn't seemed well. Compared to Natasha, Brigitte had a new appreciation for Nikolai's first two wives. If not for Natasha, Nikolai would still be dancing at the Mariinsky Theater, carrying on in the tradition of Christian Johansson, Pavel Gerdt, and Marius Petipa. Not wasting his talents at the Narodny Dom.

She thought of what he'd been wearing. Wool britches with both knees patched, a grey wool sweater with holes under the arms. Natasha, on the other hand, wore a fine silk dress. Nikolai had needed Brigitte's protection all these years, as much as she had needed his.

She heard movement behind her. Mr. Reznik stood with Chana as two dark shadows. She pulled the curtain closed. Mr. Reznik lowered his head and put his hands together as though to pray.

"Madame, forgive me. Please accept my deep gratitude." In the dimness of the room, he looked smaller. If she did not know his voice, she might believe he was not the same man whom she'd sought out that morning for help.

"Chana will stay here with me, now," she told him.

The shadow shape of Mr. Reznik's head nodded. "Yes, that is safest for us all." Chana left his side and went to sit on the sofa, picking up her doll and holding it to her chest. Mr. Reznik said, "I think it best that you tell the Akrona you evicted us. We will find other lodgings."

"Where will you go?" she asked.

"G-d will provide. Can Chana stay with you until we prepare to leave Russia? I will pay you, as I can, for her provisions."

Brigitte nodded.

She stepped back towards the window and peeked out to the street. "You should go now. Chana, say goodnight to your grandfather."

Chana obeyed by jumping up onto the sofa, walking across the cushions, and leaning forwards toward Mr. Reznik, who caught her and held her in a tight embrace.

"Do not cry, *Dedushka*," Chana said. "I am just downstairs. Now I am a proper Russian girl, I am safe."

"*Laila tov*," Mr. Reznik said, kissing her forehead. "Sleep well, *Neshemele*."

With both of her hands, Chana gently pulled his head down by the ears and kissed his forehead.

In the middle of the night, Brigitte rose and tiptoed to the sofa where Chana gently snored. She went again to the windows as she'd already done several times since tucking Chana under her blankets. The night offered nothing but the disquiet of her worries. Yet, her heart felt stronger from the single moment she touched Nikolai's face.

FEBRUARY 1917

The Rezniks moved out, finding a room at the Jewish almshouse on Liniya Street across from the Neva River in the Vassievsky Ostrov District.

Brigitte had enough money to feed Chana; this didn't concern her. She worried about finding food to buy. The merchant who made her favorite fish soup had not set up his stall in the market for weeks. Bakeries closed earlier every day, posting SOLD OUT signs in the windows. At the midday meal served at school, she began slipping bread and a bit of boiled meat and potatoes into her bag.

Friday night, after the Rezniks moved, Chana asked if they could light candles for the Sabbath. "We do not know when the Akrona might come back," Brigitte answered. "How will you explain celebrating Sabbath?"

Chana tilted her head in thought, a gesture that Brigitte found endearing. "Candles are cheaper than the fuel for the lamps."

Brigitte brought plates to the kitchen table. Chana brought two white candles in silver holders. She struck a match, lighting them. Then she put her hands over her eyes. *"Barukh atah Adonai Eloheinu, melekh ha'olam, asher kid'shanu b'mitzvotav v'tzivam l'hadlik ner shel Shabbat."*

The musical words soothed Brigitte.

"It is for the mother to bless the child of the house," Chana instructed. "Bless me."

Her commanding manner amused Brigitte. "I ask G-d to bless you," she said.

Chana shook her head. "Say, 'May G-d make you like Sarah, Rebecca, Rachel, and Leah.' They are good women in the Torah. Ask G-d to make me strong and righteous so I grow up to be a good woman, like them and you."

Brigitte burst out laughing. Chana scowled, sobering Brigitte. "May G-d make you like Sarah, Rebecca and Rachel, and Leah."

"Now say, 'G-d bless you and protect you. May G-d's face shine toward you and show you favor. May G-d look favorably upon you and grant you peace.'"

As Brigitte repeated the words, she felt a settling, as if a piece of her soul slipped back into place after a lifetime of misfitted vexation.

The Rezniks were to visit the next day if they could. Chana brought a chair to the window. After a while she would rise, going to the kitchen to look out the window there. "Where are they?"

She complained so often, Brigitte finally scolded her and made her sit on the sofa.

By late afternoon, Brigitte left to find food for the week. When she returned, Chana came rushing out of the kitchen and hugged Brigitte around the waist. Brigitte kissed the girl on the cheek.

"Nikolai Gustovich was here. But not *Dedushka* or *Muter*."

"Nikolai came here?" Her heart leapt up. "What did he say?"

"He said the Akrona are following him, so he decided he should act his part. I like him as my father," she added. "He left you this." She handed Brigitte a letter.

She opened it hungrily.

To whom it may concern,
My daughter, Anna Nina Nickolaiyevna Legher, lives with my sister,
Brigitte Gustoevna Legher whom I have chosen to be her guardian.
With this letter, I confirm that I am the child's father. Nickolai
Gustovich Legher

Brigitte put the letter in her pocket. Though happy to have proof to show the Akrona, should they return, she had hoped for more. For him to ask her back into his life. For him to ask for his old room back because he needed a place to escape his wife.

"Let's make our meal." Brigitte showed Chana a bright red tomato from the basket. The old Jewish woman still grew them in the winter.

CHAPTER 23

Petrograd, February 1917

Two days later when Chana and Brigitte returned to the house in the evening, Chana discovered a note from her grandfather hidden underneath her doll's skirt. Mr. Reznik had retained his key to the apartment.

"He says they were watched on Sunday. This is why they did not come." Chana smiled with relief. "He left money." She handed Brigitte three rubles.

The money troubled Brigitte. The sooner the Rezniks saved enough, they could take Chana, and Brigitte could be relieved of the fear only the girl's mother should bear.

"*Dedushka* says we should meet them at Ostrovskovo Square, Sunday at 11 o'clock." Chana frowned. "That's so long from now."

Thursday morning, the first fingers of sunlight streamed sideways into the kitchen window. After weeks of leaving the house in darkness, the light at half past eight felt like a sacred gift from a benevolent god. Chana held Brigitte's hand as they walked together to the electric tram, a mode of transportation Brigitte resisted, fearing electrocution. The horse-drawn carriages were far fewer now. Many horses had starved to death.

With the tram overcrowded, Chana sat on Brigitte's lap, though with her long legs, she was nearly as tall as Brigitte. Chana's body heat staved off the bitter winter cold. They left the tram and walked to the day school where Chana had enrolled. She kissed Brigitte's cheek and disappeared inside.

Despite Brigitte's severest criticism, her students seemed to have forgotten their left from right. Brigitte gave up before the class concluded, sending them all to the floor for stretches.

At the midday meal, she put the boiled potatoes in her bag. Madame Chikaskia, who had become noticeably thinner, her cheeks caving, gave Brigitte an unreadable look. She too took her potatoes, tucking them in a bag. "Do you want your bread?" she asked taking it off of Brigitte's plate. Brigitte snatched it back. "I have grandchildren to feed," Madame Chikaskia pleaded. "You are alone."

"I am caring for my niece."

Madame Chikaskia eyed her suspiciously. "You are a liar," she said, her eyes glittering.

In her afternoon class, the pianist, Mr. Mokorov, arrived before her and sat sullen, reading a newspaper. A few moments later the girls shuffled in. Brigitte's hopes that the morning classes had been an anomaly fluttered to the floor. Once they were all lined up at the barre, Mr. Mokorov began to play the music, as Brigitte counted out loud and called out the positions.

The sound of shouting out on the street could be heard over the piano. Garbled slogans mixed with single words. *Down. Tsar. Bread.*

Leyla spoke without permission. "They are saying 'give us bread.'" She went to the window, followed by the rest of the girls.

Brigitte pounded her stick against the floorboards, bellowing for them to remember themselves.

Mr. Mokorov struck a succession of wrong notes, craning his neck to see outside. "It is a demonstration, Mr. Mokorov," Brigitte chastised. "This is not new entertainment." Consternation laced her words. "If you are worried about missing the performance below, there will be another a block away this weekend. You may watch on your own time."

The shouting outside grew even louder. Angry chants of "Give us bread" competed with the plinking of the piano, Brigitte's voice, and the scuffling sounds of the little girls' ballet slippers.

For the remainder of the day, her students were distracted by the noises of the demonstration happening on Nevsky Prospekt. The walls of the school, ever a fortress, now seemed porous, as angry voices penetrated the steady beats and counted tempos.

The next morning, the sound of the gramophone in the *Chambre de Joie* roused Brigitte. Chana often woke first to begin morning exercises. Even though the sky had yet to welcome the sun, the day held a promise of something fresh, a compelling optimism. Had she had a good dream, Brigitte wondered, that put her in such a bright mood? She could not resist the urge to dance.

Chana played the Rimsky Korsakov record. Going to the center of the room, Brigitte began moving freely in her nightgown, like Isadora Duncan. Her entire body felt liquid. Chana twirled around Brigitte; twirling and twirling; she started to giggle, adding fresh notes to the melody.

Spontaneously, the dancers reached out to one another, their fingertips meeting, but they did not clasp hands. Carried by the currents of sound, from one end of the room to the other, flowing, ebbing, touching, letting go, they spoke in a shared language.

The record finished. They fell to the floor with Chana resting her head against Brigitte's narrow shoulder. "I love you, Auntie," she said tilting her head up to kiss her on the chin.

"You will be prima ballerina absoluta one day," was Brigitte's response.

The tram did not come at its usual time. A man with a pockmarked face and sinister eyes growled at them, "No rides today. You don't want to go down that direction." His voice sounded like deep church bells clanging out a warning. "Trouble yesterday. More trouble today."

Petrograd always had trouble somewhere. Storms, blizzards, floods and violent men made up the shades of grey in Petrograd's stone blocks and gilded trim.

"A walk in the sunshine will do us good. We'll be late, though. Come, quickly."

A small brigade of Cossacks armed with shashkas rode by on horses. Chana stared up at them in their fine uniforms.

"Keep your eyes down," Brigitte said in a hushed voice. One of the soldiers smiled, and Chana waved at him. Brigitte grabbed her hand and held it. Petrograd seemed a difficult enough place to keep one's self intact. How would she ever keep Chana safe? Leaving Chana at her school brought a reprieve from the constant vigilance of spotting danger before it stole the girl away.

When Brigitte had nearly reached Theater Street, she saw again the Cossacks. Passing by the Lomonosov Bridge and the snow-covered bust of Lomonosov, by himself in his little square, she felt the tension in the crowd. Men, women, and children walked towards Nevsky Prospekt, like spectators on their way to a parade. The ringing notes of a speechmaker created a hum behind the percussion of the horses' hooves, muffled by the compacted snow and ice.

The air in the school held a new scent that morning as if the noise and commotion a block away rattled loose the old dust and perfume that had long clung to the tops of windows and rafters, finely sifting through the thin winter's light. Some of her students were missing from class, and at the mid-day meal, many of the teachers and staff were absent.

"Strikes and riots make empty classrooms," said a thin pencil of a man, the mathematics teacher. She had never once heard him speak. He sat at the furthest end of her table and did not look up from his plate.

"There have been strikes for months," Brigitte said. "Why should our students be involved?"

He looked up at her, his expression filled with condescension, reminding Brigitte why she had so loathed mathematics and mathematics instructors. "The crowds are out of hand. We are losing a war. The tsar has turned over the running of the country to a German whore and a mad monk, who is now thankfully dead." He curled his hand into a tight fist, putting it on the table beside his plate. "Have you noticed there are fewer chairs in the school? Where do you think they have gone? You may think the chairs have been sent out for refurbishment. Each day there are bodies of those who have starved to death in the night lying in the street. But perhaps our tsar has decided it is time to polish the chairs my students sit upon."

Brigitte felt chastised and culpable. She dropped her gaze to the boiled potato and cabbage, a thin slice of beef.

"Those chairs have become firewood. Have you noticed the tree stumps? Have you seen the queues of people lined up in the dark and cold of the night in front of bakeries?" He sneered at her. "You live your whole life as the privileged prostitute to our Little Father Russia, with no concern about the feeding of your family, or your son being sent to the front before his sixteenth birthday. You wonder where everyone is? You wonder why they do not come to class? They are hungry. They are dead!"

He stood and picked up his plate, hatred for her in his large, bespectacled eyes. He pushed back his chair, which scrapped loudly across the floor, caught on a board, and fell backward with a bang that caused the few others in the room to jump.

If he were alive, Brigitte would have gone that moment to see Leonid, to rest her cheek against his fine white shirt and smell the power of his protection. Then she thought of Sergei and how she had never again felt safe once she'd given her heart to him. She rubbed her eyes, her grief swelling into a crashing wave.

Those left in the dining room emptied their meals into oilcloths and bags. There had been no fuel delivery for a long while. She'd been keeping the heat low, but now the boiler had gone out completely. That evening in the cold kitchen, Chana retold stories she'd heard from her classmates. She cataloged the mothers, fathers, and brothers who had been injured during demonstrations. Thankfully, she did not mention a single death. Brigitte wondered if this was because none had died, or if the students who had such a story to tell were not in school. Chana shivered as she talked, despite wearing her coat.

The Rezniks left their brazier in the apartment above. Brigitte halted Chana's chatter about the police attacks and told her to get a lamp and light it. "We are going upstairs," she stated.

"Do you hear something?" Chana rushed from her chair. "Do you think *Dedushka* is here?"

"No, but he left us a way to get warm."

Blankets and pillows were more easily transported up, than the brazier down. She wished she had one of the chairs the mathematics teacher spoke of. She had only her furniture. "What did your grandfather use to chop wood?"

"His hatchet. He left it in the passageway." She dashed out of the room, coming back with it. "*Dedushka* said I should aim for the head if the Akrona caught me hiding there. He said a man of split mind is easily escaped."

Brigitte shuddered at the thought of sweet child, like Chana, needing to defend herself in such a brutal fashion.

"There is more in the passageway. Muter left us a basket. Should I fetch it?"

Brigitte nodded absent-mindedly. Chana came back holding a laundry basket filled with crackers, jars of applesauce, and dried fruit and nuts. Letting out a deep sigh, Brigitte felt tears sting her eyes. At that moment it hit her just how bad things had gotten, and she was not prepared. No Gustave or Nikolai or Leonid. Just her. And she was responsible for the life of a child.

"Tuck that away until we need it," Brigitte instructed.

Within the hour Brigitte's old bedroom began to warm up. She'd brought up the samovar and made them tea. Chana lit two candles and covered her eyes with the palms of her hands. The sun had set on that Friday evening. The Sabbath began.

All of Saturday they stayed near the stove. Chana played with her doll. Once Brigitte ventured down to her part of the house for firewood. She selected the wood from the telephone box. Her service had been cut off when Leonid left her. As she began to chop it with the hatchet, her normally quiet street seemed full of sound, voices. Leaving the wood for a moment she cracked open the front door, peeking through. Smoke rose in the sky from a different part of the city than where the factories were. A building on fire? A crowd, men and women walked as a group carrying shovels, hoes, sticks.

Two automobiles sped from opposite directions, both veering crazily. They swerved to avoid one another, causing one of the cars to careen toward her house, crashing into a thick tree stump. A boy flew out of the car and lay motionless on the boulevard. Four other boys, no more than twelve, poured out and ran.

A woman carrying a creamy white muff approached the boy and rifled through his pockets. She took his boots, then casually strolled away.

Brigitte closed the door, then went to the windowsill and pried up the loose board reaching in for the money kept there in a beaded purse that Leonid had given to her. The purse, itself, was valuable; perhaps worth more than the sum it held. She tied a ribbon around the clasp and tied the ribbon to her waistband, tucking the purse into her corset. From a drawer in the wardrobe, she took her documents. She pulled down her satchel from the top shelf and began filling it with both her and Chana's clothing. Fetching the sewing kit and her jewel case, she made her way back up to the bedroom where Chana slept in a nest of blankets.

Back in her old bedroom, she wished Nikolai would come to wake her up from a nightmare and tell her of his misadventures. As the light of the day faded behind smoke and clouds, Brigitte stayed busy sewing the last of her jewels from Leonid into the lining of her and Chana's coats.

The sounds of a city in a battle with itself went on through the night. Brigitte rocked Chana in her arms and told her folktales of Baba Yaga and *Marya Morevna*, the warrior queen. Chana reminded Brigitte three times before she fell asleep that on the morrow, they were to go to Ostrovskovo Square.

"The world has gone mad outside. Best to let the crazy ones wear themselves out, first. Perhaps next week."

When she woke in the morning, winter had again gained entrance inside. Her thoughts went first to what she might chop up for a fire. The table in the hallway?

"Chana," she rolled over to wake her. Chana was not there. She called her name again. Sitting up, listening. The house was quiet. The streets were quiet. The stove and the samovar were silent. "Chana, are you downstairs?" She rose, moving towards the bathroom and the secret passageway.

Chana's coat was not on the floor where Brigitte had finished with it the night before. Neither was Chana's doll in the place where the girl had slept with it tucked under her arm.

Brigitte threw on her coat and boots and rushed out the door, stealing a precious second to lock it behind her. The people out on the streets were her mirrors, terror-stricken men and women searching for loved ones. Calling out names, eyes frantic, filled with fading hope. Three men wheeled a cart loaded with bodies. Street by street, windows had been smashed, stores looted, shelves emptied.

When the church bells began to peel, she wished she could hear them as she did a samovar, a sound of comfort. The bombastic ringing mocked the destruction below the church's tower.

Some of the streets were barricaded with burning automobiles and debris. Would Chana be lost on her way to Nevsky Prospekt? To Ostrovskovo Square? Perhaps she would give up and return home.

She reached Sadavaya Street before she found clear passage to turn towards Nevsky Prospekt. Sunlight glinted off the crosses of St. Nicholas Cathedral's golden domes. A portion of the crowd was turning into the church. Brigitte searched among them for any signs of Chana, not expecting to see her there. Chana would not pray to the Orthodox god.

A young man drove by in a delivery van. He passed Brigitte, then slowed and stopped. Leaning out of the window, he shouted, "Mother, let us give you a ride."

Her distrust gave way to her desperation. She climbed into the passenger seat vacated by another young man, who crawled into the back, then leaned close to her shoulder.

"Nevsky Prospect," she told the driver.

He shook his head. "That whole street is set up like an encampment. We can get you as far as the Apraksin Market."

"I did not dare venture out yesterday. What has happened?" she said.

"The Cossacks and soldiers are deserting. Fighting with the people, now. The pharaohs are holding on and some soldiers, too. They say the tsar is on his way from the front. If he makes it to Petrograd, we will kill him and his German wife."

As he spoke, he reached over and patted her knee. By the look on his face, she saw he felt the pieces of jewelry sewn into the hem of her coat. His gloves were red with dried blood.

"You will pay for your ride, Mother?" he said, his face contorting now from the young fresh-faced student into a devil.

"Let me off here."

He swerved to avoid hitting a woman bent over a man's body lying dead in the street. The woman keened, lost to the world around her, having no recognition of how very nearly she'd been killed herself. Brigitte was thrown against the driver and held onto his arm to keep her seat. He lifted his hand from her leg, laying on the horn.

A cacophony of wailing, shouting and church bells blasted all around her, a desperate alarm.

"Let me out," Brigitte demanded.

"Your knife, Yuri," the driver said reaching behind him. Yuri handed it to him. The driver used it to slice the hem of her coat, steering with one hand, the van swerving precariously. Her jewels poured out onto the floor. Yuri dove forward to catch what spilled, pushing Brigitte to the side. She could see that the driver would not stop, or if he did stop, she would be further accosted, and every last ring found.

She opened her door and leapt, falling to the ground. Yuri jumped after her, but she was quicker, a ballerina who spent nearly every day of her life thinking about how her body moved amidst the bodies of other people. Before Yuri could grab her, she reached the sidewalk and slid into the crowd.

"Down with the tsar, Death to the tsar!" Shoved from behind, the crowd carried her towards Nevsky.

A dragoon regiment began to shoot into the crowd. Pushed to the side, Brigitte found herself up against the wall of one of the shops whose windows were shattered. Climbing over the sharp glass, she dropped down inside and huddled in a corner, covering her ears, but able to see the street, hoping to spot Chana.

The dragoons pushed the crowd west down Nevsky away from the statue of Tsarina Catherine. Brigitte climbed through the storefront window tearing her nightgown on a spike of glass. She kept close to the walls of the buildings as she moved in the opposite direction, towards the square. Just beyond a spot on the wall smeared with frozen, congealed blood, was the doll, Chana's doll, her face smashed in, arms outstretched. Brigitte snatched it up.

"Madame Legher!"

Turning towards the voice, she saw Mr. Reznik across the street with Klara a half step behind him, both of them running towards her. An explosion rent the air. All sound, Brigitte's breath, the dust sucked into the reverberation. Klara flew off her feet, higher than any dancer could leap. Mr. Reznik ran, his eyes pinned to Brigitte, pushing her towards the wall and covering her body with his, as he reached back behind him for Klara's hand, as though it had slid away from him. He leaned away from Brigitte, turning to look back.

"Klara!" he screamed. He rushed to her body. With the delicacy of a midwife, he picked her up, carrying her to the sidewalk. Klara's eyes were open, wide with shock.

Zeev appeared out of nowhere, shoving Brigitte aside to get to his mother, an unearthly sound coming from him.

A policeman rode by on a chestnut mare, his pistol out, aimed directly at them, a look of defeat shifting to defiance. Zeev left his mother's body in his grandfather's arms and rushed at the police officer. Before he made more than a few steps, the policeman aimed his gun. The shot became an earthquake in Brigitte's body. She threw herself to the ground. Zeev smashed to the bloody cobblestones, his head bouncing once before slamming down. Blood bubbled from his lips.

Brigitte crawled to him, shielding him with her body. Mr. Reznik put Klara down and came to his grandson's side, grabbing his arm, and dragging Zeev out of the street, and to his mother. The police officer kicked his heels into the horse's flank and cantered away.

Zeev moved his lips trying to say something. Mr. Reznik's eyes were closed tightly. Brigitte took Zeev's free hand. "Chana," he said, his voice rough. "Inside a crashed car. Just there," he tried to point with his eyes, but they rolled back and lost focus. "Chana," he said.

Rushing out into the street, Brigitte nearly tripped over the body of an old man, his arm severed at the shoulder. She went to three different vehicles, burned out, twisted, and bent. As she made her way to a fourth car, a new round of firing started. Brigitte dove into the car, covering her head with her hands; whizzing bullets flew past, followed by yelps and screams. Looking out through the shattered windshield, she saw a crowd gathering around the police officer who had just shot Zeev. He waved his pistol in the air, shouting threats, his face streaked with tears. The crowd rushed at him, pulling him off the horse as it reared and whinnied.

Away from the mob, she saw a black Renault leaning at an angle, wrapped around a lamppost. She ran from her hiding place to the car and pulled the door open. Chana was curled into a tight ball, her hat pulled down to her chin, her arms over her head.

Climbing in beside her, Chana stiffened and jerked away. "Let's go home, now," Brigitte said. Chana shook her head, hooking a foot around the gear lever when Brigitte tugged on her arm. "Your *dedushka* is waiting for you at home," she lied. She could not imagine leading Chana to Mr. Reznik, her dead mother, and dying brother. "He is waiting for us."

Chana shook her head, refusing to move. Another great explosion sounded, followed by the crowd screaming in unison.

"*Neshemele.*" Mr. Reznik's deep voice sounded from behind Brigitte. "Come along."

Chana pulled up her hat, and pushed past Brigitte, rushing into Mr. Reznik's arms. He picked her up and carried her towards Sadavaya Street.

Brigitte ran behind him. "Just a few steps more and we can make it to the ballet school. I know a way inside."

He halted and let her get ahead of him, then followed. She ran as fast as she could past the statue of Tsarina Catherine, who had become a captive audience for the revolutionaries. Theater Street was eerily vacant. Brigitte went to a door at the far end. Nikolai showed her how to jiggle the handle to open it back when they were students. The door went no farther than a storage room, explaining why decades passed and the lock was never fixed.

Inside the storage room was a short half door that led to the boiler room, and from there, one could access the main hallway.

The three of them made their way across the building, exiting on Lomonosov Square with the bridge across the canal in sight. Chana clung to her grandfather, terrified. Her white mittens were stained red. Whose blood? Brigitte prayed to never find out.

They ran across the bridge. Ran as long as their breath held out, then walked back to Krasnoameyskaya Street and Brigitte's house. The boy Brigitte had seen thrown from the car still lay on the ground, his body frozen solid, his eyes open and vacant.

At her front door, she fumbled in her pocket for the key, then held the door open for Mr. Reznik and Chana. Inside, she collapsed to the floor.

She sat uncomforted, sobs convulsing her whole body. The incessant barking of a dog finally led her back through the jumbled images, back to her senses.

In the *Chambre de Joie*, the secret panel leaned against the wall. Brigitte climbed through, pulling the panel into place behind her.

In her old bedroom, Mr. Reznik sat amid the blankets that had been her bed the night before, rocking Chana.

"Is she alright?"

"Never again will she be alright." His voice broke. "Nothing again shall be alright."

Chana reached up, touching the side of his face, stroking his beard. She began to sing the lullaby Brigitte had taught her, the one Nina sang to her youngest children.

I've hired as nannies for you, the Wind, the Sun, and the Eagle. The Eagle has flown back home. The Sun has hidden under the waters. And three nights later, the wind is rushing away to her mother. The Wind's mother has been asking, where have you been for so long? Have you been fighting the stars? Have you been chasing the waves?

Brigitte moved closer to Mr. Reznik, putting her hand on his back, kissing Chana's head. He reached for her, drawing her into the circle of his arms, strong, warm, and more tender than any embrace she'd ever known. Brigitte sang with Chana the last part of the song.

I haven't been chasing the sea waves; I haven't been touching the gold stars. I have been guarding a baby and rocking gently her little cradle.

CHAPTER 24

Petrograd, February 27, 1917

Brigitte whittled off strips of wood from the doorframe of the *Chambre de Joie* with a sharp knife, collecting the smallest shavings, and started the fire in the brasier. Watching Mr. Reznik sleeping, his breath puffing through his lips, steadied her. When they woke, only he accepted the steaming cup of tea she offered, and a bowl of applesauce laced with boiled nuts, taken from Klara's basket. Chana refused. Mr. Reznik thanked Brigitte, touching her hand, his eyes moist.

As the day wore on, the agitation of watching the faces of those in deep grief drove her out to find more food. Smoke hung heavy in the sky making her eyes water. Even the sun hid, seeming to have no desire to witness the destruction below.

When Brigitte reached Sadavaya Street, a couple she recognized from the shop where she bought her gramophone records passed by. The wife wore the traditional kokoshnik headdress. The man touched his hat in greeting. "He has risen," he said, smiling. Brigitte, confused by the Easter greeting, responded as she'd been taught. "He has risen indeed."

"He has risen. He has risen indeed." The perverse holiday found celebrants singing around bonfires lit in the middle of the streets, warming their hands, wearing their best shubas, dyed bright red, bright blue, the fur on the inside, keeping them warm.

Two large women, breathing heavily, rushed by Brigitte. Both wore coats too small for them. From behind, men shouted; the women began to run. A gang of six men, wearing no coats, no gloves, or hats, caught up with the women, knocking them to the ground. A crowd instantly gathered to watch, as the women's hats were pulled from their heads and their coats torn open. Brigitte drew closer unable to resist the shocking sight of women being attacked in broad daylight.

"Stop," Brigitte screamed at the men. "Stop it," she shouted, but her words were lost in the frenzy of cheers. She pushed her way into the center of the throng. "Stop, stop!"

When she got close, she saw the women, now stripped nearly naked, had no breasts, but hairy chests.

"Death to the Akrona. Kill them!"

One was Officer Sobetivich, who had fixed her boiler. Disappointed, Brigitte saw the other man, whose face was bloodied, was not Lt. Dimivich. She walked away from the bloodthirsty mass kicking the men to death.

At Yusapovsky Park the promenade of celebrants was again amenable, smiling and strolling as though it were Easter morning and they had all become aristocrats. "The city is ours," a group of women called out as they moved along the street together, their arms entwined. They handed out red ribbons; helping to tie them around the recipients' arms.

"Christ is risen!" A woman pressed a ribbon into Brigitte's hand. "Wear this and you will be known for your loyalty to our new Russia. No one will bother you." Brigitte tied the red ribbon around her arm.

On the other side of the park, a crowd clustered at the doorway of a restaurant. The owner, with bloodshot eyes, shouted an invitation to eat. "In honor of the great day of freedom, come inside."

She joined the line making its way past a series of tables laid out with glasses of kvass, plates of pickled fish, and meat pies. Brigitte filled her coat pockets, while those behind her shoved her forward. Taking the kvass, she drained the glass. The owner's wife collected the dishes. Brigitte gave her the glass. "He is risen," the woman said, her eyes betraying her terror that any moment the rebellion would destroy her business.

Returning home, her pockets full, the house was empty. Chana's basket and her dance shoes were gone. The stove had nearly grown cold upstairs with only a few glowing embers. Mr. Reznik had reclaimed his granddaughter; Brigitte's help was no longer required.

She sat in the cold parlor holding a pillow to her chest, trying to think of something good. She should go upstairs; make up the fire. Instead, she went to the dining room, curling up on her bed, pulling her coat tight, exhausted by the grief boiling in her chest.

Waking her from a light sleep was the sound of someone pounding on the front door. "Everyone outside." The wood around the door splintered.

Brigitte jumped up, rushing into the kitchen. Before she could shut the door, she was grabbed from behind. "Out of the house." A soldier wearing a dark green overcoat lifted her off her feet. "Neighborhood is being cleared."

"I live here. My things…" She wanted to get her satchel.

He pointed his rifle at her. "Who else is here?"

She shook her head, so startled by this angry man, she couldn't move until he shoved the barrel of his gun into her chest. "Move!"

On the street, her neighbors spilled from their houses.

Screaming followed by a gun blast. The throng rushed forward. She ran with them, as fast as she could. An old man fell. She saw him too late; her foot had nowhere else to go, her boot landing square on his back. If she looked behind to see if she'd hurt him, she would fall under the boots of the others.

As though they had run into a brick wall, the panicked crowd stopped. Bursts of gunfire sounded in front of them. The mob squeezed together. She had no way out, no side to slip off to, no retreat, no forward advance. Collectively curling into an inconspicuous ball, the people of her neighborhood crushed together. Unable to breathe, she felt dizzy.

The street fight swirled around them. One by one, the frightened neighbors peeled away, running or getting caught in the crossfire and dropping to the ground. A space opened in front of her. Across the street was a deep window well. She sprinted towards it, diving for safety, the sound of bullets pinging off the heavy stone foundation above her head.

Brigitte prayed, "Into thy hands, O Lord Jesus Christ my God, I commit my spirit. Have mercy on my soul. *Shema Yisrael. Adonai Eloheinu. Adonai echad.*"

A field gun rolled by, two soldiers pushing and loading at the same time. An explosion sounded so close her ears rang for long minutes.

Blood flowed in rivulets over snow and ice, over the exposed cobblestones. A young blonde woman lay dead, near enough that Brigitte could reach out and take the pocketbook that she'd flung in front of her when she fell. Her eyes and mouth were open. Her teeth were broken, bleeding. Tears trickled down the woman's cheeks, but the light of life was extinguished.

"*Shema Yisrael. Adonai Eloheinu. Adonai echad.* Do thou thyself bless me, have mercy upon me, and grant me life eternal." She mouthed the words, unable to look away from the dead woman, afraid to leave the window well. The construct of time broke. Her legs became numb from cold, but she didn't dare move while gunfire and the field gun shook the ground.

In the fading light of day, Sergei emerged through the smoke, holding out his hand. Calling her. She stood, going with him to the barre in Gustave's room. Nikolai was there waiting. In unison, they began exercises. She turned at the sound of Gustave's voice, "You are monkeys." Giggling, they arched their backs and hung their arms limp. Folding their tongues up under their upper lips and making monkey sounds. Gustave roared with laughter. Nikolai picked her up, putting her over his shoulder. She was puzzled by the scent of him, like cigarettes and fear. "You are so easy to lift," he said.

Then she was standing at her kitchen door. She realized she had no key. Turning, she asked Nikolai if he still had his. No one was there. The door to the Reznik's apartment had been partially torn off its hinges. She pulled herself up the steps. Inside her bedroom, she wrapped a blanket around her shoulders. Not a blanket at all, but a fur coat, one she hadn't worn in years. She could not explain to herself where it had been stored or where it had come from. Taking the coat, she went to the secret passageway, listening at the bottom of the stairs, but hearing nothing from the *Chambre de Joie* except the muffled firefight out on the street. Taking her satchel, she put it under her dress.

She closed what was left of her front door on her way to her cot. Shrouded in the coat, her back to the world, eyes closed, and holding on to her satchel, her only plan — to wait for her brothers to return.

The next morning, the sun shone through the windows, bright, silent. Panicked, Brigitte jumped out of bed. She'd be late for work. Her entire body screamed in pain, as she collapsed on the floor. Her hip especially hurt. Putting a hand down to massage the muscles, she winced. Her hands and feet were numb with cold.

The oven upstairs held heat. She needed to get to work. Students would be expecting her. She could get warm at school. Eat the midday meal there. Hot potatoes. If she left right away, she would have time to ask for a cup of tea from the kitchen.

She hid the satchel in the passageway. She would wash at school. There, she could collect herself.

On the street a police officer ran by, going into an apartment building. Brigitte noticed another policeman on the roof pointing his rifle at her. She wished in her heart, that last place in her body that hadn't given in to the cold, that he would pull the trigger. When he didn't, she kept walking.

As she reached the end of the street, the muffled sound of gunshots bled into her damaged ears. Looking back over her shoulder, the officer on the roof tumbled to the street. She felt nothing.

At the state library across from the school, the double-headed eagle that had hung over the entrance signifying the building belonged to the tsar, lay on the cobblestones, partly covered with a soldier's greatcoat. The street itself was deserted; with not an automobile, carriage, or person in sight. She pulled on the door that she'd walked through every working day for the past twelve years. It was locked. Posted beside the door a sign read:

> *The Imperial Theater Schools have passed to the authority of the Provisional Government. Defend it as national property.*

Another sign beside it was handwritten. *All Imperial Theaters and Schools Are Closed.*

She tried the next door and the next. At the third door, she attracted the attention of three men wearing a strange mix of Cassocks' *papakhas* on their heads and Imperial guardsmen's red jackets. They carried rifles with bayonets.

"You cannot go in," one of them shouted. She could barely hear; her ears still rang.

"I am a teacher." Her voice echoed in her head.

"Not anymore," one replied, pointing his gun at her. "This building belongs to the people."

Brigitte nodded in consent, turned, and walked the length of the street with the symmetrical yellow buildings on either side of her; the buildings that were perfect in every mathematical way.

She wandered along the Fontanka Canal, the sounds of the city muffled and distant.

"Shoot the policeman! Shoot the pharaoh!" A boy in good leather boots, still shiny with newness lifted a pistol. He stood amidst a group of happy children. Boys and girls circled one another. To these children, the day was a holiday with distracted adults and no school.

Brigitte looked into their faces as she got closer. Some were clean and well-dressed. Others wore rags and had runny noses and red splotches on their white cheeks. They played together as equal friends, playmates, boys, and girls, wealthy and poor. There were ten children, all between seven and twelve, she guessed. She wanted to be a little girl again. Go back and play with children who were not special. Not perfect. Not working their hearts out trying to figure out how to fly.

A peasant boy pretended to be shot, dramatically falling to the ground, jerking twice before lying still. She was nearly upon them now and thrilled to see how the boy came suddenly alive again. The children squealed in delight. The boy had a jolly face, open and excited. He took the hand of a little girl, smaller than himself, and raised it as if together they were somehow victorious in this game of make-believe.

Brigitte's heart lifted. Loose fragments of hope stirred in her breast. "Shoot the pharaoh," the children chorused. The boy holding the pistol pulled the trigger, followed by a loud report, throwing the boy off his feet. The little girl with her hand raised collapsed into a heap, blood pouring from a wound in her chest. The boy who had held the gun dropped it. The children scattered, including the new assassin, leaving behind the tiny girl, struggling to breathe.

Brigitte ran to her, kneeling on the street and lifting her head into her lap. The little girl's eyes already grew dark and distant.

Brigitte began to cry. "May you be like Ruth and Leah and Rachel," she whispered. "*Shema Yisrael. Adonai Eloheinu. Adonai echad.*" The lullaby Pytor Tchaikovsky wrote came to her, the one Chana sang to her grandfather, the one Nina had sung.

> *"Welcome sweet sleep; Nannies three watch over you. Wind, sun,*
> *and eagle. The eagle flew home; the sun hid over the water; the wind,*
> *after three nights, comes racing to his mother."*

The girl's eyes became more focused. "I see them, all three of them." Brigitte could barely hear her. "I see the sun and the eagle. I feel the wind."

Brigitte repeated the verses countless times as the girl's blood seeped out, as her eyes closed. She sang until someone came, lifting the girl out of her arms. She did not look to see who, but heard the question, "Your daughter?"

Brigitte stood on cramped legs, waiting a moment for the blood to flow, so she could walk away.

"No, I have no daughter."

With reverence, an orthodox priest held the girl's body. He carried her to a wagon, laying her carefully alongside other bodies. A nun carried a bucket and offered Brigitte a ladle. "The water is clean and safe to drink," she said.

Brigitte drank, her thirst fierce.

"There are beds in the church if you have nowhere to go. There is hot soup," the nun said loud enough for Brigitte to hear. Then the nun's countenance shifted, growing lighter. She spoke but Brigitte struggled to understand her. A fragment of prayer, perhaps.

"Leave everything you know behind," was what Brigitte heard her say. Brigitte looked at the woman's mouth, trying to read her lips. She could not make out any more of the woman's prayer.

Handing back the ladle, Brigitte thanked her. She looked at the little girl on the wagon, one dead body amongst three.

She shook her head. She would not follow the dead to the church.

CHAPTER 25

Delray Beach, Florida, USA, February 1, 1952

The canvas, yellow-and-blue striped beach chair had been set up for Brigitte by Chana's youngest daughter, Caroline. A tall, lithe thirteen-year-old, Caroline, nicknamed Carrie, inherited her mother's perfect turnout, though she could care less. She had her father's fair coloring, red hair, freckles, and dark eyes that flashed when her mood changed. Brigitte thought of Carrie's eyes as warning signs, like the clever traffic signals that went from green to red.

All of Chana's children visited Auntie Gitte, as they called her, over spring break, beginning when Merritt, Chana's oldest was able to ride the train by himself. Beverly had another year in high school. She did not have a perfect turnout, but loved ballet.

This was the first time the girls came without Merritt, now a freshman at Boston University. Brigitte could not say that she missed him so much. While they loved one another, he had outgrown her, forgetting how to talk to old ladies in any meaningful way.

Carrie wanted to swim, and Bev had attached herself to Brigitte's neighbor's handsome grandson, Robert. From her vantage point on the beach, Brigitte could see Bev and Robert sitting side by side on Brigitte's lavender bath towels.

Meanwhile, Carrie, who abided by rules well, could only swim in the ocean if someone was watching out for her. Brigitte watched. What would she do, she wondered, besides sound the alarm, if Carrie's red head stopped bobbing? She'd learned to swim at the age of fifty-five, which thrilled her. But diving into the Atlantic Ocean to rescue a girl a full six inches taller than herself? Brigitte knew they would both drown.

Brigitte pulled her straw hat down lower over her eyes so she could see through the glare of the sun. There were only a few bathers at midday. Local children were in school. Vacationing families used the public beaches further north. Those between the young and old, the men of Chana's generation, were dead, killed in the Great Wars, including Chana's husband. Those left behind had the responsibility of working, supporting their families, and rebuilding. They had no time for beaches in springtime in the middle of the day.

Brigitte sat nearly every day listening to the waves. Each time she lowered herself down to the sand a small sob would escape her. The first time Chana had been with her. She'd asked Brigitte tenderly, "Are you hurt?'

Brigitte couldn't explain the feeling of grief leaving her body, finally allowed safe passage, here in paradise. Each moment of joy freed her from a moment of sorrow.

When they were newlyweds, Chana's husband, Julius Widerman, invited Brigitte and Mr. Reznik to Palm Beach to meet his parents. Nervous about meeting her in-laws, Chana begged Brigitte to come. "They will hate me. The way Julius talks, they must think I'm a backward-Russian refugee. The Widermans have been in America for five generations."

The trip from Boston had been comfortable in Julius's Nash Ambassador, a fine automobile by anyone's standards, fifth generation or not. Brigitte imagined Leonid would have such a car. Mr. Reznik alone seemed unimpressed, falling asleep on rides in any vehicle that lasted more than ten minutes.

They had stayed in travel lodges, enjoying a fine adventure of diners and sightseeing. What Brigitte could not get over was the ease of traveling by car, leaving on their own schedule, with no waiting, no official documents granting permission. Julius would stretch his legs after a feast-like lunch at a roadside restaurant, smile at Chana, and hold out a hand to Brigitte to help her rise from the table. He paid for everything, which impressed Brigitte, but not Mr. Reznik, who more than once commented to Brigitte that the man would be bankrupt before the first anniversary.

Brigitte liked Julius' charming manners. She was sad he'd been killed; a sweet man who, for so much of his life, knew nothing of war, fighting, killing, and death.

Julius's parents had been gracious hosts, speaking slowly, which Brigitte appreciated as her English was formative.

They settled on Delray, a village to the south. The Widermans introduced Brigitte as a Russian ballerina, and the artistic community in Delray embraced her as a treasure. A prominent artist paid her to sit for a series of paintings. Brigitte relished the attention. Mr. Reznik inquired about buying one of the paintings, but they were sold as a collection to Consuela Vanderbilt.

Mr. Reznik built her a ccottage near the ocean, much smaller than her home in St Petersburg. She had no *Chambre de Joie*, but she'd outgrown barre exercises. Long hours walking on the beach brought her deeper peace. Mr. Reznik, in their escape from Russia, had been shot in the thigh, leaving him with a pronounced limp, so Brigitte walked alone.

Julius went to war the summer Carrie turned two. Chana sent the children to stay with Julius's parents, leaving her free to run the ballet school Brigitte had started in Boston. Chana became Anna to everyone but Brigitte. Even Mr. Reznik called her by her new name.

When Julius was killed, Chana came to the cottage to grieve. For weeks they walked the beach, often in silence. Brigitte understood the strength it took for Chana to return to Boston, growing the dance school into even greater success.

Glancing at Beverly and Robert, Brigitte noted that there seemed to be a proper distance between the two young lovers. No stolen kisses or wayward hands.

Her attention strayed to a young woman strolling by, a beachcomber. The woman stopped, looked at Brigitte, and waved as if she knew her. She did look familiar. The woman sprinted up the beach, greeting Brigitte, by name.

"I'm sorry," Brigitte said. "You sound Russian, but my memory is not so good. What is your name?"

"Zosia," the woman said.

"You are too young to have been one of my students."

The woman said something Brigitte couldn't understand. She reached down to Brigitte, touching her cheek. "*Mameleh*." The young woman said a bit more, then patted Brigitte's shoulder and walked past her chair so Brigitte could not see her go without turning around.

She sounded Jewish. Perhaps from the synagogue. What had she said, Brigitte wondered. She repeated Zosia's words in her head. "*Mameleh! Ikh hab azoy lang gevart aoyf meyn sfetsyeln. Mir veln bald zeyn tsuzamen.*" Brigitte puzzled over them. *Mameleh*. Little mama. *Bald zeyn tsuzamen.* Together soon. Brigitte couldn't figure it out. It made her head hurt to try.

The sun seemed particularly bright, even with dark sunglasses and her hat pulled down. Too bright. It gave her a headache. She drifted a bit, closing her eyes, thinking about the pain in her head, wondering how she'd find the energy to walk two blocks to her cottage to get a glass of water and a heroin tablet. She corrected herself. They were called aspirin now. Heroin, it had been discovered, was a terrible, addictive drug. The only ones who used it now were jazz musicians.

"May I sit?"

Brigitte knew the voice in an instant. Putting her hand up over her brow, she could still not make out his features, just his dark shape with the sunlight shining behind him.

"Yolya! Is it you?"

He sat down in the beach chair Carrie had set up for herself, and she could see him.

"Nickolai!"

"Brigitte Gustoevna," he sang. "Legher," he finished.

Reaching for his hand, he clasped hers. "All these years, Yolya. How did you know where to find me? I am so far from St. Petersburg."

"I followed my heart."

"I've missed you," she said, tears blurring her vision.

"Tell me, how were you able to leave St. Petersburg?" He smiled, but his eyes were serious, almost stern.

"How did I leave? Like everyone left."

"Not everyone left. Natasha and I didn't go until 1923. It became unbearable."

Brigitte sat up straight in her chair, looking him square on. "How could it have been bearable for you in 1917?" She wanted to chastise him, to tell him how much she had needed him, his help, his friendship, in those last horrible days. But he'd only just sat down. She held her tongue.

"We last spoke exactly 35 years, to the date. You brought Anna to me on February first." Nickolai wore a pair of white slacks and a white tee shirt. He took a pack of cigarettes and a lighter from his pocket. "Would you like one?" he offered. Without thinking, she took the yellow cigarette, forgetting that she'd quit.

"The cigarettes here are all the same color. All white," Brigitte said. "Everything in Florida is white. This yellow makes me think of the school on Theater Street."

"They changed the name of the school. And the street."

"I never understood the need to rename everything. Petrograd, Leningrad?" Brigitte inhaled the smoke. "Did you ever wonder why no one ever walked down Theater Street? We all walked around toward Lomonosov Square, even when it would be faster to cut through. Did you know the buildings there, the ballet school and library, were designed to demonstrate perfection? The street is as wide as the buildings are high, 22 meters, making a perfect square. The length of the buildings is ten times their height, 220 meters."

"Architects often have curious ideas of what makes something beautiful."

"I have a theory of why no one used that street. Perfection is off-putting."

He nodded and smiled. "That has been my experience too."

"Is Natasha with you?" She hoped the answer would be no.

He sighed. "She is in London, running my school, teaching my curriculum, using my name to attract students."

He looked remarkably good. Much younger than Mr. Reznik, who had surprised her when she finally got around to asking him his age by revealing he was only three years older than herself. He'd looked ancient lying dead in the hospital bed, his face clean-shaven to remove a tumor from his neck. She would have rather never seen him without his beard; it made him look weak. The strongest, bravest man she'd ever known; he never woke from the surgery.

Nikolai asked again, "How did you leave St. Petersburg?"

"Are you here to confront me? Is that what this is? After all these years? Are you finally ready to have it out with me? To hear me confess to killing Sergei?"

He looked thoughtful. "I forgave you years ago. Before you left Russia. Even before you brought the girl to me. Life went on, didn't it? At the time it happened, that seemed impossible. One day, without knowing how, the anger simply was no longer there."

A sob caught in her throat. "Why did you not come to tell me?"

"Foolishness. Pride. You'd stopped dancing. I knew you must have died every day to go to school and teach, but not to dance. Not just I knew. Everyone did. They would ask me about you. Alfred Bekefy told me all the time what a dog I was to you."

"Alfred," she said, her voice soft. "Is he alive?"

"The Siege of Leningrad took him. My daughter with Antonia also died. Joseph Kchessinsky, too. So many. A million people starved to death."

Brigitte's eyes filled with tears. Nikolai pursed his lips, an expression of his she'd forgotten; it meant he was working to control strong emotion.

"Do you remember the train tickets you were given in Crimea?"

Brigitte remembered, but how could he know about them? "The tickets the boy gave to us in the station?"

"We were there together. Alfred, Natasha and me. We saw you. You, Anna, and a man, the Jew."

"My husband."

Nikolai nodded, as though he knew she'd married. "We were inside the restaurant, waiting to board the train. We had a choice, though. I'd been offered a place with the Bolshoi." He paused, putting his cigarette out in the sand. "Natasha wanted to leave. She had been ill and her parents had already fled. We all had offers from the Bolshoi and we had three tickets for that train."

Brigitte remembered the messenger boy dressed in a man's coat, wearing a hat too big for his head. He'd called her name, "Mlle. Legher." Chana heard him, touched Brigitte's sleeve, and pointed. She let the tears spill down her cheeks. When she made it to Delray, she'd given up hiding her tears. They felt good, like taking a deep breath.

"We could see you from the window of the restaurant, looking so worried and resolute. I felt Sergei standing next to me as I drew in my notebook a caricature of you. I'd not seen your face in years. Sergei stood beside me, chiding me. Crazy to say, but it is true. I looked at you, then down at the drawing, and it had been finished. My hand never moved past the outline of your head and that insane scarf you wore over your hair. Sergei goaded me into giving you our tickets. He said I should go to the Bolshoi, and set you free."

She looked out to sea. Through her tears, she could barely make out Carrie. "We had been waiting in that station for nearly a month, assured of passage on a ship to America if we could only get to the port."

Nikolai said, "How did you leave St. Petersburg?"

Brigitte floated back, her body rising from the chair on the beach, as quickly as a thought. Back to her *Chambre de Joie* where she said goodbye to her home, took one bag, and walked to a stranger's house where Chana and Mr. Reznik waited for her.

"We stayed at a safe house for Jews only. We were to travel together. With no warning, they turned us out, telling us to fend for ourselves, and if we could make it to the port in Feodosia, tickets would be waiting for us."

She had often wondered at the chances of finding Mr. Reznik out on the street the night she wandered away from the ballet school. What provenance brought them together and allied them in their escape? When they were put out on the street, Mr. Reznik took them to the pink and white synagogue with the blue dome, where refugees could rest.

"We were out on the street looking for a way to eat, to feed Chana," Brigitte continued telling her story to Nikolai. "A shopkeeper had his fill of revolutionaries feeling entitled to his goods without paying. He'd beaten three men, by himself, such was his fury. He had a pistol and shot at the thieves as they fled down the street. One of the bullets hit Mr. Reznik in the thigh. A curse that turned into a blessing."

The feeling of Nikolai so close to her was the strength she needed to continue. "The shopkeeper saw he wounded an innocent man and brought us into his home. He called a doctor, who extracted the bullet. We were fed and given a warm place to stay. I asked the shopkeeper for help." Brigitte paused, pursing her lips. "We waited a week. Finally, a delivery van with tea the shopkeeper sold arrived and he secured the three of us transportation to Moscow. From there, I sold a piece of jewelry that I'd sewn into Chana's coat for train tickets to Crimea.

"I never told Mr. Reznik how I got that ride, Nikolai. We were married by then, you know, although we had not yet become man and wife." She stopped talking, thinking about the simple ceremony performed by the rabbi who smiled as he sang the *Sheva Brachot,* the seven blessings. Mr. Reznik had kissed her, and such was the truth on his lips, she fell in love.

"The shopkeeper had a subscription to the ballet. He remembered me. I don't know how desperate he must have been to want me. Revolution does not make one beautiful." She could recall the shopkeeper's features. His eyes were too close together. So thin and tall, he seemed to be a walking skeleton. She'd been afraid of him. "I refused. For the first time in my life, I refused to sleep with a man even though I was desperate for what he could do for me. I knew refusing his bed meant that Chana might not be saved. Still, I refused him. I made no excuse. I did not say I was diseased. I said no. He did not press me further. Then we talked. We talked of the fighting.

Of all that had changed. We talked about things we missed. Of things we had not had time to miss, but we would. Every night while we waited for the truck, I met with the shopkeeper in his storage room, and we talked like old friends." She looked to Nikolai to see his judgment. He had tears on his cheeks. "I knew my refusal may get me killed. May get Chana and Mr. Reznik killed if we couldn't leave the city. I did it for myself. I had to save all of myself or none of myself before I could save anyone else. I do not apologize, Nikolai. In the end, we were all saved. We got that ride. But first, before I saved Chana and Mr. Reznik, I saved myself." She picked up a handful of sand, sifting it through her fingers.

"I would have helped you."

She had been waiting for his accusations. She hadn't expected these words.

"You would have helped me?"

"I helped you with Anna." She heard his hurt and pain. "I had that Akrona following you jailed for being a double agent. Dimivich. I reported that I had seen him talking to someone behind the theater in German."

"You did that?"

Nikolai's serious expression transformed into a grin. "I too can ruin lives."

"His life needed ruining," she laughed.

"The shopkeeper told me something that helped me leave Russia." She thought now of the man, his name lost to time, but not his face, not his words. "His father had been part of the diplomatic service. They lived for a long time in China. When he was twelve, the family returned to St. Petersburg. He cried to his mother that he did not want to leave his home in the mountains. He spoke mostly Mandarin, preferring it to Russian. His mother told him, "It's as simple as this." Brigitte looked out at Carrie diving into a wave. "Leave everything you know behind."

"Did you take nothing?"

"Nothing. Not the language. I danced to new music." She laughed. "I must tell you, after all the years of hearing the same exercise songs, Rosemary Clooney is a relief and a joy. I left the Russian god of the Orthodox Church. I left you, Yolya. I left you behind. I had to."

Nikolai tenderly wiped a tear from her cheek.

"Mr. Reznik pretended to believe me when I told him my mother was a Jew from Kyiv."

"You became a Jew?"

"I became myself."

"You loved him?"

"In a quiet way. I thought I needed a man to be safe. Papa, Leonid, you, Sergei. I was terrified of losing protection because I was not what I was supposed to be. With Mr. Reznik, I had no fear. There is more room for love when there is no fear." The emotion rose in her throat. For a time, she couldn't speak. Nikolai took her hand, putting it against his chest, where she could feel his heart beating, slowly, almost erratic, as though it skipped beats. "I love you all. Mr. Reznik, you, Sergei. I always will. Forgive me. I was all the wrong things and that made it impossible to fit perfectly into your lives. A Jewish orphan, an imperfect dancer. A terrible teacher. Being all of that, for a time, I was Legher. I belonged to you and Sergei. Belonging to you both for a little while, I thought that was enough. Then one day, I became Brigitte Reznik and it was enough to be an imperfect Jew with a child to raise. Chana grew into such a beautiful dancer. Her perfect turnout. A good woman. Brave. Independent. A wonderful mother."

Carrie came out of the water, walking towards them.

"Someone is waiting for you. She is just over there," Nikolai said.

"Carrie?"

"Your *muti*."

Brigitte leapt out of her chair. She knew her now, the beachcomber. Zosia. *Muti*. As if it had been only hours since her mother's last kiss, she knew her. The scent of her. The feel of her arms. Brigitte saw her, radiant and smiling and she ran into Zosia's outstretched arms.

"*Muti*. When I danced, you were with me."

Light filled Brigitte's whole body, lifting them both high like birds in flight.

ACKNOWLEDGMENTS

The Class of Perfection was born in 2008 as part of an exploration into Past Life Regression therapy. I had begun work on learning to be a PLR therapist with Dr. John Amoroso through Atlantic University in Virginia Beach, VA, and was guided in a past life regression by Dr. Brenda Cennedy in Minneapolis. That is when I first met Brigitte. Five more times I would be regressed to a past life in St. Petersburg and learn more of Brigitte's story.

I'd like to thank Dr. Amoroso for opening up so many new worlds for me to explore. Lydia Spencer was a guide on one of those regressions. In some ways, her words were the ones that opened my heart to Brigitte and helped me find the courage to tell her story.

Linda Henry and Kirsten Stasney, my writing partners, were the only two of my early readers to push through the novel when it was double the length, and far less polished. They have been my faithful friends, confidants, and encouragers. Thank you, my dear sisters.

I want to thank those in my writing groups over the years who read pieces of the novel, giving me invaluable feedback and asking great questions. I wish to thank the Jackpine Writers Bloc and especially, Judy Merrit and Marsha Wolff. In Florida, I'm grateful to have been invited to join Valeria Wenderoth's group. Thanks to Valeria, Tobias, Arthur Doweyko, Bob Smith,

Sarah York, and others in the group whom have come and gone over the last years. Especially thank you to Cindy Schwartz for the edits and feedback. Thank you to Sarah Dornin. I cannot tell you how much the gift of your time and talent as an editor, as well as your friendship, has meant to me.

Thank you, Sandy Andress, and to all the women in the Artist's Way Group. You made me a better writer. Thank you to my friends and beta readers, Sandy, Julie Spiesel, Kay Keyser, and Linda Smith. You helped me be brave.

Thank you to my best writing teacher, friend, and mentor, Mark Vinz. I hear your voice in my head still. It is like music.

I thank my husband Keith for prioritizing a writing space for me when he remodeled our home.

I thank my daughter, Hannah Ekren, who lives and breathes stories. Countless times she came to my rescue, saved me from myself, and used my own parenting tricks against me. Brilliant child. My son, Samuel Ekren brought his filmmaker's sensibility to my scenes and helped me to see them beyond the voices in my head.

I thank my dad, David F. Martin, for telling an interviewer back in the 1970s that perhaps his youngest daughter would be a writer. He read my first novel, written when I was thirteen, gave me a spelling list, and his comments on what was good and what I might do to make it better. He believed.

Lastly, I dedicate this novel to my mother, Patricia Martin. Besides Linda and Kirsten, she was the only other one who read all 773 pages of the original manuscript. When she finished, she put her hands on my shoulders, looked me in the eyes with so much love, and said, "This needs to be published."

She is the mother Brigitte was always searching for.

ABOUT THE AUTHOR

Cynthia Ekren lives on an island in Florida. She grew up in North Dakota, ran a fishing resort in Minnesota, and later, earned an MA in Transpersonal Studies from Atlantic University. She is a Tarot card reader and animal communicator. A 13-time Nanowrimo *winner*, she shares her home with her husband and two dogs, River and Figaro.

www.ingramcontent.com/pod-product-compliance
Lightning Source LLC
Chambersburg PA
CBHW070604300726
48975CB00006B/1713